This Game Has No Loyalty

WRITTEN BY
JUNE

Editor: Carla M. Dean (www.ucanmarkmyword.com)

Printed in the United States of America

First Edition

ISBN#: 13-digit: 978-0-9827-6790-0
10-digit: 0-9827-6790-0

Published by: FourShadough Publishing, LLC

This Game Has No Loyalty

Acknowledgements

What can I say? Listen. I've been on a long, difficult journey and on that journey I've made many mistakes, suffered huge losses, fought countless battles, endured tortuous situations, and experienced excruciating pain but throughout it all, I don't regret anything that I've been through because it molded me into who I am today. I've learned lessons and I've become stronger mentally and physically because of it. I don't hide behind anything I've done; I face it head on, the only way to deal with life.

Mother – Your faith in the Almighty and your endless prayers for me is what spiritually kept me grounded through my years. Thank you mother for trying to raise 4 children to be positive and successful with the little resources you had when we came to this country some 30 years ago. You wanted to give us a better life and provided, to the best of your ability, for your family through hard work and perseverance. I thank you.

Dina (Sis) – Wow…you have always been my best friend (I think we were supposed to be twins). Throughout our years we've remained closely knit. Thank you for your support and confidence in my abilities. Thank you sis for being there for me in my darkest hours and providing the tough love that only you are able to give to me. You are my rock and I love you for that.

Cirilo (my other big bruh) – I took a lot from you when we were younger, you fueled my thirst for education and reading. It is you that made me an organized and structured person. I thank you for that.

Nathan (my youngest older brother) – You are hands down the most supportive person in my life. With every idea I've approached you with, you've never denied me, put me down or told me it was far-fetched and not feasible. I may be slightly older than you but you have taught me so much through your wisdom. I appreciate all you've done for me and for being there to hold me down when I was experiencing hardship. I will never be able to repay you for that. Thank you babe bruh, I love you.

Sha-Juan, Shaaid, Shadiya, and Shamel (the four Sha's) - Shajuan, my baby girl, you were one of daddy's first inspiration to change his life, your birth is responsible for making me the man I am today. Shaaid, my lil' man, I see myself in you when I was your age. You are my manchild and you helped me realize a man has to be present to raise his son, I will not fail you son. Shadiya my second baby girl, you are so intelligent, sweet, and respectful. I am proud of you and know your success is already cemented for your future. Shamel (Man-Man) my last boy, you are defined through me. I see so much of myself in you, its like looking through a mirror. I am proud of all of you and my love for you guys is eternal, equal, and ever present.

Cuwan, Chanae, Mark (my other three) – Cuwan, I'm hoping you learned from your mistakes. Remember, you make the choices in your life. I hope this book will incite some of the realities of the environment in which we grew up. You have the ability to change and control your destiny, be strong and be a leader. Chanae, you have grown up to be a beautiful young lady, continue to stay focused on your dreams. You have the right idea, enjoy life but don't forget your responsibilities. Mark, you are the one that will shock the world. You have talents beyond measure. Don't forget that education is key. I love you all.

Millette – We've been together over a decade and you've given me two boys that I love very much. The support you've given me before and during this project is what helped it come to fruition. I must thank you for that. Remember that time heals all wounds and when we know better we do better. The world is waiting for you and at your disposal. I congratulate you on all the progress you've made thus far. I love you.

Donnell (D-Boy) – We've been homies for an eternity. You've been by my side throughout my entire life. Throughout our years, we've experienced a lot together and grew to be responsible men to our families. You are my brother from another mother and I thank you for being a true homie and holding me down when I had no one else.

Peaches (Sara) – We've both made a beautiful daughter together which was my one of my strongest inspirations to change. You have remained my best friend throughout the years and I cherish our relationship. You have always been the shoulder I could lean on and be myself without worrying if I looked weak. I thank you so much for being real throughout our friendship.

Norris, Monica, Tuwoski, thanks for reading my manuscript and giving me honest feedback, you are one of my first supporters. Adrian (A.D.) you are my homie for life, we've been through so much together and I cherish our friendship, thanks for being a true friend. My Little Washington family (L dub), Eva Keys, Peaches, Ziggy, Rat (Mouse), Stacy Keech, Faye Keech, Sleepy, Stick Man, Omar (Scarnitti), Bunky, Beanie (Bink), Big A, Johnnie Lonnie, Cool Whip, Mikki, Ant, Al Green, Shawn, Bolo, Sammy, Eric T., Fruit, Pat W., Tasha, Aimee P., Lil D, Alton R., Flava Man, Niyoko, Kelly, and the rest of the L dub crew y'all know who you are, if I missed anyone, my apologies. You all made me feel like I was born and raised in L.W. I love you all for that and I'm glad throughout the years we maintained our friendship.

To my homies from 'round the way – Ramel, Ra Dollar, Detail, Cleve, Bazz, DuSha, Big Moe, Billy Bang, Big L (Larry), B.Z., Sheeny boy, Shrimpo, Crazy Ty, Sunshine, Uncle D, Jamel, my homie Divine, Barry, Cee, 1100 (keep pimpin'), Big Stubbs, Mizzo, D-Nice –don't let the time do you, and the rest of my homies (you know who you are), this is about us for us, ya heard!

Lady Scorpio (Brooklyn) – Special thanks to you for being one of my first supporter on line and now a true big sis, thanks from my heart and soul.

Tameeka – Thank you for your support. You have really been a very important person in my life, thank you so much.

My Facebook peoples, myspace homies, C2C, all the book clubs, all my readers and supporters, thanks for the love and support you've shown me by reading my excerpts and commenting honestly. Without you guys, this would not be possible; I thank you all from the heart.

G.C. Miller (older bruh) – I held you last because the last shall come first. You are my role model. Although many may not understand you and see you as complex (I once did), I thank you for your overall support and teachings of life to me. I hold you dear and I'm glad you've embraced me and cared enough to assist me in getting ahead and being successful. You can easily take up a whole page so I'm going to cut it short and tell you that I love you and thank you for being there for me.

Special shout out to any mother's who read, This Game Has No Loyalty. If you enjoy this book, pass it on to one of our male youth. Give it to them, tell them to read it in the bathroom, read a page a day, read when they're on the bus, on the train, in the car, or whenever they have some down time. Trust me, once they read it, you will open a door in them that may have been locked. Reading invokes change mentally. You will be surprised.

Dedications

This book is dedicated to Eric Jerome Keech, (my best friend) who left us way too early in this lifetime. You have inspired me to write in hopes of reaching the misguided and misinformed youth in words, their words and our words, which they can relate to and gain a true understanding of what really happens behind the scenes on the mean streets of any hood. You've left a lasting imprint on the souls and minds of those who knew and loved you. You will continue to live on through your son, Jahiem and daughter Erica.

I love you Black and you are never forgotten, you are a true soldier in our war of survival. I also dedicate this book to all the fallen soldiers that left this world early because of the game, there are too many to name but I will name a few...Tyran, Kirk, Eugene, JoJo, and many more. God Bless you all.

“June has written a good book, with the added suspense in the end making for a great cliffhanger. I'm looking forward to the continuation of this story. ” **- Carmen - OOSA Book Club**

”This Game Has No Loyalty is an action-packed novel with so many twists and turns, you'll be asking yourself who really is loyal after all, only to discover that the game really does have no loyalty. If you are going to be in the game, the lesson to be learned is: DON'T TRUST ANYONE...even the ones you think have your back, just might be the enemy.” **- Apex Reviews**

“June delivered a well-written story in 'This Game Has No Loyalty.' His characters are so real, I could feel myself liking some and hating others and just plain not trusting some. He thoroughly showed you how deceiving the streets can be and the effects of it. He didn't hold back, just told you like it was. While I was reading the book, it was like seeing a movie unfold before me as all the hate and betrayal started unfolding before me. Thanks June!!!”
Mashawn – SBS Book Club

“This was without a doubt one of the best books I've read over the past few months. It's set in the late 80s and everything was pretty much on point from the Guess and Karl Kani gear to the reference of slangin' off the pager. I do question the "Captain Save-A-Ho" reference because I think that was more 1993. Regardless, the book was tight - well written, intriguing from the jump and most important - real.” – **DaRevew**

BAPTISTE HOUSING PROJECTS BROOKLYN, NY 1990-91

Lakim and Kendu sat on the benches in the back of Lakim's building smoking a blunt and drinking a forty- ounce of Old Gold. It was almost midnight and in the back where they were sitting, it was packed with young men and women talking, drinking, and smoking marijuana while listening to music blaring out of the window of a tenant on the first floor of the building.

"Yo Du, pass the blunt. You sucking on that shit like a Hoover!" Lakim said to his friend Kendu.

"Chill, man. You just passed it to me," Kendu replied, sucking as much smoke into his lungs as possible.

"Shit, you already steamed it down to a roach," Lakim remarked, as the now small blunt was finally passed to him.

As Lakim sucked down the last of the weed, Kendu switched his attention to the girls dancing and shaking their ass near the back exit of the building.

"Damn, them shorties over there is holdin'," Kendu said to Lakim.

Lakim brushed some ashes off his pants and looked at the girls his friend was referring to.

“Damn! What they putting in the water making them girls fill out like that? Them bitches thick as fuck. You can stand here and sightsee, but I’m gon’ try and get with one of those fat asses tonight,” Lakim said, starting to walk over to where the girls were dancing.

Kendu got up from the bench to follow him, when he heard his name being called. He turned to the voice and noticed one of his old friends from high school approaching.

“What’s up, KB?” Kendu greeted his high school buddy by slapping him five.

“Ain’t much. Just chillin’,” KB replied.

Lakim gestured to KB with a nod of his head as acknowledgment.

“I ain’t seen you in a minute. Where you been, bruh?” Kendu asked KB.

“You know my M.O., kid. Still stickin’ up spots and robbing these fake-ass drug dealers,” KB replied boldly.

“I hear that,” Kendu responded.

“I hear that fly shit, too, but ain’t no fake-ass drug dealer over here,” Lakim said, taking offense to KB’s comment.

“Nah, kid, I ain’t talkin’ ‘bout you. You fam,” KB replied.

“Oh, I thought you was trying to play me,” Lakim said.

“So y’all dudes getting money out here now, huh?” KB asked.

“Look, kid,” Lakim said, showing off a wad of bills. “I made this today, and I just came out at seven!”

“Damn, the crackheads bringing money in a Brinks truck?” KB asked jokingly.

“Nah, kid, but they coming with Hefty bags of that dough for these jacks, and I’m running out. Matter of fact, I betta go beep my man so I can re-up,” Lakim said.

“Who you slinging for?” KB asked.

“My man Junior from the Fort,” Lakim replied, while counting his money again. “Damn, I didn’t know I made this much money already.”

“Damn, he getting money over on this end like that and this ain’t even his hood?” KB asked.

"Yea, he bubblin', too. Yo, I gotta go beep this dude right now. I need some more work. I can't afford to run out now," Lakim said, as he walked toward the corner to use a payphone.

KB had a gleam in his eye because the guy Lakim was talking about sounded like someone his colleague Stump would be interested in. So, he pushed to get more information about the guy by probing Kendu while Lakim went to make a phone call.

"Yo, Du, who this dude La talking 'bout? You fucks with him, too?" KB asked Kendu.

"Yeah, I fuck wit' him sometimes. I made like fifteen hundred today gettin' rid of that shit," KB replied proudly, deliberately lying about the amount of money he made.

"Word, kid? It's money out here like that?" KB asked, amazed.

"Yeah, muhfucka, the heads don't stop chasin' this shit. Plus, the shit we got is the bomb, a scud missile," Kendu bragged.

"I didn't know you was a worker bee. I thought you was holding your own self down. What happened?" KB replied smugly.

"I'm gettin' money, that's what happened. Can't you tell?" Kenu pulled out a mountain of bills from his pocket.

"A'ight, muhfucka, I see you gettin' paid. Where La said he from again?" KB asked.

"He from Fort Green projects, but he sometimes stays with his girl, Shondra. You know, the dark-skinned bitch with the fat ass," Kendu told him.

"Yeah, I know her. Her brother is Ru-Ru, right?"

"Uh-huh. I think he been dealing with her a coupla years now," Kendu informed him.

"Does he live in the crib with her?" KB continued with his questions.

"I think he might, 'cause he out here hustling every day, all day," Kendu replied.

"You cool with him?"

"He a'ight, but he not my man like that," Kendu answered.

"Him and your man La tight?" KB inquired.

"Not like that. La's my main man. He just works for him," Kendu clarified.

"In that case, would you be willing to set the muhfucka up to be robbed?"

Kendu's face screwed up. "Hell no, I ain't setting my man up to get robbed. Is you crazy?!"

"I'm not talking 'bout your man La. I'm talking 'bout the muhfucka y'all work for."

"What I'm gonna get if I do that?" Kendu replied with interest.

"You get a percentage of what we get from the muhfucka," KB lied.

"And how much is that?"

"You tell me. Where do he keep his money, in his girl's house?" KB asked hungrily.

"I don't know all that, but I know he be having a lot of money on him when La goes to him to re-up. Matter of fact, tomorrow's the first, and that's probably when he goes to get his big package that he gives me and La. Plus, he goes and pick up money from everybody that owes him. The muhfucka keeps the crackheads' welfare cards so he don't have to worry about them not paying him the first and fifteenth of every month," Kendu told him.

"You know the heads that owe him?"

"Shit. Everybody that smokes out this muhfucka owes him," Kendu replied.

"Do you know the ones he picks up from?" KB elaborated.

"I don't know all of them, but I know a couple. He's definitely gonna pick up from this closet-smoking bitch named Lizzette that lives on the other side. He always gives her credit, and I think he hittin' it on the low," Kendu answered.

"A'ight, I'm gonna let my man know what's up with him, and we gonna watch his moves early in the morning. Then we gonna need you to set him up when we find out when he picks up his package."

"A'ight, just make sure I get my cut, and don't try and beat me outta my share," Kendu said.

"Don't worry, son. I got you," KB replied.

"I hope you have some heavy iron with you 'cause he got mad guns," Kendu warned.

KB pulled out a black .38 revolver and showed it to Kendu. “I keeps my toast on me at all times!” KB said, feeling a surge of power.

He pointed the pistol in the air and let off three shots into the night sky. Everyone, including Kendu, scattered for safety. KB smirked wickedly, then walked away. He was on his way to call Stump and tell him about Junior.

CHAPTER 1
IT'S ALL OVER; I GOT YOU

Junior was ready to go in the house after serving his last customer, but before he made it to the entrance of his girlfriend's building, he heard gunshots that sounded like they came from the building across the street. Everyone standing in front of the building with him ran off in different directions. Junior ran into his girl's building, then peeked out the door to see if he could get a glimpse of the shooter. He didn't see anyone and figured whoever was shooting was merely testing out their new toy, something common in the hood.

A few minutes later, a police cruiser drove slowly by the building. In the hood, the police usually never got to trouble that fast. For that to happen, they had to already been in the area patrolling when they heard the gunshots. They never did get out of their vehicle to investigate; they just circled the block and shined a bright light at the building across the street.

Once Junior knew the police were gone, he went into the house to get his gun from his girlfriend's room. She was fast asleep, or seemed to be, and didn't stir when he came in or when he went into the closet. He took out a duffle bag full of automatic guns and revolvers. He chose a black .357 revolver with a rubber handle and stuffed it into the pocket of his Fila sweatpants. Then he went back out as silently as he came in.

He opened the back door of the building and stood by the benches near a black gate that traveled around the side of the building. He pointed the gun in the air away from the windows in the projects and let off four thunderous booms from the snub-nosed revolver. The fire from the barrel lit up the cool summer night. After the echoes from the blast subsided, he looked around, hoping someone recognized him. He wanted them to know his gun had a bigger bang just in case someone had ideas of fronting on him. Satisfied he sent his own message, he went back into the house, got into bed with his girl, and fell asleep.

Junior woke up to the familiar smell of bacon and eggs. The scent traveled from the kitchen to the room in the back where he slept. He turned over, stretched, and then sat up in the bed. He reached for a clip of a Newport that was half smoked in the ashtray. He lit the tip, took a long pull, and blew out the smoke as he got out of bed. He knew Shondra would be coming in soon with his breakfast, so he went to the bathroom to wash his face and brush his teeth. When he returned to the room, he slipped on the Fila sweatpants he had on the night before and headed to the kitchen.

Shondra was standing over the stove in a tattered floral print housecoat with a tear in the side that revealed her brown skin. Her body was tight. She had firm breasts with perky nipples that showed through any light clothing she wore, and a small waist accentuated her nice, round hips and bubble ass. Junior loved her. She was his queen, best friend, and confidante. She was his Bonnie and he, her Clyde.

He grabbed her gently from behind and wrapped his arms around her waist, letting his hand rest in the comfort spot of her crotch. She squirmed slightly and threw her head back to his shoulders, revealing her discolored wino lips acquired from drinking hard liquor straight from the bottle when she was younger. He gently kissed her on the temple as he grabbed one of her breasts. While caressing her, he felt a rise in his sweats. She quickly turned to face him and put her tongue in his mouth, moving her snatch around until she felt his hardness. He grabbed her ass with both hands and drew her to him hard, moving in a

circular motion as he enjoyed their good morning kiss. She moaned as their bodies moved as one. He stiffened more, alerting him it was time to take things a step further. He pulled the snaps of her housecoat and revealed the two beautiful stacks that jumped out at him in eagerness to be held. He moved her over to the sink and put his mouth on her breast, sucking her nipple gently. Suddenly, the smoke alarm went off and they both stopped abruptly. His breakfast was burning.

"See, boo, you made me burn your bacon," she said, her breathing slowing back down to its normal pace.

"Fuck that bacon. That's not what I was trying to heat up," he said, patting her ass.

"Well, at least all the bacon didn't burn. You want me to make you some more, or is this enough?" she asked, showing him the portion that wasn't burnt.

"It don't matter, Mooka," he said, walking back to the bedroom.

Shondra's room was steel gray. He had painted it that color but couldn't remember his reason. Now, as he looked around, he realized it was a very depressing color. He had also put down a gray carpet with black specks because he wanted to make the room comfortable and give it a different look and feel from the rest of the rooms in the apartment.

"Here, boo," Shondra said, placing the plate of food on the edge of the bed.

Junior picked up the remote and turned the television on to *Jerry Springer*. He loved watching this talk show because Jerry always had some crazy people on the panel. Junior ate his breakfast while he and Shondra watched the show together. The caption on the bottom of the television screen read, "Revealing Secrets: My Girl is a Man."

Shondra lay down, her head resting on his lap. "What happened last night, boo? I heard gunshots," Shondra asked, while gazing up into his eyes.

"Some stupid-ass muhfucka showing off his new gun," he replied, as if he wasn't troubled at all.

“You gotta be careful, baby. You know they don’t really like you around here.”

“Like I give a fuck. Ain’t nobody gonna stop me from gettin’ this money unless they willing to lay down.”

“I just want you to be careful, that’s all, boo.”

“Get up, Mooka. I gotta get dressed. It’s the first of the month,” he said, placing his finished plate on the bed.

Junior already knew most of the guys around her way didn’t like him, and it wasn’t just because he was hustling over there. It also had something to do with him being with Shondra.

He sat on the edge of the bed and thought back to how he met Shondra four years ago in the summer of ‘86.

Junior met Shondra one summer while hanging in Baptiste Projects. He knew a couple of the guys from around there through one of his high school homeboys who lived there since he was in public school. Since Junior lived in downtown Brooklyn, he always wanted to find a girl in the area so he could have somewhere to lay up when he didn’t feel like taking the long ride home on the train.

Puerto Ricans predominantly inhabited Baptiste Plaza Projects, so Junior always thought he would end up with a Boriqua mami, until he noticed a girl buying an ice cream cone at the Mister Softee truck. He rarely saw black girls in the projects, and the ones he did see usually acted like they were Spanish. The first thing he noticed was that she had a fat ass. He asked his homeboy did he know her, and his response was that she was a firecracker, a little on the wild side. He had gone to public school with her brother back in the day and remembered she was always fighting.

Junior walked over to the ice cream truck and tried to kick it to her.

“What’s up, miss? Can I talk to you for a minute?” he asked, as she turned around and looked into his eyes.

“Excuse me?”

“I mean, are you in a rush or something? You got a minute to talk so I can get to know you?” he asked her.

"Not really. My man is waiting for me. And who are you anyway?" She began walking back towards her building.

"I don't mean no disrespect, ma, but I just noticed you and wanted to get to know you."

She stopped, turned around, and looked at him.

"Okay, mister, here's your minute."

Her response caught him off guard, but he recovered quickly.

"I don't know you and I know you don't know me, but I think we should get to know each other. I want to know everything about you that you're willing to reveal, and the things you conceal I will learn about later as we get to the next level of understanding one another. All I need is a chance, and if you're not willing to take a chance, give me the opportunity to develop a friendship with you that is like no other friendship you've had with any dude. So, can we get to know each other, luv?" He spit sixteen bars like he was in a recording studio.

She smiled a wide grin and shuffled on down the street without saying a word.

"Hold up!" he yelled, running behind her. "Why you slidin' off like that, ma?"

"My man is in front of the building,"she turned and said to him.

Junior caught a glimpse of a guy standing in front of the building she was walking to. He was a light-skinned guy with a dark Caesar haircut and was sort of on the heavy side. Junior followed behind her and watched as she and her man went inside the building together. Although her grill wasn't all that attractive, Shondra had a nice shape, and the roundness of her ass made him want to pursue her.

Junior made it his business to go by Shondra's building the next day. He kept passing by all day hoping to see her. On his way back from the store on Siegel Street, he saw her walking with a little girl towards the Chinese restaurant. He decided to follow her and then act like he just happened to bump into her, but it didn't work because she spotted him before he could get to her.

"Are you following me?" she asked as he came up on her.

"Yeah, you busted me," he said, smiling. "I just wanted the rest of my minute."

"Well, my man didn't appreciate you following me last night."

"Like I said yesterday, I ain't tryin' to be disrespectful, but fuck him. If he didn't like me following you, he shoulda said something to me."

"Look, I don't want no problems with him, so you need to keep it movin'," she said, then she grabbed the little girl's hand to cross the street.

"Look, ma, I ain't trying to get you fucked up. I just want to get to know you. Is something wrong with that?"

"Yeah, the problem is that I already have a man."

"And how long have you had that problem?"

"You ain't funny," she said, smiling. "Seriously, he's real jealous and I don't want no problems. That's all."

"Look, let me worry about that problem. I can handle myself. Can you?"

"I ain't worried about me. I'm worried about you."

"Now look, ma, if you trying to get out of your fucked-up relationship by getting me to beat your man's ass, just let me know so we can cut this shit short."

She laughed real hard at his comment, then stopped in front of the restaurant and looked him in his brown eyes.

"Get a pen and give me your beeper number. I'll beep you when he leaves later on tonight, a'ight?"

Junior went into the restaurant to get a pen, then gave her his number and walked away. He knew he had her. There was no way she could resist his chinky, bedroom eyes.

Later that same night, Junior was standing in front of a bodega on Graham Avenue talking with some guys when Shondra paged him. There was a payphone on the corner, so he was able to return her call quickly.

"Hello. Can I speak to Shondra?"

"She's not here. Who's this?"

"Can you tell her that Junior called?"

"I sure will. Where you at right now?"

"I'm on the corner of Humboldt Street. Why?"

"This is me, crazy. Didn't I just beep you? How you didn't know it was me? You forgot the sound of my voice already?"

"I shoulda known it was you by that sweet voice," Junior said, trying to recover. "I just needed to make sure it was you and not your moms or somebody else."

"You crazy, boy. What you doin' right now?"

"I'm out here chillin' on the ave. Why, what's up?"

"Come to the back of my building so we can talk, if you ain't too busy."

"I'll be there in thirty seconds."

Junior walked to the back of her building and waited by the benches for her to come outside. When she came out, she walked over to him and sat down beside him. She looked at him, smiled, and grabbed his hand in hers.

"I've been thinking about you ever since you gave me your beeper number. I couldn't get you out of my mind. I don't know what to expect, but I like how you came at me."

"Whoa! That's deep, ma. I didn't know you was feelin' me like that. After you told me you got a man and shit, I thought you and him was tight like that. I didn't think I had a chance."

"You know everything ain't what it seems. I do have a man, but he been actin' up lately, doing foul shit. So, we 'bout on our way to a breakup. I always said if I found a nice guy, I might hafta speed up the process. So now that we're here, what's up, daddy?"

"I ain't tryin' to step on homeboy's toes, but if his shit ain't right, then he gonna hafta get lost. I'm saying, baby, what you want to do?" he asked, dragging her up from the bench and pulling her close to him.

"I'm down for whateva," she replied.

"Let's get outta here then," he said, leading her through the building.

"Hold up, daddy. Let me go get my bag," she said, as she went to her door.

While Junior was waiting in the hallway for her to come out, he saw her man come into the building. He walked right by Junior and entered her apartment. Junior didn't know what to do. He didn't know if he should stay or leave, but decided to stay in case something jumped off.

Junior walked out of the building and sat down on the bench to wait for her. Shondra lived on the first floor and her living room window faced the back of the building. When Junior heard her man arguing with her, he went up to the gate, peeked in the window, and watched as her man shook, then slapped her in the face. He saw Shondra run out the door and into the hallway, screaming as her man followed behind her. Then Junior did something he had no business doing. He went back into the building. He didn't know what he was going to do, but knew he didn't want to see her get her ass beat by her man.

"Get the fuck off of me, motherfucker!" Junior heard Shondra screaming.

"Get ova here, bitch!"was the response from her abuser.

When Junior opened the door to the lobby, he could see her man choking her by the exit. He wanted to do something, but didn't want to seem as if he was coming to her rescue. So, he walked into the lobby as if he were cutting through the building. Her man didn't stop choking her and she looked like she was about to pass out, so Junior asked him what was wrong.

"Yo man, she 'bout to pass out."

Her man turned around, not taking his hand from around her throat. "Yo, mind your fuckin' business, a'ight?"

Junior looked at Shondra, whose eyes were pleading with him to help her.

"I'm saying, dude, she a girl. You gotta take it easy or you gonna really hurt her!"

"Didn't I tell you to mind your fuckin' business, muhfucka?" her boyfriend barked.

"I'm just looking out for you, dumb ass, so you don't catch a murda charge, but if you don't want to listen, fuck you!"

Her man suddenly released Shondra and directed all his concentration on Junior.

"Yo son, who the fuck you supposed to be, Captain Save-a-Ho?" He was now walking toward Junior.

Junior timed him perfectly and caught him with a hard right hook to his temple. Unprepared for the blow, the guy fell backward onto the stairs behind him. Shondra was on the floor catching her breath and holding her neck with both hands. Junior ran over to where the guy stumbled and commenced to hitting him with lefts and rights while he tried to cover up the blows. Junior stopped when Shondra got to her feet and started to stomp her man.

"You fat bastard! You think you gonna keep beatin' on me like that?" Shondra screamed.

Her man groaned at every foot that caught him in a tender spot. Abruptly, she stopped and ran into her house. Junior backed up and waited for him to get up, not knowing if he would charge after him or go after Shondra. While Junior waited to see what his next move would be, Shondra returned with two big steak knives in both hands and lunged at her man as he struggled to his feet. Junior tried to get to her before she plunged the knives into her man, but he moved too slowly. Shondra slashed her man on his back with one knife and the other one found itself buried in his thigh. He let out a loud yell as Junior grabbed, then pulled her away from her victim. She fought with him furiously, but he held her tightly as her man hobbled to the entrance of the building, trying to get away before she carved him up like a Thanksgiving turkey. Junior held Shondra tenderly as she buried her head into his chest and wailed.

"Alright, baby, it's all over. I got you," he said, comforting her by rocking her back and forth in his arms.

That incident consummated Junior and Shondra's union, and because of what happened, some of her ex's homeboys held animosity toward Junior. He started to hustle in front of her building shortly after getting together with her, which made them dislike him even more because he pioneered the drug game in their projects and he wasn't a resident of the hood. None of them said anything to him directly, though, because of his street credibility.

Junior was skillful with his fight game and was known to bust his gun if necessary. The guys around the way protested silently amongst themselves, but would do subliminal things to let Junior know they didn't like him. For instance, when he would go in at

night, they would rob the crackheads that came looking for him. He would find out when the crackheads told him the following day that they were robbed or bought soap, and Junior would tell them not to buy anything from anyone out there when he wasn't around. It actually benefited him because he was able to get all the money that came through there since the crackheads didn't trust anyone but him. Everything they tried to do didn't bother Junior because he wasn't going to let them or anything else stop him from getting his money.

Shondra came back into the bedroom with a glass of Pepsi and interrupted Junior's daydream. He grabbed the glass out of her hand and took a deep swallow as he stood up.

He stood 5'4" and was built like he worked out, although he didn't. He had broad shoulders and a wide, firm chest with muscular arms attached. His complexion was a tint lighter than caramel and his teeth were pearl white. His chinky eyes were complemented with long, curly eyelashes that made him look sexy whenever he blinked slowly.

Shondra lusted at her beautiful specimen of a man, then suddenly disrobed and pushed him down flat on the bed with his feet still on the ground. She straddled him and positioned herself so she could feel him stiffen. He grabbed her by her hips, brought her down to him, and kissed her lips softly. They moved as one for a moment, and then she pulled his sweats down to his thighs, grabbed his pole, and stroked it. He moaned a little, enjoying the sensation she sent through his body. Junior felt a snowy feeling coming over him and quickly repositioned himself so he wouldn't explode prematurely. The way she handled his body would make any man blast off unexpectedly. She was just that good.

He grabbed her hands, stretched them above her head, kissed her neck, and licked around her mountains, working his way down to her valley. She squirmed with each lick, and the movement of her body enticed him more. He moved his hands down to her waist and caressed her ass, then moved them to her thighs and opened her legs slightly so he could view her hairy cavern. He licked her clit and rotated the tip of his tongue around her opening, listening

for the grunts and moans she released from every good feeling. He proceeded to suck on her clit and moved his tongue rapidly like a hissing snake. He gripped her legs firmly and locked onto her like vice grips. She moaned out in pleasure as she creamed on his chin. He then flipped her over on her stomach and slid his pole inside her pulsating hole. She let out a howl, then relaxed. He went in and out her slowly, feeling her wetness while the friction sent waves of satisfaction through his body. As the sensation increased, he moved more rapidly until he fell limp inside her.

Junior rolled over on his back for a minute to catch his breath. She held him close and put her head on his chest, as they both lay naked in ecstasy.

"Damn, boo, you make me feel soooo good," she whispered in his ear.

"I love making you feel good," he replied, his breathing returning to normal.

"Don't forget to give your moms the five hundred for the rent. You can get the money out the safe," he told her, as he got up and went to the bathroom.

"Can I have some money so I can buy me some sneakers?" she asked, while going to the safe hidden in the closet.

She rarely asked for money, and that's how Junior knew she truly loved him solely because of his character. Most broads wanted dudes that had bank, but she was different. And although she didn't have shit, she wasn't a gold-digging whore.

"Take what you need," he replied. "Just make sure you lock the closet when you're done."

Junior had an everyday routine when he came out of the building. He always checked the back and front of the building for anything or anyone that looked suspicious. A lot of the guys in the hood respected or feared him, but he had to be real careful of the snakes that did you dirty behind your back. That's why he was always on the lookout for the stick-up kids and the police. He didn't want to get caught slipping. It wasn't easy being in the game. Only three years into it, he wasn't even considered a vet yet. He was still trying to perfect his craft by taking things slowly and taking advice from his cousin Craig who was a "boss" in his hood.

One of the most important things for Junior was to try and be observant of everyone and everything around him. He couldn't trust shit.

Nothing seemed out of the ordinary on this day, so he walked to the back of the building. As he approached the opened back door, he saw Sugar coming through the lane. When she saw him, she put up one finger to let him know how much she wanted to cop. He nodded at her and looked around to make sure there were no police around or on the roof looking down at him. Then he went back into the lobby so he could make the transaction on the inside.

"What up, Suge? I got it good for you, baby."

"Let me get one, my sweet prince."

When he held his hand out for the money, she stuffed her grubby hands into her pocket and produced some folded bills. She passed him the wrinkled money and he counted it to make sure it was the exact amount.

"Didn't I tell you stop bringing me this wrinkled-up money?"

He hated wrinkled money because it took too much time to unfold and count, and at any moment you could get caught if Jake (the police) came into the building.

"Wait right here," he told her, while walking to the mailbox to get his stash. "Here, baby," he said when he returned. "And the weight is nice, so don't stand there staring at it like you gonna get another one."

She took the product in her dirty hands and looked at it, plucking the bottom of the bottle with her finger like so many veteran crackheads to see if the little rocks inside settled down.

"Come on, baby, you can do me better than that," she said.

"Look Suge, I'm just coming out. Don't give me no drama this early."

"That's right, baby, and I'm just coming out, too. So, I want my first hit to be major," she replied, her smile revealing her missing teeth.

Sugar's beauty was destroyed by her addiction to the little, hard rocks. She was once a beautiful Puerto Rican woman about a year ago before her druggie boyfriend introduced her to the drug

for his own selfish reasons. He was unable to support his own habit, so he figured he would turn her out and once she became addicted to the drug, he would use her to sell her body or provide oral services for money to get high. That lasted for about three months until she realized she was the only one making money to support their habit. So, she got rid of him.

When she first got hooked on the drug, every motherfucker that ever wanted her sexually paid for her services. She was the most desirable crackhead at that time and was rewarded for her amazing skills both sexually and orally. As time passed, her beauty and physical attributes faded from the excessive use of the drug, and she was unable to support her habit by performing sexual favors around the way. She was reduced to going on the "ho stroll," a designated block for women that were strung out on drugs. Sugar would turn tricks with Mexican immigrants and other strung-out druggies, and because of the volume of partners she had, she was believed to have contracted the "monster."

"A'ight, fuck it, Sugar. Give it back and I'll see you later on," he told her, digging in his pocket to get the money she had given him.

"Please, baby, just let me get a better one and I'm gone."

"I'm not fucking wit' you, Sugar. I got shit to handle and you holding me up. Take it or leave it."

"Okay, baby, but you owe me," she said, while heading for the front entrance. "Be careful. You know it's hot out today. It's the first."

Sugar was referring to the narcs. They would be out in force trying to make busts because they knew the first and the fifteenth of every month were when welfare checks came out and most drug users would be out trying to score.

"I know, baby. Thanks for letting me know."

Junior was on his way to the other side of the projects to pick up money owed to him. He was going to Lizzette's, who lived on the fourth floor in his homeboy's building. She was a closet smoker who wasn't strung out on the shit yet, but if she continued to use, it would just be a matter of time before she looked like Sugar or worse.

He walked up the steps to the third floor, walked to the end of the corridor, and knocked three times. When she came to the door, he could hear her opening the locks, and then she opened the door wide, which was her way of inviting him in without actually saying so. He stepped inside and looked around before going all the way in. He wanted to make sure she was alone.

"What's up, papi?" she asked with her strong Spanish accent.

"You," he replied quickly, looking at her stunning figure.

"Give me a second to get dressed. I was making some breakfast," she said, walking back into the kitchen. "You not in a big rush, are you?"

"Nah, not really."

She was wearing thin yellow shorts that showed the roundness of her ass, and she couldn't have been wearing any panties as short as the shorts were. Her white T-shirt was dingy, but Junior only noticed her nipples poking out of the thin fabric. Her skin was pretty. She had a butterscotch complexion and not one blemish on her body. She was damn near perfect.

Although he loved Shondra, the man in Junior always wanted to sample her goodies, but she never showed any interest in him like that, and he didn't want to use drugs as a vice to persuade her. He didn't want her to think he was a trick.

"I'm sorry, papito. Ju wan' sonthin' to drink?" she asked.

"Yeah, something cold if you got it."

"I have only Kool-Aid, sherry flavor."

"That's good. Thanks."

She poured him the drink and then passed it to him, but the red fluid in the cup looked like an oil spill, which killed his thirst immediately. So, he sat the cup down on her center table.

"Look papi, I'm gonna take a quick shower before we go to the check-cashing place, okay?" she asked, walking past him.

"Sure, hun, but don't take too long in there," he replied, watching her ass jiggle as she went into the bathroom.

Once she was out of sight, Junior took the cup of Kool-Aid and emptied it out in her sink, washed the cup, and then deposited it in her dishtray. Her apartment was very tidy, but her furniture was battered and old. The couch was dingy beige with stains on the pillows. The tiles on the floor were clean but also had visible stains on them.

About fifteen minutes had passed, when he heard the bathroom door opening. He purposely sat facing the bathroom, hoping to steal a glance of her naked body. She emerged from the bathroom with a small towel wrapped around her upper body, and he watched her go into her room.

"Hey Liz, can I use your restroom, ma?" he yelled out to her.

"Sure, papi, go ahead."

Junior had never been past her bathroom before, but he had hopes of getting past it one day soon. He really did have to urinate, though, so he went into the bathroom and relieved himself, leaving the door open in case she wanted to come in. The bathroom was pink and very clean. It smelled like apples and cinnamon, and the aroma made him want Lizzette more. After flushing and washing his hands, he walked out of the bathroom slowly, still hoping to get a glimpse of her putting on her clothes in her bedroom. Suddenly, she came out in her bra and panties.

"Oops! I thought you were out the bano already," she said, not trying to hide herself.

"I'm sorry," he replied, his eyes fixed on her goddess-like shape.

She gave him an alluring look like she wanted him, so he went for it. He moved to her slowly, his eyes fixed on hers to make sure he was reading her signals right. When she moved toward him, he grabbed her shoulders, gently pushing her up against the hallway wall. He could hear her breathing getting heavy, and he gently kissed her while letting his hands explore the regions of her body. His heart was racing, but he kept his composure. He couldn't lose control, not when he finally had her. She smelled sweet and was soft to the touch. Her hole was already wet, so he played in her with his middle finger while she moved with his motions and moaned as they kissed. He slid down on the cold tile floor and laid down. She followed his lead, and he kept the pressure on by continuing to kiss her passionately.

As he began to pull down his sweats, she whispered in his ear, "Ju have a rubber, papi?"

He didn't have a rubber and wasn't sure how he should reply without looking desperate for the skins.

"You clean, right, mami?"

"Yeah, papi, but that's not it. I need to protect myself, and ju do, too. I don't want any bambinos."

"Ahhh, come on, Liz. I'll pull out before I nut."

"No, papi. If you don't have nothing, we can't do nothing. I want to, but I need to make sure we do it the right way."

"A'ight, mami, let's finish this another time," he said reluctantly.

"But, damn, you big, papito. I wanted you inside me," she moaned, as she got up and went into the bathroom.

Junior walked back to the living room and tried to pull himself together. She came out of the bathroom and then disappeared into her room. After getting his senses together, he walked to the front door as she came out of her bedroom. She was fully dressed and was looking edible. She had on black riding pants that showed the curves of her body and made her hips stick out like gun holsters. She had on a long, white T-shirt that covered the front of her, slightly revealing the V-shape pussy print in the tight, black pants.

"How I look, papi?"

"Like a Puerto Rican queen, baby," he replied, turning the knob on the door. "Now let's get to the check-cashing place before it gets crowded."

CHAPTER 2
I'M THE LANDLORD OF THE HOOD

"Where the fuck is this dude at?" the six-foot tall, stocky guy asked. He was talking to KB, a short guy who was on the chubby side, but not really overweight. "I'm getting tired of waiting, KB."

KB was the flunky or TIT (Thug In Training) for Stump, the six-foot tall, thug lord of his hood. Stump was a career criminal with armed robberies, grand theft auto, grand larceny, and attempted murder on his long list of crimes. He was just coming home from doing four years on a three-to-six for armed robbery. He lived in Bushwick Projects, which was one block away from Baptiste Plaza Projects. He was well known and feared for his crimes in the neighborhood. He had more enemies than friends, and the enemies that lived in the neighborhood preferred to stay away from the places he frequented to avoid a disastrous confrontation.

Stump had been shot over five times about five years ago. Half the hood was glad when they heard he had been shot, and many wished him dead. His enemies breathed a lot easier and hoped for his demise. The few friends he did have were devastated, some saying they expected nothing less because of the kind of life he was living. But, Stump survived the attack, and that made him look almost invincible and unstoppable, increasing more fear of

him. A lot of people began to think if Stump could get shot over five times in his upper body, live, and then come right back to the hood to wreak havoc, he had to be indestructible. He had stayed in the hospital only six days, and when he came home, he seemed to be more ruthless and dangerous than before. Stump was a real thug - a true thug to the death.

KB, on the other hand, wasn't anything like Stump. He wasn't built for a life of crime, but wanted to portray that image to the people that knew him. When he was younger, he wasn't much of a threat and always looked up to the "bad boys" and liked the attention they received from other people. He also lacked confidence when it came to girls and never really had a girlfriend. He saw hanging with Stump as his way of building his confidence, gaining respect, and getting girls. He was looking to earn some recognition in the hood, but never expected to get in as deep as he did.

"Go 'round the corner and see if you see that muhfucka, K," Stump told KB.

"A'ight."

KB went around the corner, but instead of looking to see if Junior was coming, he went into the store. While he was in there bullshitting, he never noticed Junior and Lizzette coming out of her building.

"Hey papi, I want to see you later on tonight and not just for business," Lizzette said to Junior seductively.

"No problem, ma. I want to finish what we started up there with no interruptions. Feel me?"

As they got closer to the corner, Junior started ruffling through his pockets looking for her welfare card.

"Shit, I think I left your card home," he said, a little frustrated. "I have to go get it. You just go ahead to the check-cashing place and stand in line. I should be there before you get to the window."

"Okay, papi. It's probably crowded by now anyway."

Junior kept walking straight toward his girlfriend's crib, while Lizzette turned the corner and began walking toward the check-cashing place. KB emerged from the store just as she turned the corner. He caught a glimpse of her beautiful shape, not knowing it

was her, and walked behind her quickly to get a full-body view. When he finally recognized who she was, he hurried to Stump to let him know.

"That's the bitch he be seeing on the side," KB pointed to Lizzette and told Stump when he finally made it where he was standing.

"That's the bitch, huh?" Stump asked, watching her cross the street. "She don't look like no fiend to me. You sure she fuck with that shit?"

"Yeah, man, she gets high, and I saw him go over there earlier."

"Well, where the fuck he at then?"

"I don't know. I didn't see him with her, so he musta left."

***

Shondra was in the shower when Junior got to the crib. He went into the bedroom and looked on the bed and floor for the missing welfare card. Unable to find it, he unlocked the closet to see if he'd dropped it in there. When he didn't see it in the closet, he became worried because he needed it in order to get the money owed to him.

"Ay Mooka, did you see a welfare card anywhere in the room?" he yelled to Shondra, who was still in the shower.

"Huh?"

Junior walked over to the bathroom and opened the door. The steam from the hot shower billowed out like a backdraft. The thick, white smoke stifled him as he asked Shondra again if she had seen the card.

"Oh yeah, boo. I put it in your black Fila jacket hanging in the closet."

He could hear the water beating off her body, and he could see her silhouette through the thin shower curtain. He was getting excited, but refrained from his impulses because he was in a rush. He would have to take a raincheck and come back to tear that ass up later.

He returned to the bedroom, and as he checked the pocket of the jacket, he looked up on the shelf at the pistol he shot off the night before, along with two nine-millimeter automatic Glocks and a .38 snub-nose revolver he had taken out and forgotten to put back in his duffle bag. He kept guns in the house in case he ever had beef in the streets, but so far, he never had a reason to use them and hoped he never would. However, after what happened last night, he had a strange feeling things were about to change. Then, all of a sudden, the thought gave him a strong urge to take one of the guns with him.

After finding the card in his jacket, Junior stood in front of the closet contemplating on whether or not to take one of the guns. His reasoning for taking the gun was because it was the first of the month, the day all welfare recipients received their check, more notoriously known as Mother's Day in the hood. On this day, more thieves would be out in flocks looking for a quick stick or quick lick to scam unaware women out of their money. Having a gun would give him the leverage needed to thwart any possible attempt of robbing him. His reasoning on not taking the gun was because he had on sweats, which provided no support if he carried the gun in his waistband. Another reason was the increase of police patrolling the hood. They, too, knew that on the first most welfare recipients received their budgets. A majority of those recipients were strung out on drugs, and the cops would be looking to bust a user for copping or catching a dealer making a transaction. He was having a hard time trying to decide because his reasoning on both sides was valid. Then he thought of something he was told by his cousin Craig. *It's best to have a gun and not need it than to need one and not have it.* Needless to say, Junior took the gun.

Shondra came into the room smelling like Dove soap with a towel covering only a portion of her voluptuous body, showing off how firmly shaped her breasts and hips were in the terrycloth fabric. Junior looked up at her and lusted, but pushed his desires to the back of his mind because he had more important things to take care of at the moment.

***

The check-cashing place was packed with customers trying to cash their welfare check, Social Security check, or employment check. Some of the women picking up welfare checks had on their houseclothes, wearing house slippers with headscarves tied up on their heads. The younger females were there with their infant children or toddlers dressed in the newest fashions, proof of what they spent the free money on. The people picking up their Social Security checks were older or disabled, and the working part of the crowd was dressed in company uniforms or in slacks and shoes.

After spotting Lizzette, Junior walked over to her while she spoke in Spanish to another woman and placed the welfare card in her hand. She turned to him and smiled lovingly.

"I'm going to stand outside and wait for you," he whispered in her ear.

She nodded and continued her conversation with the Spanish woman. Junior walked out and stood by a payphone on the corner just as his beeper went off.

Junior checked the number in his beeper and then fumbled in his pocket for change to return the call. Once he dialed the number, he turned around as he spoke to the person on the other end. Being so observant, he noticed KB and Stump standing on the corner a couple of blocks away. He looked at the two, and when he hung up, he stood there and continued to watch them. He knew Stump from his rep on the streets, and it was highly unusual for him to be out so early because he was known to commit his crimes later on in the day. He also recognized the guy Stump was with on the corner. He was the guy Kendu, one of his workers, hung out with from time to time, but Junior had never seen him with Stump before and that, too, was unusual in itself. Junior tried to figure out what the two were up to this morning, but more importantly, he knew their connection spelled trouble. They had to be scheming on someone or something in the immediate area, and he hoped it wasn't him.

Lizzette came out with Junior's money bundled up in one hand and a receipt in the other. Junior took the money owed to him and

whispered something in her ear. Then she walked off in one direction, and he in the other.

Stump and KB were still standing on the corner hoping to run into Junior.

"You know what?" Stump asked KB. "You would think he knew I was waiting for his ass today. Shit, I just want to talk to the brotha 'bout some things I been hearing about him in the hood."

"Things like what, dawg?" KB asked, engaging in the light banter Stump was starting.

"I heard the muhfucka been making some cream out here in the hood and ain't paid me no rent yet."

"Is that right? But why would he pay you rent, Stump?"

"'Cause I'm the fucking landlord of the hood, that's why. That muhfucka ain't even from around here, and he making money out here like he paid dues already. Fuck that. He gotta pay or change locations."

"I feel you," KB said. "They said he make like five hundred on a bad night."

"That's why he gotta pay to play. He can't be out here blowing up without giving back to the fuckin' community. I'm not having it!"

Stump had a fetish for robbing drug dealers and mainly focused on the big fish, the ones that supplied the product. He would occasionally rob a street peddler as a bonus since their operation was always done out in the open, making them easy targets. He would rob the ones in his neighborhood because he didn't like drugs being sold where he lived.

Lizzette was walking past the bodega when KB noticed her.

"That's the bitch he was with this morning," KB told Stump.

"I know," Stump replied. "Go ask her if she knows where Junior is when she comes out."

"A'ight."

Lizzette was buying some milk, eggs, and bread, when KB opened the door and walked into the bodega.

"You want me to help you wit' your bags, miss?" KB offered.

"No, I'm okay. Thank you," she replied.

"Oh a'ight. Ummm…I wanted to talk to you when I saw you earlier, but I saw you wit' Junior. I didn't want to be disrespectful, so I didn't say anything. Since he's not wit' you now, I figured I could talk to you, unless he's your man. Is he your man?"

"Que?" Lizzette asked in Spanish.

"Junior…is he your boyfriend?"

"Oh, Junior…yes, yes, I know Junior. He very nice guy," Lizzette answered.

"So is he your man or not? I mean, is it okay for me to talk to you?" .

"No, I…ahh…no…I don't know," she responded in her worst English.

"I'm talking about the guy you was wit' earlier, a lil while ago?" KB reiterated.

"Today? Yeah, I see him today, but I don't know where he at," she replied, as if she didn't understand what he was trying to ask her.

"Oh…okay…sorry to bother you, luv."

KB gave up and walked back to Stump to tell him what Lizzette had said.

"That bitch was lying through her fucking teeth. Acting like she don't understand English. I saw him go to her building early this morning and he didn't come out," he said to Stump.

"Ah, shut the fuck up. You don't know if he came out or not 'cause your dumb ass wasn't paying attention. He mighta came out and you just didn't see him," Stump retorted. "Fuck it. I'll get him later on tonight or tomorrow. But, if I catch him later and my pockets is fucked up, then ain't no telling what will go down."

***

When Junior got back to Shondra's place, he went into the bedroom closet to stash the money he picked up from Lizzette in his safe. While he put the money away, he couldn't help but think that seeing Stump and KB was confirmation of the funny feeling he was having that morning. Although nothing happened, he was sure they were up to no good standing on that corner scheming.

Junior pulled out a bomb of work, put it in a plastic bag, and then stuffed it inside the front of his pants. Shondra was sitting on the bed dressed in Crème European silk pants with a matching top watching television. She had on two pairs of doorknocker earrings, and three modest-sized gold chains adorned her neck. One chain was a herringbone Junior bought off a crackhead for one hundred dollars, which appraised for eight hundred when he took it to the scales. It had a heart pendant outlined in diamond chips hanging from it. The second chain was a Figaro with a crucifix pendant, and the third chain was an eighteen–inch medium-sized Cuban link with a diamond pendant of a Nefertiti head.

Shondra wore the finest apparel because Junior loved for her to look good. Aside from that, it was a statement in being hood rich. You dressed as if you were royalty, you wore exorbitant amounts of jewelry for no real purpose, and you bought expensive electronics that cost more than the rent you paid. All this was done in an attempt to separate you from the reality of being poor and trying to act rich but not knowing how to be rich. It was all smoke and mirrors in the hood. No one was educated on how to live. You were happy just existing.

With all Junior bought and did for Shondra, it didn't change her. She was still the humble, sweet, loving girl he met three years ago.

"I thought you were going shopping? I see you got all dolled up," Junior said before leaving out again.

"I am. I'm waiting for Gloria to come downstairs. Then we goin' downtown and pick some things up."

"Oh, okay. What you goin' to cop down there?" he asked, forgetting what she had told him earlier.

"I want the new Carolina Blue Air Max. They not even out yet, but my homegirl got me the hook up in Dr. Jay's downtown."

"You know what, pick me up a pair, too, but I want all white ones."

"Okay, boo. I'll get what you want if they have them."

"Thanks, baby."

Shondra sighed heavily when Junior left out the door. She was concerned about him. The night before she had heard gunshots and

became afraid because she wasn't sure if he was involved. That night she waited patiently for him to come in, and when she heard the front door close, she breathed a sigh of relief but acted like she was asleep. She heard him open the closet and ruffle around in some bags, then he left. Not soon after she heard more gunshots that terrifid her.

Since he started hustling in her hood, he didn't allow her to be out late at night because he felt she was a target for anyone that wanted to get to him. She was a hustler's girlfriend, so she had to play her position, which was to not question him about his business. He made it clear that if he didn't tell her anything, it was best for her not to know. Although it was hard to follow his rules, she respected and trusted his word.

Every one of Shondra's old boyfriends was always from different neighborhoods, and the guys in her hood never liked that fact. The ones that liked her could never get past the friendship stage with her because she wouldn't talk to anyone in the area romantically. Shondra's looks weren't what made her so sought after. What was attractive and intriguing was the fact that no one in the hood could ever say they hit it, which made her somewhat like wifey material. Shondra was not known for sleeping around and didn't have a bad rep or carry the moniker of being a whore. She wasn't stuck up, had a beautiful shape, and most importantly, she was friendly and demanded respect. What she was known for was her temper and her impeccable fighting skills. Most of her fights were violent because she fought like a beast in the wild, making sure her opponents came out looking other than themselves. She had gained respect from every girl and many of the women in the PJs, and although she was a really nice person, females knew not to fuck with her because of her brutal fighting skills.

Shondra didn't care if the guys around the way didn't like her man. She was behind everything he did one hundred percent. She had his front and his back, and would not let anything happen to him if she was able to prevent it. She was down with him to the bitter end. She was his eyes and ears on the streets. She was someone whose word he could trust, and she loved him dearly because he loved her unconditionally. His making her feel

beautiful boosted her self-esteem. She cherished their relationship because he was a good man to her and did things with her that she never experienced with any man before him.

CHAPTER 3
YOU TRYIN' TO SET ME UP

Junior ran into Lakim as he came out of Shondra's building. "What the deal, dun-dun?" Lakim asked, slapping Junior five.

"Ain't nuthin', kicko I got you," Junior told him. "Come on. Let's go take care of this in the building."

After they boarded the elevator, Junior pressed the button for the sixth floor. They got out when the doors opened, walked to the stairway door, and made the transaction inside the stairwell. First, though, Junior walked up some of the stairs leading to the roof to make sure no one was up there getting high. He didn't like to conduct business inside apartments because he felt it was a "get had" spot. If you handled business in an apartment, it wouldn't be long before someone peeped it and set you up. He figured if he was in the building, he could hear anyone coming up the stairs or coming off the elevator, which would give him time to get away or deal with the situation.

Lakim pulled out a bankroll and counted out forty-two hundred dollars in small bills.

"Kendu's in here, too, but he still got a bomb left. I knocked all mine off last night."

Junior counted the money and put the roll in his pocket, then pulled out the Ziploc bag full of work from inside the front of his

sweats and handed it to Lakim. Lakim looked at the bag, then stuffed it inside his jacket.

"Yo, why don't you hit me off with more work?" he asked, not waiting for an answer before continuing. "I be knocking off like five G's every two days, and you still spoon feeding me, bruh."

"You want me to hit you with a ten-G pack?" Junior asked, tilting his head and looking at Lakim sideways.

"I'm just saying, yo, when I finish my last pack, I always got to find you, and I be losing money on the block like that. Like, I finished my pack last night after you went inside, but I couldn't re-up because you don't want nobody knocking on your door after you go in for the night. I lost like five hundred easy last night, and I'm a late hawk. You know my motto, kid. I don't close; I doze. Ya feel me?"

"Why didn't you just get Kendu's work and knock it off then?"

"'Cause that dude don't be out late like me. He mostly be out in the morning and go in when he make like four hundred or something. That's why it takes him so long to knock off his pack."

"Aight, check this out. Take whatever Kendu didn't finish and knock off the pack I just gave you. That should be about seven G's worth of work. If I see you Thursday to re-up, then I'll keep you on that, cool?"

"A'ight, but Du gonna be vexed if I take all his work and he don't get no re-up. You know what I'm sayin'?"

"Tell Du come see me 'bout that. I need to talk to him anyway."

Besides Kendu moving his work slow, Junior wanted to see him because he had a bad feeling after seeing Stump and KB together earlier. He knew KB hung out with Kendu, so he was going to see if Kendu said anything to them concerning his operation. Because of his rep, Junior knew if Stump heard about him making money in the hood, he could be expecting a visit from him very soon. The more he thought about it, the more urgent the need to talk to Kendu became.

As of late, Kendu had been acting a little suspicious, too. He wouldn't be around as much, and he was taking an unusually long time to knock off his packages. Then he would come up extremely

short with bullshit excuses. Junior began to feel that something shady was about to go down soon. With the random shots fired the night before, to seeing Stump and KB on the corner, it was all telltale signs of something bad happening.

Junior processed things realistically because he wanted to be one step ahead of the bullshit. He was a naturally cautious guy and stayed on point most of the time, so he wanted to make sure he wasn't caught slipping if in fact someone was scheming on him. There was so much on his plate he had to worry about – the cops, the crackheads snitching, stick-up kids looking for a quick stick, and just the run-of-the-mill haters to name a few. Shit was really hectic out there in the concrete jungle.

***

Shondra opened the door when she heard Gloria yelling her name in the lobby for her to come out.

"Damn, girl, you deaf? I been calling you for ten minutes," Gloria remarked to Shondra when she opened her front door.

"Shut up, bitch. That's why they say we so damn ghetto. We done forgot how to knock on doors like normal muhfuckas," Shondra said, locking the door behind her. "Not to mention how much we fucking curse."

"Come on, ho, let's get moving before them real ghetto bitches buy up all the shit in the shoe store," Gloria replied, and then they left to go to downtown Brooklyn.

Shondra was in Bakers Shoe Store looking at some sandals, when a guy with a mouth full of gold fronts came up behind her and rubbed himself on her ass.

"Damn you soft, mama," he whispered in her ear.

Shondra reacted so swiftly that the blow threw him off guard and he fell back into a display of shoes.

"What the fuck is your problem, muhfucka!" she screamed, searching for the box cutter Junior always made her carry in her Gucci purse.

"What the fuck you hit me for bitch?" he protested, getting up from among the spilled shoes on the floor.

"Is you crazy muhfucka? You not my man to be rubbing up against me like that!"

"I made a mistake, bitch. It's crowded in here!"

Gloria was rushing from the front of the store trying to see what the commotion was all about.

"What's wrong, Shondra?"

"That stupid muhfucka over there tried to cop a feel on me like I'm a ho or something. That bastard don't know me or what I will do to his faggot ass!"

"Fuck that, you ugly bitch. I was just trying to get past your ugly ass!"

The manager of the store came and got between Shondra and the guy right before she could swing the box cutter.

"Wait! Don't do something you'll regret later," the manager said, grabbing the hand that held the razor.

"Get the fuck off her!" Gloria screamed, pushing the manager off of Shondra.

As a crowd gathered in front of the store, the guy who had grabbed Shondra slipped out of the mayhem unnoticed.

"Where the fuck he at? I should have sliced off his two-inch dick, with his bitch ass. That's why I don't like coming down here. These disrespectful muhfuckas don't know how to act. They think every girl they see is a ho or something. And what the fuck was his black ass doin' in a woman's shoe store anyway?"

"You ain't lying, girl. Fuck it. Let's get outta here," Gloria said, walking towards the entrance of the store.

"Damn, I forgot to get Junior his sneakers. Let's go to Tom Dick's around the way and get them," she told Gloria, as a cab pulled up.

"I'm wit' that," Gloria responded.

***

Kendu was sitting on his bed watching TV when he heard a knock on the door.

"Who is it?"

"It's me," Lakim said.

Kendu opened the door to let him in and then headed back to his room that was only furnished with a twin mattress and box spring that lay on the floor, and a thirteen-inch black and white television that sat on a broken wooden dresser. Lakim sat on the edge of the unmade bed, picked up an unlit blunt in Kendu's homemade ashtray, and lit it.

"What up, man?" he asked, taking a pull of the blunt before passing it to Kendu.

"Ain't nothin', man. I'm just chillin'. What's good wit' you?"

"I just got right. How much work you got left?" Lakim asked bluntly.

"I still got like a half a bomb left," Kendu said, putting out the blunt.

"Today's the first. You 'posed to get right. Why you ain't on the block getting that easy bread?"

"That money ain't goin' nowhere, man. Them heads want that shit 'round the clock. I ain't stressin' trying to get rid of that shit in no hurry."

"Well, give me what you got left and I'll knock it off. Plus, Junior wanna holla at you."

"What the fuck he want with me? He wanna know why I ain't on the block, huh? I'm getting tired of this dude actin' like he my boss and shit. And I'm getting tired of him stressing me about getting rid of this work. This ain't no real job where I punch a fuckin' clock or get docked for coming to work late. He act like it's legal to do this shit! He really got this shit twisted."

"It ain't like that, dawg. It's called fast money, and that's all he trying to do. If you making it slow, then you holding up the process, you feel me?"

"You act like you on his love. Let me find out." Kendu shook his head. "Did he send you over here to get his work 'cause I'm moving it slow? He scared to tell me himself? Faggot-ass muhfucka!"

"Come on, Du, you know how it is when a muhfucka want they money. They don't want to wait, and they definitely don't want to hear excuses."

"You know what? Fuck this! Take this shit!" Kendu pulled out the work from under his mattress. "I don't need this bullshit from that muhfucka. He thinks he's the man out here anyway, and he ain't even from our hood!"

Looking at Kendu, Lakim could see he was upset and was overreacting, but there seemed to be something else contributing to his anger, something more than what he was letting on.

"It ain't like that, Du. You know how the game is. Do you and the man got beef or something? I mean, the way you sounding off, you make it seem like he did something foul to you." Lakim tilted his head. "Did something go down between you two? Did he violate or something?"

"Man, La, you lost to this shit. That dude ain't nobody. All he doin' is making money in our hood and giving us the crumbs from all the bread he making. Shit, we can do this shit on our own and run his ass outta here."

"Yeah, you right, but what did he do to you to make you flip like this? Something had to happen to make you start talking like this all of a sudden when just last week everything was gravy."

"This ain't all of sudden, homeboy. You know the boys ain't never like him like that. His ugly-ass girl is the only reason why nobody ain't moved on his punk ass yet. I'm telling you, La, brothers is ready to move that muhfucka out the hood. So, you better keep it real out here or they gonna think you down with him."

"Damn, I knew the boys 'round here wasn't really feelin' him, but I didn't know they was talking like that. I mean, dude is mad cool and ain't never fucked with anybody out here. All he do is smoke that good choke and drink his beer. Which one of the cats out here sayin' they ready to move on him?"

Kendu lit the blunt again and took a deep breath. "It ain't just a couple dudes. Everybody saying they ready to move on him…the whole projects…bitches, too."

"Get the fuck outta here, man. You gotta be bullshittin'. The whole projects can't be saying that because I ain't heard nothing. But check it, Du. Fuck them other cats. I'm talking about you. Why you salty with Junior? While none of these dudes 'round here

getting no money, he came through and put us on. When you short with the dough, he don't beef. He tells you to double up on your next pack. Du, you know you my man and I'm down with you, kid. Just tell me what the problem is."

"Yo, why is you actin' like that muhfucka's sponsor? You carrying on like he saved your life or something. Come on, La, don't change sides, man. Dude ain't worth it." Kendu looked Lakim straight in his eyes. "I don't like him because I don't like how he thinks he can throw his weight around like he the man and he really ain't. That's what my problem is with him. Fuck him, La. He ain't no fuckin' body."

Lakim shook his head as he got up off the bed, picked up the work, and headed for the door. "Yo, Du, I can see why you upset, but you really going about this the wrong way, homeboy. Don't get caught up in the hype with these cats, because they don't have no real ambition. If they did, they would be out here slinging, too. Look at shit for what it really is."

"Yeah, a'ight. Don't get too tied up with your homeboy. You know you one of us kid, and when shit hits the fan, you know nothing is gon' happen to you. You hear me?" Kendu asked before Lakim reached the front door.

"I hear you, son. I'm not getting caught up."

As he walked to the elevator, Lakim concentrated on what Kendu said to him. Kendu was sending out bad vibes and something was about to go down, and when it did, it was going to change everything in the hood. Shit was about to get real fucked up out there, and Lakim had to make a choice. He rode down the elevator wondering if he should inform Junior about what Kendu was saying or if he should back off from Junior. Whatever he was going to decide, he needed to do it fast because time wasn't on his side.

Junior was coming from the other side of the projects from collecting money that was owed to him, when his beeper went off. When he checked it, he recognized Lizzette's code and already had an idea what she wanted. So, he turned around and headed towards her building. When he got to her floor, he fixed the gun in his waist and then knocked on her door.

"Come in," she said.

He turned the knob of the brown metal door and walked into her apartment.

"What's up, ma?"

"You were right, papi," she said, coming from the back of the apartment wearing a see-through shirt with no bra and panties. "The short guy was asking me questions about you."

"What did you tell him?"

"I don't tell him anything. I just listen to what he ask me about you."

"What did he ask you?"

"He ask me if you my boyfriend and if I see you early today. I tell him I see you, but then he ask me if I know where you go. I tell him no, but he don't look like he believe me."

"Did the other guy say anything to you?"

"No. He just whisper something to the other guy, and he stay outside and just look at me. Wha, they no like you or sunthin'?"

"I don't really know because I don't know them like that."

Junior didn't want Lizzette to know what he was really thinking, so he avoided answering her question. One thing was for sure. His suspicions were now confirmed aobut Stump and KB.

"Well, what you got good for me, papi?" she asked, walking to the back room of the apartment.

"Whatever you want, luv."

She returned with a small plastic bag, then sat down on her couch.

"Give me five." She poured the contents of the bag on the oval glass center table.

Junior pulled out six of the skinny, clear plastic bottles and placed them on the table.

"Okay, papi." Her eyes got big after seeing the drugs. "I'm gonna get right. I hope you don't mind."

"Nah, go ahead. Knock yourself out," he said, getting up from the couch.

"Where you goin'?" she asked, splitting open a cigar with a rusty razor.

"I gotta jet. I got some shit I need to take care of on the other side. I'll be back later if you need me."

"I thought you was gonna stay a lil while with me. I hope I'm not turning you off doing this."

"Come on, ma, I ain't no judge. I sell the shit," he replied, as he changed his mind and went to the bathroom to relieve himself.

When he returned, she was crushing the small white rocks in a dollar bill. He stood and watched as she emptied the contents into a cigar that was filled with weed. She rolled up the cigar, then put it in her mouth and twirled it around, allowing her saliva to act like glue and seal the edges. She looked up, her head half-tilted, and then lit the cigar. She drew a deep breath, blew out the smoke, and sat back looking like she just orgasmed.

Junior looked at her, wondering how the hell someone so beautiful could be on that shit. It was so powerfully addictive, and it slowly stripped its users of their self-respect. It turned them into different beings that would sell their souls to the devil to acquire a false sense of euphoria. She looked at him, took another deep drag, and blew out the smoke again. He started to smell a sweet, tangy aroma, signaling him that it was time to go.

"A'ight, ma, I'm out. Hit me on my hip when you need to see me again."

"I need to see you now," she responded seductively, rubbing her breasts and smiling a crooked smile that formed from the effects of the drug numbing her mouth like Novacaine.

"I'll come back later on. I just gotta take care of some business real quick," he said, closing the door behind him.

Lizzette sighed when he left. She was usually able to use her body to get guys strung out with her so they would supply her with free drugs until they went broke, but Junior seemed just a little too focused to get pulled into her trap.

Lakim was coming out of the building after serving a customer, when he saw Junior coming up the block.

"Whaddup, kicko?" Lakim asked.

"Nothing. I just left that Puerto Rican broad's crib making a sale. It's fucked up to see how that shit can fuck up some perfectly good ass. The bitch was getting fucked up with me in there. I don't trust bitches like that, 'specially when they know I can supply their ass with the shit that keeps their pussy wet," Junior said, chuckling.

"I got that work from Kendu. He had a buck left," Lakim said, getting down to business.

"Did he give you the rest of my money?"

"Nah, he said he would give it to you himself later on," Lakim lied.

"You told him what I said?"

"Yeah."

"What he say? Was he mad when you took the rest of the work from him?"

"Yeah, man, he was heated, but I told him he was slowing shit down 'cause he takin' his time to get rid of the work. He tried to tell me why he wasn't finished, but I wasn't really listening to what he was saying. I was trying to get the work so I could come out here and get this money."

"So you a'ight now?" Junior asked.

"I'm good. I made like six already, so I'm 'bout to go to the crib and get something to eat, then come back on the block lata on."

"Cool. I'm going up to Williamsburg to go pick up the rest of my money. I'll be back in a few. I'll see you on the block when I get back."

***

Shondra and Gloria were walking up Graham Avenue talking about going to club Red Parrot that night, while Kendu was standing on the corner of Siegel Street talking to KB.

"My man La came to my crib and told me that muhfucka don't want me to work for him no more because I move his shit too slow. I started not to give him the rest of the work and tell him to tell that muhfucka come see me if he wanted it, but I figured I'd just keep the dough I already got. He thinks I'm his son or something. And he a coward for sending my man to do shit he scared to do himself. I know he scared of me. I'll fuck his ass up

and he knows it." Kendu waved his hands in the air as he talked. "He sent my man because he knows if he came at me with that bullshit, he would have problems. I hope that muhfucka do come and ask me for that money so I can beat flames outta his ass. I'm telling you, KB, he be knowing who to go to with that bullshit."

"I hear you talking, bruh. About how much shit he be moving out here?" KB asked.

Kendu shrugged his shoulders. "I don't know, maybe about eight, nine G's a week."

"You and your man La the only workers he got slingin' for him?"

"Yea, I think it's only me and La right now. The muhfucka greedy. He sells most of his shit himself. He got La working my building, 155, and 215. I work my building in the day, and sometimes I go in front of 300 and catch the heads going to Bushwick, but I do it when shit moving slow. I ain't out here like my man La, every day and every fucking night like I'm a basehead. Junior hustles in front of his girl's building during the day, and at night, he slings outta the back. He usally sits on the benches all night and waits on some cat to come through from Tompkins."

"Oh, so he don't be by himself when he out here slingin'?" KB questioned.

"Sometimes me or La will be out here with him, but when it gets late, some dude from Tompkins usually comes through and chills with him. I guess he comes through to hold him down or something."

"Who the dude is?" KB asked.

"I don't know who he is but I know he from Tompkins," Kendu told him. "My man La told me that."

"Do that cat be out there all night with him?"

"I don't know. I don't hang with him like that. I just smoke his choke up and drink all his beer. Then when it's all gone, I jet."

Shondra and Gloria walked past Kendu and KB while they were talking. Kendu glared at Shondra as they walked by, and Gloria stared KB down. Gloria thought KB was cute, while Shondra returned Kendu's glare.

"Stump ready to move on that dude, you know?" KB told him after the girls passed them.

"I hear you. I don't like that faggot-ass muhfucka no way. When y'all ready to get at him, let me know, 'cause I'm down for whatever."

"Ain't that his wisdom that just walked by with that dark-skinned chick?" KB asked.

"Yeah, that's his bitch. I don't like her fronting ass either. She be actin' like she all dat, and she used to be a bum-ass bitch back in the day."

"He must be getting money, 'cause they look like they just came from shopping with all dem bags they had. Plus, she's dressed fly as fuck," KB acknowledged.

"Yeah, yeah, his trickin' ass probably is giving that ho all his money. That's why he stressin' me for his money and shit."

"I'm saying, though, she draped in jewels and the whole nine," KB elaborated.

"Fuck that bitch, son. She ain't nobody. She ain't shit either, just like her punk-ass man."

When Shondra and Gloria got in her house, Shondra threw the bags on her bed and Gloria turned on the Sony radio/CD/cassette player on her dresser.

"Let me call my baby to let him know I'm home," Shondra said, picking up the phone.

"You gonna tell him about what happened downtown?" Gloria asked.

"Hell yeah! He know a lotta people and we was downtown where everybody hangs out, and if somebody he knows seen it and tell him instead of me, he gonna be pissed off with me."

"Well, you got a good man, because most muhfuckas wouldn't give a fuck," Gloria said with attitude.

"You right, most muhfuckas, but not my muhfucka," Shondra said, smiling and dialing his beeper number.

Gloria began dancing to the music playing on the radio. "Don't forget to tell him that you want to go to the club tonight, too, bitch," she said, shaking her round hips to the rhythm of the music.

"We going. Don't worry, ho."

Shondra pulled out the Nike box with Junior's sneakers in it and put it in the closet on top of his other sneaker boxes. She had also bought him a matching Nike shirt.

"That color is nice," Gloria said.

"I know. I got good taste, bitch."

"What you gonna wear tonight to the club?" Gloria asked.

Gloria didn't have as many clothes as Shondra, but everytime they went shopping, Shondra would always pick her up something because Gloria wasn't financially able to buy expensive clothing nor did she have a man that splurged on her.

"I didn't even think about it yet. I might wear that purple, buttersoft leather dress with the back out and my Nine West hooker boots."

"You gonna be a fly bitch with that on. I really want to go so I can dance and enjoy myself. You know what? We should ask them bitches across the street to go with us so we can really party. What you think?" Gloria asked.

"I was thinking about that, too. We can make it a girls' night out. By the way, you see that guy we passed on Graham Avenue that was talking to that dirty-ass Kendu?" Shondra asked her.

"Yeah, I don't like Kendu. You see how he looked at you all funny and shit when we walked by? But the guy he was standing with was kinda cute. I was going to say something to him, but that jealous-ass Kendu probably woulda cock blocked."

"I think the dude he was with is from Williamsburg," Shondra said.

"Yeah, I believe he is," Gloria responded.

"I heard the dudes from over there are real grimy. I heard they be beefing with the guys from our projects, trying to set them up and shit," Shondra told her.

"I heard that, too."

"I don't know him, but I been seeing him with Kendu a lot in the back getting high and shit. Kendu always look like he up to no fuckin' good. You gotta watch his greasy ass," Shondra said.

"You right 'bout that Kendu, but the guy he was with, I think he's cute. The next time I see him, I'm gonna make it my business

to get with him, that's if he's by himself," Gloria said, shaking her wide hips.

"Well, don't give the pussy up until you at least get his name, ho," Shondra chuckled.

"You don't worry about who I put this good pussy on, bitch. The only thing this pussy worried about is if he's hung like a horse."

Gloria envied Shondra's relationship with Junior. She never found a man to treat her the way Junior treated Shondra. Alhtough she had a shiny, black complexion, Gloria was still very beautiful and had an hourglass figure. Her face was perfectly round with full lips, a straight nose, and a good grade of hair, thanks to her Cherokee heritage. When she was younger, Gloria was loose and had been dogged out by a lot of guys from the projects. She was labeled a ho because she was so easy to bed down. Her low self-esteem was a result of being raped as a child by most of her mother's boyfriends. To add insult to injury, her mother would mentally abuse her by calling her "blackie", "tar baby", and "inkspot" because she hated the fact all her boyfriends seemed only to want to be around her because of how well developed her daughter was. Gloria soon began to desire the affection and attention she was missing from home and sought it from anyone who would tell her that she was pretty or that they really liked her. That was all it took for her to put out and give her body away.

It got around fairly quickly that Gloria was an easy lay, and every guy in Baptiste was in her ear trying to sample her goods. She loved the attention. Her reputation for her mean head game and her freaky activities between the sheets soon spread throughout Baptiste and to the neighboring hoods like a wildfire. She was compared to the porn star Vanessa Del Rio because of her willingness to do threesomes and have gangbangs. She was so caught up in all the attention she was receiving that she never realized she was being abused physically and mentally by her sex partners. Her reputation was being trashed, and she had no idea of the adverse effect it would have on her life.

One day, one of the guys she saw regularly called and said he wanted to see her. She wasn't doing anything, so she agreed to

meet him at his house. When she got to his room, he lit a blunt and they got high and had sex. After they were finished, he asked her if his boys could get down, but she refused his request. He was not happy with her response and tried to smooth talk her into changing her mind, but her mind was made up.

Upset, he stormed out the room and returned with seven guys. Upon seeing them, Gloria gasped, fearing the worse. The look on the guys' faces said they were not in the mood to hear the word "no". She got up off the bed and went for the door, but one of the guys blocked her exit. Another guy put his finger over his mouth, motioning for her not to make any noises. Her heart started to beat quickly and her mouth got dry as a desert. Suddenly, it became hard for her to swallow. She couldn't believe what was about to happen. She never fathomed anything like that happening to her. She backed up, moving away from the pack of wild boys who were ogling her body hungrily. Unconsciously, she backed right up to the bed and fell backwards. Someone mounted her almost immediately, and she closed her eyes and lay still, letting each rapist assault and abuse her temple savagely.

When they were finished with her, she was left sprawled on the bed, ravaged, like she was the victim of a terrible car wreck. Gloria was left alone in the room naked, cold, and numb. She felt worthless and contemplated on ending her life. She rose to her feet and walked out the door half-dressed. She wandered out into the building's hallway aimlessly, unaware that she was suffering from shock. When she walked out the building, the frigid November breeze brought her back to reality as she tried to cover up with what little clothes she had on.

Shondra happened to be coming from Cooper Projects, when she noticed Gloria walking in the direction of Baptiste. She walked quickly to catch up to her so they could walk home together, although she distanced herself from her in the past because of her bad rep. When she caught up to Gloria, she realized something was wrong and flagged down a cab, taking her home. Shondra cleaned her up and gave her pain pills. When Gloria finally came back to her senses, she was laying in Shondra's bed having her hair stroked by Shondra.

Shondra never asked her anything about what happened. She just took her under her wing and taught her how to love and respect herself. She made her realize she was searching for something outside of herself she always had on the inside. When Shondra was finished with her, Gloria was a totally changed woman with a brand-new outlook on life and a better understanding of herself. This is when Gloria and Shondra's friendship was cemented. Shondra was there for Gloria. Even when some guys tried to break Gloria's will, she continued to support her effort to change until everyone soon realized Gloria was a changed woman.

***

It was late in the afternoon. Stump got up and sat on the edge of his bed yawning. He had come home and dozed off because he had gotten up so early to see about the guy KB had wanted him to rob. His catnap wasn't sufficient and he was still feeling a little fatigued, but he wanted to go back to Baptiste and find Junior. Stump hated drugs, but most of all, he hated drug dealers. He had lost his mother to an overdose when he was seven years old.

The dealer that sold her the lethal dosage was his father, and he had left her to die. Stump remembered standing in the doorway of her bedroom as he watched his father pack his belongings, while his mother lie shaking and foaming at the mouth on the cold, wooden floor. The dealer never noticed his son, motionless, tears streaming down his cheeks, standing there watching, but unable to utter a single word. The dealer grabbed the dopefiend's "tools" and any other evidence that could prove he had been a witness to her death. Then he rushed out of the bedroom, literally knocking young Stump to the ground.

The front door slammed closed and Stump made it to his feet, slowly walking into the bedroom to try and help his dying mother. He cried out her name in desperation, but her eyes stayed rolled up in her head, showing only the white portion while her violent spasms continued. Young Stump heard the door slam again and

the noise made him jump. When he turned around, his father grabbed him forcibly by both arms and lifted him up in the air, shaking him violently.

"You betta not tell nobody I was here, you lil bastard, or you'll wind up like your dopefiend mama!" his father yelled.

Young Stump was speechless and scared shitless. The dealer put him down and pushed his face toward the colorless corpse on the floor.

"Look at her! If you say anything to anybody, this is what's gonna happen to you!"

Horrified, when the dope dealer released him, Stump scurried to the corner and slid down the wall, staring blankly into space. His father looked at him, satisfied he would be in the clear, then left for the final time. When the police and paramedics arrived five hours later, they found the overdosed woman sprawled on the floor and young Stump in the same spot huddled up in his own feces and urine. He was in complete shock, which may have been the reason they didn't ask him any questions about what had happened to his mother.

Ever since that tragic event, Stump couldn't stand anything or anyone that sold or used drugs. It bothered him to think about the day he witnessed his mother's murder, but that experience made him wary about trusting people and hardened his heart.

He went into the bathroom and washed his face, then put his gun in his waistband. He returned to his room and grabbed his jacket off the chair next to his bulletproof vest before heading toward the door. Prior to walking into the hallway, he checked to make sure his gun was off safety and then bolted down the stairs to the lobby of his building.

***

Junior had just reached Williamsburg, when he felt his beeper vibrate. So, he went into the corner bodega to get change for the payphone. After dialing Shondra's number, he listened to her tell him about her episode when she went downtown. He was only half

listening, though, because he was thinking about what Lizzette told him about KB and Stump. Once he told Shondra he would be home after picking up his money, he walked up the street to the building where the guy that owed him money lived. After he picked up his money, he headed back to Shondra's house.

Kendu was in the lobby of Shondra's building with Joyce, a booster from Baptiste who was strung out on crack. He was looking at some items of clothing she was trying to sell to him.

"These shirts are hot and dey just came out, so ain't nobody got 'em yet. I took dem scrait outta da box in da stockroom, so these muhfuckas not even on display yet," she remarked about the Georges Marciano shirts she had in a Macy's bag.

"They a'ight. How much you want for this black and blue one?" he asked, holding one of the shirts up to his chest to see if it was his size.

"Gimme twenty dollars and two nicks."

"Two nicks and twenty dollars?" Kendu asked.

"Yeah, man. These not even out yet. You'll be da first muhfucka wit' it. Shit, I can get thirty dollars easy for one."

"Yeah, but they don't have a price tag on them, so you don't know how much they really cost. They might only be thirty dollars for one, and I'd be gettin' beat," Kendu replied.

"Boy, I jus' tole you dat I got dem scrait from da stockroom, so dey ain't gon' have no tags on dem. Come on, man, you know Guess cost sixty dollars off top. So, stop frontin' and give me da twenty and two nicks."

"A'ight, Joyce, but look, I gotta give you the nicks when I come from the crib and I don't have no money on me right now," Kendu told her.

"Nah, man, you gotta give me all mines right now," she said, putting the garments back in the bag.

"See, Joyce, see how you tryna play me like a crab. I'm not going to beat you outta your shit!"

"Come on, muhfucka. I wanna blast off and you bullshittin'. I wanna take a major and you talkin' reckless. Fuck it. I'm gonna go see La. He always holdin'. Shit, you ain't neva got no work when I come to cop from you. Is you smokin' your own shit?"

"Fuck you, you crackhead bitch!" Kendu said, throwing the shirt on the floor and stomping on it.

"Ah! Why you gotta do dat dumb shit for, muhfucka?" she asked, picking up the shirt and trying to clean it off. "Did I hit a nerve or sumthin'?"

As Kendu walked out the building in a huff and headed for his building, Joyce grabbed up the clothing and muttered to herself, "That muhfucka in the closet!"

Kendu was furious and slammed the door to his bedroom. He opened the closet door and went into the pocket of a jacket that was way in the back. He pulled out a cigar and a small, clear, glassine bag. The small mirror from off his nightstand was placed on the unmade bed, as he split the blunt open and emptied the contents of it into a brown paperbag. He poured some of the stuff from the glassine bag onto the mirror, put a dollar over it, and used a lighter to crush the small rocks into a powder. Then he took the razor, scraped the white powder together in a small mountain, and licked the residue off the dollar bill. The weed in his pocket was poured into the cigar. Then he scooped up the white powder with the dirty razor and sprinkled it over the weed in the cigar. He scooped up some more and spread that evenly over the reefer, then used his index finger to pick up the remainder and licked the residue off his finger. Finally, he rolled up the cigar, transforming it into a woola blunt. He lit it, inhaling deeply and holding his breath, trying not to let any smoke escape his lungs. He held the smoke in for as long as possible, then exhaled as the cloud filled the dimly lit room. He continued to smoke until the blunt was burning his thumb and index finger.

The combination of the weed and crack gave Kendu an immediate rush, and he began to feel lightheaded. He tried to get comfortable on his bed, but for some reason, he couldn't find a position that suited him. He kept looking around as if he lost something, and then his mind told him he was bugging out from the drugs. He laughed to himself, then tried to enjoy his high. His mind was flooded with all kinds of thoughts. He was sitting in a room getting high because he didn't want anyone to know he was smoking crack, and another crackhead had just called him out. His anger began to resurface.

Kendu blamed Junior for getting him addicted to the shit he was smoking. If Junior never gave him the packages to sell, he would never have met that bad-ass Puerto Rican bitch that showed him how to tap the bottles and increase his count. While she showed him how to tap the bottles, she offered to suck his dick for a hit. The average man would never know she was smoking because she looked so damn good and kept her body tight. It was a good feeling to get served by a bad bitch like Lizzette. It was mad dudes 'round the way that wanted her. Even the Puerto Rican cats sweated her when they saw her walk past in some skintight jeans.

Lizzette was the one who got Kendu addicted. One day, he went to her house to serve her, and while she got high, Kendu rolled a blunt. She came over to where he was sitting, sucked on his earlobe, and asked if he wanted some head. He thought fucking was next after she sucked him off—at least that's what he was expecting—so he told her yes and waited to see how much it was going to cost him, but she never said anything. She just took off her stretch pants and oversized T-shirt and started rubbing her pussy in front of him. Kendu was aroused and started stroking his manhood in preparation for what was to come next, but then she did the okie doke. She told him she wanted to take a hit first because it made her more horny and wet. He fumbled in his pocket and took out one of the tapped capsules he had made from Junior's pack. She took the capsule, put it in her mouth, and then sucked it like a lollipop. She was mindfucking him.

As he sat there massaging his piece, she asked him if he had anymore weed. When he told her he did, a smile grew across her face and she set her plan in motion. Kendu pulled out the weed and a blunt, and then she asked him to fix it up for her while she crushed the rocks into powder. He did as he was told. Then she took if from him when he was done and prepared it to be smoked. He lit it for her, and as she put it in her mouth, she got on her hands and knees and crawled to him, the blunt dangling from the side of her mouth. Kendu waited on her to reach him as he inhaled

the sweet smelling smoke. When she got to him, she pulled off her panties and stood over his dick, positioning herself right over his pole. He grabbed her by her waist and tried to bring her gently down on his tool. As he did that, she put the blunt in his mouth. In that moment of weakness, he "ate the forbidden fruit."

It seemed like an hour had passed while Kendu sat in his room, high and blaming his fuck-ups on Junior or anyone else he could think of. He was in denial big-time.

He heard a faint knock on the door and sat still, trying to hear if someone was outside his room. After about ten minutes of listening, he got up to see if anyone was actually there, but when he opened the door, there was no one there. He closed the door, sensing his own paranoia. He walked over to his cracked, full-length mirror and gazed at his reflection. The guy in the mirror had eyes as wide as saucers, white lips, and didn't resemble Kendu. The guy in the mirror looked tired, confused, and in desperate need of help. Kendu grabbed the mirror and threw it to the floor - seven years of bad luck.

***

Shondra explained to Junior what happened downtown more in detail when he came to the house. She also told him of her and Gloria's plan to go out dancing at the Red Parrot that night. Junior really didn't like her going out, but he didn't want to act like he was her father by telling her not to go. She was already dressed and looked good in the leather outfit she had on. Her ass stretched it out, and it clung to her thick thighs like Spandex.

"With that dress on, a muhfucka might kidnap your ass if you don't give him no play," Junior said to Shondra.

"Oh boo, nobody out there wants me. Plus, this rock on my finger lets them know I'm taken."

"Bullshit. Look what happened today downtown. That dude wanted to put your lights out because you wouldn't give him no rap."

"That's true, but I put that shit in check with the quickness. I just don't like the fact that muhfuckas think they can say and do whatever they want to a female. I get tired of that shit."

"Then why you going to a club where there ain't nothing but muhfuckas like that?"

"It's just me, Gloria, Cheryl, and Elaine going. It's girls' night out, and we ain't all hung out together in a long time, baby."

"Yeah, but none of dem bitches got a man, and you do. Their whole purpose on going would be to meet guys."

"You right, boo, but you don't got shit to worry about 'cause I love you and I'm not looking for nobody else. I'm just going to listen to some music and have some drinks. That's all. I know you trust me, baby. I would never step out on you, ever."

"I'm just saying, them chicks you hang wit' is wild, 'specially Gloria. She a straight ho."

"Come on now, you don't have to disrespect my homegirl like that. She not like that anymore, and even if she was, you know I ain't no follower and I definitely ain't no ho. If anything, I'm the chief and they the Indians."

"I ain't call you no ho. I was just saying…ahhhh, fuck it," he said, knowing he wouldn't be able to win the argument.

She walked over to the closet and pulled out the sneakers and shirt she bought him earlier, hoping it would change his mood.

"Look, I bought you the shirt to match the sneakers. Try it on so I can see how it looks on you."

"That's cool." He grabbed the shirt and looked at it. "Yeah, it'll fit. What time y'all leavin'?"

"'Bout eleven o'clock, and I'll be back 'round two or three in the morning. All right?"

"A'ight, I'm out. Take this," he said, giving her some money. "Buy your own drinks." Junior gave her a long, sloppy kiss and headed out the door.

"Thank you, daddy. I love you."

There weren't many people out, and the night air was thick. Junior went to the store to get a forty-ounce of Old Gold, then went to his regular spot on the benches behind Shondra's building. He cracked open the cold beer, tilted the bottle up to his mouth,

and took three long gulps. As he put the top back on the bottle, he noticed one of his regular customers standing by the back door of the building. The customer flashed three fingers as he approached Junior. They went into the vestibule of the building and made the transaction smoothly, then Junior returned to his spot on the bench. He guzzled down some more of his beer and waited for the paperchase to begin.

Lakim was coming out of his building, when he saw Kendu coming up the block. He was on his way to go chill with Junior behind Shondra's building, but when he saw Kendu, he changed his mind.

"Yo La, where you headed?" Kendu called out to him.

"Nowhere but right here, bruh," La replied.

"Did you see Joyce?" Kendu asked.

"Yeah, she had some fly-ass Guess shirts. I copped four of them."

"You know that crackhead bitch ain't want to let me go for ten dollars?" Kendu remarked.

"Word? That's fucked up."

"You just comin' back out since the last time I saw you?" Kendu asked.

"Yeah, man, I had to cop some Z's since I been out all last night. I'm 'bout to go get me a beer and some choke from the black gate."

"A'ight, let's go," Kendu said, and they both started walking in the direction of the weed spot.

As they were walking, someone called out Kendu's name. When they turned around to see who was calling him, they noticed KB standing on the corner with Stump.

"YOOOOO!" Kendu called back to them. Then he turned to Lakim. "Let me go see what these dudes want. I'll catch up with you in a minute."

Kendu jogged toward them, while Lakim watched. Seeing Kendu running over to them spelled trouble. Lakim turned back around and kept walking to the spot. Shit was about to be fucked in the hood, and it looked like Kendu was going to be the start of it. He figured Stump was the one Kendu was talking about when

he said motherfuckers were ready to move on Junior. Stump was a dangerous and ruthless motherfucker, but he wasn't sure if Junior would be an easy win if he didn't come correct.

Lakim copped his smoke and headed back around the way to the projects. When he got to his building, he checked the back to see if Kendu was out there. He was beginning to feel uneasy. He was used to seeing KB with Kendu from time to time, but seeing Stump meant danger, especially after how Kendu had been acting. Everyone in the hood knew how Stump got down. If he heard somebody was getting money in the hood, he was on them like a fly on shit. Kendu had to have told him that Junior was getting a lot of money, and from what Lakim was taking him every four to five days, he would be right. Junior had Baptiste on lock, but now it seemed that Stump wanted a cut of the dough, or just wanted a big payoff. Either way, it was looking grim for the home team.

"Damn!" Lakim said out loud, not realizing he was talking to himself. "Why this dude got to go and fuck wit' them grimy-ass muhfuckas? He know they don't give a fuck 'bout him like that. Damn, Du!"

Lakim decided right then that if something were to happen, he would have Junior's back. He was just stuck between a rock and a hard place when it came to him telling Junior what Kendu said about him. Kendu was his childhood homey and Junior was just his boss. His loyalty to Kendu went as far as their friendship. He tried to fool himself into believing that telling Junior wasn't being disloyal. As far as he was concerned, the only thing he had to remain loyal to was the *money*. Lakim didn't want to go against the grain, but the reality behind it was that his love of money was truly stronger than his friendship with Kendu. Junior looked out for him when it came to money, so that's where his loyalty was really vested. What Kendu was plotting to do was impulsive, and Lakim believed he had the right idea but was not using the right resources and wasn't thinking straight. Kendu was just reacting, and reacting without a plan could prove disastrous.

Stump, KB, and Kendu walked over to an adjacent building while talking.

"Did you see Junior yet?" KB asked Kendu, as they all took a seat on the benches in the back of the building.

"Nah. He should be in the back of 110 by now. Did y'all check over there?" Kendu replied.

"Nope. Wasn't that La you was walking wit'?" KB asked.

"Yeah, we was going to cop some smoke and some brew."

Stump didn't say anything. He just sat quietly and listened to them, while periodically feeling for his gun.

"You know we ready to get at that dude tonight, right? You still down wit' it or what?" KB asked.

"I already told you I'm with it. I'm down for whatever."

"A'ight. We gotta find out if he out here first. You need to go and see if he's in the back of that building, then come back and let us know. If you don't see him when you go over there, just wait 'til he comes, then come back and let us know. You got it?" Stump spoke sternly.

"I hear you. I'll just go over there with La when he comes from the store. He usually goes back there and smokes wit' him," Kendu informed Stump.

"A'ight then, we gonna chill right here in the cut and wait for you to come back. Listen, make sure you come back and let us know something," Stump warned.

"I gotcha, man, trust me. I'll be back so we can get that muhfucka," Kendu said, walking off.

When Junior saw a figure coming from the street side of the building, he rose from the bench to try to figure out who was coming toward him. As the person got closer, he recognized him.

"What up, Du?" Junior asked, slapping him five.

"Ain't nothin'. What up with you?" Kendu answered.

"Same ol', same ol'."

"You seen La?" Kendu asked.

"Nah, not since earlier. He said he was coming through later on, though."

"Oh yeah, he told me that you wanted to see me about somethin'."

"Yeah, let me go take care of this custy real quick and then we can talk, a'ight?" Junior said, walking toward the building to serve someone that was waiting impatiently for him.

Kendu sat on the bench and looked at Junior with disgust. He hated how he acted like he was so cool. This made him want Stump and KB to get him that much more. He was going to sit with Junior until Lakim came by so he could warn him about what was going down because he didn't want Lakim getting caught in the middle.

After serving the customer, Junior walked back over to the benches, sat down, pulled out a half-smoked blunt, and lit it. He took a couple of drags, then passed it to Kendu.

"I want to talk some business wit' you," Junior began.

"I'm listening," Kendu said, while looking behind him to make sure no one else was around.

"When I first hit you off with work, I told you that if you wanted to make money you would have to be dedicated to what you do. In the beginning, you was flipping more than La, but then you just slowed down out of the blue. I'm not trying to put a rush on what you do, but what I'm concerned with is what made you slow down so much. To me, it seems like you loss interest or somethin' or you makin' too much dough. Is that what happened?"

Kendu couldn't believe he was talking to him like they were at a fucking board meeting.

"Nah, I just had other shit I been taking care of, that's all," Kendu replied, flicking the finished blunt in the grass.

"Why you ain't just tell me? I mean, I don't want to know your business. It's just you coulda told me you had some other shit to do, and I woulda worked something out with you until you got ready to get back to working. You know what I'm saying?"

"I know, but everything is all right now." Kendu was not feeling the conversation. Junior was really taking that boss shit to heart.

"It's just that when I'm done with my package and you still have work left, I have to wait on you to finish so I can go re-up, and that slows down the process. I gotta make sure my count is right with the losses and everything else. I can't go to my connect

for less than what I usually cop because I won't be able to get nothing on consignment. So, if I come short, I'm gonna be short and will wind up having to make two or three trips for nothing. You feel me?"

"I hear you. I got the rest of your dough upstairs. I'll give it to you tomorrow, unless you need it now."

"Nah, I'm good right now. So what's up? If all your issues is cleared up, you ready to get back on the block again?" Junior asked.

"Not right now. I'll let you know when I'm ready," Kendu replied.

"That's cool. Just let me know when you ready to get started again. You need any extra money or anything? I can hit you wit' a lil something if your pockets ain't right."

"Nah, man, I'm okay, but good looking out." Kendu was getting furious. He didn't like Junior trying to son him.

"Well, just keep what you got, and when you ready to start up again, let me know."

Junior still wanted to ask him about Stump and KB, but didn't feel the time was right.

They sat on the benches talking shit for a little while longer, then Junior heard a horn beep. He looked over to the street and excused himself, telling Kendu he would be back shortly. Kendu rose to his feet to dismiss himself, but Junior was insistent on him waiting until he came back.

"Hold up for a minute. I just gotta tell my cousin something real quick."

"A'ight, I'ma chill," Kendu said reluctantly.

Junior walked out to the street, while Kendu watched to see where he was going. He noticed Junior walking towards the corner and observed him talking to someone in a 190E Mercedes Benz with alloy rims.

Junior got into the red car and immediately turned the music down. Craig, Junior's cousin, was pumping "New York State of Mind" from Nas' *Illmatic* album. Craig was a dark chocolate brother with a smooth complexion and wavy hair. He was tall, thin, and good-looking. He lived and hustled in Tompkins Projects

in Bed-Stuy Brooklyn. He usually came through to check on his cousin because Junior was fairly new to the hustle game. He didn't want Junior to slip and make rookie mistakes while he was out there, because in the game, any mistake you made could prove to be fatal.

Craig would put some of his money with Junior's to help Junior get his weight up. Then they would take turns going to cop. He didn't really approve of Junior selling, but felt if Junior was going to be in the game, he should learn it from somebody that would keep his best interest at heart. There was so much shit to watch out for in the game that you needed eyes in the back of your head to see everything that came at you. You had to be one step ahead of everyone. You had to think like your worker, like the detective or cop that wanted to bust you, like the motherfucker that wanted to rob you, like the dude that was jealous of your status, and most importantly, like the woman you slept with.

"How you did this week?" Junior asked Craig.

"I did a light fifty-seven thousand. What you do this week?"

"I did like eighteen thousand, give or take a G. You know I gotta pay my workers and I had some losses, so I made a little less."

"Me too, and you know my team bigger than yours. Anyway, I got my shit sucked so good today. I mean, that broad sucked me so good, I thought she had a degree in cocksucking from Big Dick University," Craig said, grabbing his crotch and laughing.

"Yeah, well, I got this Spanish mami that got a bangin' ass. I almost laced her, but she wouldn't let me go raw."

"Is you crazy muhfucka? You betta' not fuck none of dem broads raw. You know they can give you some shit you can't get rid of," Craig told Junior.

"I know, man. I was slippin', but she look good as hell and the ass is soooo fat."

"Yeah, but you can't let that shit cloud your judgment, kid. It's all good when you hittin' it, but three days lata' you gonna wanna kill the bitch 'cause she fried you."

"I can dig it," Junior replied.

"Just think about if you brought something home to bugga."

"It's Mooka, you stupid muhfucka," Junior corrected him.

"Oh, my bad," Craig said, laughing. "Nah, but for real, you gotta think about that shit. She not gonna wanna hear no sorry and shit, so you better think with the right head from now on."

"You right, cuz. I'm 'posed to see the broad tonight before I go in. Shondra went to the club and she ain't comin' in 'til late, so I got a chance to go hit that real fast."

"You love playin' dangerous games, cuz. Why in the world would you fuck with somebody that lives in the same PJs as your girl? That ain't nothin' but problems, kid. You need to go somewhere else with that shit, and she's a crackhead. You know how they blow the spot up when they want a hit."

"I ain't worried 'bout no bitches. If she try to flip out on me, I'll tell Shondra she lyin' 'cause I won't give her no credit."

"A'ight, whatever, muhfucka. Don't say I didn't warn your ass when Shondra got your nuts in a grinder," Craig said, laughing. "Now come on and let me count out this money for you."

Craig reached in the backseat and pulled out a brown paper bag full of money.

"I be trying to get these dollar bills changed over so my knot won't be so fat. I'm tired of counting all these ones," he said, pulling out four stacks of bills.

"I know. I be telling the heads I don't take dollar bills at night. I make them change that shit, and I definitely don't take loose change," Junior said.

"Well, that's all of it. When you going to go re-up again, or is it my turn?" Craig asked.

"You know it's my turn, muhfucka. You ain't funny. I think we need to up it to at least five keys now. We see Cheech almost three times a month, and I'm starting to hate goin' up there so many times in a month 'cause it be so fucking hot out there with the po-po and TNT. What you think?"

"I think you're right," Craig replied. "I'm tired of going up there my damn self, but who the fuck we gonna trust with all this dough?"

"Nobody." Junior tried to stuff the money in his pants, but it wouldn't fit.

"What you doing with a tool on you? You got beef out here?" Craig asked after spotting the gun in Junior's waistband.

"I hope not. I just got a feeling that something shady is 'bout to go down."

Craig looked real disturbed by Junior's statement.

"What you mean you got a feeling? Did something happen out here recently to make you feel like this?"

"Not really. It's just that some cat out here been asking 'bout me, ya know. That Puerto Rican girl told me this dude named KB was asking her about me. Him and this other dude, Stump, was on the corner of Graham Avenue when I went to the check-cashing place this morning to collect my money from her, and when she was on her way back to her crib, he started questioning her and shit," Junior said, fixing the gun in his waist.

"Who are they?" Craig quizzed.

"I seen KB before hangin' with Du, the kid that works for me. I think he's from Williamsburg. He ain't no real threat, but the other muhfucka he was with is the one to worry about."

"Why? Who the fuck he 'posed to be?"

"I don't know him like that, and today was my first time seeing him around here. From what I hear, he one of dem stick-up kids that's always into some shit. He don' robbed almost every muhfucka that sling in this hood and getting paper. I heard some cats shot him up, but they said that shit only made his ass worse," Junior replied, trying not to sound worried.

"You know where he rest at?" Craig inquired.

"I'm not really sure, but I think he's from Bushwick projects or somewhere in the Bushwick area. The dude that I see with KB sometimes is in the back. He works for me, so I was gonna ask him some questions on fam. You know what I mean?"

"I feel you, but I don't think you need to talk to him. If something is going down, he gon' be hip to it when you start quizzing him. Let me talk to him and find out what's really going on 'round here," Craig suggested.

"Nah, cuz, I got it. If you ask him any questions, he definitely gonna know I suspect something. I'm not gonna ask him straight up. I'm gonna beat around the bush and see if I can get any

information out of him. Matter of fact, let me go holla at him now before his ass leaves," Junior said, grabbing the door handle in the car. "I kinda think he know somethin' 'cause he been actin' suspect lately. He been slow getting my money to me and I ain't been seein' him around like before. You know you can tell a muhfucka actin' funny by how they change up what they do. He don't even hang around me like he used to and shit. I been peepin' his flow, and he been actin' real shady these past couple of weeks."

"Well, I'm gonna run up to my man's crib on Broadway real quick and get me some heat so I can hold you down tonight, a'ight?" Craig said, starting up his car.

"Cool," Junior replied, then stepped out the car.

Carrying the bag of money, Junior went through the front of the building so Kendu wouldn't see what he was doing. He went into Shondra's house and put the money away in the safe. Then he headed to the back of the building to finish quizzing Kendu. As he got closer to the back door, he could hear Kendu yelling. He pushed the door open slightly and could see Kendu with Lakim. They were having a heated argument. Junior tried to strain his ears so he could hear what they were arguing about, but he couldn't. So, he opened the door a little more, but when Kendu saw him, he walked off quickly.

"What up, La? What was all that about?"Junior asked.

"Ahh, it wasn't nothin', man." Lakim sucked his teeth.

"Why Du just walk off like that? He looked real vexed," Junior asked, keeping his eye on Kendu as he walked away.

"Look, Junior," Lakim started, "I need to tell you something. I think Du is trying to set you up. I'm not a hun'ed percent sure, but he been saying some ill shit about you."

"Like what?" Junior asked, his full attention shifting to Lakim.

"Like when I went to go get the rest of the work from him, he just started talking reckless and shit. I asked him did you say something to him for him to be feelin' all salty and shit, but he just said 'fuck you' and then started sayin' that muhfuckas 'round here was ready to move on you and shit…"

Junior stood frozen listening to everything Lakim was telling

him about Kendu. His heart was beating fast as hell, and he was becoming a little nervous knowing what he was thinking all along was now confirmed. He continued to listen intently, knowing his life was about to take a drastic change.

"He even told me that I better stop hangin' 'round you before they move on you, or I might get it, too," Lakim finished.

Junior was speechless, but he couldn't show Lakim any weakness. He had to stay in control and make sure his response was strong and direct, with no indication of fear. He knew what Lakim was doing could jeopardize his rep in the hood, and he really didn't want to involve him because he knew the outcome might turn deadly. He had to make sure Lakim stayed confident so he wouldn't think he made a mistake by telling him about the setup.

"This is what that muhfucka told you just now?" Junior didn't realize he was yelling.

"Yeah, man, he was acting like the shit about to go down now and…" Lakim trailed off from what he was saying as he began to wonder if he had done the right thing by telling Junior.

"WHAT!" Junior screamed. "That black muhfucka! Where the fuck was he going, La?" Junior grabbed his gun from his waist and headed in the direction Kendu was walking when he left.

"Chill, son. I know you heated, but you gotta think first," Lakim said, trying to stop Junior from leaving.

"Yo, get the fuck off me! I looked out for that faggot-ass muhfucka and he tryin' to set me up. That's some real crab shit. That's my word. I'm gonna put a hole in that dude's wig and leave his ass leaking on the sidewalk. Get the fuck outta my way, La!"

"Come on, Junior. He probably want you to go looking for him. He probably hopes you go looking for him so he can ambush you in the building or sumthin'. Just chill, man, and think for a minute," he coerced Junior.

Lakim was right. Junior was just reacting. He wasn't thinking logically or strategically. He knew Kendu couldn't be the mastermind of this shit. He was too slow. He was just a pawn in this setup. Junior had to think. He had to devise a plan on how he would move, where, and when. He didn't know how much time he had left to think of a plan, but he needed to move soon. He needed to calm down, and he needed to cool out for a minute.

Junior sat on the bench and looked down at the gun in his hand. After looking up at the roof from instinct to see if any police were watching, he blew out a long sigh. In all honesty, he wasn't prepared for what he knew he had to do. He wanted to leave and say "fuck it", but he was already knee deep in the game, and if he abandoned his spot, his rep would be ruined and he would lose what little respect he had in the hood. If he just left, when motherfuckers found out, he would be looked upon as weak and would have every punk-ass criminal trying him like a winning slot machine in Atlantic City.

Kendu was furious; he couldn't believe Lakim was defending Junior. Lakim was acting like Junior was more his homeboy than Kendu was. Kendu tried to warn Lakim to leave Junior alone because Stump and KB were ready to get him. When he told Lakim, he had the nerve to argue with him, and then tell him he was jealous of Junior. Secretly, he *was* jealous of Junior. Kendu hated the fact that Junior had so much love in his hood, more love than he had, and he was born and raised in Baptiste. The proof was how he had his man Lakim turning on him. Kendu also hated the fact that Junior was making major paper in his hood and had a girl from around his way. Shit, there were a thousand reasons why he was jealous of Junior.

When Kendu got to the back of the building, KB and Stump were on the bench talking.

"He out there. I just left him," he said, as he walked up on their conversation.

"Okay. Who's out there with him?" KB asked.

"My man La. You know, the one I was walking with earlier. He's out there with him right now. I told him to get ghost because I didn't want him to catch no fever when y'all go over there."

"You told him what we plannin' to do?" Stump asked, his brows lowering.

"Yeah, that's my man. I had to let him know so he don't get caught up in this shit."

Stump stood up and instantly slapped the shit out of Kendu. The blow caught Kendu off guard and knocked him to the ground.

"What the fuck is wrong with you, muhfucka?" Stump boomed. "You put him on to what I'm 'bout to do? Huh?" He grabbed Kendu and held him by his collar. "You might be tryin' to set me up for all I know. How the fuck you gonna tell somebody what the fuck I'm gonna do? Did you tell the police, too?"

Stump smacked Kendu again, and Kendu's bottom lip swelled up immediately as he stumbled backwards, unable to defend himself because Stump never let him regain his balance.

"You dumb bitch. What the fuck was you thinkin'? I didn't tell you to go ova there and tell nobody shit. I told you to see if the muhfucka was out there, nothing else!" Stump screamed.

Stump was deadly serious about what he was saying. Most criminals were caught because of another person running off with their mouth before anything even happened.

"Suppose he tell the muhfucka we trying to get what you told him, huh?" Stump yelled, grabbing at Kendu again, but Kendu got to his feet and wiggled out of Stump's grip.

"Look, man, he not gonna tell Junior shit," Kendu cried, as he backed up out of Stump's reach.

"How the fuck you know?" Stump was still trying to get a hold of Kendu.

"'Cause that's my man. KB, tell him I ain't tryin' to set y'all up. Please, man," he begged.

KB was just watching. He wasn't going to agree with anything because he didn't want to catch a backhand from Stump. Those blows looked like they hurt.

Stump finally got a hold of Kendu and punched him hard in his face. Kendu let out a loud yelp and covered his face in anticipation of more blows to his head. He couldn't fight Stump back and just wanted him to stop. He wished he had never told Lakim anything, but even more, this ass whooping made him wish he hadn't told Stump that he told Lakim about the set up. He was going to be in bigger trouble if Lakim told Junior, because that would definitely be the end for him. Stump was not the one to play with.

“You better hope that muhfucka not hip to what’s about to go down or you’re a dead man,” Stump said, as he let Kendu drop to the ground.

“You think we should still go ahead and get this dude?” KB asked cautiously.

“Fuck yeah! And this talkin’ ass muhfucka gonna lead the way!” Stump said, grabbing his gun.

Kendu was getting to his feet, trying to regain his senses.

“I’m not tryin’ to set you up, man. I wouldn’t do that. That’s my word on my momma.”

“I don’t want to hear that shit. Just show me where he at!” Stump boomed.

“He’s in the back of the building with La,” Kendu whimpered.

“I want you to go back ova there and tell him to come inside the building. I’m gonna lay in the building once I see you go through the front. I’ll have the drop on him. It should all come as a surprise for his ass, but if it doesn’t, that means you or your man gave him the heads up, and in either case, all y’all gonna be dead men tonight. You hear me, muhfucka?” Stump pointed his gun at Kendu’s head. “Don’t do nothing other than what I just told you. I’m gonna be right behind you, so you ain’t gonna get far if you try to run.”

Kendu didn’t know what he had gotten himself into and wanted out of it immediately because it turned into a lose-lose situation for him. He was so afraid that he didn’t know what to do. He wasn’t one hundred percent sure that Lakim didn’t tell Junior, because when he was trying to tell him what was about to go down, Lakim was acting like he was on Junior’s side.

Kendu didn’t have a gun on him, so if he just walked up on Junior, there was no telling what his reaction would be. Kendu’s heart was racing, and he couldn’t see a feasible way out of his dilemma without getting hurt or killed. He was deathly afraid. The tables had turn on him. He was in a world of shit and was sinking fast.

CHAPTER 4
WHY YOU PULLIN' OUT ON ME?

Junior and Lakim were standing on the corner - Junior with a gun in his hand, and Lakim with his back against the black gate. Even though they were both on alert for anything or anyone suspicious, Junior was secretly praying nothing happened. He wished what Lakim told him was all bullshit, but that was wishful thinking on his part. It seemed to him that Lakim was going to hold him down because he didn't have to tell him what Kendu was up to, and he definitely didn't have to stand there with him, knowing something was supposed to jump off. It was as if Lakim didn't care what the outcome was going to be. It was hard for Junior to believe someone would go against their childhood friend for a stranger, and that raised some questions on Lakim's loyalty, not just to Junior but also to his friend. In the meantime, Junior was just glad Lakim was on his side this time.

Junior's mind was racing a mile a minute. He was trying to figure out what he was going to do. He knew he had to warn Shondra because he didn't want her caught up in anything, and he didn't want anyone to use her to get to him. There was no telling how grimy those guys were.

Junior and Lakim stood silently on the corner like sentries, looking up and down the block. Junior saw headlights coming

from the south corner of the building, so he put his back against the wall and held his gun. Lakim saw his reaction, but because he didn't have a gun, he moved closer to the entrance of the building in case something jumped off. As the car got closer, Junior realized it was his cousin and pointed around the corner to let him know to park on the side of the building.

"That's my fam, La. Chill right here for a sec. I'm just gonna let him know what's goin' on, okay?"

"I got you, kid," Lakim said.

Junior handed his gun to him.

"Hold on to this. If you see Kendu or any of dem other cats, holla so I'll know, but if you don't have a chance, I don't have to tell you what to do."

"Right," Lakim replied, holding the gun firmly in his hand.

When Junior turned around, Lakim pointed the gun in his direction, but only to check to see if it was loaded.

Junior walked around the corner as Craig was getting out of the car dressed in a black fatigue suit with a gun in his hand.

"I saw you with the heat in your hand when I was coming up. I was thinking something went down already. Did you see that kid yet?"

"Nah. My man La just told me the dude's tryin' to set me up to get robbed. He said the muhfucka told him the shit 'pose to pop off tonight. He told me soon as you pulled off. Can you believe that shit? You know I'm gonna blow that muhfucka's head off when I see him, right?"

"Hell yeah, I believe it. What makes you think these cats got love for you in their hood? All you are is a money machine for the dudes that work for you, kid. These muhfuckas don't give a fuck if you live or die. The only thing they care about is if you still gonna hit them off with work. Smarten up, cuz. This game has no loyalty, and the hood don't have no love for you. The sooner you realize this, the better off you'll be, 'specially when shit like this pops off. Where does this dude live? Let's lay in his building and wait for him to come in or go out."

“No. He just told La, so he might be expecting me to move like that. You feel me? So, I’m trying to think on which way we should move on this clown.”

“So what we gonna do? Just sit here like ducks waiting on somebody to pick us off?” Craig asked, frustrated.

“What you think we should do then, Craig?” Junior asked.

“I think we should go to his crib, drag him out the house, take him on the roof, and blow the back of his head off. That’s what I think we should do!”

“Yeah, I know, but we can’t do that right now. I don’t know if he’s expectin’ me to react all crazy without thinking and run over to his building and turn it into the O.K. Corral. I should chill right here like I normally do and see what move he makes. I mean, I know something’s going down, so it ain’t like I’m gonna let him catch me slipping. I got my man La in the front of the building looking out, so he gon’ holla if something ain’t right. You know what I mean?”

“You trust that muhfucka? Shit, he could be tryin’ to set you up, too. You’re forgettin’ this ain’t your hood. This they hood. They gonna stick together. I don’t trust none of dem dudes when it comes to beef. I think you already slipping. Don’t let fear interfere with your better judgment, cuz. That shit can have you layng real still in a pine box.”

“I hear you, Craig, but that dude ain’t like that. For one, he got love for me. He’s in the front lookin’ out for them muhfuckas right now.” Junior was praying he was right and that the betrayal stopped at Kendu.

“Whateva. If you feel he gon’ bust his gun with you, then fine by me. Go ahead. I’m gonna keep a close eye on him just in case. You know what I’m saying?”

“Come with me to the crib real quick so I can get my other toast. I let La hold onto the other one,” Junior told Craig.

“You gave the muhfucka your gun, too? Is you a’ight, cuz?” Craig said, feeling Junior’s forehead like he was checking his temperature.

Kendu could see Lakim standing in front of the building. He was nervous but had to go over there. Stump and KB were in the

building across the street watching his every move. He walked slowly, his hands showing so Lakim could see he was unarmed, but as he got closer, he noticed a gun in Lakim's hand, which caused him to stop abruptly.

"What up, La? Why you pullin' out on me?" Kendu asked, the palm of his hands open.

"Get lost, Du. I'm not trying to hear shit you gotta say right now, dawg," Lakim told his childhood friend.

"Come on, La, you my man. Let me holla at you for a minute."

"I'm tellin' you, Du, don't come over here, son. Get gon' before Junior comes out here and sees you," he warned, noticing the bruises on Kendu's face as he inched closer.

"You told him what I told you?" Kendu asked.

"Yup. You going 'bout this all wrong, man, and I ain't wit' it," Lakim responded.

"You told him? Aaaahhhh shit, La, you just got me killed."

"Fuck it, son. You played yourself. Just get lost before this dude comes back out here. I'm trying to warn you, man."

When Junior and Craig came out the house, they went to the back of the building because they heard Lakim talking to someone.

"I think he's talking to Kendu," Junior guessed.

"I'm goin' 'round the other side. You take the side your man is on. When I see him, I'm blastin'. Once I let off, just make sure he's not comin' in your direction," Craig said, cocking his gun, then trotting to the other side of the building.

Junior pulled out his big silver gun, cocked it back, and held it down by his waist. He walked along the other side of the building to where Lakim was. When he reached the corner of the building, he peeked around slowly. He could see Lakim with his gun drawn, telling Kendu to leave. Kendu was walking slowly toward Lakim with his hands outstretched and seemed to be pleading with him. Junior watched closely.

There was no one out except for a few Puerto Rican kids who noticed Lakim holding a gun and decided to watch and see if some drama unfolded from a safe distance across the street, while cowering behind parked cars. Just then, Junior heard what sounded like an explosion. He saw Lakim back up towards the entrance of

the building. When Kendu took off like a jet across the street, Junior realized Craig had started shooting at him. Then Junior heard two or three more thunderous booms. Kendu was now across the street and running in Junior's direction. When Junior saw Craig giving chase with his gun pointed at Kendu's back, Junior jumped into action and let off shots toward Kendu, who was running and ducking at the same time.

"Don't let that muhfucka get away!" Craig yelled.

Junior was in pursuit and heard some more loud blasts, but these were from a different gun. His adrenalin was pumping. He glanced in the direction of the noise and saw a tall figure running behind his cousin letting off a barrage of shots.

"Somebody's bustin' at you. Watch out!" Junior screamed to Craig.

Junior turned his gun toward the tall figure and let off shots in his direction. The figure ducked behind a car, and Junior made sure Craig was out of danger. By now, Kendu had cut through the back of a building, and Junior continued his chase with Craig following close behind him.

"Who the fuck was that bustin' at me?" Craig asked when he caught up to Junior.

"I don't know. I think it was one of them cats that was with Kendu," Junior said, breathing heavily.

"Come on! We can't let Kendu get away. I'm gonna kill that muhfucka," Craig said with determination in his voice.

"He went into that building," Junior said, pointing his gun at the back door.

"I don't think he got a burner on him or he would have been bustin' back at me," Craig analyzed.

"Fuck it. Let's get outta here 'fore the police come. We'll catch him on the late show another night!" Junior said.

They ran back toward Craig's car, and as they crossed the street, they heard more shots. Turning around quickly, Craig emptied his clip at the tall guy shooting at him. Junior stooped behind a car to get a good look at the guy shooting, and then Lakim came running out of the building busting in the tall guy's direction.

"Come on, muhfucka!" Lakim yelled.

"Let's go!" Craig called out to Junior.

Junior rose slowly and let off three more shots, then quickly made it to the other side of the street where Craig was putting another clip in his automatic.

"Come on, man, we gotta get the fuck outta here before the fucking police come!" Craig said, running toward his car.

"Yo, I can't leave La like that, man. He still bustin' at them muhfuckas!" Junior cried out.

"Man, fuck that dude. We gotta blow," Craig said, while pulling car keys from his pocket.

"Go start the car, man. I'm gonna go get him. He gotta come with us!" Junior said, going back to where Lakim was.

Junior could hear more gunshots as he ran through the back of the building.

Lakim was hiding behind one of the columns in front of the building, peeking to see if the guy shooting would advance on him. He had no idea how many bullets he had left in the gun and didn't want to waste what he had. He was petrified, his heart was beating rapidly, and his legs felt weak, but he had to hold on. He was never in a shootout before and didn't know what to do next, but instincts told him in order to stay alive he would have to hold fast.

"Yo, La!" Junior yelled from inside the building. "Come on, man. Let's get the fuck outta here!"

It was as if he heard an angel speaking to him. Lakim fired off the last shots and watched the slide on the barrel of the automatic freeze in an extended position, letting him know the clip was empty. He ran into the building and followed Junior to Craig's car.

As Junior and Lakim ran to Craig's car, Craig yelled for them to hurry. As soon as the pair reached the car, Craig pulled off and made a right turn towards Bed-Stuy.

"Did you hit anybody?" Lakim asked Junior.

"Nah, but I was trying to get a headshot on Kendu!" he replied.

"Who the fuck was the kid bustin' at me?" Craig asked.

"That was Stump," Lakim replied.

"So Kendu *was* trying to set me up. I should have killed that muhfucka!" Junior cried out.

“I was trying,” Craig said, “but the other dude that was shooting threw me off.”

“When Du was walking up on me, I heard somebody let off and I ran in the building. I didn’t know who was bustin’ off, so I stood by the mailboxes thinking somebody was going to come in the building. I was gonna blast they ass as soon as they came in the building,” Lakim told them.

“That was me. I didn’t know if Kendu was holdin’ heat or not. I was aiming for his melon, but I wasn’t close enough,” Craig said.

“Yo, when that muhfucka heard them shots, he jetted the fuck outta there,” Junior said. “I started chasing him until I saw Stump bustin’ at Craig. I can’t front, he had some big shit and it was loud. His shit sounded like a cannon. I think he had a fifth or a .44.”

“Yo, you know you can’t go back over there right now. Not ‘til shit cools down,” Craig said to Junior.

“I know, man, but my girl lives over there. I don’t want nobody trying to do something to her trying to get to me, and I can’t let them stop me from getting money.” Junior was visibly upset. “Fuck them! I’ma just hafta be a lil’ more careful, that’s all!”

“You buggin’. It’s gonna be hotta’ than fish grease ova there. You gotta be easy, cuz, ‘cause if you go over there slippin’, you gon’ fuck around and get locked up, or you might get your ass flattened,” Craig said.

Lakim was sitting in the back not saying anything because he was wondering what he was going to do now.

***

Stump was furious. He couldn’t believe Junior and his crew had the heart to shoot back at him. The first shots let him know that Kendu had lied. He had underestimated all of them and didn’t expect them to react the way they did. They were prepared for battle. When Kendu walked over to the building, Stump had told KB to wait inside the building while he went to investigate who was shooting. When he got outside, he saw Kendu running and somebody chasing after him. He shot at the guy that was chasing

Kendu, and then he heard return fire from someone else. That's when he realized they were prepared to go all out and that he really wasn't ready for an all-out gunbattle. He had rushed his decision to move on Junior and only moved that quickly because he didn't want to wait any longer. He had bigger things lined up. He expected to get the drop on him and just rob him and be over it. Stump had to respect Junior because he wasn't a pushover like the other cats he had robbed in the area.

"Where the fuck is Kendu?" Stump screamed at KB when he got back to the building.

"I don't know, man. What the fuck happened out there?" KB asked.

"Muhfuckas was expectin' us. They saw Kendu and just started blastin' off!"

"I heard. It sounded like Beirut out that muhfucka. How many of them was it?" KB quizzed.

"It was a dude in all black bustin' at Kendu, another guy I couldn't see too good, and I guess the other guy was Junior. Kendu's homeboy was in the front of the building bustin' at me when I started licking at the dude in all black!"

"That must have been Lakim," KB guessed.

"I don't know his name. All I know is I'm gonna put Kendu to rest and then flatten the other muhfuckas that was bustin' at me. When Kendu told us that he told him, I had a feeling his man was gonna tell Junior what was going down. I shoulda just waited and caught him sleeping."

Police sirens could be heard in the distance, so they decided to go to one of KB's friend's house so Stump could stash his gun.

Kendu had run to one of his friend's apartment to get a gun and change his shirt, but by the time he headed back downstairs, he could hear the screech of walkie-talkies and people talking in the lobby. He figured the police had come on the scene and was looking for witnesses to what happened. He quickly returned upstairs and put the gun up, then waited a while before going back to his building.

He walked over to his building slowly, trying to blend in with the crowd that had formed, then slipped into his building without being questioned by the police. His heart was still racing as he entered his apartment and sat on his bed thinking about how his childhood friend had betrayed him. He couldn't believe Lakim had flipped on him. Lakim was his enemy now. Although Lakim never let off a shot at him, he did have a gun pointed at him, and that was something he never thought would happen between them. Kendu was enraged.

Kendu originally thought Stump was the one shooting at him, until he glanced over his shoulder and saw a guy in all black chasing him with a big-ass gun. When he realized it wasn't Stump, he tried to get the fuck out of dodge, and while he was running he noticed Junior was shooting at him, too. He never actually saw Lakim shoot, but he might as well have since he was with the crew that was busting at him.

***

Shondra was thinking about how mad Junior was going to be because she was coming in later than she had originally planned. She was having such a good time with her girls that she had lost track of time. When the cab pulled up in front of her building, there was a crowd out front and police cars on the sidewalk with their lights flashing. Her mouth got dry and her heartrate increased. She immediately thought the worst and wasn't prepared for any bad news.

"Stop the car!" she screamed to the cab driver. "Let me out!"

After the cab driver pulled over behind a police car, Shondra snatched the door handle, breaking one of her manicured nails. Gloria paid the fare and followed behind her, while Shondra ran up to a girl who lived in her building.

"What happened out here?" she asked the girl.

`"I don't know, girl. I just heard a bunch o' shootin' out here. It was loud as hell, too, because that shit woke up me and my son."

"Did you see who…I mean, do you know if anybody got shot?" Shondra quizzed.

"Not that I know of. I just know there was a lot of damn shootin'," the girl replied, taking a long pull from her cigarette.

Shondra walked quickly to her building and broke one of her heels as she entered the lobby.

"Shit!" she squealed.

When she got in her apartment, she yelled out for Junior but didn't get an answer. This worried her more, and she rushed into her room for any signs he had been there. Gloria was right behind her to make sure she was all right.

"You have to calm down, girl. I know what you thinkin', but you ain't really sure what happened out there. Just call him and see if he knows what happened."

"I know, Glo. I'm scared," she said, shaking nervously. "I don't know if he's okay."

"I know, girl, but you also don't know if he was mixed up in that shit out there."

"I know he was 'cause he's not here. Where the hell is he?" Shondra began crying.

"Give me his beeper number so I can beep him for you," Gloria said, picking up the receiver to the phone.

With a worried look on her face, Shondra lay down on the queen-sized bed she shared with Junior. She was trying not to think the worst, but couldn't help it.

"I shouldn't have went out. I shoulda stayed home. At least I would know if he's okay or not."

"Look, Shondra, you buggin' out. You can't do this to yourself. One, you don't know what happened, and two, you can't blame yourself if something did happen. You had no way of knowing. You're not God."

CHAPTER 5
TAKE A PICTURE, SWEETIE

It was late in the afternoon when KB came out of his house the next day. His mother had been trying to wake him up earlier to answer the phone calls he was getting, but he was worn out from the night before. He had a feeling it was Stump calling because he rarely received phone calls at home. He was wearing a long-sleeved Polo logo rugby, Used jeans, and a Polo ski jacket. It wasn't that cold out, so he went back upstairs to take of the jacket.

The phone rang again when he walked into his house.

"Hello?"

"KB?" Stump asked.

"Yeah, what's good, man?" KB replied.

"Where you been? I been callin' you all morning." Stump sounded a little annoyed.

"Shit, I was knocked out. What's up?"

"Did you hear anything about last night?"

"Nah, I ain't been out," KB responded.

"So you ain't hear nothin' about Kendu?" Stump asked, wanting to find Kendu.

"Nah. I was gonna go by his crib to see if I could catch up with him," KB told him.

"Okay, 'cause I wanna know what the deal is with that joker. I shoulda put a hot one in his ass last night. Them dudes was on point," Stump said, frustrated.

"I know, and I didn't even have a burner on me to help you out."

"Meet me by the projects in twenty minutes and I'll go with you to see Kendu," Stump instructed.

"A'ight. I'll be waiting for you in front of Adbul's."

"Cool. I'll see you in twenty," Stump said, then hung up the phone.

KB tucked his burner in his waist and headed for Baptiste.

Lakim was lighting a blunt when Junior came back from the store with a turkey and cheese hero. They were in Tompkins Park waiting for Shondra. Junior had spoken to her when she beeped him last night. He was taking every precaution and told her to bring the money, guns, and drugs he had stashed in her house in case someone started snitching. He also told her not to tell anyone what little bit he told her about what happened last night, especially her homegirl, Gloria. Times like these were when he realized she was a real trooper, because she always followed his directions to the nine and came through for him when he needed her.

"I don't think nobody gonna say it was us that was shooting out there last night," Lakim was saying to Junior.

"You never know. Them faggot-ass muhfuckas might. You know they don't like me like that. They'll be glad for me to get locked up," Junior said, taking a bite of his sandwich.

"I'm not sweatin' that shit. All I'm thinking about is this money," Lakim replied, blowing the white smoke out of his lungs.

"Me, too. I'm not gonna lay low too long because I don't want nobody trying to take over my spot. I'm the one who got that traffic coming through heavy like that in the projects. It's too easy for somebody to just set up shop and take all my custies. Right now, I'ma work off my beeper 'til we find out how hot it is ova there," Junior explained to Lakim.

"I don't really give a fuck. I rest in those PJs. Them dudes not gonna run me out my own hood!" Lakim replied defiantly.

"I hear you, La, but it wasn't them dudes that was bustin' at us," Junior reminded him.

"I know, but I been livin' there all my life and I don't have nowhere else to go. I can't stay ova here forever. I know them dudes probably mad at me 'cause I fucks with you on the money tip, but I don't give a fuck. I ain't neva had no beef with them cats like that, so I should be okay going back ova there. I know Kendu did some foul shit and I know he gotta get his, but his hand called for it," Lakim said to Junior.

"A'ight, La, I got you, man. Just let me find out if they callin' out my name 'round there first, and either way it goes, you can go back out there and I'ma let you run the spot. I just gotta be sure I don't send you out there blind and put you in jeopardy. Believe me, son, I'm not gonna let nobody stop the flow of my dough!"

"That's what I'm talking about. Fuck them punk muhfuckas. This shouldn't stop us from eating. If anything, we should be able to eat lovely now that they know we ain't no pushovers," Lakim responded, passing Junior the blunt.

When Shondra saw Junior, she ran toward him with her arms outstretched and held him tightly.

"Are you okay, baby?" she asked, worried.

"I'm good, Mooka. Did you find out anything?" Junior responded.

"Mmmmhmm. Talking-ass Terry was telling Gloria he heard some guys from Bushwick was trying to rob you and that y'all was shooting out."

"Did he say any names?" Junior asked.

"No, he didn't say any names," she replied.

"What about the police? Did he say the police knew who it was?"

"No. He said they was asking people, but he don't think anybody said anything."

"Good. No police came to your house, right?"

"No. They was just outside asking people questions. Oh, I'm sorry, La, how are you?" Shondra asked, remembering her manners.

"That's a'ight. I understand. I'm okay, Shondra," Lakim replied with a chuckle.

"What you gonna do now, boo?" she asked, turning her attention back to her man.

"I don't really know yet, but I do know I gotta get Kendu and the muhfucka that was bustin' at us. Anybody call they name out or anything?" Junior already knew it was Stump, but he just wanted to hear if the hood knew.

"Not that I know of. They never said Kendu's name either. Was he the one that tried to set y'all up?" Shondra asked Junior.

"Yeah, he the one that sicced them muhfuckas on Junior!" Lakim blurted out.

"I can't stand his dirty ass," Shondra said. "You know that same day when me and Gloria went shopping, we saw him talking to some guy and he gave me the dirtiest look. I shoulda known something was up right then."

"Well, fuck him. He gonna take a dirt nap when I catch up to his greasy ass!" Junior said.

Then he grabbed the bag Shondra was carrying and inspected the contents before they all walked off to Tompkins Projects.

***

KB waited for Stump in front of the bodega on the other side of Baptiste. Things had gone wrong last night and had gotten out of hand. He hadn't planned for things to go south, but knowing Stump, he wasn't going to stop until everyone involved was dead, and KB wasn't prepared nor wanted any part of it. Hanging with Stump involved criminal activity but not to the degree it was going to reach. Now he had a dilemma. He had to find a way out before he ended up doing a life bid behind bars or up in Dante's Funeral Home.

"What up, boy?" Stump asked as he approached KB.

"Ain't shit. You holdin'?" KB inquired.

"Always. Did you see that bitch-ass Kendu yet?" Stump asked, tapping both sides of his waist to let KB know he had two guns on him.

"Nah, I think he blew. I doubt he gonna be out here."

"Well, let's go to his crib just to be sure," Stump said, walking in the direction of Kendu's building.

When they reached Kendu's apartment, Stump knocked on his door. Noone answered, so they left and sat on the benches in the back of his building. Stump wanted to wait to see if Kendu showed up.

While they were waiting, a young kid walked up to KB and asked him for fifty cents. KB went into his pocket and gave him a dollar bill. After the kid took the money, thanked him, and started to walk off, KB had an idea and called the kid back.

"Yo, shorty, do you know a guy named Kendu that live in this building?" KB asked, pointing to the buiding in front of him.

"Yeah, I know him," the kid responded.

"You seen him today?" KB asked.

"Nope. I don't think nobody's gonna see him no time soon," he replied, looking at Stump.

"Why you say that, lil man?" KB asked.

"'Cause I know," he replied, still looking at Stump.

"How you know?" KB tried to get him to look at him.

"'Cause he's my brother," he replied, looking at Stump as if he was waiting for a reaction.

Stump lit up like a lightbulb.

"Do you know where he at?" Stump interjected.

"Yeah, he at my cousin's house," the kid said, twisting his mouth in a scowl.

"And where's that at?" Stump asked, his interest peaking all of a sudden.

"Why you want to know?" the kid asked, looking Stump up and down like he was sizing him up.

"I need to give him something," Stump said, sensing the little boy didn't trust him.

"Give it to me, and I'll make sure he gets it," he replied, holding out his hand.

"How 'bout I give you something for yourself and you tell me where your cuz lives at so I can give Kendu what I got for him myself?" Stump suggested.

"That's cool, but I'm still not gonna tell y'all," he replied, shifting his eyes from Stump to KB.

"Look, shawty, if you don't tell me where your cousin lives, I'm goin' to make it so you don't see your mama no more!"

"Fuck you! My mama dead!" he said and ran off.

"Go get that lil muthafucka so I can get the address from him!" Stump yelled.

"Chill, man. He ain't gonna give you the address now, even if we do catch him," KB reasoned. "At least we know where Kendu at."

"Yeah, but what good is knowing he's at his cousin's house if we don't know where his cousin lives? We need to find that out."

Stump decided to wait around all night. He wanted to be sure Kendu didn't tell his brother to say he was at a cousin's house to throw them off his scent.

Two weeks later…

Steam seeped from the pots on the stove and the kettle was whistling, informing Gloria that the water was boiling. She was cooking dinner and making tea for Shondra. She brought the tea out to Shondra and sat down beside her on the couch.

"I can't believe it was some guys from Bushwick trying to rob Junior," Gloria said.

Shondra remembered what Junior told her about not giving up any extra information on what happened that night he had the shootout.

"I'm so scared for Junior now," Shondra replied, sipping the hot tea Gloria had given her.

"I know, girl, but you know guys bound to get into some shit sooner or later."

"Yeah, but you never think it'll be your man or someone that close to you," Shondra said.

"Think about it. 'Member when they killed Byron in front of the building? I didn't even know he was selling drugs until the police found all that money and shit on him," Gloria reminisced.

"I always wondered how he drove all dem pretty cars, though. He was so cool. His sister Alyssa always stayed to herself, too," Shondra added.

"I heard she's runnin' his business now," Gloria said. "I don't know how true it is, but you know how the streets be talkin'."

Shondra frowned. "Well, I don't want anything to happen to my baby, and I hope the guys that tried to violate stay the fuck from 'round here."

"You want to smoke?" Gloria asked, pulling a plastic bag full of weed from her Louie Vuitton purse.

"Yeah, I need something to calm my nerves and shit."

Gloria ruffled through her purse and pulled out a blunt.

"Shit, it's broke. I'm gonna run to the corner and get another blunt and something to drink. You want anything?"

"No, I'm okay with this tea," Shondra replied, lifting the cup and taking a sip.

After the door slammed, Shondra laid her head back and thought about how her man was getting along without her.

The store on the corner was closed, so Gloria had to go to the twenty-four hour store on Graham Avenue. As she turned the corner, she saw KB walking toward her.

Oh shit, it's that cute-ass guy, she thought.

She fixed her hair and slowed her walk to a sexy gait, trying to entice him. KB noticed her and he could see the roundness of her hips in the tight Calvin Klein jeans she was wearing. When he got close enough, she dropped her purse purposely, turned around, and then bent down to pick it up, giving him a full view of her perfectly round, apple ass.

"Damn, lady, you can hurt somebody wit' all dat," he said, bending down next to her.

"'Scuse me?" Gloria remarked.

"I'm saying, you bending down and exposing all dat ass is dangerous."

"I dropped my purse, sweetie. How else am I supposed to get it?"

They stood up at the stame time and he moved closer to her.

"I would have gotten it for you if you gave me a chance," KB told her.

"Second time's the charm," she said, dropping her purse again.

KB bent down and picked it up, but didn't give it to her.

"I see you like playin' games, huh?"

"I don't play games, hun. I'm grown," she replied.

"Was that some type of trick to see if I would pick it up?" he asked, holding the purse out to her.

"Like I said, hun, tricks are for kids, and I'm grown." She grabbed her purse and continued to walk toward the corner.

She thought he would walk her to the store, but she noticed from the small talk that her game was a little more advanced than his. She turned around to see if he was coming behind her, but he was just standing in the same spot watching her.

"Take a picture, sweetie. It'll last longer."

KB was checking out her fine body. He couldn't believe somebody as fine as her would even be interested in someone like him.

"Hold on, chocolate. Where you going?"

Got him, she said in her mind. "I'm going to the store.'

"Let me walk with you."

Gloria stopped and waited for him to catch up to her.

"What's your name, lady?"

"Gloria. What's your name?" she returned his question.

"Keith, but everybody calls me KB. You live around here?"

"Yeah, been living here all my life. You ain't never seen me before?"

"Nah, 'cause I'm not from around here," KB responded.

"Well, where you from?"

"I'm from Williamsburg."

"Oh, okay. What you doing over here so late?"

"I'm just chillin'…on my way back to the crib."

Gloria put two dollars in the square, Plexiglass cube of the store window.

"Let me get a Philly and a sixteen-ounce Pepsi," she told the Arab man behind the glass.

"You smoke choke?" KB asked her.

"Duh, yeah! What is that, a trick question?" she asked. She couldn't believe that everything coming out of his mouth was so lame. His talk game was whack.

"Why you so uptight, luv? I'm just trying to make conversation."

"I'm sorry. I ain't tryin' to be mean. I'm just joking with you."

As they started back toward the projects, KB grabbed her hand suddenly and stopped her in the middle of the block.

"Look, luv, as you can tell, I'm not really good when it comes to kicking it to a female, so I'm just gonna be forward with you, if that's alright."

Gloria looked into his eyes and could tell he was serious.

"Go ahead, hun. Say what's on your mind."

"I like the way you look, I like the way you dress, and I like the way you talk. I want to get to know you better. I don't know if you got a man and I really don't care, but if you feel close to how I'm feelin', I think we should see where this takes us."

Gloria was taken aback. It wasn't that what he said was so powerful. It was just the realest and most honest line she had ever heard from any guy that had ever tried to talk to her before.

"You know something, KB. I like the way you look, too, and I like how you're kickin' it to me right now. So, I do want to see where this goes. And by the way, I don't have a man."

"Good. So what do we do from here?" KB asked.

"I don't know. Why don't you give me your number, and I'll call you tomorrow so we can hook up."

"Sounds good. Ay, I noticed you didn't say you like the way I dress. Is there something wrong with my gear?" KB stepped away and crossed his arms.

"Nah, baby, you dress fine. You dress real fine." Gloria smiled wide as she walked to her building.

Shondra was lying on the couch nodding off, when Gloria walked into the apartment.

"Girl, you ain't gonna believe who I just ran into on the way to the store!" Gloria shrieked.

"Who, Glo?" Shondra asked with sleepiness still in her voice.

"'Member that guy who was with Kendu a coupla weeks back when we came from shoppin'? Well, I just kicked it to him and got his number. I'm 'posed to hook up with him tomorrow. He is so fine," she said, twirling around like a high school girl in love.

"That's cool," Shondra remarked dryly.

While Gloria was talking about how she met KB, Shondra was deep in thought. She was too wrapped up thinking about Junior to really pay attention to anyone or anything else. She was so worried about him that she couldn't partake in her friend's good fortune in hooking up with a guy she seemed to really like. Gloria continued talking, not realizing that Shondra was a million miles away. Finally, after Shondra stopped responding to anything Gloria was saying, Gloria realized Shondra wasn't listening to her story.

"Are you okay, girl?" Gloria asked.

"Huh? Oh, I'm so sorry, Glo. I'm just sitting here thinking about my baby," Shondra replied.

"I understand. Come on and smoke some of this blunt with me. It'll help clear your thoughts."

"I think that's what I need to help me stop worrying 'bout him so much."

Gloria took a deep pull of the cigar filled with marijuana and fell back onto the couch next to Shondra.

"Damn, that's some good shit!" Gloria said.

"Mmmmmhmmmm," Shondra replied, blowing a cloud out of her mouth and nose.

"Yeah, this is what you need to get your mind right," Gloria added, filling her lungs with more of the ghetto herbal medicine.

"I know. I don't want to worry, but I can't help it. I just keep thinking something bad is going to happen to my baby. I don't want him to get hurt or get into any trouble. You know what I'm sayin', Glo? I just want things back to the way they used to be." Shondra sighed.

"I know, baby," Gloria said, as she grabbed Shondra and held her close to her bosom. "I know."

***

Lakim was impatient and ready to start making money again, so he and Junior were discussing how Junior wanted things to run. Junior wanted to make sure everything ran smoothly for both of their sake. Lakim was so thirsty for money that he didn't care about anything. He just wanted Junior to send him back with some work. His money was getting low, and he was tired of staying at different people's cribs.

"Look, Junior, I'm just ready to get back ova there. I'm tired of stayin' up in that lady's crib like that. I mean, I appreciate your cousin letting me chill, but I need to get back to the hood and get this money."

"I hear you, La. I just wanna make sure this shit gonna run like clockwork 'fore I send you back out there. You know what I'm sayin'?" Junior said to him.

"I hear you, man, but we been over this shit already. I need to get back on the block before dudes start makin' moves out there. Then there's gonna be more beef, ya feel me?" Lakim was insistent as well as impatient.

"A'ight, let's just go over this shit one more time. I need to be sure you understand what it is I want you to do. You gotta stay low until I handle this shit with Stump and KB. Once I find out at least where one of them rests, I can light that ass up and then move on to the next target," Junior explained.

"Shit, Stump lives in Bushwick Projects. I think he stays in building 821," Lakim informed Junior.

"You knew where that muhfucka lived at? Damn, you shoulda been told me that." Junior looked at Lakim suspiciously. They had been talking about it nearly a month and he never once brought it up.

"I just remembered that shit when you was talkin' to your cousin the other day and he said something about a bitch he was fucking from Bushwick. I meant to tell you then, but I forgot. Well, now that you know, let's smoke him, and when people find out his ass got wet up, ain't nobody else gonna try no shit like that with us no more."

"You right about that, but I don't want you to be down with that. I'm gonna take care of it myself. I'm gonna catch his bitch ass sleepin'," Junior said.

"I can dig it. That's smart. Once I get this work and go back ova there, I'll find out what floor he lives on," Lakim told him.

"Cool. Let's split this work up so we can get back to business."

Junior went into his backpack and pulled out ten thousand dollars' worth of work for Lakim.

"Get them two young dudes that live in Lizzette's building to get down with our team to work this shit off for you. You pay them twenty-five percent off every hundred. Give them shifts so there'll be work out there twenty-four seven. There will always be work out there, so money will come hand over fist. You down for that?" Junior asked.

Junior had been thinking about implementing this plan since the shootout. He figured he could have someone else working the block for him, while having Lakim pick up the money and give out the work.

"As long as I'm gettin' this paper, I'm alright with whateva," Lakim replied.

Junior gave him the package and cab money to get back to the projects. After Lakim left, Junior called Shondra's house.

"What's up, baby? I know I ain't been returning your beeps, but I'm trying to take care of this shit so I can come back home to you," Junior said to her when she picked up the phone.

"I know, boo. It's been about a month and I've been worrying about you, especially when I beep you and you don't call me right back."

"Don't worry about me, baby. I'm a'ight. Shit, I'm more worried about you. But, look, I need you to do me a favor."

"Anything you need, boo," Shondra cooed.

"La just told me what building Stump lives in, but I need to find out where the other guy that was with him lives. I know he stays in Williamsburg, but I need to know what building. So, keep your ears open for any info for me. I'm gonna body both them muhfuckas, but I want to get the easiest one first. You know what I mean?"

"I understand. You know something…Gloria met the guy that was with Kendu. Remember that day I told you I passed him when we came from shopping? The guy that was with him that day?"

"Oh yeah, I remember. That's KB. He's the one that was with Stump that morning. She kickin' it with him now?"

"She told me that she got his number the other night and that she was supposed to be hangin' out with him that next day. I can ask her to find out."

"Nah, I don't want you to ask her because I don't want her to know he's the dude I got beef with. She might tell him, and that'll fuck everything up. I don't want him to be hip to what's about to happen to his ass. This is real serious, Mooka. I'm gonna kill that muhfucka."

"Oh please, Junior." She started to sob. "Please, no. I don't want you to do nothing to get yourself hurt or locked up. Please, baby, can't somebody else do that?"

"Nah, I gotta do this one myself 'cause them muhfuckas violated. Ain't nothin' gonna happen to me. They the ones that's gonna get it. That's why Gloria can't know why you askin', feel me?"

Junior never imagined he would be planning to kill someone. He had been a little naïve to the game and thought he would hustle without any problems because he thought he was smarter than the average hustler. His mind was changing now, and he was feeling he didn't have a choice in what he was about to do.

"Okay, Junior, I'm gonna see if I can find out where he lives for you without letting her know why I'm asking."

"Look, Mooka, I know that's your girl and everything, but you can't tell her shit. I can't trust nobody right now on this but you. Do you think she knows he was down wit' Kendu setting me up?"

"No, I don't think so. If he says anything about that, I'm sure she'll tell me."

"What about Kendu? You seen him around there lately?" Junior asked.

"I haven't seen him. They sayin' he went down South, but I don't know how true that is. You know how muhfuckas be talkin'."

"A'ight, that's cool 'cause I just sent La back ova there with some work. I'ma get that bitch-ass Du, too. I figured he was gonna get ghost, so I'll just catch his ass after I take care of dem other two faggots. They the real threat. But, trust me, once I take care of them, I don't care what part of down south he at. I'ma go down there and bury him, too!"

"So when am I gonna see you, baby? I miss you so much. I'm used to you sleeping next to me, and I'm lonely without you right now," Shondra said sincerely.

"Soon, ma, real soon. Let me take care of this business and we'll take a trip to VA or something. Just you and me, a'ight?" Junior coaxed her.

"Look, Junior, I need some dick, straight up. I don't mean to sound like that, but I'm horny as hell for you."

"Damn, baby, I'm sorry. I been so caught up in this shit that I'm slippin' on my duties to you as your man. Matter of fact, take a cab to Five Towns Motel in Far Rock in about a half hour, and we can spend the weekend out there. I'll take care of that ass, a'ight?"

"Say no more, baby. I'm packing my overnight bag as we speak."

"I'm gonna leave right now. Just beep me when you're on your way so I can be outside waiting for you," Junior told her.

After hanging up, he grabbed some cash and went outside to find his cousin to see if he could give him a ride to Far Rockaway, Queens.

***

Kendu was getting worse. His habit was costing him over two hundred dollars a day, and he was broke. He'd been wearing the same clothes for over a month and was pawning his aunt's valuables to support his habit. He realized shit was getting out of hand when the younger drug dealers around his aunt's way started disrespecting him and treating him like a fiend. One day when he went to cop from one of them and was two dollars short, he asked the youngster could he bring it back later.

"Yo, you act like I got a license to sell this shit or something," the young dealer had said. "You betta go suck a dick for the rest or take your bum ass somewhere else."

Kendu was hot as fire while listening to the guy disrespect him like he was a crackhead. At that moment, he felt like grabbing him and beating him within an inch of his life, then take his money to show him what he was really about. However, he just didn't have the heart to do it at the time.

Kendu didn't realize he was falling deep into depression. His life had changed so drastically in one fateful night. He made a bad decision in getting mixed up with Stump and KB, and now his best friend was his enemy. He was a ticking timebomb and was on the brink of losing control. His thoughts were solely geared toward getting high in order to escape the reality of his present situation. It wasn't evident to him that the disrespect he was experiencing was because he had the traits of someone strung out on crack. He was in denial. The reality of his situation was that he felt he didn't have anything more to lose. He had gone too far and was spiraling out of control. His life had changed for the worse, and he was at the point where he didn't give a fuck what happened anymore, which was a dangerous mindset for a man faced with his dilemma.

He had just used up all the fuel in his lighter, so he walked toward Key Food Supermarket to steal another one. On his way to the store, he spotted the same young drug dealers across the street standing on the corner talking to a girl.

"Ayyyy yooo!" Kendu called out to him.

The guy looked around and noticed Kendu across the street.

"What man?" he yelled back, looking up and down the block for police.

"I need to see you. What's up?" Kendu screamed.

The guy remembered Kendu because he had been copping from him all week. He told the girl he was talking with to hold on while he went to make a sale. As he crossed the street, Kendu quickly dug in his pocket for some money to flash on him, then pulled out an orange box cutter. When the guy got in front of him, he had a serious look on his face.

"What you need, muhfucka?" he growled.

"I want to spend twenty dollars. You gonna give me a play, right?" Kendu asked, licking his crusty lips.

"Look, man, don't waste my fuckin' time because I got shit to do. You get four jacks and that's it," the young hustler replied.

As the hustler picked out four capsules to sell to him, Kendu opened the box cutter, which made a loud clicking noise as the blade revealed itself from its orange hiding place, and then he brought it down across the young guy's face with one swift swing.

"OOOOhhhhhh shiiit!!!" the pre-teen hustler screamed, dropping the bag and backing up.

His face opened up, exposing his pink flesh that soon turned red and started leaking like a broken kitchen faucet. Kendu scooped the bag off the ground and dug his hands in the young dealer's pockets. Then he stepped back and brought the sharp blade down on the dealer's hands, which were covering his gash.

"Yeah, muhfucka, now look at you!" Kendu yelled.

After watching the baby-faced boy screaming in pain, he made a mad dash back to his cousin's house. He left the juvenile hustler on the corner bleeding like a pig as the girl across the street came over screaming, "Help! Help! Somebody please help him!"

The injured youngster continued to scream, blood streaming all over his hands as he held his wound tightly. The hysterical girl looked in the direction of where Kendu ran. Then she dashed over to a payphone and dialed a number, paying attention to the building Kendu ran inside.

When he got inside his cousin's house, Kendu started to think about the repercussions that were sure to come if anyone recognized him as the one who slashed the young hustler.

I bet them muhfuckas know I ain't no joke now, though, he thought to himself, while opening the door to the room he was staying in.

"Damn, that lil dude had a lot of dough on him," he said aloud, while counting the bloody bills.

Kendu had close to one thousand dollars when he finished counting and almost five hundred dollars in product. He had hit the jackpot. He figured the young boy's boss would find out what happened and there was sure to be problems. However, as quick as

the reality of that thought entered his mind, it left because he had enough money and drugs to do what he wanted. He was going to make sure he saved enough money for a bus ticket to North Carolina where he would go and stay with his uncle. He planned to get off the drugs, clean his act up, and then come back to Brooklyn to get his revenge on Stump, Junior, and Lakim. Yeah, that was his plan.

***

Three days passed and Kendu's plan was derailed. Instead of putting money away for the bus ticket, he spent everything getting high. He hadn't slept and was completely out of money. He had even pawned some of his aunt's valuables while on his binge and was feeling guilty. While sitting on the edge of her bed, he decided he was finally going to leave for North Carolina. He just needed to pawn a little bit more of her things in order to get enough money for a one-way ticket.

As he rummaged through her closets and drawers, he learned he had pawned everything of value. He kept looking, though, until he heard a knock on the door. He started to panic because no one ever came to his aunt's house, especially since she was out of town. Quickly, he went to his cousin's bedroom to get a bat just in case it wasn't a pleasant housecall. While heading to his cousin's room, he heard the front door crash open. An older guy, with a long scar from his temple to the bottom of his chin, rushed into the apartment, pointing a massive gun at Kendu.

"Don't move, motherfucker, or you're dead!" he screamed, moving towards Kendu slowly.

Scared to death, Kendu put his hands up. "What's goin' on?" he asked, his voice quivering with fear.

"You 'bout to find out! Is anybody else up in here with you?" the intruder shouted, his eyes darting left and right quickly while he kept the big .45 auto trained on Kendu's head.

"N-n-n-noooo, nobody's here but me," Kendu stuttered.

The gunman moved within an arm's reach of Kendu, then swung the gun at his head. Kendu felt an immediate pain on the

left side of his head and dropped to the parquet floor, rolling onto his back and clutching the spot where he was hit. The scarred gunman kicked Kendu and then he felt the cold steel of the barrel pressing against the back of his head. Someone else entered the apartment, and when Kendu looked up and saw the young guy that he had robbed and cut, he knew it was over for him.

The gunman kicked Kendu again, then looked at the young dealer and asked him, "Is this him?"

"Yeah, that's that fuckin' crackhead that sliced me," he said, hock spitting on Kendu and feeling the scar on his face pull.

"Please, man, please!" Kendu begged, rubbing the knot on his head.

"Shut the fuck up!" the gunman yelled. "Where's the shit you took? You better pray you still have some of it, 'cause if you don't, you gon' meet the devil!" the gunman said between clenched teeth.

"It's in the room in the back under the mattress. Please, man, I'm sorry. I fucked up. I was high on that shit. Please, man. I can work it off for you. Please don't kill me, please," Kendu begged.

There was no possible way Kendu would still have any of the work or the money, but the gunman wanted to check if there was antying else of value in the house he could take for reparation.

The young drug dealer went into the backroom to search for anything worth taking.

"Make sure you don't touch nothing with your bare hands in there," the gunman yelled.

"I'm not. I got my gloves," he responded.

The gunman made Kendu sit on the couch in the living room and kept the gun pointed to his face. Kendu could see nothing but the black hole and the long, black barrel. He had the worse feeling in his stomach. He couldn't stop shaking, and his heart rate had sped up like a revving motorbike. The gunman held the gun on him and glanced toward the back to see if his accomplice had found anything. When the youngster came back from the room, he was heated because there was nothing worth taking.

Kendu was squirming on the couch, his body trembling uncontrollably. He had spent the money and smoked all the product. He was trying to think of something he could give them

that would compensate for the shit he took, but he had sold everything of value.

"Look, man, I can get the money back for you. All you have to do is make a call. Please, man, don't kill me!" Kendu was reduced to real tears.

"I wish you shut the fuck up!" the young drug dealer said and punched Kendu in his face with a hard right.

Kendu felt the end was near. They were going to kill him even if they would have gotten all their shit back in full. He mustered up all the heart he had and tried to think of a way to get out of the deadly situation he was in. Since he had nothing to lose, he was going to try something that would come as a surprise to the gunman. He just had to wait for the right moment, and the way shit was looking to him, he didn't have any time to waste.

The gunman was standing over Kendu, now pointing the gun at his chest. He had a look of death in his eyes and a firm grip around the handle of the .45 caliber automatic pistol. His hand was steady, showing he was not new to holding a pistol in his hand. The young thug was busy ruffling through Kendu's pockets looking for money. He stepped across Kendu's legs to get to the other pocket and momentarily blocked the vision of the gunman. That's when Kendu saw his chance.

In what seemed like slow motion, Kendu grabbed the barrel of the gun as the young thug stepped across his legs. Catching the gunman by surprise, he held onto the gun as the gunman tried to unsuccessfully pull the trigger. Kendu held on with both hands and tried to yank it from his grip. The young thug started swinging wildly at his head, while Kendu and the gunman tussled for possession. Kendu wouldn't let go. He held on because his life depended on it.

The gunman was yelling for his accomplice to help him. The youngster ran to the kitchen, and Kendu could hear the clanging of utensils. He had to get possession of the gun or he was definitely going to be killed. He turned his body sideways and bit down hard on the gunman's hand. Within seconds, he had the gun in his hand. He turned the weapon on the gunman and was about to pull the trigger, when he felt a sharp pain in his back. The young thug was

stabbing him repeatedly. He turned around and pulled the trigger, but the shot missed the young thug. He squeezed off another shot before falling facedown from the stab wounds in his back. The young thug had dropped the knife when Kendu turned around and ducked behind a china cabinet when the first shot was fired. The scarred gunman, who was on top of Kendu as he fell, snatched the gun from his hand.

"I should shoot your ass for almost getting me blasted!" the gunman screamed at his cohort.

The gunman turned his attention back to a fallen Kendu. He placed the barrel of the gun to the base of Kendu's head and made sure there would be no more mistakes. The boom from the gun was loud, and Kendu's brain matter splattered across the nicely shellacked parquet floors.

"Take the knife with you and leave," he told the young thug. "I gotta clean some of this shit up. Now go!" the gunman yelled, while looking down at the corpse.

He took a towel from the bathroom and wiped off the doorknobs in the house. He went into the kitchen and wiped down the drawers and then took out every utensil and put them in a plastic bag. He went into the bedroom and wiped down the headboard, the bed rails, and all the knobs to the closets. He walked past Kendu, being careful not to step in the dark red blood that oozed out of his head and made a puddle in the middle of the floor. He didn't want his boot prints to play a part in the murder investigation. He grabbed the front door knob with the towel and walked out of the apartment, closing the door behind him

***

There were red and blue flashing lights in front of the three-story brownstone, and a crowd had gathered around the yellow police tape, eager to find out what happened inside the building. Many of the people from the neighborhood were thinking the worse since this was not the first time they were witnessing a crime scene. A black van with the word CORONER painted in white letters on the sides pulled up among the police cruisers and

unmarked detective vehicles. Two burly men got out of the van, pulled out a stretcher, and went up the steps of the brownstone, disappearing through the doors.

"What happened in there?" someone asked.

"I don't know, but I heard some gunshots. They must have come from in there," an old lady commented, as she pointed to the brownstone.

"Whatever happened I know somebody in there is dead. You see that black van that pulled up? That means there are dead bodies in there," someone else added.

"Who lives in that building?" another person asked.

"Ms. Brown owns the building, but I think she moved to North Carolina over a year ago. I think she left the building to one of her sons, but you don't see him much. I don't know who else lived in there, though," a next-door neighbor said.

There was silence as the stretcher came out with a body covered by a white sheet. No one in the crowd knew who the person was under the sheet. They whispered and asked questions, but no one had a definitive answer. Many of the people out there were making their own assumptions on what had happened, but no one actually knew who was murdered and why.

In the crowd, there was a group of young men standing around not saying anything. One person in the group knew exactly what happened in the house. The person under the sheet was the guy that had robbed and cut him four days ago. The young guy with the newly acquired scar stood in the crowd with his friends and looked on, acting as bewildered as everyone else. He was only there to see if anyone had any idea about what happened. He vowed he would get the guy back; he couldn't let him live after that. When he came out of St. Mary's Hospital after getting his face stapled, he told his older brother, Drez, who was the drug supplier in the area, what had happened and who did it. Drez promised him that he wouldn't have to worry about it anymore.

Kendu was dead at only nineteen years old. It seemed like he never had a chance. He was just another black youth that got caught in the fangs of a life void of love, discipline, and truth. He grew up not knowing the love of a mother because she died when

he was eight, right after giving birth to his little brother. He and his brother went to live with their grandmother who worked to support them, but unfortunately, she was never home due to her hectic work schedule. So, they were forced to raise themselves. Kendu had to learn the streets and made his own rules as he got older. He didn't adhere to anyone else's rules because there was no one to enforce discipline. His only truth was the sad reality of his doomed life. He was not taught he could be anything he wanted to be. There was no father figure to guide him, so he lived lies to compensate for all his losses. Kendu was a typical guy that grew up in the hood and never had many opportunities in life. Had he chosen a different path, things may have turned out different for him, but the last chapter in his book of life was written when he heard that final knock on the door.

CHAPTER 6
I'M READY TO PUT Y'ALL ON

Lakim went on the other side of the projects to find the two homeboys Junior wanted him to use to help get rid of the work. The guys were little terrors. They were young with a lot of heart, not afraid of anything. They had always wanted to get down with Lakim before, but he never thought about them selling for him since he worked for Junior. He did give them work before and paid them fifty bucks, but he couldn't keep that up because it ate up his profit. Lakim was greedy and wanted all the cash. Now that Junior wasn't going to be around for a while, he was going to be the heavyweight in Baptiste. He was going to have boss status.

Lakim was eager to get started again, and although he was aware of the danger of having beef with Stump, his desire for money was more. He would just be careful and make sure he kept a gun on him at all times. Stump was a dangerous dude and Lakim had to make sure he wasn't caught sleeping or his dreams would become permanent. If Junior moved too slow in taking care of Stump, he was going to put his own plan into action to take him out.

"What up, Rock?" Lakim asked, approaching the young guy wearing a Yankee baseball cap.

"What up? What's poppin'? I heard you was bustin' your gun at some cats a month or so ago. You need me to body somebody for you?" Rock asked, motioning like he had a gun in his hand.

"Nah, that's a'ight, kid," Lakim replied, laughing lightly. "I got some good news for you and Dusty, if y'all wit' it."

"What is it?" Rock asked.

"Where's Dusty? I want to tell y'all at the same time."

"He upstairs wit' a dirty. You know he like trickin' up his money on them bitches," Rock said, chuckling. "Matter of fact, let's go up there and throw a monkey-wrench in his shit real fast."

"You crazy as hell, Rock. Dusty gon' kill you if you stop him from bustin' a nut and he payin' for it."

"That dude ain't longwinded like that. He probably finished already and only been up there five minutes," Rock said, laughing loudly.

They rode the elevator up to the third floor. Dusty's grandmother had lived in the building since they were built over twenty years ago. His mother died from a drug overdose when he was two years old, and his grandmother had been raising him ever since. She was hardly ever home because she was a live-in home health aide for a wealthy family that lived on the upper westside of Manhattan, which gave Dusty free run of the house.

Rock stayed with Dusty because his mother was strung out on drugs. She was a bonified dope fiend, and Rock never acknowledged her as his mother since he was a pre-teen and old enough to understand that she loved her high more than she loved him. He called Dusty's grandmother "Momma". She had taken him in because she was aware his mother didn't take care of him and she wanted to help out. She loved both boys like they were her own, cared for them financially with what little she had, and gave them guidance whenever they needed or asked for it.

Rock opened the door and went straight to the back, while Lakim took a seat in the living room. The house was well kept, considering two young boys stayed there. Dusty came into the living room in his multi-colored boxers, then hugged Lakim and slapped him five.

"What up, La? Yo, I thought you got hit up in that shootout!" Dusty exclaimed.

"Nah, ain't shit happen to me," he replied with bravado.

"You know how these muhfuckas be stretching shit. They was sayin' you got hit and was in the hospital. They said Kendu caught one in the back and died on the way to the hospital. Then they said Junior was shooting at the police and they cornered him and locked him up on attempted murder charges," Dusty reported.

"Wow! Muhfuckas can tell some whoppers. That shit sounds like it came straght out of a movie. You know these dudes don't really be knowing shit. Wasn't nobody even out there when that shit went down. Kendu told me before the shit went down that everybody from the other side of the projects was down with it because they don't like Junior." Lakim explained.

"Fuck dem crab-ass muhfuckas. They mad 'cause Junior getting that paper in the hood, and they don't know how to embrace him. So, they just go against him. I heard them talkin' and shit, but I never fed into it because Junior mad cool with me. He always look out for me when he sees me and he always hits me off wit' some ends when I ask him. Them dudes just hatin' 'cause they don't know how to get no paper out here. I did hear that Kendu flipped the script on you and shit. What went down with that?" Dusty asked.

"He came up to me and told me that Stump wanted to rob Junior and that he was down with that sucka shit. Du was working for Junior, too, so I couldn't really figure out why he just flipped like that. He told me to stay away from Junior because he didn't want me to get caught up in that shit, but I thought about it and told Junior what was going down before they aired him out. Junior went and got right, then gave me some iron to hold shit down. His cousin came through, and we set it off out there like Scarface. I was bustin' at Stump and the whole shit." Lakim added color to his story to make it more exciting.

"You was bustin' at Stump?" Dusty asked, somewhat surprised.

"Hell yeah! That muhfucka was trying to kill us. I was trying to make him disappear for good!"

“I don’t understand Kendu. I mean, that was your man. Why would he just flip like that?” Dusty asked.

“Because he a closet smoker!” Rock said, coming back into the living room. “Joyce told me he was smokin’ that shit, kid.”

“Word?” Dusty asked.

“That’s my word. She told me that shit a while ago. She should know. She smokes her damn self, and I guess a crackhead can recognize another crackhead by how they act,” Rock assumed.

“Do you think he’s really smokin’?” Dusty asked Lakim.

“I don’t know and I can’t really say. Just like Joyce can’t really say unless she saw him smoking that shit. You know what I mean? All I know is that he was actin’ mad funny about givin’ me the work and money all of a sudden. But you know something? None of that shit really matters because he not gon’ come ‘round here no more no way. Let me tell y’all what I came here for. You still got a broad back there, Dusty?” Lakim asked, peeking down the hallway.

“Yep, and I just got some brain for free,” Rock said, laughing.

“You got head for free from her? That bitch ain’t gettin’ nothin’ else out of me with her raggedy ass.” Dusty was upset.

Lakim cut to the chase. “Look, boys, I’m ready to put y’all on if y’all ready to start working.”

“Hell yeah!” they both said in unison.

“Let me tell you how it’s going down. Y’all gon’ to work in shifts. That way somebody will always be out there with some work twenty-four seven. I want all the heads to know that our operation doesn’t close. Whatever time y’all choose you gon’ have to stick to it. No excuses. My operation has to run like a real business. Any competition is gonna be knocked out because the shit I got is top quality, and I’m putting more weight on the bottles, so the heads are going to be getting more bang for their buck. So what y’all think?”

“I’m down. I’m gonna stick to whatever schedule you give me, bruh,” Dusty replied quickly.

“Ditto,” Rock agreed.

“A’ight, cool. I’m gon’ set y’all up tomorrow. I’m gonna take the morning, and y’all can split between the night,” Lakim said.

"I'm gon' hit y'all with your packs now. You take twenty off every hundred you sell. Right now, it's gon' be a little slow, but once the heads know we back out here, it'll start clicking like I had it before."

Lakim offered them less than the twenty-five off every hundred Junior told him to give them. His greed for money even had him taking a shift, when all Junior wanted was for him to distribute the work and pick up the money.

"Let me tell that bitch to get outta here," Dusty said to Lakim. "You want to get some face, too, before I send this slut home?"

"Nah, man, I just want to take care of this shit, so I can go home and bag up the rest of the work I got," Lakim informed him.

"A'ight, man. She got a fat ass, though." Dusty tried to coerce Lakim.

"I ain't gonna lie, La. For an older broad, she real nice. You can't even tell she smoke that shit. I woulda hit it, but I didn't have no rubber," Rock chimed in, trying to help convince Lakim.

The Puerto Rican woman was on the bed putting on her bra when Dusty entered the room.

"I thought you were finished. I'm going back upstairs. Who else is out there?" she asked suspiciously.

"Only my man and Rock. Why you suck his dick for free and you make me pay?" Dusty asked her.

"He lie and tell me he gonna pay me, but he just leave the room after I finish and he no come back," Lizzette told Dusty.

"Well, you shouldn't have did shit without asking me first," Dusty said, upset Rock got served for free.

"I'm sorry. I think since he your friend he no lie. I don't like to do all the time. I only do when I need money to get high. You understand, yes?" Lizzette said.

"Yeah and no. You shouldn't be using that shit no way, as fine as you are. If you wasn't on that shit, I would make you my girl and take care of you. I'm about to get put on, so if you straighten yourself up, maybe that can happen. But, that means you can't be sucking dick and giving up that good pussy for money or crack."

Lizzette's mind went into overdrive when Dusty said he was going to be working for his man. Her habit was getting worse, and

it was becoming difficult for her to hide the effects of the drug. She was losing weight and her skin was turning pale. Since Dusty lived in the same building, it would be convenient for her to cop the beige rocks and keep her habit a secret. Yes, this would camouflage her addiction, and no one would really know what she was doing.

"I understand what you say, Dusty, but you no understand me. I no do this all the time. I just do when I need money. I no want everybody to think that I will do all the time, you understand?" Lizzette lied in her worst English.

"A'ight, fuck it," Dusty said, giving up. "As long as I can still see you when I need to, I don't care. I was just trying to look out for you. I gotta take care of some business, so you have to leave. I'll tell them to go in my grandma's room so you don't have to be embarrassed at him looking at you. That okay wit' you?"

"Okay, fine. I get dress now," she said, as she put on the rest of her clothes.

Dusty walked out the room to tell Lakim to go in his grandmother's room so she could break out and they could finish their business. She walked out nervously, glancing at the door to see if anyone was looking at her as she departed.

"You know we didn't finish and I already paid you, so you know we gotta take care of this a lil lata', a'ight?" Dusty told her when she got to the door.

"No problema, papi," she said, flashing a smile and palming her round ass. "Just come up to my place when you're done or have the time."

"I'll knock on your door around eleven tonight. That ain't too late, is it?" Dusty asked.

"No, just come by. I'll still be up."

Lizzette was almost to the point of being strung out. She was performing sexual favors for money so she could support her habit, and she particularly chose Dusty because he was young and innocent. He didn't have a girlfriend and was inexperienced, so she used that to her benefit to get money out of him in order to keep from having to go on the "hoe stroll". She liked Dusty because he was always willing to try something new, and when she gave him the combo – pussy and head – he was weak to all her demands.

As she climbed the steps, she thought about how men were weak for flesh and how quickly she turned them out. Dusty telling her that he would be selling just made it more convenient for her to get high. Now she wouldn't even have to leave her building.

When Dusty came into his grandmother's room after seeing Lizzette out, Lakim had the work on the bed and was splitting it up for Dusty and Rock.

"Come on, man, let's go in my room. If my grandmom catch us in her room doin' this shit, she'll fuck all of us up."

Dusty's room was well furnished. He had a black lacquer headboard, armoire, and two matching nightstands on each side of the bed. It was rare to find a young guy this clean and organized, but it was all thanks to his grandmother's upbringing. Junior had made the right choice in choosing him to be down with him.

Rock and Dusty were both given a one-thousand-dollar package and were told by Lakim to only take two-hundred-dollar bombs at a time so if anything went wrong while they were on the block, they wouldn't be totally assed out. He also told them that they would each have to put twenty dollars off every five-hundred they sold towards a lawyer, so if they were ever pinched, they would have their own attorney. This was something Lakim thought of, not Junior. The problem with public defenders was that when it came to drug cases, their first solution was to have their defendant plead guilty to a lesser charge. A paid lawyer fought against any kind of conviction.

Lakim schooled the young men on what they were expected to do, all the while acting as if he was the mastermind and boss of the whole operation. When Lakim was done, he and Rock left, while Dusty lay on his bed thinking about all the money he was going to make, finally.

***

Gloria and KB were getting tight. She really liked him, and he seemed to be into her just as much. He didn't really talk much

about himself or his background growing up. He seemed more interested in her and what she wanted. He catered to her like a waiter in a fine restaurant. Gloria had never been treated so nicely by any man before KB and finally understood why Shondra loved Junior so much. She and KB had spent everyday together since the night they met, and up to that point, they hadn't done anything more than swap spit.

They were coming from seeing a movie one day, when KB asked her if she wanted to take the relationship to the next level. She told him yes if that meant she was going to be his main girl. She wanted their relationship to be exclusive.

KB hailed a cab from 42nd Street and told the cab driver to take them to the Hilton on 53rd Street and Sixth Avenue. One of the things Gloria really liked about KB was that he wasn't afraid to say what was on his mind. He didn't pull any punches. He just laid shit right on the table and wasn't afraid of the repercussions.

The cab pulled up across the street from the hotel, and they got out and walked into the entrance of the building. Gloria had never been to an expensive hotel before. Most of the guys she used to be with took her to the four-hour spot or even fucked her in their homeboys' houses.

KB walked in, while she stood in the lobby looking at the clean carpet and the people coming inside the hotel with their luggage being carried by bellboys. Gloria was so impressed that she planned on giving him the colossal fuck of his life. She was going to make sure he would never leave her after she threw that good pussy on him.

They both boarded the elevator after KB checked in. The brass in the elevator was so shiny, it looked like gold. When they got into the room, KB went to the bathroom and immediately jumped in the shower. It was on. From instinct, Gloria peeled the top cover back to look at the sheets – no stains. They were white and smelled summery fresh. She picked up the remote and turned on the television. She flipped through all the channels, and there weren't any pornos showing at all. This was no bullshit. This was the real deal.

Gloria was glad she had on her matching bra and panties,

because if she didn't, there would be no way she would let KB see her undress. Shondra told her that anytime she went out with someone, she should always have matching underwear, void of holes in case she wanted to have sex. It made the guy know he was dealing with a woman that took pride in her appearance and hygiene.

KB came out of the bathroom with a towel wrapped around his waist. He had a hairy chest and a nice physique for a short guy, although he had a little potbelly with visible stretchmarks by his love handles. She could hear the shower was still running as he uttered one sentence: "I left it on for you." Then he walked past her and lay on the bed, dripping wet from his shower. She complied and went into the bathroom, where she removed her tight-fitting dress and underwear. She looked around and found a shower cap, then jumped into the steamy, hot shower. The water felt good beating against her body, and she was getting horny thinking of how KB was taking control of the whole night since he made it official between them. Damn, she was happy. She finally had a good man.

After her shower, Gloria got out, stood in front of the mirror, and admired herself. She had a banging-ass body. She had an hourglass shape, and her ass was perfectly round. Her breasts were full, and her nipples were perky and always hard. She wrapped the towel around her body, but it didn't cover her completely. So, she decided to go without it. She toweled dry, but made sure to leave her skin a little moist with drops of water so it would glisten slightly. She walked out of the bathroom, went straight to the bed, and lay down next to KB, pulling the sheets over her. KB had dozed off but awakened when she got in the bed.

"Damn, Gloria, you're bad as hell," KB said, not fully awake yet, but getting a glimpse of her goddess-like shape.

"Well damn, KB, you just don't care what you say, huh?"

KB got under the covers, took his towel off, and moved closer to her. She felt something hard against her thigh and moved slowly toward the bulge. He grabbed her shoulders and pulled her closer, kissing her on the mouth and neck while running his hands down the small of her back and over her ass. He caressed and squeezed

her ass cheeks as he rubbed his hardness on her thigh. It felt good to her, and she moaned a little, grabbed a handful of KB's ass, and squeezed. He positioned himself so his shaft was over her shaved snatch. She felt the throbbing of his meat on her, then pushed her cat against him hard. KB moved toward her, grabbed her breast with one hand, placed his mouth over her hardened nipple, and sucked it gently. She gasped as she felt the warmth and wetness of his tongue. He rotated his tongue around her areola, then sucked her nipple softly. She whined with delight and grabbed his thick pole, rubbing it on her wetness. He cringed from the feeling and allowed her to take control.

"Give it to me," she whispered in his ear, as she sucked his earlobe hard.

He inserted himself into her slowly and could feel the moisture of her hole engulf his manhood. He moved in and out of her slowly, savoring their defining moment and basking in its ecstasy. Gloria let out low moans of delight as he quickened his movements, and she held him close to her so he wouldn't slip out of her sloppy wetness. She gyrated her vaginal area to enhance the feeling. As they became one, they both began to move rapidly in unison.

"Oh my God! I…I'm about to cum!" Gloria shrieked.

"Hold on, baby. Wait for daddy. Don't cum yet!" KB bellowed, the feeling coming to him almost immediately.

"K, baby, you're makin' me feel sooooooo goooood!" she wailed, as her legs locked and her body began to shake.

"I feel you, baby. I can feel you cummin'!" he squealed in her ear.

The feeling lasted almost a full twenty seconds, and then they both lay on their backs when it was over.

"Damn you good, Gloria," he said after catching his breath.

"You so damn big," she replied, squeezing his semi-hard pole.

KB turned to Gloria and positioned her head on his broad chest. While she thought about how good his pipe game was, they both dozed off to sleep.

When Gloria woke the next morning, KB was gone, and she had a fleeting thought that maybe he wasn't special and that all he

wanted was to hit it and split. However, that thought changed when she saw a note he left on the nightstand saying he had gotten an important page and had to leave in a hurry. It said he didn't want to wake her up because she looked so peaceful sleeping. He left a one-hundred-dollar bill for her to take a cab home. She felt bad that he had to leave, but figured it must have been important for him to leave her alone in the room, especially after the night they shared together.

Gloria sat up in bed and saw a breakfast cart sitting off to the side. There were waffles, Canadian-style bacon, fresh strawberries and cantaloupe, and freshly squeezed orange juice. She jumped in the shower, and when she was finished, she sat down on the bed and ate her breakfast as she dialed Shondra's number. She was beaming, and Shondra sounded genuinely happy for her. Gloria gave her the minutes of her night with KB.

"Is he there right now with you?" Shondra asked.

"Nope. He must have left bright and early this morning," Gloria said, her mouth full of waffles.

"Oh. Did he say where he was going, or he just left you there like that?"

"He left a note saying he got an important call and had to go," Gloria replied, taking a drink of her orange juice.

"So that's your man now, huh, girl?"

"Mmmmhmmm, yeah, girl. And he slayed me after he made it official. God knows he's big as hell," Gloria shared.

"He can't be bigger than that mule Junior got between his legs," Shondra challenged.

"Well, I can't say 'cause I ain't never seen what your man got, but I know MY MAN is big as a horse," Gloria replied, laughing.

"I'm glad for you, Glo. I hope he's really the one, and I hope he makes you happy and keeps you happy. You really deserve that. So tell me something about your new man. I mean, I never met him, and you know I got to check him out to make sure he's doing my girl right."

"I know, girl, but he kinda funny when it comes to talking about himself like that. He seems a little anti-social and shit. He

say he don't like meeting people, but I told him he had to meet you 'cause you my sister," Gloria told her.

"What he say when you told him that?" Shondra asked.

"He said if we tight like that, he knows he gotta meet you then. He said he's a little shy about meeting you because he wants you to like us together as a couple. He promised me that he'll meet you real soon, though, because he knows it's important to me."

Shondra continued with her questions. "So where does he live?"

"He lives in Williamsburg with his mom. I think he stays there with her because she sick or something. I ain't really sure. Like I said, he don't really talk much."

"Well, if he's staying with his moms 'cause she sick, that says a lot about what kind of guy he is. You know what I mean?" Shondra said.

"Yeah, I guess. I really like him, girl. He's like the first guy that ever treated me like he gives a fuck about my feelings, not just getting into my draws."

"I feel you, Glo but you gotta be careful. Sometimes it's good in the beginning and then shit changes. Just be careful how fast you let yourself go," Shondra warned.

"I guess you right, but I'm hoping things between us will be something like you have with Junior. I want a man that loves me unconditionally and treats me that way no matter who we're around, like how Junior treats you," Gloria said honestly.

"I know what you mean, Glo, but you know he wasn't like that 'til we put in mad time together. We went through our shit and worked it out. We still gon' go through shit. It's a process. There were times I thought we were gonna break up, but our love for each other kept us together. I had to swallow a lot of shit and he did, too, but there has to be boundaries, baby. There has to be a line you draw that cannot be violated for no reason. We've been through a lot and weathered the storm. That made us closer. Glo, I want you to be happy, baby, I just don't want you to get hurt by no sorry-ass muhfucka again," Shondra stated sincerely

"Thanks, sis. I know you only looking out for me. I'm gonna take my time. I just hope he's for real."

“Well, for one thing, you need to know a little bit more about him. You know what I’m saying? You should know as much about him as possible. That’s how you’ll know if he’s real or not.”

“That’s true. We’re gonna have to sit down and talk about a lot of things. I just hope I don’t push him away.”

“Shit, if that’s the case, you need to find out now so you’ll know,” Shondra urged her.

After talking for about an hour or so, Shondra made plans for her and Gloria to meet and get their nails and hair done.

“When you get here, just knock on my door. I’m gonna make the reservations as soon as I hang up,” she told Gloria.

“All right. I’m gonna finish eating this good-ass breakfast and check out of this room at eleven. I’ll come straight to your house because I already took a shower. I’ll be there in the next hour or so,” Gloria told her.

“Okay, baby, I’ll see you then,” Shondra said, then hung up.

Shondra went to her closet and pulled out some Jesus sandals and a white linen Ralph Lauren short set she had never worn before that Junior bought for her from Bloomingdale’s. After showering, she called her Dominican hairdresser located in Harlem and made appointments for her and Gloria. Once she hung up with her hairdresser, she paged Junior and put on her outfit.

CHAPTER 7
THAT'S WHAT I DO BEST

Stump couldn't waste any more time looking for Junior and Kendu over the shootout they had. He still had to get money, and doing capers was where he made his money. Robbing local dealers was something he did just to past the time, but he always had big jobs from his boy Drez.

Stump was standing in the middle of the living room explaining to his crew sitting on the couch the plan he had devised. All three men were sitting side by side listening to him intently, hanging on his every word. The men were all hardened criminals; they were guys Stump had an affiliation with from doing bids in Sing Sing and Attica.

Ray-Ray was a career criminal. He was muscular from being in and out of jails from the age of fifteen, and he used his size to intimidate his victims.

At 280 pounds, Roughhouse was the guy that gave Stump his respect when he did his first bid. Stump had a run-in with him while going through processing in Elmira, and he and Roughhouse fought over some money. Roughhouse was known for his hand skills up north, but Stump changed all that when he broke his jaw with two wicked right hooks. Stump used to box Golden Gloves and was a prospect for the Junior Olympics until he got locked up. After breaking Roughhouse's jaw, he caught another charge, was sent back to Rikers Island, and was given an additional three years on his sentence. When he got to Sing Sing, he ran into Roughhouse again and they finished what they had started on the yard. In that encounter, Stump broke Roughhouse's will instead of his jaw. Roughhouse lost his credibility and began to run with Stump's crew.

The last guy, Murda Mike, lived up to his name. He was a cold-blooded murderer, but he miraculously had never been convicted of any of the bodies he slumped because there were never any witnesses. The only way the police could get him in jail was by crooked practice. They planted everything from drugs to guns on him and got him a five-to-fifteen year sentence for conspiracy to commit murder. Murda was heartless and the worst motherfucker to run into late at night. They said when he was locked down in Sing Sing, he got stabbed in his stomach and now had to wear a shit bag. He never let that cripple him, though. Instead, it made him more dangerous. It was rumored that he killed more motherfuckers than cancer itself.

All the men in the room respected Stump because he was all about business. He never let emotions get in the way of what he needed to do. They all knew from experience that Stump feared nothing and no one, including himself. When you dealt with a man that was not afraid to die and had literally cheated death numerous times, you were basically dealing with the devil, and none of them wanted to be an enemy to the devil, no matter how tough they thought they were.

As Stump continued to lay out his plan, there was a knock on the door. All the guys sitting on the couch got up, almost in unison, and pulled out their guns. Stump walked slowly to the door but kept his back against the wall. He had a black snub-nosed .44 Bulldog with a rubber pistol grip. As he got closer to the door, he yelled for the person on the other side to identify himself.

"It's KB."

"Oh, it's my man from 'round the way," he informed the guys.

They relaxed after hearing that and put their guns back from where they were concealed. Stump turned the knob on the door and pulled it open. KB was startled because Stump was pointing the gun to his face.

"What the fuck is up?" he asked Stump, his hands raised to his face as if he could deflect a bullet if it was discharged.

"You tell me. Where you been? I beeped you over an hour ago," Stump replied, his eyebrows furrowed.

"I was with my lady, man, damn. I just left her in the city. We were at Olive Garden eating dinner and shit when you beeped me. I had to leave her and take a cab straight here. You know how dem yellow cabs don't like bringing blacks to the hood," KB explained.

It seemed every time he was out with Gloria having a good time, Stump always beeped him and interrupted their time together. He knew Gloria was getting tired of him running and leaving her whenever Stump beckoned.

"Okay, I'll give you a pass this time, but in the future, make sure you at least call me back and let me know something. You don't know if it's an emergency or what, so it's critical you call me back and give me a time. I set my clock to what you tell me, a'ight?" Stump said to KB.

KB could tell Stump was serious as he lowered the gun and let him enter the apartment. KB slapped everybody five, introduced himself, took a seat, and was briefed on what Stump was plotting.

Stump was planning to rob a coke spot Drez had told him about that was in the neighborhood. Stump had been watching it for two weeks and already had his crew picked out. The spot was camouflaged as a twenty-four hour bodega. There were always two guys inside, and the drugs were located in the basement of the store. They had a particular clientele and only sold weight, so it was hard to get inside the store once they closed the gates at night. The only way to get them would be in the afternoon when they least expected a hit, because the store was usually busy in the early mornings and late afternoon. What was so attractive about this particular stick was that they could each walk away with over fifty thousand dollars if everything went smoothly. This caper was worth putting his revenge of Junior on the back burner. He hadn't forgotten about him and had plans to still take care of him, La, and Kendu.

KB was going to be the wheelman as well as the lookout man. He was slated to get an equal cut like everyone else, although Ray-Ray didn't agree with him getting the same amount since his job was least dangerous. Stump explained the importance of each person's job. The robbery couldn't go smoothly if any one of them weren't present.

"Look, Ray," Stump said, "when we come out of the store wit' all that dough, where we goin'?"

"We gonna get in the car and peel out," he replied, looking at KB.

"Can you drive?" Stump questioned him.

"Hell yeah, I can drive. Like a bat outta hell!" Ray-Ray responded braggadoshishly.

"Okay, to keep the peace, you can be the wheelman and KB can be the shooter," Stump suggested.

"Nah, man, I need to hold the iron in my hand. That's what I do best. That's my thing. You know that, man!" Ray-Ray insisted.

"Oh okay, now you understand!" Stump turned and addressed everyone. "I handpicked all of you specifically. I know what each of you is good at and capable of doing. I need the best men, and I believe I have the best. We all have things we're good at, and there are other things that we can do but may not be the best at. That's when you need help to balance the shit out. That's what I did when I chose this crew. So, understand one thing. This shit will not fly unless everyone handles their job to the T. We are all counting on each other for this shit to go without a hitch. Does everyone understand me?" Stump preached.

There was no doubt in anyone's mind that this was a big lick. They knew they would have to be on their jobs and not slip, because one slip could be fatal for the whole crew.

CHAPTER 8
LET ME GET A HAM AND CHEESE

Circling the block in the stolen white commercial van, KB slowly drove past the store to see if there were any people inside. The rest of the guys were in the back of the van wearing masks and checking their guns to make sure the safety was off. This was crunch time, and there was no room for mistakes and no time to back out. They were pumped and ready to take the money and leave without any casualties. Stump knew the guys they were about to rob were not going to go out without a fight. He anticipated it, but didn't tell any of this to his crew because the caper was already dangerous and he didn't want to add an edge. There was way too much money involved for anyone in his crew to second-guess themselves.

"Y'all ready?" Stump asked, putting a live round in the chamber. "Park ova there by Lindsey parking lot and keep the van running. Don't turn that shit off for nothing. Got it, KB?"

"I got you, man. Don't worry. I got my end covered," KB replied.

"I gotta make sure you can see us comin' out that muhfucka. Once you see us, mash the gas and pick us up!" Stump explained.

"I gotcha, man. I'm not gonna fold on you. Trust me."

KB pulled the van into the lot and parked between two other cars to look inconspicuous. The back doors opened and the crew

jumped out. Ray-Ray, Roughhouse, and Murda Mike all walked toward the store. Roughhouse was to go inside first and order a hero sandwich to keep whoever was behind the counter busy. Ray-Ray was to go to the back of the store by the cooler and act like he was buying beer. The back was where the door to the basement was. Murda Mike and Stump would come in last and announce the stickup once Rough and Ray had it secured.

"Let me get a ham and cheese hero with lettuce, tomatoes, extra mayo, salt, pepper, oil, and vinegar," Roughhouse told the man behind the counter.

"American cheese?" the Dominican man asked, as he turned his back to put on the clear plastic gloves.

"Yeah, American cheese, and can you heat it up for me?" Roughhouse added.

"Mmmhmm," the man answered, as he cut the Italian bread down the middle with a large butcher knife.

When Ray walked into the store, he went straight to the back and began looking at the selection of malt liquor in the cooler. While back there, he spotted the door on the floor that led to the basement. It had a padlock on it and was partially covered by empty boxes. Stump and Mike pulled their masks over their heads and pulled out their guns as they walked into the store. As the store door closed behind them, two Dominican men parked in a black Acura Legend with tinted windows observed the two men putting masks over their faces.

"Turn around and let me see your fuckin' hands 'fore I blow your face off!" Stump screamed to the man behind the counter.

Mike went around the side and kicked open the door to gain entrance behind the counter. Stump slid the duct tape over the counter to Mike, who pulled off a piece and put it over the petrified man's mouth and then duct taped his hands behind his back.

"The keys are under the sink, man, in a blue cup," Stump informed Mike.

"I got it," Mike reported, while heading toward the back.

Roughhouse and Ray-Ray were moving the boxes by the time Stump and Mike got to the back of the store.

"Roughhouse, you stay up here and keep whoever comes in this muhfucka inside. Don't let them leave," Stump directed.

"I gotcha," Roughhouse replied.

After Ray got the lock off the door, they all stood back and pointed their guns at it.

"It should only be two men down there. I'm going first. Y'all just hold me down," Stump told Ray and Mike.

Stump went down the stairs leading to the basement and turned on a light that was hanging by a chain. As he got to the bottom, he gestured for the other two to follow. He walked down a long corridor and could hear voices as he got closer to an opening where a light was shining. He turned around and put his index finger over his mouth, signaling his boys to be quiet. Ray and Mike followed behind him, moving silently like a cat preying on a mouse.

"They in there," Stump whispered, pointing to the opening at the end of the corridor. "I think they counting money."

When Stump got close enough to the doorway of the room, he could see the silhouettes of what seemed like two men and heard them speaking in Spanish. He pulled out his second gun, the .44 Bulldog, and jumped into plain sight, pointing the guns at three guys sitting around a table of money and powder cocaine. Instinctively, Mike was at his side with a .357 Smith & Wesson pointed at the men, and Ray was on Stump's other side with a nine-millimeter Beretta.

"Get down on the floor, NOW!" Stump screamed at the top of his lungs in his fiercest voice so there would be no questioning his seriousness. "If you move, you die, muhfuckas!"

Ray pulled out a black bag from his back pocket and went to the table.

"Anybody else in here wit' y'all?" Mike asked no one in particular.

"Hay nadie aquí pero satisfacemos no nos lastimamos," the short one replied.

"Oh, these muhfuckas want to play like they don't speak English, huh?" Mike said to Stump. "I think I better teach them the languasge I'm speaking real fast!"

"Hurry up and get all that shit!" Stump told Ray.

"It's a lot of shit, man. I think we might need another bag," Ray said, filling up the bag. He wanted everything - the drugs, money, and the jewelry the guys had on.

"Just fill up the bag and worry about the rest later!" Stump replied, with his guns still trained on the three Spanish men. "Where's the tape?" Stump asked Mike.

"Man, I left that shit upstairs. Damn!" Mike exclaimed.

"I need to tie these Germans up so they don't get frisky," Stump said.

"Fuck it. I'll help Ray and you hold them down," Mike replied, as he went over to assist Ray with putting the money and bags of coke into the black garbage bag.

The guys in the Acura knew the spot was being robbed. When they saw Stump and Mike put their masks on, they made a phone call to their boss. They got out of the car, pulled out two big knives, and then headed for the entrance of the bodega. The taller man looked inside and could see Roughhouse standing by the counter eating a sandwich. He waited to see if any of the other guys were around but didn't see any of them, so they rushed inside. When they got into the store, Roughhouse pointed the gun at them and ushered them behind the counter.

"Get behind the counter, boys,' he said, waving the gun toward the side of the counter.

"What's happening?" the slim one asked, hiding the knife behind his back.

"Don't worry about all that. Just get behind the fuckin' counter and you won't get hurt!" he said, his mouth full of the hero.

The taller one, noticing Roughhouse wasn't aware they already knew what was going on, lunged at him and plunged the knife into his chest. The short one brought his butcher knife down on the hand with the gun and it fell to the floor. Roughhouse backed up as both men continued to stick him with the knives in his midsection. He was fighting back and was able to hit the short one. He didn't know how many times he was stabbed, but he could feel himself getting weaker.

"Die, mudderfucka!" the taller one screamed, as Roughhouse hit him with a hard right to his temple.

The man fell to the ground out cold, and Roughhouse turned his attention to the short guy who showed no sign of fear. He looked at the Ruger on the floor and at the Dominican behind the counter who was frozen with fear. He watched the man on the floor that he had just knocked out to make sure he was really out cold. When his eyes darted back to the short guy, he could tell they were both thinking the same thing. Roughhouse kicked the gun toward the entrance of the store. The short Dominican hit Roughhouse again in his side. He winced from the sharp pain but concentrated on making it to his gun.

Stump, Ray, and Mike were wrapping things up, when one of the guys on the ground got up from where he was sitting. Mike instantly pulled the trigger of the .357 magnum, and the guy's body literally lifted off his feet and was thrown into the wall. He fell down face first to the ground, and the gaping wound in the back of his head released a steady flow of thick, red blood.

"Ah shit, we gotta off all of them!" Stump said.

"I'm heading upstairs, fellas. I'm gonna see if Roughhouse is okay," Ray said, heading for the corridor.

"We're right behind you, kid," Stump replied.

"Usted los individuos va a pagar esto con su vida," the dark-skinned Spanish guy said.

"What, you fuckin' maggot!" Stump yelled and placed his gun behind the man's head, then pulled the trigger. Stump didn't understand what was said to him, but he didn't like it.

As the other man on the ground began to weep uncontrollably, Mike pumped two shots into his back, then stood over him and finalized his death with a bullet to his head. Ray was headed upstairs when he heard the shots. Although he cringed from the explosions, he knew they were home free. Mike looked at Stump, and then they headed down the corridor to meet Ray and Roughhouse.

Ray dropped the bag when he saw Roughhouse on the ground tussling with a Spanish guy. He saw blood all over the floor and another Spanish man lying on the ground not moving. Seeing Ray running to his partner's aid, the guy struggling with Rough broke free just in time to jump up and stagger out of the store. Ray emptied his gun at the fleeing man but missed as the guy slipped out the door untouched. Roughhouse was coughing up blood, and Ray tried to pull him to his feet, but he was too heavy. Ray struggled with him until he had him sitting in an upright position.

"We gotta go. We gotta get you to a hospital, man!" Ray screamed.

When Stump and Mike came up, they saw Ray trying to pick up Roughhouse.

"Get him outta here!" Stump ordered Mike, while picking up the bag Ray had dropped. "What the fuck happened up here?"

"Some German stabbed him up. One of them on the floor," Ray replied.

As Mike helped Roughhouse out the door, Ray ran out to make sure no one had heard or seen what was happening and to look for the van, but he didn't see it in the parking lot down the block. There was no sign of KB anywhere. Mike was helping Roughhouse along in the direction of the parking lot, but Rough was on wobbly legs and couldn't move fast. He was mumbling something to Mike, but Mike was concentrating on getting to the van as quickly as possible.

"Is the van out there?" Stump asked Ray, as he came back into the store.

"I don't know, man. I don't see him. I thought he was supposed to be watching for the first guy to come outta the store," Ray said nervously.

Stump told Ray to go where the van was supposed to be. When Ray walked out the store, he heard the boom of a gun going off and knew the guy on the ground was now dead if he wasn't before. Then he heard another boom moments later, which meant the guy behind the counter had met the same fate. Stump made sure there would be no witnesses. The sirens were getting closer, and it would only be a matter of time before the police arrived on the scene. So, Ray took off running to the parking lot and Stump was right on his heels.

"Let me go, man. Go ahead. I can make it to the van," Roughhouse gurgled to Mike.

"I can't leave you like this, man. Just try to move a little faster," Mike urged.

"Just go!" Roughhouse knew he was slowing everyone else down, and he didn't want everyone to get caught on account of him.

Mike left Roughhouse leaning on a fence and ran toward the parking lot as the sounds of the sirens grew closer. The van pulled up on the corner where Ray and Stump were running and slowed down so they could get in.

"Where the fuck was you, muhfucka?" Stump demanded to know from KB.

"The traffic police came into the parking lot and made me move because I didn't have a parking sticker. So, I just circled the block and saw y'all two running," KB explained.

"Rough is stabbed up bad, man. We gotta go get him!" Ray said to KB.

KB made a U-turn and headed back toward the bodega. Mike was running up the block, and when he saw the van, he ran into the street to make sure they saw him. When KB slowed down, Ray opened the back door for him to get in.

"Go get, Rough!" Mike cried out to KB with a look of desperation on his face.

KB could see Roughhouse running and falling down. Roughhouse could see the van and was trying to make it to where it was, but his legs wouldn't let him go any further. He got to his feet again and tried to hop to the van. He was losing a lot of blood exerting all this energy. The van seemed so close, but his vision was getting blurry and he kept choking on his own blood. Roughhouse heard the sirens behind him and knew it was too late for him. He wanted them to wait, but at the same time, he wanted them to go. There was no saving him, not now. It was too late. The sounds of the sirens were deafening, and the blue and red lights could be seen flashing off the buildings. All the guys in the van were looking at him as he fought to make it to them.

"We can't get him!" KB broke the silence in the van. "We'll all go down if we do. There ain't no time!"

"Don't leave him, homey. He came with us and he's leaving with us. We not leaving nobody behind, cuz!" Mike said, his eyes filling with tears. It was weird to see Murda Mike, a man who killed with ease, getting emotional over death.

"We can't, man. We don't have no time, and we'll get busted if we go get him," KB said almost in a whisper. "Look, the police are already in front of the fuckin' store."

It was then that KB realized the seriousness of the situation. He was the only one speaking up because the rest of them didn't want the responsibility of making the call on leaving Roughhouse. KB turned the van around and sped off toward Broadway. Ray, Stump, and Mike looked out the back window of the van and watched as Roughhouse fell down for the final time, never to get back up again.

CHAPTER 9
HERE, LOVE, DON'T LOSE IT...

The unmarked police car rode past for the third time. The detectives were looking for someone to run in so they could get off the hot streets, go to the air-conditioned office, and do paperwork, not to mention the streets were more dangerous this time of the year. There were more people on the street when it was hot than when the weather was cold. And more people meant more problems and much more aggravation. Most detectives on the force just wanted to finish their tour and go home to their families, but there were a few that wanted promotions or used their status as law enforcement to exact revenge on people that treated them inferior while going to school.

Taylor and Burke were homicide detectives that used unauthorized tactics to pry information from suspects to help them solve their cases. They were notorious for threatening people and planting evidence if they didn't get the results they were looking for. This action came from when they were both beat cops. They constantly fucked with young guys that didn't have a clue about the law and the rights that protected them under it. Once they had the suspects in custody, they would sit them in the back of their unmarked car, ride to deserted factories, and tell them that they had a choice to tell them what they wanted to know or wind up dead. They easily recruited informants this way, which made their job much easier when they were out on the prowl for an arrest.

"Why the fuck they keep passin' through?" Lakim asked no one in particular.

"I know. It's not sweep week. That's next week," one of the workers said.

"Ain't none of y'all lil dudes dirty, right?" Lakim asked.

"Nah, we clean. We don't hold no more since they got Rock with that bullshit-ass possession charge," the lieutenant of the workers said.

Rock had gotten caught with half a blunt in his pocket, and the detective that caught him found some vials of crack in a tennis ball in the grass next to where he was standing and tried to pin it on him. Rock had a paid lawyer, so his charge was dropped from felony possession to a misdemeanor and he was given community service for having the half-smoked blunt.

"Yo, La, come here, man," Rock said, as he opened the door of the Lincoln Mark V he was driving.

He had gotten the car from a crackhead that owed him three hundred dollars. When Rock threatened to hurt the man, he gave Rock the car to clear up his bill.

"Whaddup?" Lakim asked.

"I just heard Kendu got murdered, kid," Rock told him.

"What?" Lakim replied, shocked.

"Kendu is dead, man. They found him in Bed-Stuy in his aunt's house."

"Who did it?" Lakim inquired.

"I didn't get all the details, but I heard that it had something to do with him robbing some of the lil' drug dealers ova that way," Rock said.

"Nobody knows who did it?" Lakim questioned.

"I didn't get all that. I mess with this shorty ova there, and she was telling me about some dude that got killed in the building. When I asked did she know who it was, she said it was Joe's cousin from Bushwick. I know Kendu's cousin's name is Joe, and that's when I figured out it was Du. She said she didn't hear anything about who did it, but the streets is saying it was a boss

who did him in."

"That's fucked up," Lakim said, slumping down in the passenger seat of the car. "I knew something like this was gonna happen, because he was acting funny right before all that shit jumped off. Damn, Du!" Lakim lowered his head.

Rock drove back to where he had picked up Lakim and got out of the vehicle. Lakim stayed in the passenger seat deep in thought. He couldn't believe his man was gone and that it had ended for him the way it did. Lakim was flooded with emotions. He was thinking of how young Kendu was, how he must have felt, whether he knew he was going to die, if he was scared, and if it hurt. He also wondered if Kendu had suffered and if he felt alone in his last minutes. At that moment, Lakim promised himself that he wouldn't go out the way his best friend had gone out.

Rock was busy telling the workers to keep the customers from hanging around the building when they weren't copping because it brought heat to the spot. Just as he said that, a blue sedan pulled up and two detectives jumped out the car and walked over to where they were standing.

"How ya doin', Rodney?" the stout detective named Burke asked.

"What the fuck you dudes want? This ain't no donut shop!" Rock yelled.

"Why all the profanity, Mr. Cooper? Are we addressing you in a vulgar manner?" the slim detective named Taylor asked.

"'Cause I'm tired of y'all fuckin' wit' me when you see me somewhere," Rock said, frustrated. "Y'all want to check me and try to plant something on me like y'all did before 'cause I got a lot of witnesses out here this time."

"Well, we did have a reason to come see you, but since you insist on us checking you," Burke said, as he walked up to Rock, "turn around so I can make sure you don't have anything on you that you shouldn't have, like crack cocaine or guns."

Rock assumed the position as he had so many other times since they busted him with weed. Taylor frisked him and pulled out a wad of bills.

"Now where did you get all this money from, Mr. Cooper?" Taylor asked, throwing the bundle of money to his partner.

"Why you worrying about where I get my money from?"

"Because that seems like a lot of money for such a young man like yourself to be carrying around in the middle of the day. Reggie and me work hard every day, and we still can't walk around with money like that in our pockets."

"It's $3,750 to be exact," Burke said after counting the money.

"Whoa! That's a lot of money. Now I'm gonna ask ya again, where did you get all this money from, Mr. Cooper?" Taylor asked Rock, while continuing to check his pockets.

"It's my mother's money. I have to pay our furniture bill, Con Ed (light company), the rent, and some other stuff. Damn, man, y'all all in my fuckin' business!"

"Can your mother verify that?" Taylor asked.

"My momma ain't home. She at work. Yo, why don't y'all leave me the fuck alone!"

"There you go with that profanity again. All right, since your momma isn't home, I'm gonna let you keep the money. I wouldn't want your momma or you to have to sleep on the floor because you fucked around and got your furniture money taken from you," Taylor said.

Burke threw the money on the ground next to Rock's feet, and the money flew everywhere.

"Oops, it slipped outta my hand. I'm sooo sorry," Burke said, snickering.

Rock was clearly upset because they were embarrassing him in front of his workers. These officers were abusing their authority. The workers scrambled to pick up the scattering money.

"You know you're not paying them that much," he finished and walked off to his car.

Taylor followed behind him, then turned around. "Oh yeah, the original reason for our visit was to inform you guys that someone from these projects was murdered some days ago." Taylor looked Rock in his eyes and continued. "I'm not sure if you knew him or if he was a friend of yours, but it's a terrible thing to happen to such a young guy. We believe it was drug related, and although

you will deny you're involved in drugs, the danger that it brings is not worth dying for. So, you be careful out here, you and your friends. We wouldn't want to hear anything like that happened to you. And if you hear anything about that murder, just let us know."

Lakim was sitting in the car watching everything the crooked detectives were doing. He didn't get out when he saw them approaching because there was no need for them to know who he was. He was the backbone of the operation as far as workers knew, and since Junior wasn't around, he had to keep a low profile so the police wouldn't know he was the man in charge. The detectives would usually bust drug users for simple possession of drug paraphernalia and try to get them to reveal the man behind the workers. Most of the users didn't know, and the ones that had an idea thought better not to talk because of Rock.

Lakim didn't sell hand to hand anymore because business had picked up from when they first started, and he was paying the workers less and pocketing more. All he did was take the work from Junior and give it to Rock to distribute. He had come up quickly, and the operation had grown from moving four thousand to seven thousand dollars a day. His clientele increased in three months, so they had to make sure that after everyone copped, they left the area immediately. Lakim didn't even collect money from the workers anymore. Dusty brought all the money to him whenever the workers were finished. Lakim made sure the workers treated every user with respect, and he made examples of the ones that didn't. His operation was going better than planned, and he wasn't ready for it to end just yet. He had bigger plans ahead and didn't want anything to jeopardize his progress. The first thing he had to do was get rid of Stump, then his other plan would go smoothly.

Rock was fuming after all the money was picked up off the ground.

"One day they gonna come around to fuck with me, and I'm gonna kill both them muhfuckas!" he sneered.

Lakim walked over to Rock and pulled him by his collar into the lobby of the building.

“Look, Rock, you see they fuck wit’ you every time they see you, right?” Lakim started.

“Yeah, man, and I don’t even be doin’ shit!” Rock responded.

“That’s not the point. They know you now, so they gonna keep fuckin’ wit’ you until they get something on you. That means you gotta stay one step ahead of them. You havta make sure you always clean when you on the block. You can’t keep a lot of money on you, no weed, no liquor, nothing that gives them a reason to fuck wit’ you. If you dirty and you see them before they see you, get ghost on they ass. But, if they see you and you dirty, you gotta dash on them. Sooner or later they gonna get tired of chasin’ and fuckin’ wit’ you because they won’t never have shit on you. Outta sight, outta mind, my dude.”

“I hear you, La, but they be doin’ foul shit. They even threatened me. They told me to be careful that what happened to Du don’t happen to me!”

“They tryin’ to push your buttons, kid, but you can’t react ‘cause them muhfuckas got a job to do just like you have a job to do. Your job is a lil’ easier because you already know what they doin’. You make their job harder by making them try to figure out what you doin’. They can think what they want, son, but without hard evidence, they don’t have shit. That’s why I told you and Dusty to put money away for a lawyer. When you have a paid lawyer, all them bullshit charges get thrown out and the judge gets pissed off because they keep wastin’ his time with bullshit cases. You gotta buckle down, son. You gotta change up your format and throw them off your scent.”

Lakim was finished with his sermon for now. He wanted to see if Rock was going to take his advice. If he didn’t, Lakim would have to take his rank away or cut him loose. Lakim felt he had come too far to fail because of one man’s fuckup.

“I’m going on the other side and check on Dusty and his crew,” he told Rock. “I want you to meet me at the crib at twelve tonight, okay?”

“I’ll be there,” Rock replied.

All of a sudden, Lakim was acting like the block was hot because of Rock, and Rock didn’t like it.

***

The traffic was really heavy coming back from Virginia Beach. Shondra was in the passenger side of the rented Corvette asleep like a baby. She had really enjoyed herself with Junior. It had been months since he spent quality time with her. They were supposed to rent a condo on Virginia Beach and spend the entire time on the beach and in the room, but Junior had decided to take her to Kings Dominion amusement park, too, which was a surprise that she enjoyed thoroughly.

The New Jersey Turnpike had been backed up since Exit 3, and Junior was just making it to Exit 6 after six hours of driving. The top was down on the red convertible, and the wind was blowing gently on Shondra's brown skin.

Junior looked over at her and thought about how much she was going through and how much he actually put her through. She rarely complained about anything he asked her to do for him, even betraying her best friend's trust by getting information for him on her new man, knowing his intentions were fatal. Junior felt his life was more important than her and Gloria's friendship. Shit, she could find another friend, but if Junior died, there would be no coming back.

Junior had a lot do when he got back to Brooklyn. He knew one day his street credibility would be tested; he just didn't know when. What he did know was that he played himself by becoming too comfortable when he first started hustling, and he made a promise never to slip like that again. It had been over three months since the shootout, and Lakim was making him more money in Baptiste than he had made when he was out there himself. He had gotten kind of lazy and comfortable just bringing the work to Lakim and collecting the money. He knew he should be out there making sure everything was going right, but his excuse was that he wanted to take care of Stump first. He was waiting for the right time to get Stump because he didn't want the murder to lead back to him. Junior didn't tell Shondra everything about his plot to kill Stump. He just told her what he needed from her.

Traffic let up, and he finally made it to Exit 14C, the Holland Tunnel. He paid the tolls, then took Canal Street to the Manhattan Bridge and headed to Brooklyn. As he passed over the East River, there was a sign that read, WELCOME TO BROOKLYN. A NICE PLACE TO VISIT, A GREAT PLACE TO LIVE.

What bullshit, he thought to himself, while riding down Flatbush Avenue.

"Damn, boo, we got back fast. We almost home," Shondra said, wiping slobber from the side of her mouth.

"Eeeewww!" Junior said playfully. "You want a Lifesaver or an ice-cold bottle of Scope?"

"Oh please, you know you love the way my breath smells," Shondra replied, laughing.

"Yeah, after you eat a peppermint and drink a tall glass of Listerine. You been sleep since we left VA, girl. Why you so tired?"

"I don't know. I had so much fun at Kings Dominion and the beach. I'm still trying to make up for those all-nighters you pulled, too," Shondra responded, smiling.

"Well, you know I got a battery in my back that never needs recharging," Junior bragged, as he pulled over by a liquor store on Myrtle Avenue.

"You want something from outta there?" Junior asked Shondra, as he prepared to exit the car.

"Yeah, get me a bottle of Bailey's," she said.

"A'ight, I'll be right back."

Junior went into the liquor store and bought a small bottle of Hennessy VSOP and a small bottle of Bailey's for Shondra, then paid the Chinese man behind the counter. When he came out of the store, he ran into an old girlfriend from high school - Charlene. He remembered her nickname was Muffin. She was his first girlfriend in high school, and she still looked good as hell. She had long hair flowing down her back, with a caramel complexion, slanted eyes like a China doll, and a gold crown on the side tooth in her mouth. She was wearing some tight Guess shorts with a close-fitting Tommy Hilfiger shirt that showed off her perky breasts. The shorts

made her ass poke out like it was swollen, and her hips curved so deeply that they were busting the seams on the side.

When Muffin stopped in front of Junior, he remembered the thing that had attracted him to her the most — her legs. They snapped back because she was bowlegged, and she looked like a stallion standing in front of him. At that moment, he forgot Shondra was sitting in the car waiting for him.

"Hey, stranger. Long time no see," she said in her high-pitched voice, sounding like the singer Michele from Death Row.

"Wow, picture me seeing you after all this time. What's good, mama?" Junior said in his slickest voice.

"Damn, can a girl get a hug or sumthin'?" Muffin said with her arms outstretched.

"My bad." He grabbed her close to him, giving her a gentle but inviting hug.

"You look nice," she said, admiring Junior from head to toe.

He had on a Karl Kani jean suit with a pair of all-white Air Nikes, an eighteen-inch cable with a house medallion, a gold nugget watch, and a bracelet with JUNIOR spelled out in diamonds. Muffin could tell he was definitely getting money from somewhere with all the expensive jewelry he was wearing.

"Thanks. What you been up to, Muffin?" Junior asked, eyeing her body.

"Nuthin' much. Jus' chillin'. Looks like you been up to a lot by all that shit you got on."

"Nah, ma, I'm jus' chillin', too. Where you on your way to?"

"To my girlfriend's house. She wants to hang out. Maybe go out to the city, catch a flick, and grab sumthin' to eat. Nothin' special. Why? You want to do something?" Muffin became aggressive.

"Yeah, why not?" Junior responded.

"You got a girl or you single, playa?" she asked him.

"Um, yeah, she ova there in the car," he said, pointing to the red drop-top Corvette on the corner.

"Oh, I'm sorry, luv. I don't want you to get in trouble, so I'm gonna step off." Muffin eyes saw the beautiful car and paid no attention to the passenger.

"You ain't gotta bounce like that. I mean, you just a friend. She ain't gonna bug out because I'm talking to you or if we go out or sumthin'," Junior coerced.

"Okay, it may be like that right now, but what about lata?"

"Lata ain't here yet. Let's talk about that when we get there." He was putting his mack game down. "Why don't you give me your digits so I can get up with you lata?"

She pulled out a pen from her purse, ripped a piece of paper off the bag he was carrying, and told him to turn around so she could write her number down, using his back as support. That move was a dead giveaway. Whoever saw that would have known he was kicking it with her and that she was giving her number to him. There could be no mistake of a platonic relationship between them.

"Here, luv. Don't lose it or let anybody else get it," Muffin crooned.

Junior took the number and balled it up in his hand. There would be no way he would let Shondra find that number. He didn't want to fuck up his chances of hitting Muffin's ass again.

"When you want me to call you?" Junior asked.

"Right now, but I know you can't because," she looked at the car, "you look a lil busy. Call me when you get rid of your dead weight," Muffin sassed.

"A'ight, I'm gonna give you a call tonight. We can go out lata," he said, smiling. "What time you have to be home so I'll know how long to plan our evening?"

"My keys are my curfew, baby!" she said and walked off, shaking her ass so hard it looked like she was walking in slow motion.

Junior was in a trance as he watched her stride past the Corvette, glance at the passenger, roll her eyes upon contact, and then shake her ass even harder. When he shook himself from the trance, he realized what had just happened and knew he had to think of something to tell Shondra. She was definitely going to ask him who Muffin was. He walked slowly back to the car and opened the door, putting the bags in the backseat. He wasn't really sure if she saw anything. So, he figured if she didn't say anything,

he wouldn't either. When he got into the driver's side of the car, Shondra had her heard toward the passenger's window, so he couldn't tell if she was mad. He pulled off and sped down Myrtle Avenue toward Tompkins Projects.

"I got to stop at my cousin's house for a minute, a'ight?" he asked, breaking the awkward silence in the car.

"Mmmhmmm," Shondra mumbled.

"What's wrong with you?"

Shondra turned to him, showing her true emotions. Tears were streaming out of her eyes and her lips were quivering when she spoke.

"I don't know who that bitch was that you was talking to, but I know you, Junior. I know you'll say it was business, but I know that's bullshit!"

"Yeah, I know her. I used to go to school with her, and we were kinda cool. I ain't seen her in a minute, and she was just talkin' to me about old times. That's all. Damn, I ain't know it was a fuckin' crime to have a female as a homey and shit!" he said to her.

"I'm not stupid, Junior. She gave you her fuckin' number. I saw her writin' it down on your back, and then the bitch got the fuckin' gall to sashay past me and roll her fuckin' eyes. I shoulda got out and snuffed that bitch!" Shondra was furious. "Then you gonna get in the car and don't say shit to me like nuthin' happened, like I ain't shit. That's so fuckin' disrespectful, Junior!"

"Aaah, come on, Mooka, I ain't thinking 'bout that girl. It's not even like that. I don't know why you all upset and shit. I'm with you, baby," he said, grabbing her head and trying to put it on his shoulders, but she pulled back.

"Junior, I swear to God, if I find out that you fuckin' wit' that bitch, I swear I'ma kill you and her both!"

"Don't even worry about that shit, ma. I'm not looking for nobody. I got you. I don't need nobody else."

"I'm not bullshittin', Junior. I'm serious!"

"A'ight, ma. I hear you, and I ain't bullshittin' either."

Junior knew she was serious and he did love her, but he was just a man. He was thinking with his dick instead of with his heart.

Shondra was quiet the rest of the way to his cousin Craig's house. She didn't want Junior to violate her trust, but she knew she didn't stand a chance against the pretty, light-skinned girl with the fat ass.

Junior pulled into the parking lot and got out of the car. His cousin Craig was shooting dice, so he stood on the side and waited for him to finish rolling.

"What up, cuz? You just gettin' back?" Craig asked when he noticed Junior.

"Yeah, man, I need to get in the crib to get something," Junior replied, as he started walking toward the building.

"A'ight. These dudes trying to break me," Craig said, as he turned to the group of guys who stood in a circle waiting for him to roll again.

"Head Crack!" Junior screamed, then went into the building.

As Junior waited for the elevator, he thought about how Craig had his projects on lock with the drug trade. Anything that was sold there, Craig ultimately supplied. He had workers and sold weight to some of the local dealers. He treated the dudes in his projects well, making sure anyone who wanted to make some money had the opportunity. He had a strong crew of workers and gorillas who were not from the projects, but came to regulate whenever Craig had major beef or had to go to war. His street credibility was never questioned by anyone in the projects, but there were always the nonbelievers. He made examples of the ones that tested his position. One guy was found dead on the roof of a building with both his hands cut off at the wrists. The police found the hands in his pockets balled up with ten bloody one-hundred-dollar bills in each of them. There was a note that read, "Don't get caught wit' your hands in my pockets!" That one wicked act was how he kept potential thieves disinterested in his operation and kept his workers loyal to a fault. Craig was also likened to the Godfather because many of the tenants in the projects came to him whenever they needed a favor. He would help them with any situation - from financial assistance to personal safety - and they would be indebted to him until they paid off the favor.

Crime was kept to a low in Tompkins Projects because his operation was organized. He didn't venture out to the neighboring areas because he wanted to keep the peace. He made it a point to spread the love every chance he got. He would sponsor basketball games for the youth, support after-school programs for the community, and he even enforced a 24-hour-a-day tenant watch program. The regular blue and whites couldn't get any drug convictions because his operation was impenetrable, but he was being investigated by the feds. Craig was addicted to the notoriety more than the money, and his high came from eluding law enforcement. Junior had taken notice on how Craig ran his operation and tried to emulate some of his characteristics and procedures.

When the elevator stopped on the twelfth floor, Junior stepped out into the dimly lit hallway. He went to the exit door and walked up the rest of the three flights to the fifteenth floor. Craig had told him never to ride the elevator exactly to his floor just in case of an ambush, and that's how Junior conducted business when he was at his own spot. Craig was always thinking like that, regardless of how tight his operation was.

Junior pulled out some keys, entered the apartment, and immediately went to the alarm system on the wall to deactivate it. He then continued past Midnite, Craig's all-black pit bull. Craig had his dog professionally trained, and his attack commands were in Chinese. He was a vicious dog and only three other people besides Junior could come into the apartment without Craig.

Craig's apartment was so different, you would think you were in an apartment in Trump Towers. Craig had Italian leather furniture in the living room, with plush carpeting and a big screen television with cable. The kitchen had a dishwasher installed and all three bedrooms had king-sized bedroom sets with 36-inch Sony televisions.

When Junior walked into Craig's room, the pit bull came behind him and snarled a little. It was instinctive because no one was allowed into Craig's room if he wasn't present. It took some time, but Craig had trained Midnite to let Junior go in without him being there, and it seemed that now the dog was just letting Junior

know it was okay but not to make any funny moves. The dog was just protecting his master's property. Junior understood because Craig's room was where all the money and drugs were kept when he re-upped. But, Craig never kept all the money or drugs in there for more than eight hours.

Junior took out four thousand dollars from the safe. He was going to give Shondra fifteen hundred and then had to pay off some of the lookouts he had in Baptiste that Lakim was unaware of. Next, he walked into the kitchen and got his gun from the freezer. Craig had at least two guns in every room of the apartment, even in the hallway. Junior was getting strapped because he was going to Baptiste, and although there were guns already out there, he didn't want to get caught coming on the scene without one, just in case. Lakim had told him that nothing had jumped off since they've been back out there and that everything was fine. Junior believed him but always wanted to be prepared.

Once downstairs, Junior saw that Craig was raking the players in the dice game. Most of them had somber looks on their faces. Junior walked up to Craig to tell him that he took some money and his gun and was on his way to drop off Shondra to Baptiste.

"Yo, Tiko, take the bank for me while I talk to my cuz real quick," Craig told one of his young workers. He put his arm around Junior's shoulder and walked with him toward the rented Corvette. "You sure you a'ight going back ova there?" Craig asked, concerned.

"I'm good. I been through there droppin' off work. Plus, since La's been over there, he ain't had no problems," Junior informed him.

Craig stopped midway to the car once they were out of earshot from everyone in the parking lot.

"The one that was stayin' ova here with you after that shit jumped off?"

"Yeah, I told you he got it jumpin' over there again."

"Oh word? So shit still movin' out there?"

"Yeah, he doin' like seven thousand a week. I need to be over there so I can watch that money and the workers. You know what I'm sayin'?" Junior told Craig.

"I hear you, cuz. Just be careful. You know you gotta keep your eyes open at all times. Now you have to watch out for the Ds and the muhfucka you got beef with, and if you hear something, you gotta handle your business. Make the barrel bend. You understand me?"

"I got you, cuz. I'm seeing how shit really goes down now."

"You said you took your burner, right?" Craig asked.

Junior pulled up his shirt, revealing the black pistol in his waist, and Craig flashed an approving smile.

"So you gonna start chillin' back ova there, huh?" Craig asked. He wanted to make sure his cousin was ready and not just fronting for him.

"Not like that. I'm just gonna pick up the paper and make sure everything is everything. Then I'll be back over there full time, eventually. I want to take care of Stump first before I get back in my groove ova there. Once I handle that, it'll be one less thing for me to worry about while I'm out there. I need to take my guns back over there before I get too relaxed. I'll talk to you about that a lil later on. Okay, I'm out." Junior slapped him five and walked off.

Shondra had fallen asleep again, and Junior pulled off and headed for Baptiste Projects to drop her off and finally check on Lakim.

CHAPTER 10
NOBODY IS READY FOR CHANGE

"What's wrong, baby?" Gloria asked KB, as she got up from the bed in the hotel room.

KB had not been responding to her sexual advances for weeks, and she was worried that he might be stepping out on her like so many of her male partners did after being with her. He was sexually non-responsive, and she took that as a sign something was amiss in their relationship, but she didn't know what it was.

"You alright, honey?" she asked again with worry in her voice.

"Yeah, I'm okay," he said with no real emotion at all.

Since the robbery, KB had been uneasy because Roughhouse had died and he felt a sense of responsibility. It had been on the front page of the *Daily News* the next day, and the article said the police had promising leads on the assailants. No police or detectives had been to his mother's house inquiring, and none of the guys said anything about detectives or police paying them a visit either. Stump was acting as if nothing tragic had happened that day, and when KB spoke to him on the phone, he was already planning another job for them.

The last time KB saw the guys was when they went to Stump's house to split up the money. There was over two hundred fifty thousand dollars, and they split it equally five ways, with

Roughhouse's cut going to his mother and sister. Roughhouse's people didn't know where the money came from because Stump had someone send it to them anonymously to help with the funeral. Stump told the guys that they couldn't attend the funeral because it would probably be swarming with undercover cops looking for anyone that could give them information on the robbery, and he didn't want anyone to take the chance.

Roughhouse died a terrible death, and KB couldn't get the image of him trying to make it to the van out of his mind. Nor could he get over how he was the one to make the fatal decision to leave Roughhouse behind. It was really tearing him down mentally, but he couldn't tell Gloria because he didn't want to chance it leaking out and getting him locked up. He didn't want any mistakes or apologies. If he was implicated in the robbery, he would be going down for murder, which carried a sentence of twenty-five years to life.

"You look like you're deep in thought. I know something's wrong, baby, because you've been so restless at night and jumping in your sleep. Tell me. Maybe I can help you. I'm here for you, K," Gloria said sincerely.

"I told you it was nothing!" KB barked.

"Now I know it's really something since you flippin' on me for being concerned about you. Whatever it is, baby, I'm not the cause, and if I am, let me know and I'll change. If I did something, K, please tell me. I'll make it right, I promise. I love you, baby. It bothers me to see you like this, especially since I know you're not really like this. Please, baby, I just want to help you. Don't you understand?" Gloria pleaded.

KB didn't want her to think it had anything to do with her. He didn't want her to blame herself. So, against his better judgment, he decided to tell her what had happened. Telling her would ease his mind because he hadn't told anyone about the robbery, and it was eating away at him inside.

"Come ova here," KB beckoned.

Gloria had a look of horror on her face as he told her the complete story from the beginning to the tragic end. After he finished telling her, she sat on the bed with her mouth wide open.

She had heard about the robbery on the news but never imagined KB was involved. She didn't believe he was capable of doing shit like that. KB looked at her and tried to reassure her that he wasn't in danger of getting locked up because the police didn't have any evidence on who committed the crime. She looked at him, not knowing who he really was at that moment. KB was sort of thuggish, but she would have never guessed he was into what he just told her. Four people died because of what he did. She began to wonder if he was capable of harming her if she were to ever do anything to him that he believed warranted that kind of behavior. Gloria wasn't afraid of him, though. She was just more in shock ahout what he had told her.

"K baby, I don't know what to tell you," she finally said. "I mean, I don't know what to say to that. One thing I do know is that I will stand by you no matter what. I love you, K, and I'm going to do whatever I can to help you whenever you need me."

KB looked Gloria square in her eyes and couldn't believe he had just told her what happened that day, but what really had him bugging was that she said she was with him no matter what. He had never met anyone who felt that way about him, and he could tell she was sincere by the tone of her voice and the expression on her face.

"Yo, ma, you don't know how much that means to me. This has been worrying me because I don't want to get caught behind this bullshit, and I feel fucked up because I feel like I'm the reason my man is dead."

"Look, K, I knew something was bothering you because you been actin' real funny and shit. I thought you was seeing another bitch or something because I couldn't get you to perform in bed like you normally do."

"You know I would never step out on you, Glo. You're the best thing that I ever did. You're all I need. I love you, too, girl, for life."

They both lay on the bed, as she began to stroke him gently. He responded by moving with her hand in an up and down motion. She pulled down the zipper on his Iceberg jeans and pulled out his manhood. She slid her wet mouth over his hardness and began to suck him slowly, looking up at him while she continued to slurp him. He was enjoying it. His eyes were closed, and he was moaning every time she sucked his tip. Glad to be pleasing him, she sucked him harder until she felt his spasms. Right before his eruption, she could feel his shaft pulsating in her mouth. The lower part of KB's body began to move left to right quickly. She applied pressure to his hips and moved her mouth up and down, sucking hard as she came down. He exploded into her mouth, and she could feel the warm, creamy liquid shoot straight down her throat. It was salty, and it was the first time she had ever swallowed a baby, but her intentions were to solidify her relationship with KB. This would definitely seal the deal. She finished sucking him dry as a desert, and he became limp. Gloria got up off him and admired his limp body lying there, not able to move. She was just that good. She was good enough to satisfy her man and have him love her for real.

KB and Gloria hopped into a cab after checking out of the hotel. Gloria had her head on his shoulder as the cab sped across the Williamsburg Bridge. KB was taking her home. They were planning to go away for the weekend, so he wanted to see Stump before he left to let him know he was going to be gone for about three or four days then Stump told him there was another hit that was supposed to be taking place real soon and would let him know once he got the details. Although the last robbery didn't go right and Roughhouse got murdered, KB did like the payoff. He made more money on that one robbery than most people in the hood made in a year. The risks were high, but all he did was drive the getaway car. He really wasn't involved in the more dangerous part of the stickup, and he still got an even split. What better way to make money?

Gloria woke up when the cab pulled up in front of her building. Then she and KB got out and went inside.

"Hold up," she said, as KB pushed the button for the elevator. "Let me go knock on my sister's door and see if she's home."

"A'ight. I'll see you upstairs," he replied.

"No, I want you to meet her. She's been dying to meet you. I told her so much about us and how you got me strung out, and she wants to see the man that got her sister's nose open."

"A'ight, I'll meet her," KB said reluctantly.

Gloria knocked on the door and waited for someone to answer, while KB stayed down by the elevators. Shondra was Junior's girl, and he didn't know if she knew he was down with Stump or that he was present the night of the shootout. KB had been careful not to tell Gloria he was there that night because he wasn't sure if she would tell Shondra, and he didn't want to risk that. He wasn't sure if Junior knew he was there that night either, but the hood had a way of getting information out. Just in case, he fixed the gun in his belt and leaned against the door of the elevator. Gloria was about to leave, when she heard the locks on the door start clicking.

"Who is it?" the voice asked behind the door.

"It's me," Gloria replied.

The door opened, and Shondra's little brother, Tim, was standing in the doorway wearing plaid boxers.

"Shondra's not here, Gloria," he told her.

"You know where she at?"

"Nope, I don't know."

"All right, Tim. Whenever she gets in, tell her to come upstairs. I don't care what time it is."

"I'll tell her," he said and closed the door.

Just about the same time Gloria was talking to Tim, Junior and Shondra pulled up in front of her building and sat in the car talking. While they talked, Junior looked around cautiously to see who was out and about. He hadn't told Lakim that he was coming by because he wanted to see if the operation ran exactly the way Lakim said it did. There was a young guy standing on the corner of the building across the street. Junior eyed him as the obvious lookout. Another guy was standing in front of the building. He had to be the one serving the heads. Junior watched as a customer came up to the guy in front of the building and how he sent him inside to cop. He observed the lookout on the corner who nodded his head, letting the seller know that everything was clear to make

the sale. After about thirty seconds, he went inside the building and the lookout seemed to be talking into a headset.

Junior was surprised. It looked like Lakim had made some changes to how they served the customers, and it looked like a good system. Junior explained to Shondra what was going on, and they both watched as the two guys rotated positions so if detectives or narcs were riding by they wouldn't see the same person standing on the corner. As Junior watched them for about an hour, he realized the traffic was steady and the guys were handling their business correctly. Junior was looking at it as if he were a narc. They wouldn't be able to get them on a possession because everything was done out of sight. The operation Lakim had in place looked like it was tight.

When they got into the apartment, Shondra went straight in her room and took off her clothes to take a shower. Junior went into the room, sat on the bed, and turned on the television. It felt funny being in the room again after being gone so long. It almost didn't feel like home to him. He lay back on the bed, looked up at the ceiling, and breathed in deeply. He lit a cigarette and closed his eyes. After finishing his cigarette, he dozed off until Shondra came in from her shower. When she was inside the room, she dropped her towel to the floor and closed the bedroom door behind her. The noise of the closing door woke him up. He looked at Shondra as she got the Johnson & Johnson baby oil and sat on her bed. She poured some in the palm of her hand and massaged both hands together, then lifted one of her legs and spread the oil evenly up and down her thick thighs.

Junior got up off the bed and helped oil her body, caressing her supple breasts and kissing her neck at the same time. Shondra was getting aroused as he slid his hand down to her split, feeling her wetness mixed with the oil on his hand. She winced a little, but he continued to massage her clit as she lay back on the bed and opened her legs to him invitingly. He placed his tongue on her nipple and felt it harden as he sucked it gently, all the while fingering her sweet, wet insides. As she began moving in a circular motion, he switched nipples. Her body felt like silk and he was getting stiff as a log. The bulge in his pants was uncomfortable,

but he continued to please her. She began to move to the motions of his fingers, while he switched positions. His hands were on both nipples squeezing them lightly, and his tongue was licking the hardened clit that was poking out of its hiding place. She whined and squirmed with delight, as he continued licking and sucking gently while squeezing her nipples. She let out a loud moan and he knew she was ready to orgasm.

He jumped up off her, stood back, and watched her body trembling. She looked up at him like a wounded puppy, begging him to finish what he had started. He spread her legs wider and put his face back to where he was before, sucking and licking her rapidly. She exploded immediately and her body shook frantically. He kept his hands locked on her hips like a C-clamp, not allowing her to get away. She was fighting for him to release her, but he kept his grip on her and continued to lick her quickly. She fought so much until another snowy feeling came over her. She was having her second orgasm, and she screamed and shook even more violently than the first time. Then she relaxed after some seconds had passed. She closed her eyes, breathing hard, and her body became limp. Her clit felt raw as Junior slowed down to a light licking. She was finished.

After washing off his face, Junior went back into the room where Shondra was putting on a Nike jumpsuit.

"I'm about to go check on my work," he said, as he pinched her on the ass.

"Okay, baby. I'm gonna go upstairs and see Glo after I wash off a little. While you were in the bathroom, Tim told me that she was down here looking for me."

Junior fixed the gun in his waistband, then turned and walked out the door.

KB was about to leave Gloria's apartment, when Shondra knocked on the door.

"Who is it?" Gloria asked, as KB stepped away from the door.

"It's me, girl," Shondra replied.

Gloria unlocked the door quickly and opened it for her girlfriend. KB sat back on the couch and brushed his pants leg off. Shondra walked into the apartment and hugged Gloria by her neck.

"What's up, girl? I missed you." Shondra peeked over Gloria's shoulder, noticing KB.

"I know. I missed you too. Did y'all have a good time?" Gloria asked her.

"You know I did. Hmmm, you must be KB," Shondra said, acknowledging his presence in the room.

"Yeah, I'm KB," he replied, getting off the couch and outstretching his hand to her.

"Oh no, hun," Shondra said, grabbing him and hugging him. "You family. You got my girl all sprung and shit. So how are you? I heard a lot about you."

Shondra purposely hugged him to see if he was strapped. The hard metal gun that pressed up against her confirmed her suspicions.

"I told you she was cool," Gloria crooned.

"Yeah, I see" he said, blushing slightly.

From her initial reaction, Shondra did seem cool to him. She gave him a nice reception, when he had expected her to give off some negative vibes.

Shondra thought KB was a handsome dude. She liked his build and he dressed nice. He had a boyish look to him, and he seemed a little on the shy side.

"So, Mr. KB, you from Williamsburg I hear?" Shondra asked.

"Yeah," KB responded in monotone.

"My girl tells me that you the man in her life now. You better treat her right or you're gonna have to deal with me." Shondra smirked.

"I'm goin' to go get that blunt from the room. Don't scare my baby off now, girl," Gloria said, leaving Shondra and KB alone in the living room.

"So what you do, mystery man? Seems like you don't talk much," Shondra pried.

"I just be chillin', you know." KB was short and vague with his responses.

"How long you lived in the 'Burg?"

"All my life."

"What side you live on?"

"Meserole."

"Oh, so you must know Gino and them dudes?"

"Yeah, I know Gino. We went to the same school."

"You seem cool, KB. I hope I'm not being too nosey asking you twenty-one questions and shit, but that's my girl and I know she really likes you. I just wanna make sure you have good intentions. You know what I mean?" Shondra clarified.

"I hear you. She told me how she used to be and how you changed her. I respect that about her because she didn't have to tell me shit. On the same token, I can't say where we'll end up, but I am feelin' her, fa real. That's why I made her my girl."

"Roll this shit up," Gloria said to Shondra, as she came back into the room, passing her a blunt. "We should all go out sometime," Gloria suggested. "Me, you, KB, and Junior…as couples."

That statement took Shondra's and KB's breath away. Both their identities were now confirmed for each other. KB looked at Shondra to see what she was going to say to the suggestion.

"That'll be cool. We should hook up and go out," Shondra replied smoothly, then licked the blunt and lit it. She kept her cool because she anticipated Junior's name coming up, so she wasn't caught off guard.

"We goin' to Atlantic City this weekend," Gloria said, as she passed the blunt to KB.

"That's cool. What hotel y'all stayin' in?" Shondra asked KB directly. "Caesar's Palace's rooms are nice, especially the suite."

"I'm thinking about the Trump Plaza," KB replied, while checking his pager. "I gotta use the phone, Glo. 'Scuse me, Shondra," he said, as he got up and walked out the room to use the phone.

"Damn, he don't talk much, do he?" Shondra asked Gloria.

"Not really. I told him about that. He all anti-social and shit." Gloria sounded disappointed.

"Well, do he at least talk to you? I mean, does he tell you anything about himself, like personal shit?"

"Yeah, we talk, but he's not really big on talking."

"You need to know your man, girl. Like who his homeboys are and where he at when he's not with you."

"You don't even know where your man is twenty-four seven. You know how guys is," Gloria said defensively.

"Bullshit. I know where he tells me he is. He don't necessarily have to be there, but he do tell me, and I do know who his homeboys are," Shondra shot back.

"That's true. I just don't want to seem like I'm sweating his every move. I don't want to push him away by being too much in his business. You understand what I mean?"

Gloria was being sincere. She had always wanted a good man, and KB seemed like he was the one. He treated her respectfully, and she didn't want to do anything to mess up what she had with him, although she always listened to and trusted her best friend's words when it came to men.

"I hear you, girl, but you need to know more about him. I'm not sayin' he hidin' shit from you. I'm just sayin' you need to know who you fuckin'."

"I know," Gloria mumbled.

"Look, Glo, you know I want you to be happy. I just don't want you to slip up and make any more mistakes with a no-good-ass dude. I'm not saying that KB is no good. I'm just making sure you know more than just his name for your own benefit."

KB walked back into the room and Shondra got quiet, while Gloria stared at the floor.

"I got to make a run real quick, hun. I'll be back lata on tonight," KB said, as he kissed Gloria and headed to the door.

"Okay, baby," Gloria said, her eyes closed.

Shondra looked at him and wondered where he was going. She watched as he kissed Gloria passionately. She saw how Gloria melted right there in front of him, her emotions exposed. Her best friend was really in love. Shondra had thoughts of how Junior was so much like that, even after they'd been together over four years. Gloria went out into the hallway with KB and asked him where he was going. She was unconsciously doing exactly what Shondra wanted her to do.

"I'm goin' to handle some business."

"I'm just askin' because I hope you're not goin' to fuck wit' that guy Stump."

"That's my man, baby. No matter what happens, that's my man. You gotta understand that," he reasoned.

"I just don't want you to get into any more trouble. That's all, baby," she said, rubbing his back.

"I'm good. Don't worry," he replied, while pressing the button for the elevator.

Gloria walked back inside the apartment and held her arms out for a hug.

"What's that for, girl?" Shondra asked.

"Because I know you love me and only want the best for me."

"You know I do, girl."

Gloria hugged Shondra long and tight.

"What's wrong, Glo?" Shondra asked, her antennas going up.

"It's KB. I do know something about him, and it's bothering me."

"What is it?" Shondra asked hungrily.

"You remember that shit that happened by Lindsey Houses, the coke spot that got robbed?"

"Yeah, I think so. Didn't like three or four people get killed?" Shondra's heartbeat quickened.

"Well, KB and his crew was the ones that hit that store. They robbed and killed the two Dominican guys and one of his homeboys died fighting off one of the other Dominican guys that was killed. They had to leave him because he couldn't make it to the getaway car," she told Shondra, almost sobbing.

Shondra was shocked to hear that KB was involved in that robbery, but then her mind shifted and remembered he was capable of doing something like that because he tried to rob her man. She began to wonder whether the outcome would have been similar had KB and Stump succeeded in robbing Junior.

"Damn, that's fucked up. He don't look like that kind of dude," Shondra surmised.

"Looks can be deceiving. That's why I said you were right, because I wouldn't have found that out about him if I didn't push the issue."

“Well, tell me something. Who was the guys he did it with?”

“Some guy named Stump. He ‘posed to be the ringleader, and then there were some other dudes. I can’t remember all their names.”

“You ever meet the one named Stump? Do you know where he lives at?” Shondra asked.

“Nope, I never met him, but I do know he lives in Bushwick Projects because that’s where KB said they met to go over the details before they did the robbery, and that’s where they split up the money.”

“That’s right! The news said they got away with a lot of money. KB must have a lot of money now if he didn’t have any before.”

“Yeah, he said they came off with like two hundred thou. That’s how we goin’ away for the weekend. He said he wanted to spend some of the money on me.” Gloria blushed.

“Well, I’m gonna go back downstairs ’cause I’m tired as hell from that long ride from VA. Come down in the morning so we can finish talking, and let me know when y’all leaving, all right, girl?”

“All right, I’ll be down in the morning. See ya later.”

***

When Junior got to Rock and Dusty’s building on the other side of the projects, there were a bunch of young guys standing in the front. They were staring at him hard, and he didn’t recognize any of the faces. One of the guys blocked the entrance, making Junior go around him to get into the building. Junior braced himself to swing at the guy, but the young boy already had intentions on robbing Junior and swung on him first. The right hook to Junior’s jaw made him fall back onto the black fence. As he stumbled backward, he pulled out the silver nine millimeter and unlocked the safety with his thumb. He pointed the gun toward the guy that hit him and then fanned it around to the crowd of guys that looked like they were ready to run.

“Back the fuck up!” Junior bellowed.

“Be easy, duke,” the one that hit him said.

Junior walked up to him and put the gun to his face, patting him down to make sure he didn’t have a burner on him. Then Junior turned to the other guys and told them to lift up their shirts and turn around to make sure they were unarmed, as well.

“What the fuck? Y’all lil muhfuckas don’t know who I am?” Junior asked with a look of death in his eyes. He didn’t know if the guys were part of Stump’s goons, but prepared himself to kill them instantly if they were.

“Nah, man, we don’t know you. Who you?” one of the guys asked.

Junior looked at him and swung the gun at his head. At the same time, he squeezed the trigger, making the gun discharge. The guy dropped to the ground holding his head with both hands. The other guys thought Junior had shot their friend in the head because it happened so fast. All their expressions changed to fear.

“I’m the muhfucka that did this to you!” Junior turned to the other guys. “If y’all don’t know me, you better get to know me, or fuck around and wind up wit’ a hole in your forehead.”

All the guys looked at Junior and figured they had fucked with the wrong dude this time. They all stood there wondering if he was going to do something to them next. The young guy he hit was on the ground in a fetal position, holding his head and moaning as Junior stepped over him and grabbed him by his shirt.

“Who you down wit’? If you lie to me, get ready to close your eyes for good!” Junior threatened.

“I ain’t wit nobody. This my crew,” he squealed.

“I should kill you,” Junior whispered in his ear, his voice laced with cyanide.

“Yo, man, I swear I ain’t down wit’ nobody,” he cried. “Please, man, don’t do this to me,” he begged, while his blood oozed between his fingers.

Junior stepped over him and went into the building, then ran up the stairs to see if Rock was home. He wasn’t worried about the young monkeys, because after what he had just done to their man, they knew they were fucking with a gorilla. They would remember Junior and make sure they never made the same mistake again.

Lakim and Rock were in the hallway when Junior came out of the exit. They had heard a gunshot and were going to investigate.

"Whaddup, Junior?" Lakim asked, as he walked over to give him five.

"Ain't nothin'. I just pistol-whipped some lil faggot in front of the building," Junior responded.

"Word! What happened?" Rock asked, pulling out his gun.

"Lil muhfucka stole off on me, and I pulled out my gat and split his wig."

"Come on, let's go back down there and see who them young cats is," Lakim said, already running down the stairs. Lakim didn't like the fact that Junior had popped up on them like that.

"I handled that shit already," Junior said. "They don't want it. Trust me."

"Well, we gon' make sure them lil muhfuckas don't violate like that again," Rock said, joining Lakim in running down the stairs. "This is my fuckin' building, and I don't remember hiring no security guards."

They all ran down the stairs, but by the time they got outside, the crew of young guys was gone. There was blood on the ground, though – evidence that Junior handled the situation effectively.

"I see you put in a lot of work," Lakim said, as he headed toward the back of the building. "Them lil dudes couldn't have gotten far."

They spotted the crew of guys walking toward Bushwick Projects.

"That's probably them right there!" Rock said, running toward the guys walking.

"Aaaay yoooo!" he yelled.

When the kids turned around and saw Junior, Rock, and Lakim, they took off running up the Ave.

"Y'all better stop before I send some slugs at y'all lil asses!" Rock yelled, running with the gun in plain sight.

Two of them stopped, but the rest kept running. Rock caught up with the two and told them to tell their homeboys to stop and come back. They complied and the other three came back reluctantly, copping pleas all the way back.

"Look, man, we don't want no beef," one kid said. "Duke already busted our man in the head."

"Shut the fuck up. I want to know who the fuck y'all lil muhfuckas is!" Rock said.

"I'm Danny," the one that got his head busted said.

"I'm Fizz," the youngest looking one with braids reported.

"I'm Darrell," the third one answered, looking nervous.

"Leroy," the brown-skinned skinny one stated.

"Jeff," the shortest of the crew whispered.

Lakim and Junior stood there just looking at them. They were all no older than fourteen, but they looked seasoned like they were down for whatever.

"You let them little dudes front on you?" Lakim asked, looking at Junior.

"I told you the lil muhfucka stole off on me. Look, La, don't make me body shorty," Junior replied, his anger rising.

"Nah, man, I'm just sayin', shorty must got some heart to front on you like that. I'm not trying to play you. I'm just surprised these lil dudes was tryin' to muscle you, that's all," Lakim said, clearing up his statement.

"Why was y'all posted up in front of my building?" Rock asked.

They looked at each other, and then the one that got his head busted open spoke.

"We was tryin' to catch a vic."

"In front of my fuckin' building?" Rock asked with fury in his voice. "Where the fuck y'all from?"

"Bushwick Projects."

A light bulb went off in Junior's head. He wondered if he had made a mistake by letting them go. Stump was from Bushwick. Suppose he really did send some amateurs at him? He had definitely been caught slipping.

"Look, youngin's," Lakim started, "I understand y'all tryin' to get money and shit, but y'all can't get it over here like that." Then he looked at Junior. "If you want to make some money, then we can put y'all lil asses to work."

"We're down," the guy said, still holding his head.

"A'ight, y'all need to take your boy to Woodhull Hospital to get his head looked at," Rock told them. "And tell the doctor that you fell off the monkey bars or something if they ask how your melon got cracked."

As Rock, Lakim, and Junior headed back to the building, Lakim began telling Junior about the recent news on the streets.

"Yo Junior, you heard what happened to Kendu?" he asked.

"Nah, what happened to him?" Junior answered.

"Somebody murdered him in his aunt's crib," Lakim told him. "The police don't know who did it, but I heard one of them dudes over in the Stuy aired him out. The hood is sayin' he got killed because he started robbing those young hustlers over there, but I don't know how true that is."

"You said you thought he was smoking, right? It might be true then. He might have thought them little dudes over there didn't put in work. Who knows," Junior said, then continued. "La, I know that was your man and shit, but you know I had beef with that cat. So, I'm not feeling sorry for him like that, because if we would have bumped heads, I was planning the same outcome."

"I know. I'm the one that told you what he was up to, remember? Don't sweat that. Du had to know what he was doing if he was fuckin' with that shit. He saw how that shit fucks people up. That was my man and the whole nine, but he made a decision out here in the field and he had to pay the cost. I guess I just gotta charge it to the game." A slight bit of emotion could be heard in Lakim's tone.

"Well, it's a done deal now. You gonna hit his fam off with something?" Junior asked Lakim.

"It's just his lil brother and his grandma. I gave them a little something already," Lakim replied.

"That's peace. I'm 'bout to take care of that Stump character. I ain't forget about him," Junior informed Lakim.

"I ain't seen nor heard anything from that dude since I been back 'round here. I think he know what time it is," Lakim told Junior.

Rock was ear hustling the entire time Junior and Lakim was talking, then interjected. "If that muhfucka come 'round here bullshittin', I'ma put two slugs in his domepiece."

"Yo Rock, I gotta talk some business with La, so let us go up to your crib so we can have some privacy," Junior said.

"Cool. I'm gonna go on the other side and check up on Dusty and the workers," Rock told them.

"Ay Rock, you know you gotta put up your toast before you go over there," Lakim reminded him.

"I know. I stash it near that abandoned building before I get on the block," Rock informed him.

"A'ight, see you in a few," Lakim replied.

Junior and Lakim took the elevator up to the crib, went inside, and sat down on the couch to talk.

"So tell me, La, on the real, how is shit going out here?" Junior asked seriously.

"It's sweet. Shit is really going good. It's been hot out here recently, so I changed the way the workers handle the custies. I make sure nobody is holding and that there is a lookout for every shift. The one that serves stays out of sight in the building, and the one steering makes sure the head leaves out the back of the building as soon as they cop. We have headsets that look like a Walkman, and the lookout tells us when he sees Ds coming through. After about thirty minutes to an hour, everyone rotates their position. The money made is put in a mailbox until Rock or Dusty comes to pick it up. They usually come through every hour, or they chill over there to make sure that shit is running straight. We keep four guns out here — one stashed in the back of the building, one in the building, one across the street in the bushes, and one in a locked mailbox."

"Damn, La, I'm really impressed. I was watching how this shit was running while I was sitting in front of Shondra's building, and it looks like you got everything under control."

"We pullin' in about ten to fifteen G's," Lakim announced proudly. "I know you know by how fat those stacks of money I drop off to you been getting."

"How many workers you got out there now?" Junior asked, calculating in his head how many workers were on the payroll.

"I got eight shorties workin', but only three work the overnight shift."

"That's cool. Oh, and about them lil monkeys from Bushwick, I don't want them on the payroll. I need to take care of that muhfucka in Bushwick before I try to put work out there. You know what I mean?" Junior told him.

"I don't think that's gonna be a problem. I can have Rock and Dusty watch over them until you take care of that business. Nobody out there gotta know that's our shit."

"No, La, I don't want them dudes on the payroll. After I take care of that business, then you can recruit them, not before. You hear what I'm telling you?" Junior instructed.

"I hear you." Lakim's brows lowered.

"Once I take care of Stump, we can concentrate on expanding the operation to the other projects around us. I just found out that Gloria fucks with KB. He lives in the 'Burg. I got his card, but I still didn't find out what floor Stump lives on yet."

"Shit, we can body KB first then," Lakim remarked.

"Yeah, but I want to get the head of the snake first. You know what I mean?"

"I feel you. Once the head is gone, the rest of the body can't function," Lakim replied.

"In the meantime, we gonna get this money, but we can't sleep on this dude for shit." Junior balled his fist up. "I see you holdin' shit down lovely out here right now, but I'm gonna be on the scene again. I'm gonna let you run shit, and I'm gonna play the back so you can shine. You good with that?" Junior offered.

"This your shit, son. I'm a lieutenant and you're the general. You just keep shit comin', and I'm gonna keep getting rid of it for you."

Junior looked at Lakim, trying to figure out if he was being sincere. Junior had learned from experience that the power of money could make the best of friends turn to enemies. He was hoping Lakim was loyal. He hoped he wasn't making a mistake by leaving him in charge of the operation.

"Oh yeah, the Ds is hot on Rock over here. He got picked up with some weed, and since then the Ds been on him every time they see him on the block. He don't hold anymore, so if they roll up, they don't get him with nothing but money. When he got picked up, I used the money you told me to save in case any of us got locked up. I only spent twenty-five hundred on a lawyer," Lakim explained to Junior.

"That's cool. Now you know why I said to save that money. See how it comes in handy?"

"You right. I'm glad, too, because I sure wasn't comin' outta my pocket for no lawyer," Lakim stated.

"I can understand why you would say that, but there's something you gotta understand. Either way it goes, you have to pay, because if you don't look out for one of your own, they can turn state on you and fuck up your whole operation. So, you have to make sure you take care of them. Once they come home, then you can handle them whichever way you see fit."

"I hear you talking. You right," Lakim agreed.

"What's up with Dusty?" Junior asked.

"He be watching the workers and paying them at the end of the week. Most of the time he be with that Puerto Rican crackhead bitch from this building."

"Who, Lizzette?"

"Yeah, I think she got him sprung on the pussy. He always got the bitch in here with him late nights and shit," Lakim said, shaking his head.

"Damn, I didn't know she had him like that."

The last time Junior linked up with Lizzette, she was far gone on her drug habit. She had beeped him and he told her to meet him at a hotel on Broadway. She still had a nice body, but it wasn't as tight as it was before. When they got into the room, she wanted to get high first, and he noticed she wasn't putting it in blunts anymore. She was smoking from the pipe. It was an immediate turnoff for him, but he still let her give him brain. After he busted his load, she wanted another hit, but he wasn't about to give her any more for free. She begged, pleaded, and offered more sexual favors, but he declined her offer. Then she asked him how long he

had the room so she could get some more money. She left the room and came back about twenty minutes later with about seventy-five dollars. Junior didn't ask her where she got it. He just gave her the product and let her blast off. While she was getting high, she passed him the pipe like she was passing him a blunt. Out of reflex, he slapped the shit out of her and kicked her out of the room. He knew that was a dopefiend move, trying to get him hooked on the drug so she could smoke up all his product.

"Shiiiit, the bitch don't even give me head no more 'cause he be actin' like she's his main shorty," Lakim said, laughing.

"Well, I hope he don't let that bitch know what he be doin'. When they on that shit, ain't no tellin' what they'll do if you don't give them what they want." Junior knew what the outcome of fucking with a fine crackhead could be if a motherfucker wasn't focused.

Junior was impressed with how Lakim was handling everything, and despite his apparent cockiness, Lakim was in total control of the operation. Junior liked the fact that Lakim was aware of what was going on and made changes where necessary. Lakim had learned a lot from Junior, and he deserved to be in the position he was in. He was fast becoming Junior's right-hand man, and Junior hoped things between them wouldn't change.

They walked over to the block where Lakim was going to show Junior firsthand how things were running. Junior's pager went off and it was Shondra's code.

"That was Shondra. I'm gonna go see what she wants. I'll meet you in the back of the building in a few."

"A'ight. I'll be right here twistin' up this blunt," Lakim said, pulling out a blunt from his breast pocket.

Shondra was sitting in the living room when Junior walked through the door.

"Whaddup? Something wrong?" he asked her.

"Well, no, not exactly," she replied.

"So what's up?"

"I saw KB. He was upstairs in Gloria's house," Shondra said.

"What!" Junior exclaimed. "He still up there?"

"No, baby, he left a little after I got up there."

“He know that you my girl?” Junior asked, worried.

“Yeah, it came up in conversation. Glo was saying that we all needed to hang out together,” Shondra told him.

“What did he say when she said that?”

“He didn’t say nothin’, but that’s not what I want to tell you. When he left, Gloria told me that him and Stump are the ones that robbed that coke spot by Lindsey.”

“Word? They the ones that did that shit? One of the dudes got killed doing that shit.”

“I know, baby. That’s why I want you to be careful when it comes to KB,” Shondra said, concerned.

“He told her that shit?” Junior asked in wonderment.

“She said he told her everything, in detail,” Shondra revealed.

“He a stupid muhfucka. He don’t even know her like that. Suppose she gets heated wit’ him? His ass is finished. And they’ll charge him for all those bodies, too. He good for twenty-five to life for that shit.”

“I thought about that, too, but she ain’t gonna drop dime on him. She in love with him already. I can see it in her eyes and hear it in her voice when she speaks his name.”

“Did she say where he was going when he left?”

“No. I left right after him to let you know what I found out.”

“I need to hurry up and get those muhfuckas.”

“Junior, I got faith in everything you do. I just want you to be careful. I don’t trust him and Stump,” Shondra said honestly.

“I wonder if he told her if they planning on trying to get at me again?” Junior wondered out loud.

“I don’t know. She didn’t mention anything like that to me. As far as I know, she don’t know that KB had anything to do with that shootout with you.”

“I know that’s your girl and everything, but I doubt she would tell you if he did tell her anything about getting me, especially if he got her fucked up on him the way you say he do. There ain’t no way she gonna give up info like that. Trust me.”

“You right, baby. So what you gonna do?”

“What I need to do is find out how this money is flowing out here. That’s what I need to do,” Junior replied with urgency.

"Be careful, Junior," she said, hugging his neck. "I love you."

"You heard that Kendu got murdered, right?" Junior turned and asked her before leaving out the door.

"No, I didn't hear nothin' 'bout that."

"Lakim told me that some cat in the Stuy bodied him because he was running around robbing dealers out there."

"So how La takin' it?" she asked.

"I know that was La's man and all, but you know I was gonna set it on him for tryin' to set me up. I think La is dealin' with it, but at the same time, I ain't grieving for Du. La said that he was smoking, so he gotta charge it to the game. I think that shit clouded Du's judgment and he just started making fucked-up moves," Junior told her.

"Well, you know you can't trust everybody and everything, Junior," she said. "That was his homeboy from back in the day. They grew up together, so you know he gotta be feelin' bad." Shondra secretly felt like Junior had something to do with Kendu's death but just wasn't telling her.

"Yeah, but you know muhfuckas get older, and with age comes wisdom. I think La is starting to see that this game is real and you have to stay true to it or be its victim. Du *was* a good dude, but he let the game control his actions instead of letting his actions control the game. La knew what the outcome was gonna be when he told me what Du was planning. I guess he stayed on the winning side, for now."

"You just need to be careful, Junior. Everything is starting to change. Are you ready for the change?"

"Nobody is ready for change, baby. You just have to be aware and make adjustments. I see that everything is different since that night. That's why I'm taking these calculated steps. I'm making sure there's no mistake when I go after those dudes. Don't worry, Mooka. Change is inevitable, and knowing that change is coming puts me one step ahead of everyone else. Being ready is a state of mind. I'm processing what happened and making the necessary moves to make sure that I don't come out in a body bag. I was born ready. I got the best of both worlds, ma," he said, as he closed the door behind him.

***

KB was sitting down in Stump's living room listening intently to the details of the new robbery he was planning. He was looking at Stump thinking he was really crazy. Stump wanted to stick up a club. The same crew from the last robbery was there minus Roughhouse. It felt awkward to be sitting in the same spot again going over the finer points of the robbery, knowing what had happened the last time. Stump had set it up near perfectly. The one thing he didn't incorporate into the plan was someone coming into the spot and resisting the robbery, and that's how Roughhouse got killed.

KB noticed a new face in the crew, too, a face he didn't recognize, and Stump didn't entertain the idea of introducing him. This new face looked a little older than Stump and had a long scar down the side of his face, which made him look especially grimy and treacherous. He didn't really seem interested in what Stump was saying. He seemed more focused on Stump, and KB was wondering if Stump or the other guys peeped it. It seemed funny they weren't formally introduced, especially since KB knew everybody there but him. KB made a mental note to watch the new guy's every move when the day came to do the stickup. He didn't trust homeboy for a second.

"My man is a bouncer at Love Mansion, the club on Flushing Ave.," Stump explained. "Him and his crew will be at the front door, so it's gonna be easy for us to get our guns in. He said the owner is a big heroin dealer and keeps most of the dough from his transactions in a safe in his office upstairs, and that he picks up the money on Saturday nights while the club is in full swing. On that night, some dude is throwin' a party for his man that just came home from up north, so that can be more money because he said the dude having the party thrown for him is a big-time coke dealer from uptown. We're gonna rob everybody in the club, plus the owner. We can pull it off because there won't be no guns in there but ours, except for the owner, but I'm gonna have the drop on him."

KB looked around the room as Stump continued talking. All the guys had their eyes fixed on him as if he were a preacher giving a sermon, and none seemed apprehensive about the details of the crime, but KB wasn't feeling him when he said he wanted to rob everybody in the club. He felt if the party was for a big-time dealer, then most of the patrons would be dealers and would make the robbery much more difficult because they wouldn't be willing victims. KB was having a bad feeling about this one. He didn't want to be down, but he didn't know how to back out of it.

Stump finished explaining the details of the job and told everyone it would be about three weeks before everything went down, but he wanted everyone to meet at his house the night before the robbery so he could go over everyone's job one more time. He also wanted everyone to stay at his place on that night so they could go to the club the next morning together to check out the layout and go over how everything was supposed to go down. Once everyone agreed on the plan, all the guys got up and left. When KB was on his way out the door, Stump called him back.

"What's up, KB?" Stump asked.

"Nuthin'," KB replied.

"I still ain't forgot about those muhfuckas from Baptiste that was bustin' at me. You been 'round there lately?"

"Nah, man, I been chillin', spending that dough," KB lied.

"When I catch Junior, I'm gonna body him. He probably thinking shit is sweet because I ain't been back out there at his punk ass, but I had to take care of that coke spot first. You know what I mean? You know what happened to the other kid, right?"

"Who, Kendu? I heard somebody killed that dude," KB said.

"I know. Quiet as kept, my man Drez, the one that was in here with the long scar, is the one that bodied him. Just so happens that the faggot-ass nigga robbed one of his workers who happened to be his little brouther. He lucky I ain't catch his ass first. One down and one to go. You gotta find out if Junior still be over there getting money. If he is, let me know. I'm not gonna wait like I did the first time. You ready to do this next stick I got set up?" he asked KB, as if he knew he had cold feet.

"I'm ready. How much dough you think is gonna be up in there that night?"

"I'm thinking like 350 G's altogether. It could be more. Everybody in the club that night is gonna be a bonus, feel me?"

"That's a lot of dough, and I ain't even spent all that other dough yet," KB said.

"Shit, the last hit wasn't no real money. I probably got fifteen G's left from that shit. I don't hold onto money like that because it got blood on it. I try to spend it as soon as I get it," Stump informed him.

"After this stick, I'ma go away for a minute. You know what I'm sayin'?" KB said to Stump.

"Where you goin'? After this stick, I got another one set up, and I need you to drive for me."

"How long after? I mean, I just wanna go away for a little while with my shorty."

KB needed to get away for a while, because after what happened with Roughhouse, he realized he wasn't really into the robbing and murdering he had experienced hanging with Stump.

"I want to hit this jewelry spot after the club. My man's sister works there, and she told him that her boss be having jewelry that's imported from Italy. He be dropping off half a mil in jewels and cash to the spot."

"So when you gonna have it all set up?" KB asked, disinterested.

"Probably like a week or so after this one, but we gotta do it on a Thursday because the muhfucka only comes there once a month. He's a wholesaler for all the expensive jewelry shops in the diamond district. That's why he drops off so much shit at one time," Stump explained in detail.

"I'm down," KB said, feigning interest.

"A'ight, just make sure when I beep you on this stick, you call me right back. I'm gonna need everybody to be at my crib at the same time, so don't be late."

Stump closed the door as KB walked out.

***

Lakim and Rock were in the back of the building smoking weed when Junior walked up on them. They were sitting on some benches next to the back door with their backs to him.

"Pass Junior the blunt," Lakim said to Rock without turning around.

"Yo, how you know I was behind you?" Junior asked, surprised.

"I told you I got this shit on lock. I got eyes all over this place. They let me know anytime somebody comes through the front or back of the building while I'm out here," Lakim said, revealing the small walkie-talkie he had next to him.

"I'm feeling this. I like the way you got this shit clicking," Junior responded, passing the blunt back to Rock.

"I like it, too. It makes the po-po's job harder. They won't ever catch anybody dirty out here. I'm ready to start back doing hand-to-hand and make some extra money," Rock said, mimicking like he was serving a crackhead.

"You ready to start? Shiiit, I'm ready to start with the way things going over here," Lakim chimed in playfully. "The only thing we gotta worry about is running out of work."

"And that's not gonna happen because I got that shit on smash," Junior joined in, as he sat back and watched the heads who came through the front and exited out the back of the building.

Rock was the enforcer on his shift. He was there in case any stickup kids came or a head tried to get fast with the money. He kept a steel pipe and wooden plank with nails in the grass by the back door.

Rock once used the plank on a crackhead who thought because he was a little older than the worker that he could scare him into giving up his product for free. The worker gave the crackhead the drugs, and when the head left out the front of the building with the product, the worker radioed to Rock and told him what had happened. Rock caught up to the head as he rounded the corner and hit him in his knees with the wooden plank. The crackhead screamed as he hit the ground, holding his knee. Rock swung at his head, missing intentionally to scare him. The crackhead had his hands up in the air pleading with Rock, but Rock wasn't interested in what he had to say. All he wanted the crackhead to know was he didn't tolerate any robbing of the workers. He made him empty his pockets and took back the product the crackhead had stolen, but let him keep what he copped fairly and helped the head to his feet. Then he hit him in the gut to let him know he meant business. Rock never said a word when he beat the crackhead because he wanted the head to wonder how he knew the worker had been robbed. The crackhead wouldn't try it again and probably would warn any other unsuspecting crackheads who were thinking of robbing any of the workers that it wasn't worth the ass whooping.

Junior saw about four G's move in the three hours he was out there with them. He couldn't front. Everything was running smoothly under Lakim's command, but there was one thing that would really make everything complete — Junior had to kill Stump and KB. Eliminating them would make him feel a little safer when he was out there, and it would send a clear message that he and his crew were not to be fucked with. When he had the shootout with Stump, he was scared at first, but when he heard the sound of the gunfire, he had gotten extremely confident about what he was doing. That feeling could be contributed to him going into survival mode when thrown into a dangerous situation, but in any case, he felt in complete control of the situation.

After the shootout, Junior's attitude changed drastically. He always knew that as a hustler he would encounter many dangerous situations, but until it actually happened to him, it wasn't real. Stump opened up the reality of what Junior was doing, and if he planned to stay in the game, he had to adapt and have a killer instinct to ensure his continued existence. He had to take off the kid gloves because although he didn't think he was a major player to the dudes in that hood, he was. In the neighboring projects like Williamsburg and Bushwick, there were hustlers getting their grind on, but Junior was the first real dealer in Baptiste Plaza. Junior believed the guys that lived in Baptiste never thought about selling drugs because they didn't have a capitalist spirit like him.

As the weed took affect on Junior, he sat and thought about how he began hustling.

After living with Shondra for awhile, he noticed her older sister Dee Dee used to always have shady looking characters coming in and out of the house late at night. But, it wasn't until one night when someone came out the door looking for her that he realized she was smoking. Dee Dee didn't have the hardcore crackhead look — you know, the missing teeth, dirty clothes — nor did she have the conniving characteristics, like sticky fingers or the constant game to trick you out of your money. However, the person on the other side of the door had the seasoned look of a smoked-out crackhead. Apparently, Dee Dee must have given the crackhead money to cop so they could get high in the privacy of her room.

After a while, Junior heard Dee Dee arguing with the guy in her room about him shorting her on the weight. The crackhead apparently tapped the capsules before he gave her the drugs. That incident prompted Dee Dee to never let anyone cop for her for fear of getting beat out of her money. Once she started copping for herself, the effects of the drug started to show almost immediately. Dee Dee began stealing from her mother and started making up excuses of why she always needed money. She would sell her food stamps for cash to obtain the hard, white rocks that came in little plastic vials. Junior would watch as Shondra and her mother unsuccessfully tried to get her off the drug by taking her money away from her and trying to keep her in the house, but it was all in vain. She was already hooked to the point where she could lie with a straight face and cry on cue.

Junior never felt any real sympathy for Dee Dee because it was her choice to get involved in using drugs in the first place. He just didn't like to see what she was doing to his girl and her mother. Dee Dee would be out on "late night missions", then come in early the next morning and sleep the entire day away.

One night, Junior stood outside and watched how many times she went to Williamsburg to cop. He counted about twenty times, and it suddenly came to him that if she was copping at five dollars a hit, she was spending at least one hundred dollars. That was just

one person in the course of three or four hours. Then he wondered how much he could make if he had all the heads in the projects coming to him. That was all he needed. The next day, Junior called his man Shon from Farragut Projects. Shon was one of the biggest dealers in his projects. Junior had kept in touch with him through the years, so when he was ready to be introduced to the game, he went to see him.

"Yo Shon, I want to get started in the game," Junior remembered saying.

"Word? I thought you said you wasn't gonna fuck with this shit? What happened? You seeing green skies now?" Shon asked, wiping down his all-white BMW 525.

"Where my girl live at, ain't nobody slingin'. I want to open shop ova there."

"What projects you talkin' 'bout?" Shon asked.

"Never mind all that. Just let me know if you can put the God on or not."

"I can do that. I sell jumbos. I got the biggest nicks this side of the projects and in the Fort. That's why them muhfuckas over there hot with me now. They clientele come way uptown to cop from me."

"I got two hu'ned. Let me get forty jumbos. I'ma break them down to regular nicks and see if I can double my money and get it poppin' over there."

"A'ight, but you could come off better if you let me hit you off with a pack and we split sixty-forty. That way, you don't have to worry about baggin' shit up," Shon tried to coerce Junior.

"Nah, that's all right. I don't wanna work for nobody. Plus, if something goes wrong, that'll kill our friendship, and I like you just the way you are," Junior said jokingly.

"I hear you. You don't want to play Indian. You want to be chief. I can respect that," Shon acknowledged.

Junior took the work Shon gave him and stopped off to the smoke shop on Broadway and Myrtle to get some vials to start his new career in drug selling. Once he made it back to Shondra's room, he emptied all the vials out onto a mirror and transferred the contents into the smaller vials, doubling the amount he started

with. When he was finished, he went out in front of the building to find a crackhead to test his work. He was hoping it would be better than whatever they were copping from Williamsburg and Bushwick so he could stop the traffic and have them come to him. When the tester came back, his eyes were wide and his mouth was twisted. He was nodding his head, letting Junior know the product was good. Junior told him for every five new customers the crackhead brought to him, he would give him one free. The head agreed, and by the next morning, Junior had sold out.

Damn, *he thought to himself.* I just doubled my money in one night. This is where it's at.

Junior went to see Shon again and spent all of what he had made that night. He continued to do this for months, until one day his cousin asked him who he was copping from. Junior told him that he was getting the jumbos from Shon and breaking them down. When his cousin heard that, he laughed out loud and told him he was getting beat every time he spent a gee with Shon. He informed Junior that he could buy the product in weight from Manhattan. Junior was happy with the money he was making, but hearing he could make more, he decided to see what his cousin was talking about.

Junior remembered hearing his cousin talk about going uptown on 141st and Amsterdam. So, he immediately took a trip uptown to find out how he could score his own product. Blind to the fact of where he was going, he was determined to cut his spending with Shon and hopefully triple his profits.

That's how Shon's able to sell jumbos. Slick muhfucka, and he wasn't gonna tell me shit. He was gonna keep lettin' me cop from him at regular price, *Junior thought.*

A Dominican guy walked up to Junior and asked him if he was looking to cop. Junior was taken off guard by the shady character that was speaking to him in broken English.

"What you got?"Junior asked.

"We got hard and soft. What ju lookin' for?" the Dominican man asked.

Junior didn't know what he meant by hard or soft, so he said hard because he thought that must mean crack.

"Okay, come weet me," the Dominican said, as Junior followed him around a corner. As he followed him, other Dominican guys were yelling for him to cop with them.

"How much you spendin', papi?"Junior's Dominican asked once they reached their destination.

"I got a gee," Junior reported.

The Dominican pulled out a calculator and started pressing buttons.

"I give you fifty-nine grams, papi,"he said after looking at a total on the calculator.

"A'ight," Junior said, not knowing how much that really was.

"Give me the money,"the Dominican man said, holding out his hand.

"Nah, papi, I gotta see the shit first," Junior said, wondering if he was about to be robbed.

"Okay, papi. My name is Raul. I go get it for you. Stand in the hallway, okay?"

If Junior had given him the money first, the guy never would have come back. It would have been a rookie mistake.

"A'ight, Raul. I'm Junior," he replied, shaking his hand. "If the shit you give me is good, then you'll see me again real soon."

"I got fish scale, papi, the best perico out here. Ju be back, trust me," he said, then ran up the stairs.

When he came back, they made the transaction, and he gave Junior a Ziploc bag filled with three slabs of beige, crystallized rocks that looked as if they were cut from a pie pan. Junior put the bag in the front of his pants and got ready to walk out of the building.

"Wait, papi. Let me go first to make sure it clear," the Dominican told Junior.

Junior stayed by the door peeking out through the plateglass window. He watched as the Dominican motioned for him to come out. As Junior exited, he left in the opposite direction from which he originally came and headed to the A train on 145th Street.

Junior didn't know how much fifty-nine grams normally cost, but when he got back to Shondra's house and made the calculations, he figured he was paying seventeen dollars per gram.

He bagged up the whole thing and came out with approximately thirty-four hundred dollars' worth of merchandise, which gave him a nice profit. He almost let out a loud yelp as he thought about how he had shortchanged himself the whole time he was copping from Shon, where he was just doubling his money. Now it was on.

Junior had plans of blowing up, and he was going to use Baptiste Projects as his stepping-stone to success. He was the youngest dealer in the area at the tender age of seventeen, and he was his own boss. He was making more money than he had ever seen, and he was enjoying it. He was learning the game fast, and he soon became a threat to the other dealers in the neighboring hoods. He realized how Shon was able to sell jumbos and incorporated those same tactics, taking over the drug business in Shondra's area.

At that time, things were good, but Junior was soon to find out that nothing stayed the same forever.

CHAPTER 11
YOU GOT IT GOIN' ON

Junior dialed the number and waited for someone to answer. A sexy voice on the other line greeted him.

"Hello," the female said.

"Um, hello. This is Junior. Can I speak to Muffin…I mean, Charlene?"

"This is her. Who's this?"

She didn't recognize his voice because it was the first time he had called her since getting her number three weeks ago.

"This is Junior, ma. What da deal?"

"Nuthin'. I'm just chillin', just gettin' in the crib."

"Well, if you just chillin', I got sumthin' you can do."

"And what might that be, sweetie?"

"I can make tonight your night, or I can make it our night."

"That is so corny," she said, laughing, "but I'm with it."

"It's been a long time, Muffin. You still lookin' scrumptious and shit. I'd love to see if you feel the same."

"Whateva, boy. Just because I used to sex you back in da day don't mean you can still hit when you feel like it."

"I ain't sayin' that. I'm just sayin' we got a lot of catching up to do, that's all," Junior clarified.

"Well, if tonight's my night, I'm hungry, so let's go get something to eat."

"That's cool. When you want me to pick you up?"

"Give me about an hour. I gotta shower and get pretty."

"Shit, ma, how do you improve on all that beauty?"

"You still gamin', huh?"

"It's game if you have an opponent. It's the truth when you're dealing with someone exquisite." Junior's game was flawless.

"All right, baby, you got it. Let me give you the address."

"I'll see you in an hour," he said after she gave him the information.

Junior went to Shondra's house to tell her he wouldn't be coming back that night because he had to take care of some important business. Afterward, he went to Craig's house to take a shower and change his clothes. He was still driving the rental he had used to go to Virginia. He had paid for an extra month because he didn't want to take it back yet. As he pulled up in the parking lot of the Tompkins Houses, he looked at Craig's clean 190 E Benz and thought, *Now that would impress the shit outta Muffin.*

"Yo, cuz," Junior called out.

"What up, my dude?" Craig asked, walking over to greet him.

"I need to borrow your whip tonight. I got this chick that I want to pick up, and I need your wheels to seal the deal on the pussy."

"As long as she ain't no chickenhead, because you know they can't even ride in the backseat," Craig said, throwing the keys to Junior and laughing.

"You probably remember her. It's Muffin, the chick I used to fuck with in high school."

"You talkin' 'bout the redbone with the fat ass? Hell yeah, I remember her, and I remember you wouldn't let me hit it either."

"That was my girl back then, muhfucka, and I probably won't let you hit it now either 'cause the ass is much fatter."

"Make sure you strap up. You know how you like raw doggin' them hoes."

"Don't worry 'bout what I do with my piece, cuz," Junior responded, playfully punching at Craig's midsection.

"Ay yo, I want you to hang out with me in a coupla weeks. I'm throwin' my man a coming home party."

"You know I don't do the club scene, son," Junior said.

"I know, but you gonna be with family. Ain't nuthin' gonna jump off in there, and if shit do get outta hand, there's gonna be mad artillery in there. Let me find out you nervous about hanging out wit' your big cuz and enjoying yourself."

"A'ight, let me think about it."

"So tell me, what happened when you went back over to your spot?" Craig asked.

"Yo, La got that shit on lock. It almost reminds me of how you got shit over here clicking. He got shit running real smooth. The only thing I gotta do is collect my dough and keep work on the block. That shit is sweet, son. He got like four dudes on payroll and three soldiers on the team, and all those lil dudes is thorough."

"I hear you, but hear me real quick before you go. That shit sounds sweet, but if you not on the scene, then you won't know what's really goin' on because you absent. Just because you got extra time on your hands, don't take it for granted that everything is going smooth. Once you not on the scene, muhfuckas got a habit of changing the rules and your original setup, and if you don't agree, then you got beef. You understand me? Remember: out of sight, out of mind."

"Yeah, I got you, cuz."

"A'ight, now go ahead and bust a nut for me, too," Craig said, giving him five.

Junior rushed upstairs and took a shower, then put on an all-black velour Sergio Tacchini sweat suit, a black and white Nike T-shirt, and a pair of white Nike Air Max with the black swoosh. He pulled the strings on the sweat pants tight because he was taking his black, pistol grip, .38 revolver with him. He looked at himself in the mirror and liked how the eighteen-inch gold cable with the house piece looked against the black and white T-shirt, and how the jacket brought out the gold nugget watch on his wrist. If nothing had changed about Muffin, he knew she was a gold digger, and this outfit would make her give the pussy up because it was screaming out, "This muhfucka got money!"

Junior wasn't planning on paying for shit except dinner and a hotel room. The only thing she was going to get out of him was a

meal and a hard dick, and he expected some head along with the potential hotel visit. Junior was dressed to kill, literally, and he knew when Muffin saw him and what he was driving, her pussy would be doing somersaults.

The two-story house with the green canopy looked dilapidated and abandoned. Junior checked the address again to make sure it was the right crib and then beeped the horn. The house looked creepy, and he started to hope it was the wrong address, because as good as she looked, she couldn't possibly be living in those conditions. He beeped the horn again, then pulled out his toast and placed it in his lap for precautionary measures. Although shit wasn't looking right, the thought of beating that pussy up was all he was looking forward to.

He truned off the headlights on the car but left the yellow parking lights on. Then he got out of the car, still gripping his toast. He walked up to the broken black gate and pushed it open. It scraped the concrete because it was off the hinge. While looking up at the front door, he started climbing the steps. When he reached the top of the last landing, arriving at the battered double wooden doors, he tried to peek inside to see if the building was abandoned. As he peered through the glass panels in the doors, he couldn't see much of anything because the curtains shielded the glass. He looked for a doorbell, but the fixture on the side only revealed what used to be a doorbell. He turned around to descend the steps of the abandoned building, when he heard the door fly open. Startled, he quickly turned back around, poised to pull his pistol from his side and fire.

"I'm sorry. Are you looking for someone here?" a young woman in a pink housecoat asked him.

He put the gun behind his back, hoping she hadn't noticed it.

"Aah, yes, ma'am. I'm here to pick up Charlene," Junior said respectfully.

"Oh, you must be Junior. She's getting ready. She told me to check if you were out here because no one would be able to hear you knocking. I'm sorry. Would you like to come in?"

"Um, no thank you. I'll just wait for her in the car."

"You have to excuse the condition of the building. I just recently purchased it, and as you can see, there is a lot of work that needs to be done."

"Oh, that's no problem."

"Where are my manners? I'm Ms. Turner, Charlene's mother," the woman said, extending her hand to Junior.

When Junior used to go with Muffin, he never had the chance to meet her mother because she was always working. It was evident where Charlene got her good looks and tight body from because her mom was definitely a superstar, even in her housecoat.

Junior was holding the banister of the stairs with his left hand and the gun in his right hand, which was behind his back. He was faced with a dilemma because she extended her right hand out to him, and he couldn't use his right hand to shake because that hand held the gun.

"Hey Ma, why didn't you tell me he was out here?" Charlene asked, suddenly appearing behind her mother.

Junior saw his chance and switched the gun to the other hand, shaking Ms. Turner's hand as she turned around to look at her daughter.

"I'm sorry. I was trying to invite him in. I didn't want to just leave him standing here on the stoop," Ms. Turner replied.

"Oh okay, so you met my moms, huh?" Muffin asked, switching her attention to Junior.

Junior looked into Muffin's eyes. "Yes. She was talking to me while you were getting ready."

"Thanks, Ma," Muffin said to her mother. "Don't wait up for me. I'll be in late."

"Well, don't come in too late," Ms. Turner replied before going back into the house.

"Don't worry, Ms. Turner, I won't keep her out too late. We're just gonna catch a movie and go out to eat," Junior said, but his true intentions were to dick down her daughter with no grease.

Muffin and Junior made their way down the stairs, and as they walked to the car, Junior got a good look at what she was wearing. She had on a jean skirt that stopped just short of her thick thighs and showed off the form of her hips. Her legs were bare and

looked silky smooth. She had on a tight white shirt that exposed her belly button. He couldn't figure out if the shirt was supposed to fit like that, or if it was just too small for her. Her footwear consisted of white Reebok classics with some white pom pom socks, and she smelled of White Diamonds. Muffin looked good and smelled even better. He put his arm around her waist and palmed her ass gently to test her. Even through the denim he could feel her softness. He couldn't wait to get between her legs.

"You driving this?" she asked when she saw the car.

"Yeah, I drive this when I'm with someone special," he said, applying more pressure to the grip he had on her ass.

"So how many special people ride in here?" She looked at him and smirked.

"A couple, like my moms, sister, aunt — you know, special people."

"Okay, good answer wise guy," she said, as she slid into the passenger seat.

Junior purposely walked past the front of the car so she could get a better view of what he was wearing, then got into the car and pulled off. He was taking her to the Promenade first to set the mood. Once they got there, they walked around and looked over across the water to Manhattan. The skyline illuminated the cool night.

"The city that never sleeps," Muffin remarked, taking in the beauty of the skyline.

"I bet their light bill is high as hell," Junior replied.

They walked to the far end and looked at the ferry to Staten Island as it passed by and then gazed at the Statue of Liberty. He turned her around to him and placed his hand on the small of her back where the curve of her ass began. She nuzzled her head into his chest, gazing into his eyes, and he kissed her passionately. She pushed her front onto him and grinded against him, placing one of her legs between his so he could feel the warmth of her middle. He put his hand under her skirt and ran it up and down her thick thighs, squeezing her ass gently. She moved closer, enjoying the tingly feeling his touch sent to her kitty.

“Come on, baby,” she whispered in his ear. “Let’s go get something to eat so we can finish this on a full stomach.”

“I can get full off of you right here,” he said, as he stooped down and lifted her skirt up.

She had on a pair of fire-red bikini panties that he pulled to the side in order to insert his index finger into her awaiting snatch. She cocked her leg up on the rail, giving him room to operate, forgetting she was outdoors in a public place. Junior kneeled down and licked her clit with the tip of his tongue, while injecting his fingers in and out of her pulsating tunnel with precise movements as she squirmed and moaned with delight. When her legs got weak and trembled, he removed his tongue and took his finger out of her passageway, then looked up at her. Her eyes were closed, and when she finally realized he had stopped midway to her orgasm, she looked down at him licking the finger that was covered with her passion juices. This made her pussy vibrate even more. That was the most erotic, freakiest shit any man had ever done to her, and she wanted him to finish her off. He rose to his feet and looked at her blinking softly, then kissed her again so she could taste her own sweet fluid. Her cat was pulsating, and she could feel herself getting sticky as he rubbed his huge pole onto her through his thin sweat pants.

“DAMN!” was all she could say, as he grabbed her hand and led her like a zombie to the car.

As they drove over the Brooklyn Bridge to the South Street Seaport, Muffin thought of nothing but sexing Junior. After he parked in a twenty-four-hour parking lot, they walked to Uno’s restaurant for dinner. Once inside, Junior went straight to the bar and ordered a double shot of Remy XO for him and a Blue Hawaiian for Muffin as they waited to be seated. Midway through their drinks the waitress seated them and gave them menus. Muffin ordered the shrimp platter with butter sauce and lobster tails, while Junior had the steak dinner with a baked potato. It was always like a gold digging broad to order the most expensive shit on the menu.

As they ate, Muffin couldn’t take her eyes off Junior. He had changed so much over the years since high school. She never thought he would turn out to be so good-looking and well

groomed. His hair was cut in a low Caesar with waves spinning. They were so deep and his hair was so rich like he had Indian in his family. His attire was flawless and everything fit him well, as if it were an Armani suit tailored to his exact build. His big, bulky jewelry accented with diamond chips and the big, bulging wad of money that was evident in his pocket were the bonuses to the physical attraction she already felt for him. He was definitely not the Junior she remembered in her high school days.

The Junior of high school days was book smart. He was in all the gifted classes and excelled at every subject. He wasn't a nerd or anything. He just didn't seem the type to turn out the way he did. He seemed more like the dude that would go to college and get a job working for a big corporation. The young man sitting in front of her undeniably impressed her, not only with his looks and style, but with his sexual antics that floored her and had her wanting to get with him again. When they were together back in high school, they had sex on two occasions, and he wasn't that experienced. He would just get in and bust a nut in five minutes, if that long. The only thing he had going for himself back then was his pole. His shit was big, thick, and shaped like a hook. She looked at him now as a totally different person, a young man on the rise, and she wanted to be with him when he reached the top. All she saw was dollar signs and an easy life, and she wasn't going to let nothing or no one stand in her way of getting just that.

Junior sat back and ate his meal, thinking of nothing but finishing off what he had started with Muffin. She was one fine-ass bitch and soft as hell to boot. He was beaming with confidence and knew he had her in his clutches with the little stunt he pulled at the Promenade. He knew she probably never encountered anything like that before and would literally be begging him for the dick instead of him sweating her for the pussy.

He planned on taking her body places it never been before. Most dudes either denied licking twat or honestly didn't do it, but Junior found out early that eating pussy could get any girl sprung like a broken coil. He perfected his style of lovemaking, learning different things from prostitutes, watching pornos, and trying out new moves with Shondra. He found out if you stopped right before

a woman orgasmed, their body still went through the motions, but the explosive feeling subsided and they yearned for that climax. Once he found that out, he used it to his advantage. The bonus to that was he was blessed with a lot of beef, and his pipe game was just as good as his tongue game.

He planned on making Muffin sweat him more by taking her to a suite at the Marriott on 42nd Street in midtown Manhattan. Yes, he would spend a lot of money, but his plan was to show her the dough without giving her any. He wanted to make sure he had her mind fucked up, giving him full control of what transpired between them, because he didn't want her controlling the outcome of the night.

As he finished his steak and potatoes, he looked up at her with his bedroom eyes and flashed a devilish grin. She understood what he was insinuating from his eye language, so she finished up her platter while he asked for the check. The Uno waitress had been flirting with Junior openly during their meal. She would purposely put her back to Muffin and ask him if everything was to his liking. She came back six to eight times during the course of the meal, each time rubbing up against him with her ass, bending over revealing her breasts, and even making a comment on how tight her uniform was so he could see her camel toe through the thin black pants she was wearing. Junior didn't think Muffin peeped what was happening and didn't mention it in dinner conversation. When the waitress brought the check, he left his number on the back of the bill and a one-hundred-dollar tip that would ensure a phone call from her some time during the week. As they got up to leave, Junior pulled Muffin's chair from under her and let her lead the way out.

"Ooops, I forgot my purse. I'll meet you outside," Muffin said, doubling back to the table.

"A'ight, I'll go get the car and pick you up in the front," Junior replied, leaving the restaurant.

As she went back to the table to get her purse, Muffin scooped up the check and took the tip.

That bitch thinks she slick, but she won't get this fuckin' tip, she thought, as she picked up the one-hundred-dollar bill and looked on the back of the check. She took a pen out of her Louis Vuitton purse and scratched out the number Junior had left on it. Then she took a dollar and wrote the words: YOU'RE LUCKY I'M IN A RUSH, BITCH, OR I WOULD FUCK YOU UP BEFORE YOU GET OFF WORK! Then Muffin walked up to the register and paid for the meal with the money Junior had left.

Muffin was street smart and had peeped everything the waitress was doing all night. She was used to that type of reaction from both broads and guys. It was part of the game. Shit, that's how she and Junior were on the date they were on now. She walked past the waitress, passed her the note written on the dollar, and shot her a look that could freeze fire. As she strutted out the door, she shook her ass extra hard knowing the waitress was watching. The waitress rolled her eyes as she read the words on the back of the dollar. She would have to be more subtle the next time she wanted to get somebody's man.

When Muffin made it to the car, Junior took the FDR to the 42nd Street exit and drove up to 8th Avenue past the peepshows and nude bars. He pulled into the Marriott valet parking area, got out, and went to the front desk. He got the executive suite on the 40th floor, and he and Muffin rode the elevator up to the room. The elevator amazed Muffin. It was fully encased in glass and was built onto the exterior of the building so you could see outside onto the street while you rode up. After Junior opened the door of the suite, Muffin stood in awe as she looked at the biggest, most luxurious hotel room she had ever seen. Junior walked over to the mini bar, took out two rock glasses, filled them with ice, and poured them a drink. She didn't know how to act and didn't want him to see through that fact, but the truth was she was completely taken aback by the room. He passed her the drink and went through the double doors to the bedroom where she watched as he removed his jacket, his sidearm revealed. Yes, he was a true hustler. The gun on his hip solidified that for her. Muffin was in 7th heaven as she took a sip of her drink and joined him in the bedroom. He was sitting on the edge of the bed rolling up a blunt when she entered.

"Turn the cable on," he directed, licking the blunt.

When she walked past him, she tripped over his feet and fell hard in the space between the bed and the dresser.

He chuckled. "You a'ight, ma? You ain't even had none of this sess yet and you trippin' all over yourself."

"It's them big-ass duck feet," she said, getting up off the floor. "You meant to trip me up."

"You right, baby. What better way to make you fall for me?"

"Look, honey, you don't have to trip me to make me fall for you. You're doin' a good job already."

"You make it easy, Muff. All your beauty is magnetic and you pulling me in."

"I hope so, babes. You got it goin' on in more ways than one," she replied.

They smoked and talked about old times. The herb was making Muffin horny and she was getting wet for Junior. She took off her top and lay back on the bed, blowing O's as she rubbed her thighs. Sensing things were getting heated, Junior grabbed her hand and led her to the Jacuzzi in the adjoining bathroom. She disrobed completely as he filled the tub and the water began to bubble. She stepped in as sexy as she could and waited for Junior to enter behind her. He left and returned with two champagne glasses and a bottle of Dom Perignon in his hands.

This dude is not playin' no games. This shit he's doin' is straight outta the movies, Muffin thought.

"Damn, baby, what you tryin' to do, make me fall in love wit' you?" she asked him seductively.

"If that's what it takes to make you a part of me, then hey."

"I'm not gonna front, Junior. You really doin' it to me. You doin' and sayin' all the right things, and right now, I'm on a merry-go-round and I don't want it to stop," Muffin spoke truthfully.

His manners were working a part of her emotions she didn't want revealed, and he was doing it without sexing her first.

Got her ass! Junior thought.

"Like I said, Muff, you make it easy. You're so different from the other chicks. They look for what they can get outta a guy first before looking at what they got in him. Most girls think money is

everything, how much they can get out of a muhfucka and shit. I'm different, ma. I got a lil bit of change, but it means nuthin' if I don't get to spend it on someone that I feel is worthy. Chicks that are interested in my pockets more than the dude that's wearing the pants turn me off. I don't like females that expect clothes and jewelry as soon as a muhfucka busts a nut because that means they sellin' pussy, and if I want a prostitute, I would go on Eleventh Ave. At least I know what I'm gettin' for my money. You feel me, ma?"

Muffin moved closer to him in the Jacuzzi. He was being real and she respected his honesty. She felt like he was trying to tell her what position she could play in his life if she was going to be real with him.

Junior was playing on her emotions hard. He was hoping if he came at her with an unorthodox approach, he would have her mind, giving him total control of her actions. With what he was going through now, it would be good to have another person other than Shondra that he could trust, someone who would be willing to do anything for him so he wouldn't have to put Shondra in any danger. He felt a female was the only candidate for that kind of trust, and he was banking on Muffin. He felt females were more loyal than guys in this game only because they dealt with emotion differently. He felt if he could get a female to fall deep in love with him, she would remain loyal to him as long as her love for him stayed strong. During that time, he would be able to trust her to do almost anything for him.

Muffin was zoning. She never had a guy talk to her like that before. Junior was changing her mind about him, and she was really feeling what he was saying to her. After tonight, she was going to stick to him like glue if he let her. Although she knew he had a girl, there was something different about him. He wasn't afraid of expressing himself to her. He was open and revealed a lot to her, and that meant a lot. He was the first man to make her feel the way she was feeling, and it felt good.

She grabbed his hand and got out of the fizzy water, leading him to the bed. Junior followed her like a puppy, and when they reached the bed, she sat down and grabbed his other hand.

"I want to please you, daddy. I want to make you feel better than any girl has ever made you feel in your life," Muffin professed.

Junior stood there looking down at her beautiful face. He had sealed the deal. She was sprung. Her emotions were overflowing, and she wasn't trying to hide it.

"Daddy, I know you got a girl," she said, stroking his pole gently. "I'm willing to play second only if you guarantee me that it'll be just me and her. I can tell you're different from all the other guys I ever wasted my time with, and I want to prove to you that I can be your right hand from now on. Whatever you ask of me, daddy, I will do it without question. Just promise me that we will be together."

She put him in her wet mouth and started making slurping sounds as she looked up at him to make sure he was enjoying what she was doing. The sounds he made told her that he was into it. She sucked the head of his snake and licked around the rim with her tongue. As she positioned her head upright, she grabbed his hips with both hands and tried to insert all of him into her open mouth. She inched it in slowly, deep throating his huge mass. Growing excited, Junior started pumping in her mouth like it was her pussy, and she let him. She squeezed her jaw muscles when he pulled out and opened wide when he went in. When he started moving in and out rapidly, she knew he was close to climaxing. She felt the hot jism release into her mouth, oozing straight down her throat. This was the first time she had swallowed. She held onto him and continued slurping until he was completely drained. His body relaxed and she continued to suck on him until he started moaning loudly. When she looked up at him, his eyes were closed, showing complete satisfaction. She was pleased to know she had made him feel good.

She took her mouth off him slowly and licked up and down his shaft, then she rose to kiss him. They both fell onto the bed, and then he took control by spreading her legs and licking the inside of her thighs. She was already wet as he rubbed his finger across her clit. She winced a little and started swiveling her hips. As he put his tongue on her clit, she felt tingly all over again like at the

Promenade. He was a master at what he was doing. After licking her to a climax, he inserted his staff into her slowly, taking his time. She was beside herself with pure pleasure. He sucked her nipples gently, and then he did something she had never experienced. He put his hands under her ass and began fingering her asshole. It felt weird at first, but he was being methodical in his motions. She felt his finger enter her asshole little by little until he was working both his finger and cock simultaneously in each hole. She began to shiver as the pain and pleasure consumed her entire body. She was about to detonate like a dirty bomb and began making noises she had never heard come out of her mouth before. Then, in an instant, she was screaming at the top of her lungs.

"OHHHHH MYYYY GGGGGOOOOOOOODDDDDDD!"

She had cum so hard that her legs were shaking like someone was electrocuting her. He continued to thrust his pole in and out, quicker and quicker. She wasn't in control of her breathing. It was like she was having an asthma attack. Then she came again, screaming a second time in delight.

"GGGGGOOOOODDAAMMMMNNNIITTT!"

Her legs muscles tightened and she was finished. Junior continued stroking until he came, then rolled over beside her. She was sweaty and utterly confused. This was the first time she had a double orgasm. This wasn't fucking. This was how someone made love to you, something she never experienced before. She suddenly began to cry and couldn't stop.

"I'm sorry, baby. Did I hurt you?" Junior asked in a concerned voice, propping himself up on his elbows.

She threw her arms around his neck and squeezed tightly, placing her head on his shoulder.

"Junior, I love you," she murmured between sobs.

CHAPTER 12
TO THE LOVE OF MONEY

Things were going so good in the hood that Lakim decided to take some of the workers to Ryders, a neighborhood strip club. One of his friends from school told him they were having a lock-in, and he decided he'd take some of the workers to show them a good time. Lakim's intention was to try to build a structure of trust and loyalty among the chosen workers. He wanted to be sure when the time came for them to bust their guns for him that they would do so without hesitation.

"Y'all muhfuckas ready to go?" he asked his bunch.

"Yeah!"

They were going to enjoy themselves thoroughly because Lakim was paying for everything. They were going to be in there the whole night, and he expected to get them sucked and laid without them worrying about coming out of their pockets. Lakim chose these particular guys because they were the ones that made the most money on the block and were something like his inside informants. They would tell him everything that was going on in the hood from the workers who weren't happy, to the heads that were going to other spots to cop. Lakim liked playing the boss and liked being in total control of what happened on the block. He called the shots, and as far as he was concerned, he was the boss.

Lakim and the workers arrived at the strip club in the 1989 Acura Legend he purchased three weeks ago. When they pulled up, there were a lot of people waiting on the line to get inside. Lakim walked up to the door with his crew of four men and walked straight in, bypassing the people waiting on line. He was a regular, so he got VIP service. He didn't have to pay at the door and he had his own table. The workers had never been to the club before, so they were impressed with the star treatment extended to Lakim.

Lakim walked to his regular table, which had two bottles of Moet sitting in ice buckets waiting for him. After they sat down, he popped the cork and poured everyone a drink.

"To the love of money and power!" he toasted.

Everyone clinked their glasses together and drank the bubbly liquid down. The club was full of beautiful women in exotic lingerie, thongs, and bikini sets. Three strippers came over to the table and sat down between Lakim and his boys. They were gorgeous — big breasts, round asses, and thick thighs. The boys were drooling as they watched one of them give Lakim a lap dance right at the table, while he acted as if he wasn't interested. He did this because he wanted them to know the treatment was nothing special to him. He was used to a beautiful woman grinding herself against him. At least that's what he wanted them to think. The strippers would do whatever he wanted because he was a hustler and hustlers doled out big money. They would work their way around to all the big spenders and linger with the ones that spent the most.

Lakim's boys continued to drink and enjoy themselves. Lakim told them to go to the stage, giving each of them one hundred dollars in singles to tip the girls. They practically ran over to the stage to see which one of the fine strippers they would be able to get with in the VIP room.

On stage were three strippers who knew Lakim very well. He usually had two of them meet him at a hotel for a threesome, paying each five hundred dollars for their services. They loved when Lakim came around or beeped them for that special service. They would drop whatever they were doing because they

genuinely liked him and didn't have anyone that tipped as well as he did.

One of the girls, Bubbles, was talking with a guy who had a long scar down the side of his face. The guy was trying to get her and her friends to go with him to a hotel and have a ménage a trois. He was flashing a knot of money, but she wasn't interested because something about him didn't feel right. He looked treacherous and untrustworthy. She had experiences before with shady characters that used money to persuade her to go with them and then refused to pay for her services. This guy looked like one of those characters. She kept trying to reject him in a nice way, but he was being very persistent. Lakim walked by the stage to see how his boys were getting along with the strippers, and that's when Bubbles got his attention. When she saw Lakim, she whistled. He looked up at her and went to greet her. As he walked over to her, he palmed her soft, velvety ass and slid a twenty-dollar bill in her thong. She stooped down and whispered something in his ear and he nodded. Then he laughed and walked off to where his boys were sitting.

"Yo, my man, you know that ho Bubbles?" the guy with the scar walked up and asked Lakim.

"Yeah, what's up?" Lakim answered.

"I'm tryin' to get the ho to do a threesome with her girl, but she frontin' on me," the guy explained.

"A'ight, so what you want me to do?" Lakim looked the guy up and down, noticing the long scar.

"I'm saying, if you know her like that, just tell her I'm good peoples and that she safe with me," he said, pulling a brick of money out of his pocket to prove he had bank.

"I hear you, bruh, but I ain't that ho's pimp, and I can't co-sign for you 'cause I don't know you like that," Lakim informed him.

"My bad. My name is Drez. I got shit locked down in the Stuy," he said, extending his hand out for a shake.

"I'm La. I hustle in Bushwick, Baptiste Projects and I got that shit on lock ova there," Lakim replied, shaking his hand and letting him know he was getting money, too.

"What up, La? Look, kid, I'm trying to get these hoes to go to my hotel after this shit, and she flakin' on me. You ever got down with dem hoes like that?"

"Yeah, I got them a couple of times, but like I said, I can't really vouch for you like that."

"How about you come to the room wit' me so they know e'erything is e'erything?" Drez suggested.

"I don't know. I got my boys with me right now," Lakim responded, glancing at his crew.

"I got my boys with me, too, but it could be just you, me, and them hoes. Shit, we can bring six and make it a real party if you want."

"A'ight, let me go talk to her and see what's up," he replied.

"That's cool, fam. Come over to my table when you set it up. I'm sitting over by the VIP," Drez said, pointing to a table in the corner that was roped off.

The table he was sitting at was reserved for the heavy rollers, guys that held real paper. The people in that section usually spent no less than five thousand. This peaked Lakim's interest in him, and he decided to help him out as much as he could just so he could make himself more popular to his workers. Once they saw him over in the roped-off VIP section, he would gain more respect.

He walked over to Bubbles and asked her if she would be willing to take five of her friends to a hotel with him and Drez after the lock-in. Bubbles trusted Lakim, but she asked around and heard some things about Drez that made her uncomfortable. "I don't know, La. I heard a lot about that dude, and it ain't all good," she enlightened him.

"I hear you, baby, but I'm gonna be right there wit' you. I'm gonna make sure you safe. Don't you trust me?" Lakim asked, then directed his attention to where Drez was sitting because they were throwing massive amounts of bills in the air around one of the strippers.

"La, do you really know this guy like that? I mean, I heard he killed some guy from 'round your way a while back for robbing one of his workers. He killed him, La," she said warily to the back of Lakim's head.

"Huh? Umm nah, I don't know about that," Lakim mumbled, then turned his attention to Bubbles. "I'm saying, baby, you gonna be with me, so you safe. You don't have to worry about nuthin' happening while I'm there with you."

Knowing Drez was a real baller made Lakim gravitate to him. He had a no-nonsense look about him that would make anyone think twice about fucking with him. No one would dare fuck with Lakim if he was affiliated with a known murderer. And when he thought no one, he meant NO ONE.

"Okay, baby, I'm only gonna do this because you givin' me your word that everything is gonna be all right," Bubbles said, finally giving in.

"That's my baby."

Lakim was sure getting her to go with them would put him in good standing with Drez, especially since Drez was unable to get her to commit to going with him alone.

When Lakim walked over to the roped-off area, Drez waved him in. He poured Lakim a glass of Dom and looked into his eyes to see if he was successful in getting him what he wanted.

"It's a go?" Drez asked, blowing smoke out his mouth from the blunt he had between his teeth.

"Yeah, I took care of everything," Lakim said proudly.

"That's good. So when's it going down?" Drez asked.

"Right after the lock-in. I didn't tell her where 'cause I don't know where we goin'."

"That's cool. I got a suite at the Radisson in midtown," Drez said. "I'm gonna let my boys take my Jag, and we gonna ride in the limo I rented."

"Okay. When you ready, just come get me at my table ova there," Lakim said, pointing to where he was sitting.

Lakim wasn't intimidated by Drez. He didn't have time to be because he was too impressed by his obvious status and power. Lakim suddenly had a brainstorm, and when he and Drez freaked off with Bubbles and her friends, he was going to see if Drez would be interested in making a move with him to take over Baptiste from Junior's clutches so Lakim could be the acting boss, clear and free.

***

Something about the way KB was acting lately was making Gloria nervous. He wasn't himself for the past two nights, and tonight he was getting ready to leave her again. He told her that he wasn't going to be back until late Sunday night, and when she asked him where he was going, he wouldn't tell her anything. Gloria wasn't big on being nosey, but ever since she had the talk with Shondra, she was curious about his movements and whereabouts.

KB was in the bedroom making a phone call because his beeper had gone off, and Gloria was about to do something she had never done before. She went into the kitchen, hit the mute button on the telephone, and picked up the receiver.

"I'm getting ready to leave in a minute," she heard KB saying to the person on the other end.

"Yo, don't be late, muhfucka."

"I won't. I'm on my way out as soon as I hang up," KB replied.

"I'ma need you to pick up those other guns from my man before you come to the crib. I can't go because I'm waiting on the bouncer to come and give me the exact time to be there."

"Where at?" KB asked.

"Go to Iron Tires, the auto shop on Pierce Street. I already called and told him that I'm sending somebody to pick them up for me."

"A'ight, I'll go pick them up and meet you at your crib once I get them," KB responded.

"Make sure you take a cab from the shop. It's a lot of big shit he givin' you, and you don't need to get stopped on the street wit' all that artillery. It's enough to go to war with the troops in Vietnam."

"I hear you. I'm out. See you in a minute," KB said, hanging up the telephone.

Gloria hung up after she heard KB put down the receiver on his end, then rushed back to the living room. Now she knew why

KB was acting so suspiciously. It sounded like he was about to do another stickup.

KB was sitting on the bed thinking how stupid he was for calling Stump back when he was paged. He should have just went straight to his crib and said he never got the beep. Now he had to go pick up an arsenal of guns. It was obvious that they were the guns they would be using when they robbed the club Saturday night. He was going to be taking a chance going to get the guns, but there was no way around it. He would either do it or get done by Stump, which was not an option.

KB got up off the bed and put on his jacket. Now he had to go face Gloria and tell her that he wouldn't be coming back until Sunday, hopefully. He couldn't tell her where he was going because he promised her that he wouldn't do anymore stickups. He wished he hadn't told her about the last robbery he went on with Stump. Then he would be able to tell her anything and she would believe it. After he told her about his first robbery, she was always hounding him about getting into trouble with Stump, and she was always trying to find out where he was when he wasn't with her. He hated lying to her, but he had no choice.

"Where you going?" Gloria asked when KB came out of the room with his jacket on.

"I gotta go take care of something," he replied, not looking directly in her eyes.

"When you comin' back?" Gloria asked him.

"I'll be back lata on," KB lied.

"Why you lyin' to me, K? Why won't you tell me where you goin'?" Gloria pleaded.

"Come on, Glo, let me go and take care of my business. Don't put me through this shit."

"You know you about to go do something real stupid, K. Why you lyin'?"

"Look, Glo, I gotta go take care of some business. Just let me go without a hassle."

"What business, K? Is it wit' that killer Stump? I know you going to see him. I know you 'bout to do some more stupid shit. I don't believe you, K. You say you love me, but all you do is lie and keep shit from me. If you love me, you won't leave right now. If you really and truly love me, you'll stay here with me." Gloria's eyes filled up with tears.

KB didn't want her to cry, and he didn't understand why she was so emotional. He had something to do, and that was it. It wasn't anything for her to cry over. If he didn't go and Stump caught up with him, she would really be crying — at his funeral.

"Come on, Glo, get out of my way so I can go," he said, gingerly pushing her to the side and opening the door. "I said I'll be back. Just relax."

"You gonna just leave me like that? You don't love me, K. You don't know what love is!" she screamed, as he opened the exit door and went down the stairs. "Fuck you!" she said to herself, and she meant it.

Shondra was watching a movie on the VCR when her phone rang. She saw on the caller ID that it was Gloria calling.

"What up, girl?" she answered.

"You was right. I don't know shit 'bout that muhfucka!" Gloria wailed through the phone line.

"What you talkin' 'bout?" Shondra asked.

"KB. He goin' out to do some more dumb shit with that muhfucka Stump. I was listening on the phone when he was talking to him. The muhfucka treat KB like he his son. He told him to go pick up some guns, and he ran outta here like his father sent him on an errand. I asked him where he was going, and don't you know that black muhfucka lied to me in my face? I started to tell him that I knew what he was about to do, but I was scared he might fuck me up for listening in on his phone call. I'm scared for him, Shondra. I don't want nuthin' to happen to him. That muhfucka Stump is bad news."

"Did he say what they were gonna do? I mean, do you know exactly what they gonna do?" Shondra asked.

"No, but I know that he going to pick up a whole bunch of guns from some auto shop on Pierce Street. Whatever it is, I think it's major because the guy on the phone was telling him that there was enough guns for them to go to war."

"Damn, that's really serious," Shondra said, a little worried.

“I’m coming downstairs, Shondra. Leave the door open for me,” Gloria said, hanging up the telephone.

Good, Shondra thought. *That’ll give me time to beep Junior.*

After beeping him, she put in her code to let him know to call right back, then she continued watching *The Usual Suspects.*

Junior was on his way uptown with Muffin. They had spent every day together since the night of their first date. Muffin was in love, so in love she was willing to do any and everything Junior asked of her. He asked her to go with him to cop, and like a good soldier, she agreed. They were on the A train going to 145th Street. He had almost forty G’s on him and was a little nervous, but Muffin had his .45 auto in her purse. He showed her how to take if off safety, aim, and pull the trigger if necessary. She was down with whatever he said as long as he was with her. He would be fronting if he said he wasn’t catching a little bit of feelings for her, but he knew he couldn’t go there with her because of Shondra. He loved Shondra with all his heart, and she was his “for real” road dog. She was the one there for him when he needed someone most. No, he couldn’t violate the bond they had just for Muffin.

“This is the A train to 205th Street; 145th Street next stop. Please watch the closing doors,” the conductor said over the train’s PA system.

“Come on, ma, that’s the stop we gonna get off,” Junior informed Muffin.

“Mmmmm, daddy, I love being in your arms. You know you spoiling me, right?” Muffin purred.

“Yeah, I know, but you gotta be on point right now. We ‘bout to take care of some serious shit,” Junior said seriously.

“I got your front and your back, daddy,” Muffin reassured Junior.

Once the train doors opened, they exited the train and walked up the stairs. The sun was beaming down. It was a cool day, and there were a lot of people out on the streets. They walked up the hill toward Broadway, then turned left on Amsterdam Avenue. Junior took this route a thousand times, and every time he made this trip, he had butterflies until he made it back to Brooklyn. They

walked hand in hand like a couple and went into a corner bodega to buy some cigarettes.

"This is the first time I'm bringing somebody with me, so just relax and do what I tell you," Junior told Muffin when they got to the spot. "What up, Ponchito?" he said to a dark-skinned Dominican man. "You ready for me?"

"Jes, papi, but who is this chiquita with you?" he asked Junior, eyeing Muffin suspiciously.

"This my girl. It's been hot, so she's gonna carry my shit for me. Is that gonna be a problem?" Junior answered.

"No problema, but joo know she can't come upstairs, papi," the Dominican reported.

"Bullshit! I been coppin' from Venezuelo for years. If I can't bring my girl, then I'ma find another connect!" Junior threatened.

"Let me see if it's okay first, papi. Sigame."

They followed closely behind, and when the Dominican got to the door, he tapped on it three times and waited for a response.

"¿Quién está allí? (Who's there?)" a Dominican woman's voice asked from behind the door.

"It's Ponchito. Diga a Venezuela que su amigo esté aquí." He told the woman that he wanted to see Venezuela and that he had someone with him. "Y eso él tiene una muchacha con él." Then Ponchito explained that Junior had a woman with him.

"Un momento," the woman replied.

The door opened, and a big-bellied Dominican man beckoned Junior and Muffin inside, hugging Junior on sight and shaking Muffin's hand.

"Come in, come in," Venezuela said, showing them to the couch. "Did Ponchito give you a hard time, amigo?"

"Nah, not really. This is my girl, Charlene," Junior introduced Muffin. "I brought her with me so she can carry the shit for me because it's hot over here."

"No problem, my friend. Just last week the policia run up in my other apartment across the street. They no get nothing, but they make big mess in there. You hungry? Mia, you hungry?"

"No, thank you," Muffin replied.

"I'm good," Junior also declined.

“Okay, so let’s go into the other room. Excuse us, mia,” Venezuela said, picking up the remote control and handing it to Muffin.

Muffin took the remote and started channel surfing. She sat back and looked around the modest apartment. Pictures of Saint Mary, little statues of religious prophets, and rosary beads hanging on the frames of pictures were littered throughout the small apartment. She was looking for a family portrait, and when she didn’t see one, she figured this was just one of Venezuela’s girl’s houses.

Muhfuckas is the same no matter where they’re from, she thought.

“I want two keys,” Junior said to Venezuela, as they sat down in the bedroom that was transformed into Venezuela’s office.

“No problem. You moving up, I see. Business must be good.”

Venezuela was Junior and Craig’s connect and had the rawest coke that side of Manhattan. His coke looked like it had diamond crystals in it and was pure as a virgin in a monastery. Venezuela liked Junior because he never came short and always conducted business in a professional manner. Venezuela didn’t allow many hustlers in his home, but he had grown to trust Junior and Craig over the years and wanted to make them feel more comfortable when they did their transactions.

“How much you lettin’ me get it for?” Junior asked.

“Seventeen thousand a key. I give you extra half-ounce because I have new product from Peru, better than the other shit from Colombia,” he said, smiling at Junior. “I no have it long, so you get as much as you can before I run out. This perico will make your business do even better.”

“Let me go get the money from my girl,” Junior said, getting up from his chair.

Venezuela got up with him and went to call a runner to bring the two keys over to him.

“You hungry, ma?” Junior asked Muffin, as he counted out the money. “Because this is gonna take a little time.”

“No, I’m all right. You about to give him all that money?” Muffin asked, while looking at all the bills.

"Don't start asking no questions now, Muff. Just sit back and chill 'til we done," Junior directed.

"Oh, I'm sorry, daddy."

After Venezuela put the cash in the money machine and verified the amount, they went into a kitchen where he cooked up the two kilos of coke, then weighed it out on a triple-beam scale when it dried. Venezuela put the finished goods into a bag, and Junior took the Ziploc bag filled with the product in the shape of pies and placed it in Muffin's pocketbook. Venezuela gave Junior and Muffin a hug before going into the back room.

"I'll see you in two weeks," Junior told him as the door closed.

Ponchito was downstairs waiting for customers when Muffin and Junior got to the lobby.

"Joo straight, papi?" Ponchito asked.

"Yeah," Junior replied, the butterflies fluttering around in his stomach.

He passed Ponchito a one-hundred-dollar bill and waited for him to give him the all-clear signal. Then he and Muffin walked out hand in hand and crossed the street, heading for the train station.

"Don't look back," Junior told her as a blue and white patrol car drove by slowly.

Just then, his beeper started to vibrate and he quickly turned it off without looking, not wanting to draw any unnecessary attention to himself. He would check it when he got back to Brooklyn. Muffin was nervous because if the police were to stop them and found out she was holding drugs and a gun in her pocketbook, there would be no way around getting locked up.

"Don't be nervous, ma," Junior coached. "They not the one that jump out on people. They probably on them Dominicans' payroll."

"I'm all right, baby," Muffin replied.

When they got to the train station, the tension was eased.

"How much shit is this?" she whispered to Junior.

"Two keys," he replied, looking down the tunnel, impatiently waiting for the A train to arrive.

"That's a lot, right?"

"Ummmhmmm," he replied, not trying to engage in a deep conversation.

"I did good, right, baby?" Muffin looked at Junior through soft eyes.

"You did fine, luv. You my Bonnie," he said, reassuring her that she was more than his mule. "You wanna learn how to bag up when we get to Brooklyn?"

"Anything for you, baby, anything for you," she said, as a train roared into the station.

***

Dusty and Rock were watching the workers when they heard on the walkie-talkie that noccos (detectives) were circling the block. Rock informed the lookout to get off the corner and go across the street and sit on the side of the building. Then he told the workers in the back to get clean just in case the Ds jumped out on them. They all complied and stood in a group like cattle in a herd, watching for predators. Lakim came up and asked what was happening. They explained the police were hot, so they were slowing down for a minute.

"Yo, Rock," Lakim said, "go on the other side 'til shit quiet down on this end. You know if they see you, they gonna fuck wit' you. Take the money on the other side and go through the back when you leave."

"You right. I hate the fuckin' po po. Ay Dusty, give me that dough you got on you," Rock told his friend.

"What up, Dusty?" Lakim asked, as he turned his attention to him. "I ain't seen you in a minute. You a'ight?"

"I'm good. Just been spending time with my lady," Dusty responded dryly.

"Yeah, that bitch got you sprung," Rock chimed in.

"Chill with the bitch shit. That's my girl now, duke," Dusty informed Rock.

"Oh, now that's your girl? Man, she ain't nuthin' but a pretty Puerto Rican closet smoker," Rock said.

"Chill, Rock. Don't you see he's serious?" Lakim said.

"Don't tell him shit. When I snuff him, he'll know I'm serious," Dusty responded, anger evident in his tone.

"Ahh man, you gonna beat me up ova a ho? You my man and the whole nine. You mean to tell me you'll let a crackhead come between us?" Rock said, smirking.

"I already told you that's my lady, muhfucka. Why you just can't respect that and stop dissin' her in front of me?" Dusty eyed Rock.

"'Cause she a crackhead, that's why. Why don't you find you a regular chick to make your girl? Why you gotta go get a crackhead?"

"A'ight, y'all both chill out before this shit gets serious," Lakim said.

"Shit, he act like she somebody. Everybody 'round the way don' hit that. Even Junior done test drove that shit," Rock said truthfully.

When Dusty started walking up on Rock, Lakim grabbed him to avoid the confrontation.

"Don't hold him. Let him go. If he wants to thump over that ho, then I'll fuck him up and bring him to his senses," Rock instigated.

"Ain't near one of y'all fighting. Just chill out. Go 'head, Rock, and take that money to the other side and put it up," Lakim instructed.

Rock started to walk away as Lakim and Dusty talked.

"That's why his ass don't be out here no more. He be chasin' down that bitch. You better check to make sure he ain't in the closet with that bitch," Rock yelled out as he walked toward the other side of the projects.

"See what I'm talkin' 'bout?" Dusty broke free from Lakim and ran down the street behind Rock.

Rock didn't see Dusty until it was too late. All he felt was pain in the back of his head. Rock stumbled forward, his hands breaking his fall.

"What up, muhfucka!" Dusty screamed at Rock.

After scurrying to his feet, Rock threw lefts and rights in a furious barrage, knocking Dusty backward onto the wall of the building.

"Look, B, don't make me hurt you ova no ho," Rock said, grabbing both of Dusty's arms, "I'm just keepin' it real with you. You my fam first, muhfucka."

"Fuck you!" Dusty barked, as he wrestled free and swung at Rock's head.

He missed with a right but connected with a left to Rock's jaw. Rock winced from the blow, then continued his onslaught of punches to Dusty's midsection and face. By the time Lakim and the workers reached them, the fight was over. Dusty was threatening Rock to get off him, while Rock sat on top of him giving him hefty blows to every exposed area.

"Get the fuck off me!" Dusty cried.

"Get off him, Rock!" Lakim commanded when he reached the duo.

"I am. I just want him to understand why he got this beatdown. That bitch ain't worth it."

Rock got up off of Dusty, backed up, and waited for round two, but Dusty just got to his feet and kept with his threats.

"Look, it's already hot out here. We don't need no more heat," Lakim said. "Y'all dudes squash this shit and let's get back to business. Y'all hear me?"

"Yeah," they both replied reluctantly.

"I'm gonna talk to you in a minute, Rock. I'll meet you on the other side in a while. Just me and you." Then Lakim turned to Dusty. "We gotta talk right now. Let's walk."

As they walked, Lakim began, "Look, kid, you know Rock your man, and you know that he wouldn't say shit to hurt you. He just trying to look out for you. You gotta see the positive in what he's sayin'. Ask yourself a question…have you been out here on your shift lately?"

"Not really, but that's only because…" Dusty started.

"That's what I mean," Lakim interrupted. "You can't give no excuses, son. This is some serious shit we dealing with out here. When you not here on your shift, Rock is the one that takes your

slot and you still get paid. He sees that you slippin', and he just tryin' to get you to get your mind back right before it's too late. Ain't nothing wrong with fucking with them bitches, but you can't fall in love with them and have that interfere with your money. You gotta remember they want what you got access to, so you don't even know if she wit' you for you or for what you can give her. You feel me, kid?" Lakim found himself preaching as Junior would have done with him.

Dusty's pride was hurt. He felt like everyone was coming down on him. He didn't see Lizzette as a crackhead. He saw her as an older woman that cared about him.

The truth was that Lizzette had Dusty's mind all fucked up. She used his immaturity to get what she wanted from him. He was giving her money and product almost every night they were together. She stopped him from going to her house, using a bullshit excuse so she could spend all her time at his house around his stash. Lizzette was a cunning fox. She used her beauty and sexual experience to get Dusty to do things he normally wouldn't agree to.

One night, Lizzette used her womanly wiles to get him to do the unthinkable. He got high with her. They were having sex, and she told him if he took a toke of her blunt, it would make him last longer. He was skeptical at first, but she put a lot of pressure on him and he folded. Dusty took the blunt from her and pulled on it. The weed and crack combined together gave him an unusual high. He was speeding from the cocaine but also feeling the depressant of the cannabis. His heart rate increased, and then he was overcome with a panicky feeling. Lizzette studied his reaction, then put his dick in her mouth and sucked him to his climax. She figured if he reached his peak, he wouldn't be able to distinguish if it was the drugs or her that made him feel so good. As the night continued, they smoked more and more, getting higher and higher. Then she took him to his graduation. She introduced him to the pipe. Dusty was so high and his mind was so jumbled that he didn't realize what he was doing to himself. By the time he did, it was too late because he was hooked. She coached him and taught him how to get the full effect of the blast by holding the smoke in

his lungs for a long period of time, and before the night was out Dusty was a product of his own destructive ways. During the days that followed, Dusty found himself married not only to the drug, but also to the perpetrator of his habit. He tried to refrain from indulging, but the more he fought the urge, the more Lizzette cajoled him. It was a losing battle. In the end, he was in love with both of them – the woman and the drug.

Lakim continued to talk to Dusty, but he didn't seem interested in what Lakim was telling him. Dusty was wondering if his main man Rock really knew what was going on with him. To Dusty, his ways and actions didn't show he was strung out on the same product he was supposed to be selling. Dusty tried to focus on what Lakim was saying, but his mind was flooded with too many thoughts. He was too far gone and didn't know how to ask for help.

"I hear you, La. I know I been slippin' and I should be on top of my game, but to keep it real wit' you, she got me fucked up in the head real bad," Dusty confessed.

"That's what Rock was saying. He musta peeped it and told you, but you so caught up you not hearing him." Lakim had the feeling there was something more to what was going on with Dusty, but he didn't want to speculate.

"Look, La, I'm gonna get back on my job. You don't have to worry about this shit no more," Dusty promised.

"A'ight, I hear you, but this is the last time, Dusty. Rock been carrying you for a minute now, and I know he tired," Lakim emphasized.

"I know and I respect that. You got my word, La. I'm back to work."

Dusty slapped Lakim five and then walked off to the back of the building. It was the weekend and he needed to make some money because he had to meet Lizzette later on that night.

***

KB got out of the cab on Flushing Avenue and walked up the walkway to Stump's building. Some young guys were out there gambling as he passed by with the big duffle bag full of guns. When he got inside the building, he saw someone serving a crackhead by the stairs, which was unusual in Stump's building because he didn't allow any drug selling in front of or inside his building. When KB got upstairs, everyone was sitting around drinking and smoking weed.

"What up, K?" Stump asked, passing him the blunt he was smoking when he opened the door.

"Nuthin'. I didn't know you were slingin'," KB said nonchalantly.

"What you talking 'bout?" Stump asked him, a perplexed look growing on his face.

"I seen some young dudes serving a head in the lobby. I remember you sayin' that you told all dem young cats that they couldn't hustle in front of your building, so I figured it had to be your shit he was selling."

"WHAT!" Stump boomed. He hated drug dealers because of what happened to his mom. It didn't take any heart to sell drugs to an addict, and it didn't take any skill to make the money.

Stump opened the duffle bag KB brought in, pulled out a sawed-off shotgun, and then headed for the door. The rest of the guys got up on cue and followed him out. KB thought he was going to stay behind, but Stump beckoned him, too, because he wanted him to ID the kid that he saw selling in his building.

When they reached the lobby, no one was there. So, Stump opened the door and went outside. There was a group of young boys in front of the building, but when they saw Stump and the shotgun, they took off running.

"Don't run you little muhfuckas, or I make y'all a fuckin' memory!" he growled, pointing the shotgun in their direction. "Which one of them sold in my building?" Stump asked KB.

"That one over there," KB said, pointing the guy out as the young crew looked at him like the snitch he was.

"Danny?" Stump asked, pointing the shotgun at the young boy's head. "This my lil man." Stump looked at Danny, flames flickering in his pupils. "Why the fuck would you do that? You know I don't tolerate that shit in my building. Get the fuck in the building, all of y'all!"

The young boys all filed into the building and were shocked when they saw all the guns aimed at them. Visions of dying were on all their minds.

"Empty your fuckin' pockets," Stump screamed.

Everyone complied, and Danny was the only one with drugs on him. Stump scooped up the vials of crack and money and handed them over to KB, along with the shotgun. Then, in a flash, he slapped the spit out of Danny.

"Whose shit is this?" Stump asked him menacingly.

"La," the young boy replied, spitting out blood.

"Who the fuck is La?" Stump asked, looking each of the boys in their eyes.

"La is from Baptiste," KB interjected.

"Get the fuck outta here. Is that the dude that be with that Junior character we had the shootout with?" Stump looked at KB, then turned his attention back to the young guy. "You workin' for them muhfuckas?"

"We robbed one of their workers a couple weeks back, and to stop us from sticking them up, they gave me work so I wouldn't hit them again," the young boy Danny explained.

"So you took they shit, and then you gonna come here and violate? Is that what you're telling me?" Stump balled both fists up tightly.

"It's not like that, Stump. Ain't nowhere to sell out here, and I know nobody sells outta this building. All I was trying to do was get some clientele and then tell them I was gonna be over by the fence by the small park."

"I tell you what, you lil muhfucka." Stump grabbed him by his throat and threw him against the wall. "Tell them faggots from Baptiste that I got they shit, and if I catch you or any of your homeboys around my building again, I'm gonna dead y'all. Now get the fuck outta here!" he screamed, as he kicked Danny in the ass.

"You believe that shit?" Stump asked KB, while they went back upstairs. "Them muhfuckas must think I'm a fucking joke or

something. I see they don't believe it can happen to them. Now they all up in my projects trying to get money. They must really think this shit is over. I'm gonna kill them bitches one by one, and that's my word on my mama's grave. Before it's all over, I'ma make them projects a ghost town. I'm gonna light that shit up like the Fourth of July when I come through there gunning."

"I didn't even know they was back out there hustlin' after that shit went down," KB said.

"It don't matter. They not gonna be out there for long. This time I'ma do it right…just me and you, K. You hear me, man?" Stump said, grabbing KB by his shoulder.

"You know I'm wit' you, man."

"Well, let's deal with that after we do this stick," Stump told him.

"Did your man ever come by and tell you the time?" KB asked.

"Yeah, he said we need to be there by one. The owner comes between one and three and doesn't stay long. He drives a black Beema. We can do it two ways. We can either get him when he comes out of the club or we can go up in there and get him and everybody else in that muhfucka. I prefer to go up in there and get everybody else with him because that's how I plan to pay my man since he ain't gettin' none of that money in the safe. What y'all think?" Stump was asking everyone's opinion, but he already had his mind made up.

"I'm wit' gettin' everybody up in there," Murda Mike said.

"Fuck it. Let's go all out," Ray-Ray said.

"Let's get 'em all," Drez said.

"What about you, K?" Stump asked.

"Shit, I'm just the driver. I'm down with whatever you choose."

"Nah, kid, not if we go up in there. We need another head up in there with us. You know how many muhfuckas gonna be up in that piece?" Stump asked.

KB's heart dropped when Stump said that. He didn't want to go up in there with them fools. He wanted to stay out in the van where he felt he had a better chance of not getting hurt or caught.

He knew from the beginning he wasn't cut out to run with Stump, but his desire for recognition along with greed had gotten the best of him. He never realized he would have to get involved so deeply, but now his back was against the wall and there was no way around it.

"I know, but who gonna drive the van?" KB asked.

"You still gonna drive. You gonna be the first one to leave. I already got this shit mapped out, kid. E'erything gonna be a'ight," Stump said.

There was a knock on the door, and Stump got up to answer it in his usual style — gun drawn and his back against the wall.

"Who is it?" Stump asked.

"Stone."

Stump looked through the peephole, then opened the door slowly and greeted his friend, the bouncer. They walked to the bedroom in the back of the apartment and closed the door behind them. Twenty minutes later, they emerged from the room and the bouncer left as fast as he came.

When Stump locked the door, he went into the living room and yelled, "IT'S ON!"

CHAPTER 13
LOVE HURTS, BABY

It was late when Junior called Shondra back. He showed Muffin how to bag up, and he was relaxing in the stash house drinking cognac and smoking herb. He was going to use Muffin and make her a part of his team. No one had a female thoroughbred on their team, and Junior planned on making her the most dangerous part of his clique.

"What up, Mooka?" Junior asked into the mouthpiece of the telephone receiver.

"What took you so long to call me back, Junior?" Shondra wanted to know.

"Come on, you know I had to go take care of my business. I told you that I was gonna make a major move. Now we gonna live like real kings and queens," Junior replied.

"I hope that's all you doin'." Shondra said suspiciously.

"Go 'head with that shit. Just tell me what's wrong."

"Gloria came down here and was telling me some shit about KB. She said he was plotting to do something else with that guy Stump," she informed him.

"What did he tell her?" Junior asked, his intererst aroused.

"She listened in on his phone conversation and said he was going to pick up some guns or something like that."

"Did he mention my name or anything?" Junior asked.

"I think she said the guns was for a robbery they about to do or something. I don't know. I mean, I don't think he said your name," Shondra said.

"What the fuck you mean? Either she said it or she didn't," Junior replied angrily.

"Why you flippin' on me? If you would have called me back earlier, I would know everything because it was fresh in my mind. I'm just trying to help you, damn!"

"I'm sorry, ma. It's just that I want to get them muhfuckas 'fore they get the drop on me. I'm just a little nervous. Look, I'm trying to make some power moves, and I ain't gonna be comfortable until I know them dudes is taken care of," Junior said sincerely.

"I'm scared, Junior. You know they killed those Dominicans over in Lindsey," Shondra reminded him.

"Fuck that shit! Fuck them muhfuckas! I'ma put all them to rest when I catch them," he said defiantly.

"I just want you to be careful, baby. I'm just worried, that's all."

When Muffin came into the room, Junior looked at her and put his index finger over his mouth to let her know not to say anything while he was on the phone. Muffin, being the intellectual woman she was, figured he was talking to Shondra. She walked over to him, pulled down his zipper, and commenced to give him head. She knew he wouldn't be able to continue his conversation as long as she was sucking his insides right out of him. Junior began to breathe heavy as his conversation continued with Shondra, and he tried to contain himself, but Muffin was sucking on him like a vacuum.

"What's wrong, Junior?" Shondra asked, sensing a change in his tone and breathing.

"N-n-n-nothing, ma. Aah shit, I caught a pain in my side…mmmmm," he managed to get out. "I'ma call you lata', a'ight?"

"You not comin' here tonight?" she asked desperately.

"Mmmmhmmm, I'll be there lata. I gotta go. The pain is too much."

Shondra wasn't crazy or stupid. She heard slurping noises in the background as he hung up the phone. She knew he was there with a bitch, and she had warned him about fucking around on her. She dialed his beeper number again and again. She was going to do that all night until he came or called her back.

***

"You made up your mind?" Craig asked Junior as he and Muffin walked to the car.

"About what?" Junior asked him.

"You hangin' wit' me or what?"

"I don't know, man. You know I got to get to work with this shit I just got," Junior told him.

"Come on, cuz, it ain't like you go out all the time. You could bring your pretty lady with you, too. Don't you want to go clubbin' Saturday, ma?" Craig looked at Muffin and smiled.

"Sure, why not?" Muffin replied.

"See, your girl wants to hang, so you might as well just bring her with you so both of y'all can enjoy yourselves."

Muffin was looking at Junior. She wanted him to take her out to the club, which would give her a chance to let all the bitches know she was next in line after his girl. She loved the spotlight and knew a lot of girls wanted to be with Junior, especially since she had hooked up with him. It was always like that when a guy became a hot commodity.

"Come on, daddy, let's go out together. I like to dance, too, you know," Muffin pleaded.

"A'ight, but I'm not stayin' long." He walked over to Craig and whispered to him, "That's some foul shit you just did, but payback's a muhfucka."

"You'll get over it, kid, once you hear that loud music and see all them hoes in there on your dick. Then you'll be thanking me," Craig whispered back.

"How so? You just told me to bring sand to the beach."

"Don't worry about that. Them hoes gonna let me know, and I'll put you on. Just come and have a good time," Craig said.

"I'll be back later. I need to talk to you about some things. I just made a power move, and I want to make sure everything's gonna run right in the hood when I put it out there," Junior said to Craig.

"Shit, it took you long enough. I was waiting on you to make your move so you could come play with the big boys," Craig resplied, smiling at his young cousin.

"Whateva. I'm 'bout to blow up so fast that it's gonna make muhfuckas in the hood hate me more than they do now. I'm a major player now, baby," Junior boasted.

"On the real, we gotta talk about putting this shit together so that none of us have to be in this shit too much longer. I love the money that comes from the game, but you gotta know when to hold 'em and when to fold 'em. Shit is getting kind of thick out here, and you know election year is coming up. You fed status now, cuzzo. No more blue clothes coming atcha – all suits – so you gotta be weary of how you move." Craig saw that his little cousin's status was about to change, and he wanted him to be aware of how serious things were going to get for him.

Junior looked at Craig and was amazed at how he had changed his demeanor like a chameleon. One minute, he was talking shit about partying, and the next minute, he was talking like a scholar of the game. Junior listened intently to everything he said because Craig was a vet in the game and his shit had been running smoothly ever since his first bid. When he came home, his jail reputation followed him. He was known at every compound from Rikers Island to Sing Sing. Tompkins was a dangerous place to live with robberies and shootings occurring almost everyday, but Craig used that to his advantage. He recruited all the hardheads and offered them the opportunity to put their guns down and make some steady money. Some were reluctant, but most of them got on board and crime in the projects diminished without the help from the president, mayor, borough president, or any other politician looking to get elected for another term. Craig eventually took control of all illegal activity in the projects and gained respect from the very young or the very old. He was known to end beefs permanently, with bodies gone missing or being found dead in

other boroughs. Craig was a kingpin in the projects. He was known and respected in all boroughs, and he was the boss of Brooklyn in his own right.

***

"I'm telling you, man, I think he smokin'," Rock was telling Lakim.

"How you know for sure?" Lakim asked.

"He be actin' different and shit. He always with that bitch. I mean, always. If a muhfucka spending that much time with a broad and she smokin', he gotta be smokin' with her. That shit just don't fly wit' me, La."

"I hear you talkin', B, but you gotta be sure. You know what I'm sayin'?" Lakim warned.

"How sure you gotta be? I mean, if your man start actin' different and changing his ways, that's a sign that something ain't right. Look at Kendu. Didn't you say he was actin' funny to you?" Rock asked.

That question took Lakim back. He thought about his childhood friend and how he was actin' funny and even talking different near the end. He stopped hustling like he used to, like Dusty. Joyce had told him that Kendu never had work when she wanted to cop from him, and when she did cop from him, it always looked like his bottles were tapped. He remembered when he and Kendu were talking about crackheads and how they would never try it because they saw what the effects did to the users. They promised each other they would never try it, no matter what, but now his friend was dead because of it. If Dusty was on crack, Lakim wanted to save him, especially since he was unable to save his own best friend.

"I can't lie, son. There were signs that something wasn't right, but because that was my man, I didn't want to believe that shit was for real. I don't want Dusty to go out like that, so I'ma make sure he's smokin' before I try to help him. I can't go to him and dis him like that and be wrong. Feel me, son?" Lakim said sincerely.

"That's my dawg and I got eyes. I see that he ain't right in the head, and it ain't because he fuckin' with that bitch and she got him sprung. It's something else, and I'm not trying to lose my peeps over no bitch that's tryin' to get him strung out so he can feed her fucked-up habit. I already dealt with that shit once with my moms, so I ain't tryin' to lose the only family I got left to that shit," Rock said strongly.

"Any money been short lately?" Lakim asked.

"Nah, but you wouldn't be able to tell because he got grip and he keep a stash in the crib. I've seen him give that ho like fifty dollars' worth of work like she was on the books with us. When I asked him about it, he told me that she bought it. And the bitch smart. She keeps him away from me because she know that I be pullin' her card right in front of him. That fight we had wasn't the first time we got into it ova that bitch.

"One day, I came in the crib and the whole backroom was smoky. When I went to the back, he started flippin' and told me to get out. He told me if I violated his space again that I wouldn't be able to live there no more. The bitch came out the room and she was zoned out. I could tell she was beaming up because her eyes was wide as hell, and when she started talking, her mouth was twisted. I knew he was buggin' out because he would beef crazy when I used to ask to blow weed in the room, but he lets that bitch turn his room into a crackhouse. Believe me, son, right then I knew they was doin' that shit together. I broke fool on her, and he came to her rescue like Super Save-A-Ho. I was wondering why he would flip on me ova a crackhead smoking in the crib."

"Let's go up there now," Lakim suggested.

"He changed the locks after that. That's why I don't be ova there like that no more. I told you the bitch practically stays every night with him."

"Well, let's go to her crib and I'ma ask her straight up," Lakim said.

"What? You think she gonna tell you he smokin'?" Rock asked.

"Not just like that. You gotta know how to make people tell you what you want to know. Come on, let's go find her."

After going to Lizzette's apartment and not finding her there, they went to Dusty's house and knocked on the door. No one answered, so they went downstairs to wait out front for him. Lizzette was coming into the building when they reached the lobby.

"Follow my lead," he turned and told Rock. "Ay yo, can I talk to you for a minute?" Lakim asked Lizzette, blocking her path.

"Hi. Not right now, papi. I'm in a rush. I'll talk to you when I come back out," she said, trying to go around Lakim.

"Look, I need to talk to you right now. It can't wait," he urged.

"Okay, papi, calm down. Tell me what it is that you want to talk about." Lizzette stopped to listen.

Lakim grabbed her by the arm and pulled her with him into the exit. She started to resist when he started pulling her toward the exit because she was afraid. She wanted to scream, but she was fearful that would make matters worse.

"Where the fuck is my shit?" Lakim growled.

"What ju talkin' 'bout?" she asked him nervously.

"Don't act like you don't know, bitch," Rock said menacingly.

Lizzette's hands started to shake. She was consumed with fear, and her mouth and throat were getting dry.

"I swear I don't know what ju talkin' 'bout. Please tell me," she begged.

Lakim pulled out his gun, backed away from Lizzette, and pointed it to her face.

"I'm gonna give you ten seconds to get my work or my money. If you don't, I'm gonna splatter your brains all ova the wall." Lakim cocked the hammer back on the gun.

"I no have no work or no money for ju. I don't have nuthin' of yours. Pleeeeez, you makin' a mistake," she pleaded.

"No, bitch, you made the mistake because I went to see Dusty to get my money for the shit he sold, and he told me that he gave you the work on credit and you smoked all my shit up. So now, I want my money or my work, or you're gonna have a hole in your head," Lakim told her, gritting his teeth.

"What?" she sobbed. "He lyin'. He didn't give me shit on credit. We smoked that shit together that he had," she snitched.

"Stop lyin', bitch. My man don't smoke that shit!" Lakim said.

"I no lyin', baby. Ask your friend. He know," she said, pointing to Rock.

"Don't look at me. I don't know shit, bitch!" Rock responded.

"Yes, baby, ju know. Ju came in one night and we were smoking then." She tried to get Rock to remember.

Lizzette was afraid Dusty was trying to pass the buck to her to take the blame off him. She had to find a way to prove she didn't do it all by herself.

"Look, papi, he upstairs right now waiting for me to come back with some more stuff. He gave me this money." She pulled out some money from her pocket. "I'm supposed to get it from Louie because he said he the one that looks out. That's who he told me to go to," Lizzette told Lakim.

He knew she wasn't lying. Louie was the only worker that gave out deals.

"Give me that!" Lakim grabbed the money out of her hands.

"What else you got?" Rock asked.

"I no have nuthin' else, I swear to Mary," she cried.

"I'm only gonna tell you this once." Lakim was standing in front of her, his face and hers so close together that they were nearly kissing. "If I catch you around my boy again, I'm gonna ram that glass dick you be sucking down your fuckin' throat. Do you understand me?"

"Y-y-y-yes," she stuttered.

"Now get the fuck outta here, you fuckin' ho!" Lakim barked.

Lizzette fell over herself trying to get out of the building. She was glad she didn't get hurt, but she was furious with Dusty for setting her up like that. Lakim didn't have to worry about her seeing Dusty anymore, because after that shit Dusty lied on her about, she wasn't going to give him the time of day anyway. As far as she was concerned, Dusty was dead to her.

"I told you he was smokin' that shit. That bitch just confirmed it," Rock said.

"Yeah, that's fucked up. I don't know how muhfuckas can get strung out on that shit, 'specially when they see what it does to them crackheads."

“Now tell me how we supposed to get this dude to admit he’s smoking’?” Rock asked.

“I don’t know. I’m just gonna tell him that I know and that if he wants help, I’ll help him.”

“That shit ain’t gonna work. I told you how he flipped on me, and I’m his man.”

“That’s all I can do. But, check it. If he don’t want no help, son, I gotta cut him loose. I can’t have him on my team if he fuckin’ wit’ that shit,” Lakim said realistically.

“I know, man,” Rock replied sadly. “I don’t understand that dude. I mean, he knows what I went through wit’ my moms. He knows I can’t deal with that shit again.”

Lakim knocked on Dusty’s door and put his ear to it. He heard someone ruffling around and backed up when he heard the footsteps getting closer.

Dusty looked out the peephole and saw Lakim and Rock again. He didn’t open the door the first time they came because he was waiting for Lizzette to bring back their “get high.”

“Open the door, Dus. We know you in there,” Lakim yelled through the door.

Damn! Dusty thought to himself.

“A’ight, hold up.” He went to his room, opened the windows, lit an incense, and hid the glass pipe and other tools he and Lizzette used to get high.

“Come on, Dus,” Lakim said impatiently.

Dusty went back to the door. “I don’t want that muhfucka comin’ in my house,” he yelled to Lakim, referring to Rock.

“Come on, man, we need to talk to you,” Lakim said.

“Fuck it, La. If he don’t want me around, then I’m ghost.”

“A’ight, I’ll see you in a few,” Lakim told Rock. “A’ight. Open the door now. Rock just left.”

The locks clicked and the door opened slowly. Dusty turned around, went into the living room, and sat on the couch. Lakim closed the door behind him and followed Dusty into the living room, then sat on the loveseat across from him.

“What the fuck did Rock want? He knows he ain’t allowed in my crib no more,” Dusty protested.

"He worried about you, kid. I'm worried about you," Lakim said softly.

"What y'all worried about me for?" Dusty shot back defensively.

"Look, Dus, you know you my lil dude, right?" Lakim started. "I'm just gonna tell you what I know."

Suddenly, Dusty had a funny feeling in his stomach. His worst fears were coming true. Lakim had found out he was smoking crack with Lizzette. How was he going to deny it? How could he look at him with a straight face and lie? He and Lizzette already smoked up the rest of the package he had left, and if Lakim was coming for the money or the work, he would come up short. He was in a precarious situation and felt like he was shrinking as he looked at Lakim and waited for him to drop the bomb.

"I just saw that bitch you fuck with, and she told me some disturbing shit. First, she told me that y'all both smoked up my pack. Now, I'm gonna ask you man to man if you fuckin' wit' that shit, but before you answer, I want to tell you something. If you tell me that you not fuckin' with that shit and I find out you lying to me, I'm gonna hurt you, straight up. Now, if you come clean and tell me you need help, I'm gonna help you, and when you kick the habit, you'll still have your position here. So, tell me what's up."

Dusty put his head down.

"I need help," he mumbled.

Lakim went over and sat on the couch next to Dusty. He hugged him without saying a word. Dusty had said enough.

***

When Shondra rolled over and didn't feel Junior next to her, she jumped up out of the bed.

I know that muhfucka ain't leave without telling me shit, she thought to herself.

She walked through the house to see if he was there, and when she realized he left without at least saying goodbye, she became irate. The previous night when he came in, she had confronted him about being with someone else and he lied, telling her she was bugging. She didn't have any proof, although she knew she wasn't bugging as he asserted. She heard some slurping noises before he hung up the phone, and those sounds came from someone sucking his dick. He had left in a huff, but when he came in later that night, he made love to her and him dicking her down lovely had calmed her down temporarily.

Now that she was up and he was gone, she was pumped up again and couldn't help but think about who he was with. Shondra loved Junior and would do anything in the world for him, but she would not tolerate him cheating on her because she was loyal to him. She couldn't understand why he would do that to her, especially when she had proven her love for him endlessly. She didn't understand why guys could never be satisfied with just one good piece of ass.

"Who is it?" Shondra yelled from her room to whoever was knocking on her front door.

"It's me, girl," Gloria responded.

Shondra went to open the door, and when Gloria entered, she was in an upbeat mood.

"What the hell is wrong with you?" Shondra asked her.

"I think that instead of me crying ova some guy, I should just take it for what it's worth and move on with my life," Gloria said.

"Ohhh Kaaay…" Shondra admonished.

"I see it like this, sis. If a guy don't love you enough to keep shit real, then why push him? I'm only giving as good as I'm gettin'. I'm all cried out. I'm not puttin' my heart into somebody that ain't returning the same love," Gloria said, expressing her new attitude.

"What? Did KB call you and upset you with some more bullshit?"

"That's the point. He didn't call. He knew I was upset before he left. If he was so concerned, he would have at least called a sistah to make her feel better, but he didn't. Whatever it is he's up to, it's more important than my feelings. So, I'm sayin' fuck it. I'm not gonna let this shit keep upsetting me. I'm gonna keep going forward. Fuck this fake love shit," Gloria said triumphantly.

"All right, honey. When did you get this revelation?" Shondra asked, surprised.

"Last night. I was crying my eyes and heart out for someone who probably wasn't even thinking about me. I told myself that I was wasting my tears on someone who didn't appreciate the kind of love I had showed him, so I figured that I better learn to love myself first because I know I won't hurt me. I believe that he cares for me, but he just doesn't love me as much as I love him. So, I just can't give more than I'm getting anymore."

Sbondra would have usually found herself telling Gloria to leave KB, but she was finding it hard to take her own advice.

"What you gonna do when he comes back?" Shondra asked.

"I ain't gonna do shit. I'm gonna act the same as far as he's concerned, but I'm gonna look out for my own feelings. I'm not gonna let his actions dictate my emotions anymore. He's a man. I'm gonna give him his space, but in the meantime, I'm gonna enjoy myself. I can't lie and say I don't love that man, but I'm not gonna let my love for him make me crazy. Fuck that. It's about me," Gloria said, snapping her fingers and turning around.

"You right. We should never love a man more than we love ourselves, 'specially when they don't show us the same kind of love in return. It's fucked up that we gotta get our feelings all hurt and shit before we realize how foolish we really be actin' when it comes to these muhfuckas," Shondra co-signed.

"Well girl, I'm ready to go out and celebrate. You wanna hit the club tonight?" Gloria asked, shaking her hips. "I'm ready to get down and dance my pretty black ass off, and who knows? Somebody might notice me."

Shondra wasn't in the partying mood, but she couldn't let her girl go out by herself. So, she agreed to go with Gloria to a club.

***

"I'm trying to straighten that shit out right now," Lakim was telling someone on the telephone. "Just have your man meet me to drop off the guns." Lakim hung up the telephone and looked at

Rock. "You think you'll be ready to do what we was talking about?"

"I'm ready right now," Rock replied.

"I think we should wait a couple more days. I'll have them heaters by then. My man is supposed to be bringin' them ova later on."

"I knew this was gonna have to be taken care of sooner rather than later. Even though shit is kinda smooth out here, you have to make sure you cover all the bases," Rock said.

"I know, and once this shit is done, we gonna be on our way, baby," Lakim said, slapping Rock five.

"I'm with you all the way. You tell Junior about Dusty yet?" Rock asked.

"I been beepin' Junior today and I was hittin' him last night, but he ain't called me back yet and he was ova here last night at his girl's house. We need to get another package because we running low and that shit Dusty fucked up set us back. I hope that muhfucka don't think I'm gonna eat that loss, because I'm not. He should have been out here, too. Shit, if you didn't put me on, I would have never known Dusty was smoking that shit with that bitch," Lakim said thankfully.

"Where you sendin' him?" Rock asked.

"They got this inpatient spot up in Manhattan on 136th and Edgecombe. He'll be in there for six months. Then they'll transfer him to an outpatient spot closer to home until he's fully rehabilitated," Lakim informed Rock.

"That's cool. I'm just glad we caught him before he was really out there and strung out," Rock said seriously.

Lakim's beeper went off, and when he saw Junior's code, he and Rock walked to the payphone on the corner to call him back.

"What up?" Lakim asked.

"I got your beep. I was busy. That's why I didn't call you back. What's up? You ran out of food?" Junior asked.

"There ain't no more chicken in the freezer. I need another bird," Lakim replied back in code.

"I'll be over there in a minute." Junior replied and hung up.

Junior pulled up in his cousin's Benz, got out a block away from the spot, and walked through the back of the projects. When Lakim spotted him coming up, he got off the benches and met him halfway.

"Let's go to your crib," Junior said.

Lakim followed him to the car, and they took the short drive to his building. When Lakim got out, Junior grabbed a blue gym bag from the backseat and followed him into his building. Once inside Lakim's apartment, Junior removed the contents from the bag. Lakim stood and looked at all the bagged-up crack in awe. He had never seen that much at one time. He was wondering what Junior was up to.

"I just copped a couple days ago. This is some new product. I need you to give out some samples to the custies and see how they like it. This shit is supposed to be better than what we have now," Junior explained.

"Damn, the bottles are bigger. What happened?" Lakim asked, surprised.

"We on the come up, babe bruh," Junior said, smiling. "We 'bout to take this shit to the next level. I want to have this shit pumping through all the surrounding hoods," Junior said, pulling on a cigarette he had just lit. "Oh yeah, there's something else, La. I got this chick that I want to put on. I want her to pick up and drop off for you. I'ma need Rock to be with me over in Tompkins. You'll still have Dusty and you can let him take over for Rock."

"That's cool, but I don't think that's gonna work 'cause Dusty's all fucked up," Lakim reported.

"What you mean?" Junior questioned.

"Dusty's smoked out on that shit. That bitch Lizzette turned him out," Lakim explained. "Rock pulled my coat to it, and I handled it. Tomorrow he's going to a rehab so he can get cleaned up."

"What the fuck! What's wrong wit' these muhfuckas out here in Baptiste? Can't they see what that shit do to a muhfucka? Shit!" Junior was irate.

"I know, man. I was thinkin' 'bout how that shit killed Du. When I found out about Dusty, I wanted to make sure I did something to help him before it was too late."

"I don't really give a fuck about Du, but as far as Dusty, it's good you handled it before it got out of hand like wit' that snake-ass Du. Now I gotta rethink this shit." Junior sounded annoyed.

"Don't worry. I got things on this end, so you can concentrate on what you gotta do over in Tompkins," Lakim suggested.

"Boy, seems like you got e'erythin' covered, huh? I knew you were the right pick for this," Junior said, a little jealous of how well Lakim was handling his business.

"Man, I got you. You ain't got to worry 'bout shit as long as I'm out here," Lakim replied, not detecting Junior's annoyance.

"Let me think about it and I'll get back to you, a'ight?" Junior responded.

"Okay, that's peace," Lakim remarked.

"You feel like hanging out wit' me tonight?" Junior asked him.

"Where at?"

"Some club on Broadway. My cousin is throwing a party for his man that just came home. You want to come through? Maybe we can brainstorm together and figure out how I'm goin' to do this."

"Nah, I got this new chick I'm gonna check out tonight. Why don't we take care of this the following day?" Lakim suggested.

"A'ight then, I'll give you a hit tomorrow on what I'm gonna do. I'm out."

***

The warm water felt good against her skin as Muffin sat in her bathtub. She was taking a bubble bath before getting ready for the party. The white foam in the tub covered her naked body, revealing only her knees that popped up every now and then when she shifted her position. Her skin felt like silk as she lathered herself with the bubbly water, moving her hands up and down her thighs. She closed her eyes and began to think about Junior and how good his lovemaking was. Unconsciously, she started to play

with herself, massaging her clit and rubbing her breasts. Her nipples hardened as she pinched them gently, and her cat pulsated from the gentle touches to her middle. Muffin was fantasizing about how Junior initiated foreplay before making love to her. She tried to mimick his touches as she delved into her dream world about their intimacy. Then before she knew it, she was moving and moaning to every good feeling going through her body. As the time passed, the water gently rippled with every movement of her gorgeos body, and soon she climaxed, awakening her from her sexual dream.

Muffin dried off and went into her bedroom to lie down. She flopped down on the bed with her arms sprawled out, naked as a newborn baby. She was deep in thought about how lucky she was to have Junior come into her life again and how she didn't have any plans of letting him go.

She turned her head to the closet where the Nina Ricci silk dress Junior bought her was hanging on the door. Once she put it on, she would be the hottest thing in the club. It was a French designer dress, and she was shocked when she looked at the price tag when he purchased it. He had spent eight hundred dollars and didn't even flinch. She couldn't wait for him to see her in it because there was no denying her shape. When she tried it on, it conformed to every curve of her body.

She was shaped like a thick stripper with an hourglass figure, and her lovely looks were the bonus. She loved the way Junior lusted for her and how he never acted jealous because of his confidence, which was something else that attracted her to him. She could feel that Junior liked her, but she wasn't sure how much. She wanted to do everything in her power to please him to ensure her position, even if she was his bottom bitch in his stable of whores.

"Girl, what the hell you doin' lyin' on your bed naked like that?" Muffin's mother asked, as she entered her room.

"Why didn't you knock?" Muffin asked back, getting up and putting on her pink robe. "Damn, Ma, you don't give me no privacy and respect."

"Look who's talkin'. This my house, lil girl. I was comin' in here to tell you that Junior called and said he was coming over in about an hour," Ms. Turner said, her hands on her hips.

"Okay, I'm sorry, Ma. Thanks," Muffin said apologetically.

"Baby, you really like that boy, don't you?" Ms. Turner asked her daughter seriously.

"Yeah, Ma, he's real nice. He treats me good," Muffin replied, smiling wide.

Her mother sat on the bed. She was about to have a talk with her daughter that she wished she'd had with her before Muffin encountered all the bad men she met.

Ms. Turner was from the streets of Brooklyn, born and bred. She had her share of good men, and she most definitely had her time with the gutter motherfuckers. She had Muffin at a young age. She was only sixteen years old when she met a smooth-talking hustler named Juicee. He wined and dined her and showed her the fast life, flashing big wads of money, which enticed her. She didn't know the streets until she met him and he showed her the hustler's life at an early age. When Ms. Turner got pregnant, she lost the shape that once had Juicee begging to hit it, so he wound up straying to her best friend. She loved him dearly, and their relationship went back and forth until something terrible happened that ended their relationship for good.

Ms. Turner tried to raise her daughter to the best of her ability, but because she was a youngster herself, she had failed miserably by neglecting Muffin through the years. She never had the chance to teach Muffin to love herself first and not to look to a man for that affection. She worked long, hard hours doing menial labor, and when she came in late nights from work, she was always too exhausted to spend quality time with Muffin. This ultimately ruined their relationship because Muffin was neglected emotionally and lacked the maternal love to mold her into a woman. Ms. Turner always wanted a mother-daughter relationship with Muffin, but time had passed her too fast and Muffin grew up on her own, relying on the streets to teach her what her mother couldn't.

"Listen, Muffin," she began, "I see you have that sparkle in your eye over that boy. I just want to tell you somethin'. I'm not preachin' to you, baby. I just want to give you some advice. Okay?"

Muffin never talked to her mother much about her relationships with boys, so what was happening right now seemed weird to her, but she invited the conversation.

"I'm listenin'," Muffin replied.

"Sweetheart, there are a lot of guys out here, but I want to talk about two kinds of guys right now — the ones that respect women and the ones that women respect. I've noticed that the fella you're seein' is very respectable, but you have to be careful of his intentions. A lot of guys see women as revolving doors or as simple notches on their belts. The way you can make sure that they maintain respect for you is to keep your self-respect. Don't ever sell yourself short and never settle for less than you're worth. A real man will respect that about you."

"What if he has a girl already?" Muffin questioned.

"You shouldn't play second to anyone because that's a sign of weakness. It means that you're settling. However, if you do play second, then you should get double what the first one gets, be it emotionally or financially. And always remember your position if you agree to play second. You are limited in what you can do in that relationship, because if you don't know what part you play, if and when you slip up, he will let you know. The mistress might receive expensive gifts for substitutions of missed dates, broken promises, or the absence of quality time. Remember, if he has someone else, you will not get to spend those special times with him, like his birthday, Thanksgiving, Christmas, and New Year's. These are lonely holidays if you're the mistress. You also have to remember that you can't have another man because *he* will never be open to playing second. Baby, if you're this man's mistress, you may become dependent on him if he's taking care of you financially. You have to be careful to monitor your emotions and not let them take over, because if you do, he may see you as a liability to his relationship with his main girl and get rid of you before you can cause any problems between them."

"I really like him, Ma, and I know he has a girl, but that doesn't bother me because he treats me good and I spend more time with him right now than she does. Tonight, we goin' to his cousin's party. Wouldn't he take his girl if it was like that?" Muffin asked.

"Listen, sweetheart, you have to be able to understand your position as well as play it. You may be a trophy piece to him, to show off to his friends as someone else he's conquered sexually, I don't really know. What I do know is that you have to know where you stand and be sure that you don't overstep your boundaries. You can't become a slave to your heart. We tend to make bad decisions when we think with our hearts instead of our heads. Our judgment is clouded by emotions and feelings that could lead us to definite heartbreak. You must make sure he knows you care for him but would leave him in a heartbeat if he were to violate you in any way. And, baby, that's something you will have to stick to, because if you say it and don't act on it, that's another sign of weakness and that will be your greatest disadvantage in your relationship. It's okay to love him. It's even okay to lust after him. But, you should never become obsessed because that will destroy your virtue as a woman, and you may find yourself doing things that you wouldn't normally do out of desperation to keep him. And depending on how he really feels for you, he may cut you loose and save himself the headache of dealing with you."

"I don't want to play myself with him, Ma, but I really do like him, and I believe he will be all mine in the end. I mean, I know about his girl and all, but that's not gonna stop me from doing what I have to do to become his main girl." Muffin stated firmly.

Muffin's mother could see her daughter was emotionally caught up with Junior. From experience, most men thrived on having a woman who understood their "situation at home" because they didn't have to hide anything from them, and at times, that would lead to disrespect. It was too late to tell her daughter she was in an unhealthy relationship because Muffin was already obsessing over the guy. Experience had proven it was rare that a guy would leave his main girl if his side girl already knew about his situation. Why would he?

“The only thing I can tell you is to follow your heart, baby, but use your mind as your guide. Then everything should work out in your favor. Love hurts, baby, and it’s unlike any physical pain in the world,” Ms. Turner said, giving her the longest and tightest hug she had ever given Muffin in her life.

CHAPTER 14
WOW, Y'ALL ROLLIN' DEEP

"Get down!" Junior was yelling at Midnite.

Craig's pit was jumping on him as he came out of the bathroom from taking a shower. Midnite was excited because Junior had been playing with him a lot since spending so much time at Craig's crib. Craig had told him not to play with the dog because he was strictly there for protection and nothing more.

Junior went into the room to get dressed for the club. His cousin was already downstairs with his crew. They were all standing in the parking lot where everyone was going to leave from to go to the club. Craig told Junior he wanted to show up at the club about thirty people deep to show strength.

Junior looked out the window and saw all the guys and girls hovered around Craig. He was the center of attention, and Junior kind of envied the love his hood showed him. He wanted his small crew of men to love him and be loyal similarly, but it just wasn't like that with him. Lakim's attitude was changing, and he could tell with all the new changes that were made in Junior's absence. Junior was not a native to Baptiste, but he hung out there since he was in high school. So, he felt like he was a native.

As he thought about Lakim and his role in his organization, Junior remembered the jewel his cousin Craig dropped on him when he first started hustling in Baptiste.

"In order to get respect from the muhfuckas around there, you have to remember that you gotta gain their love and respect without them disliking you for the strong move you're making," Craig had said. "That's hard to accomplish because you weren't born and raised from there. They are always going to see you as an outsider. To counter that, you will have to do things they have to respect as men and fear as gangsters. You have to make them believe their hood is your hood. You have to make them believe you're a native to that hood. In other words, lil cuz, you have to love thy neighbor's hood. If you fail to make them respect and fear you, you will not last long out there getting money, and they will run you out or kill you. So, be careful. It's a known fact that muhfuckas get jealous where money is involved. So, you have to make sure anyone that wants to eat can be fed, or at least offer them something to keep them happy. Never put all your trust in anyone and never let them know everything. Always switch up. Never keep the same routine; don't be predictable. You will be too easy to murk. Be hard to figure out, because who you think is your friend, will fool you. This game has no loyalty," Craig said, finishing his lecture on hustling.

As Junior continued to get dressed, he couldn't get hustling out of his mind, like he made a mistake somewhere down the line. He was feeling like he had given Lakim too much control, which was causing Junior to lose his place of authority in his own operation. While he thought about it, most of the workers were really under Lakim's order.

Junior put on a blue double-breasted suit with a black silk shirt and a pair of black Stacy Adams. He complemented the shirt with a gold rope chain with a medallion and his gold nugget watch, Craig walked into the room with an impatient look on his face.

"Y'all ready to break out?" Junior asked, picking up his gun.

"Yeah, man. We was waiting on you," Craig replied.

"Before we go, I gotta go pick up Muffin from her crib," Junior informed him.

"That's a'ight. We'll follow you," Craig said, heading for the front door.

They took the elevator down and walked into the parking lot to the awaiting throng of people. Everyone was in their Sunday's best, and almost everyone had a forty ounce of beer in their hands. Junior greeted everyone. There were faces he didn't recognize, but the love was so thick it didn't matter. They all stood around talking and joking for a while, then everyone started going to their cars. Craig announced that they were to follow Junior to pick up his lady first, and from there, they would head to the club.

When Junior pulled up in front of Muffin's house, she was impatiently waiting on her stoop, but was amazed at the fleet of cars that pulled up behind him. She felt like a celebrity when she got into the car.

"Wow, who are all dem people in those cars?" she asked excitedly.

"Those my cousin's peoples," Junior replied nonchalantly.

"Wow, y'all rollin' deep."

"Yeah, that's how we roll to make sure we don't have no problems. When muhfuckas see you deep like we are, it discourages them from starting any beef," Junior said analytically.

He was trying to convince himself of that because he was really hoping nothing jumped off at the club.

***

The black van was parked across the street from the club. KB was in the driver's seat, while the rest of the crew was in the back loading up their guns. Everyone had on black pants with black matching hoodies. There was a big turnout at the club, and people were already standing on line waiting to get inside. There were so many females on line that you would have thought Eric B. and Rakim were performing that night.

Whoever's throwing that party must have a lot of love, KB thought to himself.

"You see the bouncer out there?" Stump asked KB.

"Not yet. It's packed out there," he responded.

"The bouncer said he'd come out about the time the owner normally pulls up," Stump said.

"Well, he didn't come out yet. Oh wait, that's him right there, I think," KB replied.

"Flash the headlights one time real fast. I want him to know this is us," Stump instructed.

After KB flashed the headlights quickly, the bouncer acknowledged their presence by nodding his head in their direction.

"Now we gotta wait 'til we see this dude pull up," Stump said.

"It's a lot of muhfuckas out there and you can imagine how many are already inside. How we gonna get all of them to cooperate?" KB asked.

Stump detected fear in what KB was asking, so he pulled out his gun and pointed it at KB's head.

"With this, muhfucka! You got cold feet or somethin'? I can't let you go up in there if you scared, because somebody might smell it on you and you'd be the cause of this shit not going according to plan. I'm gonna ask you one time, dawg. You ready to do this shit or what?" Stump's tone was icy.

KB's heart was racing. He didn't really have a choice.

"You know I'm down, man. I was just sayin' it's a lot of muhfuckas out there, and I'm sure your man is probably lettin' some of them in with guns."

"He ain't lettin' nobody in there wit' no heaters. I already told him we the only one in there that should have heaters. He gon' turn away anybody that holdin' heat," Stump confirmed.

The line was moving slowly because the bouncers were searching everyone before letting them enter the club. The male bouncers were checking every guy thoroughly, turning away anyone that had guns on their person. The girls had their pocketbooks checked by a male bouncer on the inside with a flashlight and a female was there to pat them down, as well.

A cab pulled up to the front of the club, two females dressed in black DKNY cat suits and hooker boots got out. Every guy on the line stopped what he was doing momentarily to gawk and lust after

the statuesque females. The two women strutted to the entrance like racehorses and disappeared inside.

Craig's crew parked around the corner from the club and entered through the back. Craig had paid the bartender to let them in because they were exclusive guests of the host. The crew of twenty males and ten females entered the club like superstars. All eyes were on them as they filed through the back door. Most of the guys had guns, as well as some of the females. Craig made sure they would be able to get their guns in through the back. He had tried to talk to the bouncer and offered him some money, but he was uncooperative. So, Craig found someone else who was willing to let him in with the firearms.

As everyone moved to make room for the others to come in and get stamped, Junior was fixing the burner in his waist. Feeling self-conscious that some of the people in the club had noticed what he was doing, he decided to give the gun to Muffin. He removed the large .45 automatic from its hiding place, put the safety on, and passed it to Muffin discreetly, who put it in the large Gucci bag she was carrying.

The inside of the club was illuminated in crimson red lighting. The music was deafening as the crew made their way past the bar. There were people on the dance floor dancing to Shabba Rank's latest hit. The smell of marijuana in the cloudy air made it evident that the crowd was doing more than dancing and drinking. As Muffin shuffled through the crowd, she began gyrating her hips and moving to the beat of the music blasting out of the speakers. Although it was a little dark, the crowd noticed Craig's crew walking toward the VIP section. There were two bouncers standing on either side of the ropes separating the VIP section from the regular crowd. The crew approached the entrance to the section, but the bouncers blocked the entrance until they got confirmation of everyone who was in the crew. Craig went to the front and showed the special tickets that were given to him, allowing him entry to the section. Everyone placed their hands under a UV lamp that showed the ink that was stamped on their hands and then walked up the steps to the VIP section. Some of the females in the club were watching to see who was being allowed in so they could put their bid in once the guys in VIP came back down to the dance floor.

The VIP section was a second dance floor in the club and very large. Once up there, you could look over the rail and down onto the crowd. There were people already sitting at the tables containing complimentary bottles of Moet. Craig saw his friend Jock, the one the party was for, and they embraced. Jock was muscular and wore a red tank top and white, baggy linen pants with red gator shoes. He had a bevy of beautiful women with him at his table. Craig introduced Junior to him and they too embraced.

The section became more packed when Craig's crew arrived, but there was standing room for the rest that couldn't get seated at the table. Meanwhile, down below in the crowd there were two females in black DKNY cat suits that were focusing their attention on Junior.

About that time, a red car with alloy rims pulled up in front of the club. A slender man dressed in blue dungarees and a white shirt got out, walked to the passenger side, and opened the door. KB and the rest of Stump's crew were stooped down on the side of the van with their guns out and their hoods on. The owner had arrived. Stump was already waiting on the side of the club for the slim man to get out of his car and enter the club. Stump wanted to get to him before he got inside because there were still people on line waiting to enter the club. KB watched as Stump coolly walked up to the man as he closed the passenger's side door. Stump whispered something in the man's ear. The man looked shock but kept his cool. Then they both walked around the building, out of sight. When the bouncer saw that Stump had the owner, he began to quickly let everyone into the club. As the last person entered through the black steel doors, he motioned to KB.

"Come on. Let's move!" Ray-Ray said, walking toward the entrance of the club. He turned around to see if the rest of the guys were following. "Come on, Drez, Mike, K. We gotta get in there so we can have the drop on them muhfuckas."

In his mind, KB was going into a death trap. There was no way they were going to be able to get all the people in the club to cooperate, but he didn't see any other option for himself.

As they stood by the door, Ray-Ray told everyone to holster their guns and take their positions once they got inside the club. The door opened, and the bouncer let them in and followed behind them without saying a word. KB made his way over to the DJ booth and Ray-Ray went toward the back door. KB never saw where Drez went. Everyone stood in their positions waiting for the sign from Stump. KB's legs felt like spaghetti, but he had to go through with it now. It was too late to back out.

Junior was on the dance floor with Muffin, when he felt a tap on his shoulder.

"So, muhfucka, this is what you been doin'?" Shondra yelled in his ear over the music.

Junior turned around and was shocked to see her standing behind him. He was caught totally off guard.

"What the fuck, Junior? You can't say shit?" Shondra screamed.

Grabbing her by the hand, Junior pulled her through the crowd toward the bar, while Muffin looked on with hatred in her eyes. As he pulled Shondra, he noticed Gloria on the dance floor in her cat suit dancing, unaware that Junior was pulling her friend. Shondra was resisting, but he kept a tight grip on her until they reached the bar.

"What the fuck you doin' up in here?" Junior screamed.

"No, muhfucka, that ain't the question. What the fuck you doin' in here wit' that bitch?" Shondra retorted.

Stump and the owner walked up the stairs to his office unnoticed by the horde that was in the club partying. As they approached the steel door, the owner was praying he made it out alive. He didn't want to make any sudden moves. He wanted to cooperate fully in hopes that Stump would just take the money and leave, and not turn the apparent robbery into a homicide. The owner opened the door to his office, and as soon as he did, Stump pulled his gun from the inside of his hoodie and stuck it to the back of the man's head. Stump made the owner open the safe, and then he tied the owner's hand with an extension cord and duct-taped his mouth. Quickly, Stump emptied the contents of the safe into a black bag. There was a lot of money in it like the bouncer

had told him, along with two complimentary guns, courtesy of an asshole that thought someone would tell him to open his safe and hand him the money. What a rookie mistake.

The owner lay face down on the ground beside a desk in the office, looking like a captured slave. Stump went over to the two-way mirror that overlooked the club. He could see out, but no one in the club could see inside. He looked out into the crowd to see if his people were positioned where they were supposed to be. He saw KB standing by the DJ booth, Ray-Ray was by the bar, Murda Mike was at the entrance, and Drez was by the VIP section. The bouncer had his boys scattered all around the club. As Stump stood there looking over the crowd, he had a strong feeling this was going to be the hardest part of the robbery, but the thought wasn't enough to deter him from the plan. He was ready, willing, and determined to go forward.

"I can't believe you dissed me like this!" Shondra was saying to Junior, tears welling up in her eyes. "I never fucked around on you. Why would you do this to me?"

"It's not what you think, baby. My cousin asked me to come at the last minute. I really didn't want to come, but he insisted. You know me. You know clubbin' ain't my thing," Junior tried to explain.

"That's not what I'm talking about, Junior. That's the same bitch that gave you her number when we got back from VA," Shondra said, turning around to try and locate Muffin in the sea of people in the club so she could point her out to Junior.

"Why don't we just get the fuck outta here so we can go home and talk? I can't hear shit in here," Junior suggested.

"Hold up. I came with Gloria, let me tell her I'm leaving," Shondra said, walking into the crowd to find her.

Shondra saw Gloria dancing with two guys. They had her in a sandwich and were grinding and groping all over her to the hip-hop music blaring. Shondra was making her way to Gloria, when suddenly the music stopped and there was a loud bang. Her heart skipped a beat when she heard the boom because she didn't know what was happening. Some people started screaming and heading for the closest exits, only to be stopped by gunmen in hoodies backing them away.

"Everybody get the fuck on the ground!" a voice yelled over the PA system.

No one moved. Then there was another loud boom. This time, everyone got low. Junior immediately scoured the crowd looking for Shondra. He wanted to make sure she was all right. His mind was racing, and then he remembered Muffin and began looking for her because she had his heat in her purse.

He noticed all the gunmen had on black hoodies with their guns out. There were two guys near him at the bar, and they were hustling people to the center of the club. Junior moved with the crowd in hopes of making it to his cousin's crew or Muffin.

"We want your money and your jewelry. If any of you dudes want to play superhero and turn this robbery into a homicide, just be sure you look around. The muhfucka next to you might be with us, so just cooperate so everyone can go home," the voice on the loudspeaker said.

Craig and Jock were already thinking of a way out of the situation. Most everyone in their crew was strapped, but they didn't want to make any quick moves because they didn't know who was down with the robbery.

"Yo, how many do you see out there with guns?" Craig whispered to Jock, who was stooping down with the rest of the crowd.

"I counted five cats in hoods, but I see about three more with guns," Jock reported.

"It's about forty of us. I think if we can get close to the dudes with the guns, we can get the drop on them. Once them muhfuckas see that we outnumber them, they might break for the door," Craig planned.

"We hafta blast 'bout three or four of them off top to let them know we not bullshittin'," Jock said. "Shit don' really changed out here, huh? I mean, muhfuckas got enough balls to rob a club?" Jock said to Craig.

"Man, muhfuckas will try anything for that scratch, ya know," Craig replied. "I'm not going out like this."

“Ain’t that one of the bouncers that was at the door?” Jock asked, as he looked over to the crowd gathering in the middle of the dance floor.

“I don’t know. I came through the back door,” Craig replied, looking at the bouncer Jock was referring to.

“Yeah, it is that muhfucka! He down with this shit, too! Fuckin’ snake! That’s why he was being so thorough at the door tonight. If it’s the last thing I do, I’m gon’ make sure I body duke!” Jock was pissed.

“Let’s make our way to the middle so we can get a good position,” Craig suggested, as he started to move to the middle of the floor with the rest of the crowd.

The crowd was complying with the gunmen. Money and jewelry were being passed to the four men with black bags. There were two guys standing around them with their guns drawn, pointing them randomly at everyone. No one in the crowd tried to make a move out of fear of becoming the first victim. The women were crying and shaking hysterically, while some of the guys had looks of revenge in their eyes. Gloria and Shondra were both together crying uncontrollably.

“What the fuck is goin’ on?” Gloria sobbed.

“I don’t know, girl. I just hope they take what they want and just leave,” Shondra replied, sobbing.

The guys collecting the money and jewelry made their way over to where Shondra and Gloria were stooping down. Gloria looked up and was shocked when she saw KB standing over her. Her eyes got as big as saucers, and she was about to scream out his name but thought quickly against it. She put her jewelry and what little cash she had in the bag, while staring in his face with the evilest glare she could give him. He didn’t utter a word. He just kept moving through the crowd as if he didn’t see her. Shondra noticed him, too, and her heart dropped. She was afraid that if he was there, then Stump would be there, too, and if they saw Junior, they would more than likely kill him.

“Oh shit!” she whispered to Gloria. “That was your man and he didn’t even say shit to you. That’s fucked up!”

"That muhfucka!" Gloria cried. "How could he do this shit? I knew he was up to something, but I woulda neva thought he would do some foul shit like this."

"I gotta find Junior," Shondra said desperately when she saw one of the gunmen hit a guy in the face with his gun for moving too slow. "If KB's here with Stump, they might kill him when they see him."

"Why would they do that?" Gloria asked, clueless.

"Look, Gloria, Stump was the one that tried to rob Junior that night we came from the club," Shondra confessed. "We need to make sure he don't see Junior."

"What?" Gloria didn't process what Shondra said right away.

"Kendu was down with them. He was the one that set Junior up in the first place," Shondra blurted out.

"Why you never told me that?" Gloria started to think. "That means you knew about KB before I met him?"

"Look, Glo, I gotta find my man before these muhfuckas find him first. We got to think of something so they won't kill him, please!"

"Hold up. You knew all this shit and you didn't tell me? Is that why you was asking me all them questions about him, so you could set him up instead? Wow. What kind of friend are you?" Gloria was disgusted.

Muffin and Junior were stuck in the middle of the crowd. She had passed him his burner and he tucked it into his waist.

"It's not a lot of them," Muffin whispered to Junior.

"I see about seven dudes with guns and the dude up in the DJ's booth," Junior responded.

"Those guys we were with, don't they have guns?" she asked.

"Yeah, and I need to find them. I know they gonna do something," Junior said, his eyes scouring the club looking for his cousin.

"They need to do something, because these muhfuckas look like real amateurs. I hate muhfuckas that do foul shit like this," Muffin said irritated.

"I know, but that's what they do. You can't knock anybody's hustle, only when it causes you grief. Oh shit!" Junior exclaimed.

"What?" Muffin looked at Junior and could see him pulling his gun slowly from his waist.

KB was walking toward Junior but didn't see him. Junior tried to shield himself from KB, not wanting him to see and recognize who he was. Junior put his head down and peeked up at the guy that was in front of KB.

"Put everything in the bag!" the gunman growled to the men and women that were stooped down on the ground. KB was standing behind him, waving the gun around the heads of everyone. Junior's heart was beating rapidly, and his hand was clammy from gripping the gun so tightly. As KB got closer to Junior, Muffin noticed who Junior was staring at. Then suddenly, she grabbed Junior's gun and squeezed off three shots in KB's direction.

BLAM! BLAM! BLAM! There was loud screaming as everyone got up and rushed the exits trying to get to safety. There were more shots fired immediately after the first three, and people were falling over each other trying to get out of the club. KB had gotten hit twice and had fallen to the ground. He was bleeding profusely from his wounds, and his gun fell out of his hand when he hit the floor. Someone had picked it up and started blasting away at the other gunmen, and all hell broke loose.

Craig had shot two of the gunmen in the head, and they died instantly. His crew was positioned around the club and had most of the gunmen at bay. Jock and his crew were shooting anyone that had a gun as they made their way to the exit. The exits were crowded from the club-goers stampeding to escape the mayhem going on inside. Craig kept his back to the wall as he moved close to the exit so he could see who was coming in his direction. The screaming was deafening, but he kept his eyes moving around the entire club to make sure no one snuck up on him. He was looking around for Junior and anyone else from his crew, but it was mass pandemonium and the people running were blocking a clear view.

When Craig made it to the exit, he caught a glimpse of the bouncer Jock was talking about. Craig stayed close behind him. The bouncer was looking nervous as he made his way through the crowd, pushing people as he headed for the bar. Craig stayed behind him with his gun down by his waist and out of clear view. The bouncer was by the door getting ready to make his exit, when Craig pulled his gun up from his waist.

"Ay muhfucka!" Craig shouted.

The bouncer turned around and was met by the barrel of Craig's gun. The bouncer dropped his hand and backed up to the door that led to his potential freedom if he could make it out. By the cold stare Craig was giving him, he wasn't going to make it home to see his kids anymore. Craig pulled the trigger, and a loud boom was heard as the bouncer was lifted off his feet and thrown into the exit door, then falling into the darkness of the night. Craig turned around briefly to see if anyone was looking, then walked over to his still-breathing victim. He kneeled down and looked at the bouncer lying on the ground shaking. Craig slowly put the barrel of the gun to his mouth. The bouncer clenched his teeth tightly. Craig forced the barrel of the gun inside his mouth, shattering his teeth in the process. The bouncer mumbled something in protest, but Craig pulled back the hammer on the gun, turned his head away, and pulled the trigger, sending the bouncer into eternal darkness. The bouncer's head exploded like a watermelon blown up by a pack of firecrackers. Craig stood to his feet and wiped the droplets of the bouncer's brain matter from his cheek before walking off into the moonlit night.

Gloria was kneeling down screaming for help for her wounded boyfriend. KB was losing a lot of blood. She was afraid to leave him there and go get help because she feared he might expire on her. Shondra walked over during Gloria's pleas of desperation.

"Get the fuck outta here, bitch!" Gloria screamed. "You wanted this shit to happen! This is what you hoped for! I hate you, you fake bitch!"

Shondra couldn't do anything but look at Gloria. Her heart dropped. She couldn't deny what Gloria was saying. The reality of what she had been trying to do rushed through her as she looked at KB on the ground dying and witnessed the hurt her friend was feeling for the man she loved.

"Who the fuck did this to him!" Gloria cried out, cradling KB's head in her lap. "Did your man do this, huh? Did Junior do this to him!"

"I…I…I don't know," Shondra stuttered truthfully.

"OOOOOHHHHH God, please don't let him die. Please, God. I'm sooooo sorry." Gloria continued to cry her heart out.

Shondra got up and went to find someone to help KB.

"Where the fuck you goin'?" Muffin asked Shondra angrily, blocking Shondra's path as she tried to leave through the entrance of the club.

"None of your fuckin' business, bitch!" Shondra barked, as she pushed her way past her.

Muffin grabbed Shondra by the arm and turned her around forcefully, pointing Junior's gun in her face. "It is my business, bitch!" Muffin sneered. "You need to leave Junior alone!"

"What, bitch?" Shondra asked, her temperature at its boiling point.

Shondra knocked the gun from Muffin's hand in a sweeping motion and hit her with a barrage of punches to her face. Shondra then grabbed her hair and swung her against the wall of the club. Muffin was dazed and slumped to the ground. Shondra stomped her in the face numerous times to seal the quick win. Muffin curled up trying to block the onslaught of kicks to her mid-section and face, while Shondra kept stomping and screaming over and over, "You fuckin' bitch!"

As Shondra continued her assault on Muffin, someone walked up behind her and hit her in the back of the head. She felt a sharp pain right before everything went blank. The person that had hit Shondra in the head helped Muffin to her feet and out of the club.

Junior saw the guy that hit Shondra, but he was too slow in getting to him as Muffin and the guy disappeared into the crowd outside of the club.

The sound of sirens could be heard as people ran to their cars trying to get away from the chaos. There were bodies lying around, some dead and others with serious injuries. After going outside and trying to find Muffin, Junior noticed paramedics and police vehicles pulling up. So, he went back inside to help Shondra, who

was lying on the ground unconscious. He knelt down next to her and put her head in his lap. When he saw two paramedics come into the club with stretchers, he waved them over to him and they took over. Junior looked at her one final time before hurrying through the club towards the back exit. Reaching the back door, he pushed it open and the cool wind alerted him of a wound he had suffered while inside the club. His shirt was sticking to the upper portion of his body from the blood. It was empty and dark in the back, and as Junior walked, he stumbled over a body. When he looked down, he was grossed out by what he saw. The body's head was blasted open and disfigured. Junior stepped over him and quickly made his way back to Tompkins Projects.

The van pulled up in front of Stump's building and everyone got out. Stump was carrying two bags, and Mike and Ray-Ray each had a bag of their own. Drez also had a bag, as well as a girl with him. They went into Stump's apartment and threw the bags on the floor.

"Now tell me who this bitch is again?" Stump looked at Drez.

"This my little cousin, man. Some bitch in the club was duffing her out, so I knocked the bitch out and brought my lil cousin with me," Drez explained.

"What about KB? Nobody knows what happened to him?" Stump looked around the room at his crew.

"I don't know. When I heard the first gunshot, I grabbed the bag I had and got to the door. We weren't the only ones with guns in there. I saw other muhfuckas in there with guns, and they was blasting, so I shot my way out the club. I ain't never see KB," Ray-Ray said.

"I saw him with some dude that must have been down with the bouncer's crew, but when I heard the all those gunshots, I ran out the booth. I hit two or three muhfuckas that was shooting, then I seen a bag on the ground. So, I grabbed it and headed for the exit. I didn't see KB after that," Murda Mike said.

"So nobody know if he dead or not?" Stump asked.

"I'm not gonna lie. I saw mad muhfuckas on the ground. I can't say if K was one of them, but there was mad bodies around

and a lot of them wasn't moving. I thought we was the only ones that was supposed to have guns in there," Drez added.

"Yeah, I don't know what happened with that, but other than that everything worked out good. A'ight, we gonna split this shit up now," Stump said.

He dumped the contents of the bags onto the floor. There was jewelry, money, and wallets in the bags that Drez, Murda Mike, and Ray-Ray had. The bag Stump had contained stacks of money.

"What about her?" Mike asked, pointing to Muffin.

"After we split the take, I'm gon' take her home," Drez said.

"Nah, she gotta get gone now," Stump said.

"A'ight, I'm gonna put her in a cab. I'll be right back," Drez said, preparing to leave.

Stump grabbed Drez's arm as he rose and whispered in his ear, "You betta make sure she don't say shit, cuz!"

And with that, Muffin followed Drez outside.

"I didn't know you was down with that shit. I thought you was getting money selling drugs in the Stuy. You got too much money to be doin' that dumb shit," Muffin said to Drez when they were out of the apartment.

"You can never have enough money. This is how I got down in the beginning. The opportunity came, so I took it. Ya know what I'm sayin'? Who was that bitch that was airing you out?" Drez asked.

"I was in there with my man, and that bitch was his girl," Muffin responded.

"Huh? That shit you just said don't make no sense. Who your man?" Drez asked, puzzled.

"Junior. He hustles out of Baptiste," she told him.

Drez tilted his head. "He got a man named Lakim?"

"Yeah, you know him? He gettin' major paper. I just bagged up some shit for him," Muffin stated.

"Yo, how close is you and that dude?"

"I love him. He got me wide open. That's why I was gonna off his fuckin' girl," Muffin stated honestly.

"Look, Muff, you need to stay away from that cat. I don't want you gettin' caught up in any shit that's about to go down with him. You hear me?" Drez warned.

Drez was Muffin's cousin, and he used to live with her when they were younger. Her mother kicked him out after she discovered his involvement in criminal activity. He was a very grimy dude, and although he and Muffin were 2nd cousins, she kept her distance. He was a live wire and was always into some shit for as long as she could remember.

"Why, Drez? What you up to now?" she questioned.

"Look, cuz, just stay the fuck away from dude. Ya hear me?"

"But why, Drez? He's so cool," Muffin asked, almost pleading.

"Let me put it to you like this. His man, La, don't want him in the picture no more, and we made a deal that if I get rid of him, then I can partner over there. I did some investigating and found out over there is a gold mine. So, I'm gonna do what I gotta do to get that money," Drez told her. "And, Muff, don't go running your mouth to homeboy for points. No pillow talk, a'ight!"

A cab pulled up and Muffin got in. As Drez closed the door, he motioned for her to roll down the window. Once she did, he emphasized, "Blood is thicker than water, Muff," and then the cab pulled away. Muffin looked out the back window of the cab and watched Drez walk over to a payphone on the corner. Drez was going to page Lakim.

Lakim looked down at his pager as it vibrated and recognized the code immediately.

"This him right here," Lakim told Rock, as they both walked to a payphone. Lakim dialed the number in his beeper and waited for him to pick up.

"What up? Everything a go?" Lakim asked.

"Yeah, I just came back from handling some shit. I almost didn't make it out," Drez replied.

"You ready?" Lakim asked.

"Nah, I'll tell you when," Drez said.

"Okay," Lakim replied, looking at Rock and nodding his head in agreement.

"I'm out. I'll beep you and give you all the details," Drez said, then hung up the payphone.

Lakim hung up the phone. "It's on! He gonna beep me back with all the info."

"That's peace. Once we get this muhfucka Stump out the way, the rest is easy," Rock said, patting the gun in his waist.

"Yeah, but Stump ain't no slow leak, so you gotta be on point," Lakim told him.

"I got this. Trust me," Rock said with confidence. "As long as your man on the inside sets him up right, ain't nothing to worry about."

"I hear you, Rock, but you gotta be careful," Lakim urged.

"I'll meet you upstairs in a minute," Rock said, as he turned to leave. "I gotta go check on that money real quick."

"A'ight, I'll be up there waitin'," Lakim told him, walking towards the building.

Rock made sure Lakim was inside the building, and then he made an important phone call.

When Junior made it to the projects, there were people standing around in the parking lot. He could see that some of the females were crying. He immediately thought something had happened to his cousin Craig.

"Damn, man, I thought you was a gon'r," Craig said when he saw Junior.

"Nah, I'm all right," Junior rerplied.

"Yo, I can't believe that shit happened," Craig said.

"You know I know who did that shit, right?" Junior exclaimed.

"Word? Who set it up?" Craig asked eagerly.

"Remember them dudes we was bustin' at a while back in Baptiste?" Junior started.

"Yeah."

"It was them. I saw one of them in there. My bitch peeped it, and when the muhfucka got close, she grabbed my ratchet and aired him out. That's when shit went berserk in there. I think she flatlined homeboy. I just saw him drop and that was it," Junior explained.

"You look like you need to go to the hospital," Craig said, noticing Junior's blood-soaked shirt. "You got hit, too?"

"Nah, I thought I did, but it must have been just a graze or something 'cause I don't have no hole in me. Duke was fucked up, though. He was spitting blood and the whole nine," Junior told Craig.

"Fuck that muhfucka! I hope he die. They killed one of my men in there. My man Jock told me the bouncers was down with it, too. I caught one of the maggots and layed him down by the back door," Craig said.

"Is everybody else all right?" Junior asked.

"Yeah, but I seriously thought you got caught up in that shit. That's why everybody out here was buggin' out. They thought those dudes bodied you. I'm glad you all right, and I'm sorry I pushed you into going out with me," Craig said apologetically.

"It ain't nuthin', but check it. I need to find out if my girl is okay. I saw this kid hit her in the head with a burner. Drive me to the hospital so I can check on her," Junior said, while checking his vibrating pager. It was Rock's code.

"Give me a sec. I want to change out of these clothes," Craig said.

"I might as well go upstairs and clean up a lil bit myself, then make this phone call," Junior said.

***

Shondra was being put on a stretcher as police and the coroner swarmed the club, collecting bodies and evidence. Her head was pounding and she was still a little dizzy from getting knocked out. The air was cool outside, and there were bystanders wondering what happened in the club. Police were questioning some of the club-goers that were wounded in the melee, and the flashing lights from the squad cars and ambulances made it seem as if the party had been moved outside. The EMT workers were asking Shondra questions, but she was too dazed to answer. Too many things were running through her mind. She was thinking about the bitch that pulled the gun on her, if Junior was okay, how her best friend

Gloria was doing, and if KB was dead. The EMT worker lifted the stretcher up and was about to put her in the ambulance, when she heard Gloria screaming nearby.

"NO, NO, NO!" Gloria yelled.

Shondra lifted herself up from the stretcher and saw Gloria grabbing an EMT worker and trying to get into the back of an ambulance. He seemed to be telling her that she couldn't ride with KB, and she was upset. Shondra was paralyzed with grief as the cries of wounded people echoed in her ears while the ambulance she was in pulled off. However, there was one distinct sound that drowned out all the other sounds. It was Gloria's wailing.

***

The money was being split when Drez got back to Stump's crib. He immediately noticed Stump putting money aside for KB.

"Anybody hear from KB?" Drez asked.

Nobody answered.

"Everybody pick out a piece of jewelry you want. We'll take the rest to the hock in mid-town tomorrow," Stump said.

Ray-Ray picked out a gold rope chain with a round medallion. Murda Mike picked out a nugget bracelet, Drez took a Figaro chain with a crucifix, and Stump selected an Italian link chain with a diamond-encrusted pendant and a herringbone chain with a crucifix for KB.

"Once we hock the rest of this, we'll split the dough. Take y'all shares and get out," Stump said.

Everyone picked up their stacks and headed for the door. As Drez started to count his money stack, Stump walked over to him and knocked it out of his hands and onto the floor.

"You think I can't count, or you think I'm trying to beat you out of some money, muhfucka!"

"Nah, man, I was just seeing how much it was. That's all, fam. All that wasn't necessary," Drez said, pissed off with what Stump did.

"Count that shit when you leave. Now get the fuck outta my crib!" Stump barked.

***

The inside of the hospital was cold. Junior hated hospitals because they had a funny smell. He walked past the security guard in the emergency room, went to the clerk, asked if they had a patient that came in a short time ago, and gave Shondra's full name.

"I don't know. There have been a lot of people who came in tonight." The clerk saw the concern in Junior's eyes. "I'm not supposed to do this, but you can go in the back and check for yourself," the clerk said, pointing to the double doors behind her.

Junior pushed the doors open and entered into the emergency area. He spotted Shondra on a bed sitting up, and when she saw him, her eyes lit up. He made his way over to her and hugged her as she cried hard on his shoulders.

"The police are here, baby, and they asking a lot of questions," she quickly told him.

"You okay?" he asked, feeling the bump on the back of her head.

The question brought back the reason she was in the emergency room.

"Yeah, but that bitch you fuckin' wit' pulled out a gun on me, Junior. She was going to shoot me."

"What?" Junior said, shocked.

"Yeah, and I knocked it outta her hand and was beating the shit outta her until somebody hit me in the back of my head."

"I'ma kill that bitch!" Junior screamed out loudly.

"I don't even know why you shittin' on me. I've been good to you." Shondra winced from suddenly feeling a sharp pain from the bump on her head.

"Look, I'ma talk to you when you get outta here. Right now, I'm gonna go handle that shit," Junior said with urgency.

"No, I want to talk about this shit now," Shondra said, but Junior vanished through the doors.

Junior parked in front of the rundown house and got out. He saw Muffin looking out of the window as he exited the car, so he slammed the door to let her know he wasn't there for a pleasant housecall. He figured she was coming down when he didn't see her face in the window anymore. He leaned against the hood of the car and waited for her to come down. One of the double wooden doors opened, and Muffin emerged from the dilapidated structure of the house, offsetting its ugliness by her radiant beauty. With the grace of a swan, she continued down the stairs. Then she saw the look of disgust in Junior's eyes and stopped abruptly at the bottom of the stairs as he advanced toward her menacingly.

"What's the matter, baby?" she asked fearfully, backing up as Junior moved closer to her.

"What the fuck happened at the club?" Junior asked through clenched teeth.

"Please, baby, let me explain before…" Muffin began.

"Why the fuck would you do that shit!" he screamed, as his open hand found her cheek and twisted her head to the left.

"Uuugh! Please, Junior! Please stop!" she cried out.

"Why should I, bitch! You pulled a gun out on my girl!" Junior growled.

"Please, Junior. I'm sorry. I was jealous," Muffin responded apologetically.

Realizing what he was doing, Junior backed away from her and turned to leave.

"Junior! Wait! Baby, please! Junior!" she called out to him, sensing she may lose him if he left.

"You fucked up, Muff. Stay the fuck away from me!" Junior threatened.

"Junior, wait! There's something I need to tell you," she screamed out desperately, trying to get him to listen to her.

The way she said it made Junior stop abruptly. Something in her tone told him he should listen to what she had to say.

"Baby, I found out your man is trying to set you up," Muffin said quickly. She began telling everything she had learned from her cousin, Drez. "…I didn't know if I should go against the grain, but I knew in my heart I had to tell you. All I ask is that you don't do anything to my cousin. That's all," she said when finished telling her tale.

Junior was heated. His cousin Craig told him not to trust Lakim from the time they had the shootout with Stump, but Junior went to bat for him and told Craig he was good peoples. Now he was faced with the same bullshit all over again.

Muffin was sitting on the stoop looking at Junior, not knowing his intentions. She didn't have any plans on what she was going to do with the information Drez had told her, but when she saw Junior was so upset about what she did to Shondra, she was desperate and told him. She wasn't sure if she made a grave mistake by telling Junior. If anything happened to Drez because of what she told him, she wouldn't be able to live with herself.

Junior was already in thinking mode. He looked at Muffin and couldn't help but thank her in his mind for saving him from another setup. There was no denying her love for him. He was feeling indebted to her for what she had told him. He walked over to her and stroked her hair gently, then whispered in her ear.

"I appreciate what you just told me, but you on probation until I take care of this shit. You understand?"

Like a humble servant, she bowed her head and invited his touch, apologizing again for what she did at the club.

"I'm not gonna promise you anything about your cuz 'cause I gotta look out for me. You feel me?" Junior searched her eyes for understanding. "I know it probably was hard for you to make this decision, but you need to understand the seriousness of what you told me. I need you to know that I cannot promise you anything."

He wasn't sure how close she was to her cousin and didn't want her to tip him off after what he just told her, but it wouldn't really matter because he already knew of the plot. He preferred the element of surprise, but if that couldn't be avoided, then it would have to be an all-out war.

"I told you because I don't want anything to happen to you, daddy, but I don't want anything to happen to my cousin either. If it's a choice I have to make, then I choose you, and if something happens, I'll charge it to the game."

Just what I wanted to hear, Junior thought. *I knew this bitch was thorough.*

"I'm out, but I'm gonna call you later on," he said.

"Okay, but please call me, and I'm sorry, baby. I hope you forgive me," Muffin said to him.

She watched the car pull off down the street and stood on her stoop wondering if she had just signed her cousin's death certificate.

CHAPTER 15
NO MORE BITCHIN'

Stump was enjoying his early morning shower. As he let the hot, steamy water beat down on his body, he wondered what had happened to KB. It had been a week since the robbery, and he hadn't heard anything from him. He sent one of his boys to his house and anonymously gave his cut from the robbery to his mother.

He grabbed a towel from the rack, got out of the shower, and got dressed in his room. He put on his bulletproof vest, a precaution he took every day after the unfortunate time he was shot up. He grabbed his twin nine-millimeter Glock automatics and tucked them inside his waistband. Then he snatched up some money and headed for the front door. He looked out the peephole, which was also part of his normal routine, then turned the knob slowly and pulled open the door. He hesitated in the hallway, thinking he had left something behind, but he couldn't remember what. So, he put the key in the door and locked it.

When Stump's door slammed, a figure in the exit staircase pulled out a gun and stood close to the exit door. As Stump's footsteps grew louder, the man in the staircase could hear his victim coming closer and he readied himself by the door. Stump walked down the long corridor and headed for the back staircase, unaware that a gunman was waiting for him. He didn't like waiting

for the elevator and rarely took it. When he went to grab the knob on the exit door, it flung open.

Stump was face-to-face with the gunman who had a big, black gun pointing right at him. Before Stump could react, the hooded gunman let off two shots to Stump's midsection, sending him tumbling backward into the corridor. The noise from the gun echoed loudly throughout the building as the gunman fired off three more shots. As one of the bullets pierced Stump's thigh, he managed to pull out both his guns and return fire while slumped against the wall. The gunman jumped back into the exit and slammed the door shut as the bullets from Stump's gun hit the metal door, creating huge, round cylinders on impact. Stump tried to get to his feet, but his thigh wound prevented him from getting up quickly, although his vest had stopped the penetration of the bullets that were targeted at his chest. The gunman in the exit attempted to open the door, and as he did, Stump squeezed off more shots to stop him from coming into the hallway. The deafening echoes from the gun blasts boomed like thunder inside the hallway of the building. The gunman opened the door and fired off a shot so he could peek into the hallway to see how badly Stump was wounded.

Stump, who was leaning on the wall, kept his guns pointed toward the stairway door that the gunman was hiding behind. There was silence for what seemed like an eternity. Then there was another loud boom, but it came from the other end of the corridor. It got Stump's attention, and he looked down the hallway. Someone else was standing at the other end, and the face seemed vaguely familiar to him. Stump then realized it was a set up because he was being ambushed. He never thought anyone had enough heart to try to hit him inside his own building.

He mustered up all the strength he had left in his body and fired two shots in the direction of the other gunman, then ran to the second exit while writhing in pain. He was feeling death coming on his heels as he tumbled down the concrete stairs, trying to get to the lobby. Hearing footsteps behind him, he stopped on one of the floors, opened, and then slammed the exit door as if he had gone out on that floor, then continued down the stairs.

The first gunman rumbled down the stairs, determined to finish Stump off, but he was thrown off by the slamming of the exit door. He stopped briefly on that floor but heard faint sounds coming from the stairwell below, so he continued down, this time treading softly so he wouldn't be detected.

Stump stopped on the second floor because of the pain in his legs and chest. He reloaded his clip, put his back against the wall, and tried to breathe in to regain some strength. He was almost to the lobby of his building, where he would be home free because he was sure one of his little homies would help him out.

While the gunman crept down the stairs, he could hear heavy breathing. As he approached the bottom of the third floor stairwell landing, he rounded the corner of the stairs and pointed his gun at Stump, who was unaware of his presence at the top of the stairs. He was surprised Stump was still standing after being hit by his powerful magnum. He aimed steadily for his head to make sure the job would be complete, then one more loud boom rattled the stairwell. The bullet slammed into the back of Stump's skull with deliberate force and traveled through, exploding through the front, shattering his eye socket and leaving facial tissue and brain matter littered on the wall. Stump's body hit the concrete with such force that his collarbone was broken on impact. Thought to be invincible, Stump's reign was over.

The gunman quickly ran down the stairs, and although Stump wasn't moving, he put an exclamation point on his work. Then he ruffled through the pockets of the corpse and took everything, even removing the guns from Stump's possession.

Once the killer finished his clean up, he ran as fast as he could to the roof of the building and crossed over to an adjoining building. There he took off his black hoodie and sweats and put them in a bag, then threw them down the incinerator on his descent to the lobby of that building. He walked out of the building into the sunlight and watched as a crowd gathered in front of Stump's building. As he walked down the lane in the direction of Baptiste Plaza, the gunman wondered if his accomplice had made it out safely, as well.

***

Lakim was sitting in his living room waiting on Rock when he heard a knock on his door. He walked to the door, gun in hand, and looked out the peephole.

"Who is it?" Lakim asked.

"Drez."

He opened the door and Drez walked in.

"So what up with this muhfucka Junior? When we gonna get at him?" Drez asked impatiently.

"I want to take care of it this week, but it can't happen over here," Lakim said. "I don't want his people to think I had anything to do with it. You know what I mean?"

"I hear what you sayin'. So where you plan on doin' it at?" Drez inquired.

"I don't know. That's what I'm thinking about now. The only place I know he hang out is in Tompkins, and it's hard to catch him on that side of town."

"I found out my lil cousin fuckin' him. I can get her to set him up so I can body him," Drez suggested.

"Your lil cousin is fucking him? I hope you didn't tell her."

"Look, muhfucka, that's my lil cuz. She family. She ain't gon' tell that muhfucka shit. And don't question me on it! You understand me!" Drez said forcefully.

"I hear you. I'm just thinking about if she did or does tell him, then what? Will you know if she did? Would she tell you?" Lakim questioned.

"She ain't gonna say shit! Maybe you ain't ready to play boss, muhfucka!" Drez shouted angrily.

"That shit don't work on me, son. My heart don't pump Kool-Aid, bruh," Lakim said defiantly.

"A'ight then, stop worrying about that bitch-ass nigga and let's set this shit up."

"I'm waiting on my man Rock so we can do this shit right."

"He didn't take care of that business yet? I practically gave you dude's head on a platter," Drez said.

"I said I'm waiting on him now," Lakim reiterated.

"A'ight. I'm tired of waiting. I say we get Junior wherever the fuck we see him. I don't have time to play secret agent with you. All you doin' is wastin' my fuckin' time," Drez said, tired of the procrastination.

"I'm just sayin', I don't want to make it a war. That'll slow down the money. It don't make sense to kill Junior over here, then it'll be hot as fish grease out here and won't nobody be able to make money."

"Is that right?" Drez asked.

"I'm just letting you know how I want it to be done," Lakim stated.

"On da real, bruh, you can't tell me shit. You ain't calling no shots if I'm laying down the murder game, so I'm really giving you a courtesy in telling you this shit!"

The knock on the door startled Lakim. He went to the peephole, and seeing it was Rock, he let him in.

Drez was still talking when Rock came into the living room and sat down. He listened to the conversation that was already in progress, and it seemed like Lakimg and Drez weren't agreeing on something.

"…and that's why we gotta do it now and not wait," Drez was saying.

"I hear you, but I don't want to take no chances on anybody linking it to me." Lakim was trying to explain his point.

"I'm not feeling what you saying right now. Sounds like you having a change of heart, bruh. I hope you not trying to flip the script," Drez said.

"Man, look, if we gonna do this, it gotta be done right, bottom line," Lakim replied, sounding like a broken record.

"Well, let's get it done then. No more bitchin'," Drez remarked.

Lakim looked over to Rock, who seemed to be listening intently.

"Yo, I'm gonna fill you in on what's about to happen, a'ight?" Lakim told Rock.

"I'm waitin' on you," Rock replied.

Lakim looked at Drez and then spoke to Rock again.

“Let me iron out the rest of the details with Drez, and as soon as we get it down right, I’ll let you know.”

“A’ight,” Rock said.

“We gonna let you know, lil man. There’s gonna be some major changes taking place very soon,” Drez added.

“I hear you,” Rock replied.

“You’ll bust your gun if you have to, right?” Drez asked Rock.

“I always bust my gun if I have to,” Rock replied matter-of-factly.

“See, that’s what the fuck I’m talkin’ ‘bout!” Drez shouted, looking at Lakim.

“Yo, beep me when y’all map this shit out. I’m goin’ on the block and check this money,” Rock said, then slapped both men five and walked out of the apartment.

CHAPTER 16
LET ME TELL YOU WHAT KARMA IS, MUHFUCKA

There was heavy police presence around the building as the two detectives walked over to the taped-off building. For Taylor and Burke this was not an unfamiliar sight. They were immune to dead bodies in the hood. It was commonplace for black males to escalate a small incident into something more serious, with murder becoming the end result. As a stretcher passed by them in the lobby of the building, Burke stopped the attendant and pulled the sheet back to see if there was a recognizable face underneath. Taylor stopped him and asked him to make a wager. If it was a convicted felon they both knew, then he would buy lunch. But, if it was someone they didn't know, Burke would take Taylor to lunch. Burke agreed and pulled the sheet off just enough to reveal the face. They weren't surprised to see it was Stump, aka Henry Billings. He was a known convict and a terror in those projects.

"Somebody must have finally got tired of his shit," Burke said, pulling the sheet back over the body.

"It was just a matter of time before somebody got to him. I guess he wasn't that lucky this time," Taylor added.

"Let's go check out the crime scene," Burke said.

They looked at the white outline of where the body rested last and observed a bulletproof vest that was obviously worn by the deceased victim.

"This is where it ended for him," Burke stated, kneeling down on the ground.

"I wonder if he knew it was his day or not," Taylor said, climbing the stairs to look for more evidence.

They went to the floor where the shooting started and there were police there already gathering evidence. Taylor and Burke looked at the holes in the exit door and the shell casings on the ground in the exit and hallway.

"Wow, I'm surprised it didn't end here. It looks like he didn't go without a fight," Taylor said.

There were no weapons, but there were plenty of shells. Taylor walked to the other end of the hallway where he discovered something unusual. There were two shells lying near the exit. He called his partner over.

"Seems like he was ambushed," Burke said upon seeing the shells.

"Yeah, seems like there were two gunmen. I guess they wanted to make sure he didn't get away," Taylor observed.

"His reputation exceeded him. There was no way they wanted him to get out of this alive. This was definitely a hit," Burke assessed.

"Seems like he got hit but was able to return fire. The shells at the other end of the hallway tell that story," Taylor said.

"I guess they didn't expect him to have on a vest. The holes in the exit door prove he was trying to sustain the gunfight. The guy on this end must have fired some shots to help the guy in the other exit." Burke was trying to figure out the last minutes of Stump's life.

"I know one thing, they were using some high-powered guns to get him," Taylor stated, looking at the high-caliber shells.

Taylor and Burke did the routine of knocking on doors and asking the tenants if they heard or saw anything, already anticipating the answer would be the same at every door. No one wanted to be a witness to a homicide because they feared

retaliation. Taylor and Burke knew most of the hardened criminals in the area, and they made it their business to keep their ears to the streets to find out who was who in the hood. They were hoping they would get a lead through one of their informants because they seriously doubted anyone was going to come forward voluntarily with any pertinent information. Although there were many that were probably glad Stump was dead, they were not going to give up any information on the assailant, even if they knew anything. If anyone told the police something and someone in the hood found out, the person would be marked for death. The code of the streets was never to snitch. Burke and Taylor knew of this code because it was similar to their "blue wall of silence", but it was mind-boggling to them that people, young and old, lived by the ridiculous code of not snitching, especially if it would change the condition in which they lived under.

The crowd that gathered in front of the building wanted to see if the rumors were true about Stump being dead. There were young and old in attendance. Some were crying and others were joking around as if his death was not serious. A lot of old people cried because there was another senseless death by the hands of one of their own. They couldn't help but feel depression and sadness from the genocide. Many of them had raised some of the kids in the neighborhood that turned out to be criminals

***

The room was silent except for the periodic beeping of the life support machine that KB was hooked up to. Gloria was sitting in a chair beside his bed keeping vigil. There were so many tubes running from him that he resembled a string puppet. He wasn't conscious and was breathing with the help of a respirator because his lung had collapsed. Gloria spoke to him and read him passages out of the Bible daily. She wasn't giving up, although the doctors were only giving him a fifty percent chance for a full recovery because of his injuries.

Gloria was getting prepared for KB's second surgery when Shondra came to visit. Gloria hadn't seen her since KB was shot

and didn't want to see her because of how she put a man in front of their friendship. Shondra entered the room, not waiting for an invitation, and placed the balloons and card she had bought on his nightstand. As Gloria gave her a wicked look, Shondra walked over to her and sat down in the chair across from the bed.

"Glo," she started, tears welling up in her eyes, "I know you don't want to see me or talk to me, but I really want you to know that I'm so sorry for betraying your trust and our friendship."

"I don't want to hear shit from you, bitch. So, please get the fuck outta here!" Gloria growled.

"Please, Glo, just give me a chance to…"

"Give you a chance? Give you a chance? Why the fuck should I give you a chance? Look at him, Shondra." Gloria pointed to KB lying in the bed. "Did you give him a chance. Did you give me a chance, huh? Did you give us a fucking chance? You was only thinking about yourself!"

"I know, Glo, and I'm sorry," Shondra said sincerely.

"You're sorry? I'm sorry, too, bitch. I'm sorry I ever trusted you. I'm sorry I ever met you, and I'm sorry you ain't value our friendship. Now get the fuck outta my face, bitch!"

That statement tore into Shondra like the slugs that tore into KB's chest. Shondra and Gloria's friendship was completely over.

***

"What up, Junior?" Lakim asked, speaking into the phone.

"Ain't nuthin'. What's up on your end?" Junior replied.

"We dry out here. We starting to lose our customers because we don't have enough work for all the shifts. I got the workers on a tight schedule, so a lot of them getting mad. Some of them going ova to the competition 'cause ain't enough work," Lakim informed Junior.

"I know shit's fucked up right now, but there's a drought because of that big bust in Miami. So, my connect don't have nothing right now," Junior explained.

"You don't have nothing stashed that you can give me to hold me down until he comes through?" Lakim asked desperately.

"Nah, kid, I ain't got shit. I gave you all I had from the last time I copped," Junior responded.

"A'ight then, man, just make sure you beep me and let me know when you get right."

"Yeah, I got you," Junior said, then hung up.

This was the second time Lakim had beeped Junior about getting some more work. Junior was waiting until there was no work over there so he could put his plan into effect. Lakim had tried to lure Junior to the projects to talk about Dusty a week ago, but Junior felt if he went there, he wouldn't return. That's when he knew he had to put an end to the bullshit. He had collected all the proceeds from the last package from Rock. He was going to cripple Lakim by breaking him down piece by piece. When Lakim called again and told him most of the workers defected to the competition because they weren't making any money, Junior knew it was time. Lakim's power was gone, and he was going to show him who the real boss of Baptiste was.

***

There weren't any workers in front of the building when two men in suits, one carrying a duffle bag, entered the building across the street. Lately, it wasn't an unusual scene for the streets to be empty because there hadn't been any work in the projects for weeks. The two men went into the building and walked up the six flights to the roof. Once they reached the door to the roof, they opened it slowly and stepped out into the cool night, walking around to make sure no one was up there. The gravel beneath their feet made a small crunching noise as they patrolled the roof. From the roof, they had a bird's eye view of the street and a good look of anything coming into or leaving the building. They also had a clear view of the building across the street, which was their main interest. The guys went into the duffle bag and took out two black work jumpsuits. They put them on and then took out two high-powered rifles with scopes on them, placing them against the wall of the roof. After they got into their uniforms, they placed padlocks on the roof doors, then took their position by the edge of

the roof and waited.

***

Junior pulled out a vest from Craig's closet. It was an official police vest that Craig had gotten from one of the girls he fucked with on the police force. He put it on over his white T-shirt, strapped it to him using the Velcro straps, and then donned an oversized hoodie. His frame looked a little bulky, but he would hide that with a leather jacket. He grabbed two .45 automatics and a .357 snub-nosed magnum revolver. He tucked the two .45's in his waist, then placed the revolver in a holster and stuffed it in the middle of his back. He looked at himself in the mirror, and satisfied with the way he looked, he grabbed his keys and left.

Junior pulled up to a phone booth, beeped Lakim, and sat in the car waiting for him to call back. He had circled the projects already and no one was on the block. When he felt the vibration from his beeper, he looked down and saw an unfamiliar number. He went to the phone booth and made the call.

"Hello?"

"Somebody just beeped me from this number?" Junior asked.

"Who's this?" the mysterious voice inquired.

"Somebody beeped me from this number. If there's somebody else there, ask them if they just beeped somebody," Junior answered, not wanting to give his name to the strange voice.

"Hold on."

"Hello," Lakim said, picking up the phone.

"Yeah, what up?"

"Nuthin'. You straight?" Lakim asked.

"Yeah, I'm straight. Where you at?" Junior questioned.

"I'm at a broad's house in Lindsey. You already in the hood?" Lakim asked.

"Nah, I'm not over there yet, but I'm on my way, though. Matter of fact, why don't you meet me on the block?" Junior suggested.

"Why don't you just come to the crib instead?" Lakim replied.

“I got some loose, so I want to go out there and let the heads check it out and let them know that shit clicking again. You can take the rest of the shit back to the crib when I get there,” Junior told him.

“I can send one of the workers out there so you don’t have to go out there yourself. Ain’t no need for you gettin’ hot for nuthin’,” Lakim offered.

“It shouldn’t be that hot out there now ‘cause ain’t no work been out there in about three weeks, right?” Junior asked.

“Yeah, that’s true. A’ight, I’ll meet you around there in fifteen minutes,” Lakim replied.

“A’ight, son.” Junior hung up and quickly dialed another number to let his people know he was on his way.

“Damn!” Lakim exclaimed, as he sat down on the couch and rubbed his head.

“What’s wrong? Was that him?” Drez asked.

“Yeah,” Lakim replied.

“Then why you draggin’ around like that? You ready to move or what?” Drez asked anxiously.

“He wants to meet in front of the building on the block,” Lakim told him.

“Okay, I’m going over there,” Drez said.

“Wait. I gotta beep Rock.”

“You do that. I’ll be in the back of the building waiting,” Drez replied, preparing to leave.

Lakim called Rock and told him the plan was going down and to meet him on the block.

Drez walked into the building and went out the front to see if Junior had arrived. There wasn’t anyone standing in the front of the building when he peeked out, but the two gunmen on the roof saw Drez and had their sights on him, following his every move until he disappeared into the building.

Junior pulled up on the side of the building and got out. He walked around to the front to make sure his cousin’s boys were in position on the roof. He looked up, and when he saw them, he put up two fingers. They replied by putting up one finger and waving it. Junior had planned everything up to now, but this was the part

he couldn't plan. He had to play this one by ear, and that's what made it so dangerous. As he stood there, he wondered if Lakim was coming himself or if he would send someone else. Junior was nervous and was taking a chance standing out there in the open.

When Lakim got to the building, he saw Drez sitting on the benches in the back. He couldn't believe the dumb motherfucker was sitting on the benches in plain sight. What the hell was he doing? Lakim walked into the building and went to the front to meet Junior. When Junior heard the door opening, he moved off the wall, wanting to see who was coming out of the building.

"What up, Junior?" Lakim asked, walking up and slapping him five.

"Same ol', same ol', playa. What's poppin'?" Junior responded.

"Waitin' on you, boss. Shit been dry. You ready to crank this shit back up?" Lakim asked excitedly.

"That's why I'm here. Go get a head so they can test it out real fast," Junior told him.

"A'ight, let me go see Pee Wee."

"Here." Junior pulled out a sample of the work for Lakim to take to the head to test.

Lakim took the product and went into the building. Junior waited for him to get on the elevator before entering the building. Then Junior walked to the back door, peeked out of the small triangular window, and noticed someone sitting on the benches. He couldn't make out a face, but he knew he wasn't one of the workers. Junior hurried back out to the front and waited for Lakim to return. He was glad Lakim didn't embrace him because he didn't want him to feel the vest he was wearing under his jacket. The roof gunmen's palms were sweaty as they gripped the long barrels on their high-powered rifles.

Lakim returned with a smile on his face.

"Damn! Pee Wee said that shit made his dick hard," Lakim said, laughing.

"Good. That's all I needed to hear," Junior replied.

"Where the rest of the shit at? I'm ready to put that shit out here now." Lakim was hype.

"I got it in the car. It's already bagged up," Junior told him.

"Good. That means I don't have to worry about doing it," Lakim responded, while rubbing his palms together.

Junior looked at the greed in Lakim's eyes and it disgusted him.

"How many workers you got left?" Junior asked.

"I'm down to three."

"Damn! Them lil muhfuckas ain't show you no loyalty. You shouldn't let them eat. You can't trust muhfuckas that'll bite the hand that feeds them. You know what I mean?" Junior said to him.

Lakim looked at Junior and hung onto his words like a trapeze artist. His palms began to get sweaty and his legs became weak. Junior suddenly grabbed him by his collar, pulled out the .45, and pulled him to the far side of the building away from the door.

"I'm gonna ask you one time, kid. That muhfucka in the back, is he waiting for me?" His gun was pressed up hard in Lakim's ribcage.

"I don't know that kid in the back," Lakim replied quickly.

"Wrong answer. Look on the roof, muhfucka! You and that dude in the back is dead!" Junior said with ice in his voice.

"Hold on, Junior. I don't know what the fuck is going on. I just came out here to meet you for the work so I can get this shit clicking again. I don't know what you talkin' 'bout. That's my word."

"We'll see. What's the signal? Is he 'posed to come out when you go back in the building?" Junior questioned.

"Man, I don't know what the fuck you talkin' 'bout. You buggin'," La said nervously.

"You know how I know you lyin', La? 'Cause if you didn't know him, you woulda asked if he was wit' me when you came through the back of the building. I don't got no time for your bullshit. If you don't tell me what duke doing back there, I'm gonna leave your brains on the wall!" Junior threatened.

When Lakim hesitated, Junior hit him in his head with the butt of the pistol, causing Lakim to let out a loud scream.

Seconds later, the front door of the building flung open and Drez emerged, gun in hand. Junior kept Lakim in front of him, pointing his gun in Drez's direction.

"What, muhfucka!" Junior bellowed.

"NOOOO!" Lakim screamed.

Junior squeezed off a shot and the bullet hit the door. Drez opened fire, hitting Lakim as Junior used him as a shield. Lakim's screams were heard all through the hood as Junior let off more shots in Drez's direction. The bullets hit the divider in front of the building, chipping away at the cement, as Drez stayed behind it for cover. Lakim dropped to the cold concrete, while Junior continued firing his pistol. The two guys on the roof couldn't get a clear shot of Drez. Their view was obstructed by the partition he was hiding behind. Junior made a mad dash to the corner of the building, letting off shots as he ran, hoping that would keep Drez from returning fire. Drez peeked around the partition and saw Junior fleeing towards the rear of the building. So, he ran inside to the back of the building with plans of ambushing him.

Junior stopped short when he got to the side of the building and double backed, peeking around to the front. His heart was racing as he looked up on the roof of the building across the street. The gunmen on the roof were waving their hands, motioning for him to go back to the front of the building. Junior ran back to the front and peeked around the corner. There was no sign of Drez or Lakim. Then the guys on the roof pointed to the far corner of the building.

Drez was peeking through the door to the back of the building, waiting to see Junior. He could hear Lakim moaning in the hallway but couldn't help him. He didn't mean to shoot Lakim, but he didn't have a choice. Lakim was propped up against the wall in the lobby, and there was a long streak of blood from the front door to where he was resting by the elevator. Drez slowly pushed open the back door, hoping to catch Junior. Then he heard a loud bang that came from behind him, and the force of the hit instantly threw him out the door. He fell to the ground and turned to look behind him, but the door closed too quickly. How did he let Junior sneak up behind him like that? He never thought to check whether Junior

had doubled back on him.

Drez's gun slid to the benches when he fell. He tried to get up, but the wound to his back wouldn't allow him to move. He was face down and could feel the burning pain in his back. He continued to try to pull himself to the benches to get his gun because that was the only chance he had to survive. Then he saw some black Chukka Timbs in front of him. He peered up and was shocked to see Junior standing over him pointing a gun to his head. He was stupefied. If Junior was standing in front of him, then who had shot him in his back? Did Lakim double-cross him?

Junior walked to the benches and picked up Drez's gun, then stood over him again.

"So you Muffin's cousin, huh?" Junior asked, turning him over on his back with his foot and pointing the gun to his forehead.

"Fuck you, muhfucka!" Drez groaned.

"I guess blood ain't thicker than water, huh?" Junior replied, and then he realized who Drez was. "You the muhfucka that pistol-whipped my girl in the club. Wow, what are the odds? Let me tell you what karma is, muhfucka. It's fate, and yours is sealed! Yo fam, La didn't tell you that I ain't that predictable? You made a fuckin' mistake when you got with La, dickhead. Y'all thought y'all was gonna take ova my shit jus' like that, huh, muhfucka?" Junior kneeled down to the wounded man as he spoke into his ear. "You didn't think shit was gonna play out like this, did you?"

That was the last thing Drez heard before everything went dark.

Junior took everything out of Drez's pockets, including his ID, and then he threw some drug capsules into the grass next to Drez. He hoped the homicide detectives would think it was a drug war after seeing the two dead bodies and close the case.

Lakim was still slumped over by the elevator where Drez had dragged him after Junior ran. Lakim didn't know how bad he was hit, but he was having trouble breathing and was losing blood. He could see Drez standing by the back door peeking out. Then he heard footsteps coming from the staircase. As the sounds grew closer, he tried to rise to his feet, hoping it was someone to help him. Rock appeared from the staircase with gun in hand, and when he saw Drez, he squeezed the trigger and Drez was thrown outside. Lakim looked up at Rock, who walked calmly over to the back door and slammed it shut.

"You a dirty muhfucka, La," Rock hissed when he turned around.

"What the fuck you talking about?" Lakim asked, his breathing labored.

"How can you be so fucking foul? The muhfucka treated you good. He gave you total control of shit out here, and your ass was frontin' like it was all you the whole time. I knew, La. I been knew you was a dirty muhfucka. You the same muhfucka that said what your man Kendu, God bless the dead, did to Junior was foul. Then you turn around and do the same dirty shit! You's a grimy-ass dude, son. And yo, let me tell you, that dude Drez…well, he the one that bodied your man Du. Did you know that, La?"

"How you know that, Rock? How you know Drez murdered my man?" Lakim asked incredulously.

"Doesn't matter now, muhfucka. He dead!" Rock barked.

"Okay, Rock, you got this. You played it right, and you played me. What now?" Lakim murmured.

"That's just it, La. I'ma leave you here to die. If you make it, then your maggot ass may deserve to live. But, trust and believe me, you won't be able to live ova here no fuckin' more, and if I see you 'round here, La, I'ma put ya lights out for good — eternal darkness, muhfucka!"

Rock walked out of the building, leaving Lakim slumped against the wall bleeding. Junior was standing in the back of the building when Rock came out.

"Where that foul-ass La at?" Junior asked.

"He dead," Rock said.

"You sure?" Junior asked.

"Not really, but if he wasn't, he will be soon," Rock said, as he counted the money Junior handed him.

"Well, one thing's for sure. He ain't running shit out here no more. Now it's time for us to blow up!" Junior said, while giving Rock the package Lakim believed he was getting.

CHAPTER 17
YOU BELIEVE HER

The restaurant was crowded, so the couple waited to be seated.

"Table for two?" the short waiter asked, as he handed the duo menus.

"Yeah." Junior replied, putting out his cigarette in the ashray provided for waiting customers.

"Smoking or non-smoking?" the waiter asked, while leading them toward the back of the restaurant to the smoking section.

"How this dude gon' ask me smoking or non-smoking and automatically walk to the smoking section? I'm going to fuck with him. Watch this," Junior said.

The waiter walked over to a table in the smoking section, stood next to it, and waited for the couple to sit down.

"Here you go." The waiter pulled the chair from under the table.

"Is this the non-smoking section?" Junior asked.

"Uh, no, this is the smoking section," the waiter responded.

"Why the fuck we ova here then?" Junior asked with contempt.

"Uh, I thought you…"

"You don't get paid to think, you get paid to take orders. How the fuck did you know we wanted to sit in this section? Did you wait for the answer? Now take us to the non-smoking section,

asshole!" Junior barked.

"I apologize, sir. I made a mistake," the waiter replied regretfully.

"See what you gotta go through just to get a nice table out this muhfucka. I swear I get tired of this kind of treatment when I'm spending a lot of dough," Junior said.

They took their seat and looked over the menu.

"Order anything you want, baby girl," Junior told Muffin.

Muffin was looking over the menu, but she didn't have an appetite. Junior was spending a lot of time with her lately, and she was enjoying every moment with him, but she knew the real reason for all the attention. She found out Drez was murdered, and Junior told her that he was there when it happened but wasn't the one that killed him. She wanted to believe him, but she was having mixed feelings because she was the one that told him about what Drez and Lakim were planning. When she told Junior, she did ask him not to hurt her cousin, but he never promised. So, she didn't know if she should believe what he was telling her.

It happened almost a month ago, and since then, Junior was spending every waking moment with her. She enjoyed the lovemaking and the gifts, but she couldn't get her cousin's murder out of her head. She was overwhelmed with guilt because if she never told Junior what she knew, Drez might still be alive. Now she was in a very awkward place and didn't know if she should leave Junior alone and tell the police, or go with her heart and forgive him. It was a hard decision for her to make, but she needed to do something because it was affecting the way she acted when she was with him.

"You ready to order?" Junior asked, interrupting her deep thoughts.

"Yeah, gimme the garden salad," she said.

"That's all you want, honey? You ain't been eatin' much lately. You on a diet or sumthin'?" Junior asked jokingly.

"Nah, baby, I'm just not hungry," Muffin said softly.

Junior knew what was bothering Muffin. She had been acting funny ever since he told her that he was there when Drez was killed. He didn't have a choice in telling her because she was the one that told him about the setup, and if he denied any involvement, he would have to worry about her snitching on him to the cops. He began to spend more time with her to keep her happy and to keep an eye on her. He figured if she was happy, she wouldn't snitch on him, and if he was always around, she wouldn't have the chance to snitch. She seemed happy most of the time. But, there were times she looked like she was deep in thought, and that's when she zoned out. This worried him because he wanted to trust her, but he had already experienced betrayal from dudes that were supposed to be true to him, and the way she was acting made him wonder how trustworthy she really was. He was glad that through it all, there was still one person he could trust his life with, and that was Shondra.

***

While Junior sat in the restaurant wining and dining his mistress, Shondra was sitting in the living room on the couch crying her eyes out. Gloria still wasn't speaking to her, and Junior was spending less time with her. She was feeling like she had lost the two people she loved the most, and then she heard a knock on her door. She walked over to the door, and without thinking, she opened it.

"Good afternoon. Ms. Brown?" the detective asked.

Shondra straightened up when she saw the two detectives at her door. She was thinking the worst, so she tried to brace herself for bad news.

"Yes, I'm Ms. Brown. Is there a problem?" she asked.

It was Taylor and Burke.

"Actually, yes. Can we come in for a second?" Taylor asked.

Shondra moved from in front of the door and let them in, motioning for them to sit on the couch.

"Would you two like something to drink?"

"Sure, thanks. Ms. Brown, I want to ask you some questions if you don't mind." Taylor was doing all the talking.

Shondra went into the kitchen, poured two glasses of Pepsi, and handed them to the men on the couch.

"Do you know someone named Junior?" Taylor asked, taking a sip of his drink.

"Yes, I do. Why?" she asked with a worried look.

"Well, Ms. Brown, we need to ask him some questions. Do you know where we can find him, or is there a number where we can reach him at home?"

"No."

"Ms. Brown, this is a very serious matter. Any information you can provide us with will give us an opportunity to try to help him. You know, give him a chance to clear up any accusations against him." Taylor put the glass on the center table.

"What accusations?" Shondra asked.

"It's not really accusations. It's more like finger pointing. Someone has mentioned his name in the connection to a murder about three weeks ago. The person that's pointing the finger isn't really credible, but we have to follow up on any leads, even if we believe them to be false. That's why we would like to talk with him so we can exclude him from the investigation."

"Well, if I see him, I'll let him know what you guys told me," Shondra replied, ending the conversation.

Both detectives rose and headed for the door.

"Okay, thanks for your help. Whenever you hear from him, you can have him call us, and we'll question him and clear his name as quickly as possible." Taylor handed his and Burke's business cards to her, then walked out the door.

"You believe her?" Taylor asked Burke once they were in the hallway.

"Hell no. The bitch is protecting him. We'll have to catch him on the streets," Burke replied.

"Well, I don't think she's going to be the one that hands him over to us," Taylor said, while opening the door to the unmarked police car.

***

The waiter brought a garden salad for Muffin and Junior had the Galleto al Balsamico Antico, which was a fancy Italian name

for grilled chicken, fried vegetables, and roasted potatoes. They both ate their meals quietly as a live band played soft music in the background. Junior decided to address Muffin's long silence.

"What's wrong, baby girl? It's like you have a lot on your mind but you don't want to share anything with me. I thought we was better than that. You know if something bothers you, it bothers me. You my lung, mama." As he spoke, he placed both her hands in his.

"Oh baby, I love you so much," she said, as she squeezed his hand. "I don't know what's wrong with me, baby. I don't want to make you feel that I'm hiding anything from you, because I will never do that. I don't really know what's wrong, Junior. So much has happened and I guess I'm depressed. I don't know."

"It's just that I'm worried about you, baby. It's like you're not happy anymore, not like how you used to be. I be trying to do things to make you happy, and it doesn't seem to be working," he said.

"No, baby, I appreciate everything you've done for me. I mean, you are the best. It's me, baby, not you."

"No, don't blame yourself. I know you've been through a lot. I want to understand you. I want to be there for you, and I want you to trust me, my words, and my actions, because it's all true to what we have built together. I want you to know that my love for you is real. I need you to feel my love, Muff," Junior serenaded.

"I do, Junior. I don't doubt how you feel for me. In the beginning, I wasn't sure, but I always wanted you to love me the way you do right now. I feel your love, baby, and I don't want that to change. You're my heart. You have my heart, Junior. You make me smile, you make me feel safe, and I love that feeling and don't ever want to lose it," Muffin professed.

"I know you're still mourning over your cousin, and it's kind of foul for you to be with the muhfucka that was there when he died. That's why I want you to know that I understand you having mixed feelings about being with me, but I need you to know and believe that I'm not the one that killed him. I would never lie to you about something like that, Muff. If it wasn't for you, shit

would have gone differently that day. So, I gotta keep it real wit' you. Do you understand what I'm sayin'?"

"I can't lie, baby. I've been feeling responsible for my cousin's death. I told you what he told me because I didn't want anything to happen to you because I love you, but I didn't want anything to happen to him either because he my family. Now I feel guilty, like I'm the one that killed him. It's because of what I told you that he's dead, and I feel like shit," Muffin said, her emotions getting the best of her.

"Come on. Let's get outta here so we can talk. I don't want you breakin' down in here." Junior stated after noticing her eyes watering.

He rose to his feet, threw some money on the table, and grabbed her hand, leading her out of the restaurant. He remained silent until they got in the car, and then he continued where they left off.

"Look, Muff, I'm really sorry that your cousin got killed, but you know something. I'm glad it wasn't me. That might sound fucked up to you, but you have to understand the game that I'm in. Muhfuckas be wantin' me dead jus' because — no reason, jus' because. Think about it, ma. My man was trying to get me bodied. This game don't have no loyalty. Finding out that your cousin got killed had to make you feel fucked up because you knew it had something to do with me. You might even have wished when you first heard about it that it was me instead of him because of your guilt. I gotta respect that because that was your family and blood is supposed to be thicker than water. I remember you sayin' that if something happened to him you would charge it to the game. Well, I had to do the same for my man La. His betrayal was something I didn't expect. I trusted him with my whole operation, and he was dishonorable. That's his charge. Imagine how I feel now, though. I'm not the one that bodied Drez, but I was the nigga he was looking to kill. Now I'm with his cousin, who happens to be the one that put me on to what he was planning to do. I feel fucked up, too, Muff. Sometimes I wish I didn't meet you so that you didn't have to make that decision. I feel like that because I feel your pain when I look at you. I don't want you to second-guess your

decision, but at the same time, I don't want you to be glad that you didn't." Junior paused. "One thing I can tell you, Muff, is that I know you love me. I know how you feel for me is true, and I trust you, baby. Believe me, it's hard for me to trust anybody after all this shit, but I trust you. I trust you because I know you love me for real."

Muffin was beside herself emotionally. Junior's statement reduced her to tears. She had grown to love him, and after hearing all this, she felt he was really in love with her. The tears streamed down like a waterfall, and she became weak. This was the feeling of true love. She didn't say anything else to him. She just leaned over and buried her head in his chest.

***

Now that Junior had made him second in command, things were looking up for Rock and he was enjoying the money he was making in the projects. The only thing that troubled him was that he was still hot as a firecracker in the hood. Taylor and Burke still fucked with him every time they saw him on the block. Now they were harassing him about a murder.

"Yeah, well, you better watch your back. Word on the street is that his friends are looking for the guy or guys that did it," Taylor said to Rock.

"Okay and you're telling me this to say what?" Rock asked.

"I'm just telling you what I heard, and it came from a reliable source. You resemble the description they gave us of the perps," Taylor responded.

"Don't we all look alike to y'all anyway?" Rock asked with his head cocked to one side.

"Smart ass! You know something, Rock. I have a strong feeling you had something to do with it, and if you didn't, you know who did. If you tell me what part you played in it now, I can promise you won't go to jail for coming forward," Taylor said.

Rock could tell Taylor was bullshitting him. There was no way he would walk if he told Taylor he was involved.

"Well, you don't have to worry about that 'cause I don't know nothing," he told the detective.

"You little bastards make me sick. You think you're so smart and slick. I really don't care what happened. It's just my job to find out, and I promise you, Rock, once I get the evidence I need to put you behind bars, I'm going to make sure they throw your ass under the cell," Taylor promised.

"Damn, man, I told you I don't know shit. Why you so mad at me? You act like it was somebody you knew personally."

"You little fuck!" Burke grabbed Rock by his collar. "You really think I won't make your mother childless?" Then he whispered in his ear, "If I catch you late at night by yourself and no one is around, your picture may turn up on a milk box."

"Look, I don't know why you screaming and threatenin' me like that. I don't know what happened, and trust me, if I did, I would tell you because the shit happened in my hood. So, please stop threatenin' me." Rock said it loud enough for everyone in earshot to hear, just in case Burke was serious and Rock wound up mysteriously dead.

"Fuckin' smart ass!" Burke said and released his hold on Rock, which sent him flying into the side of the building. "You on my shit list, you black bastard!"

After that incident, the detectives continued to come around every day, implying they were getting closer to solving the case. They kept trying to offer Rock a way out if he gave them information that would help them close the case. Rock was beginning to get nervous because if they ever found out he was involved, they would make sure he was prosecuted to the fullest extent of the law. Things were going too good for Rock now, and he wasn't looking for it to end due to him getting locked up. So, he was seriously contemplating telling the detectives something that would ensure his freedom.

Shit, Junior's the one that killed Drez. I only shot him, he reasoned.

This was the typical reaction of anyone who found himself in a precarious situation, especially when faced with extensive jail time. Rock was enjoying being "under-boss" of the operation. He

liked how all the females flocked to him, and he was definitely enjoying the money he was stacking. All that would be in jeopardy, unless he did something to secure it.

Rock was doing better than when Lakim was in charge. He was moving whatever Junior gave him like a truck driver on the Interstate. Junior had dropped off a key for him and he was already down to four O's, and he had only gotten it a week ago. Unlike how Lakim did it, Rock didn't wait until the workers were completely out. He would pay them on the ends. Junior liked it that way because he got paid first, and the workers liked it because they always had money and were able to save. Rock had gained a lot of respect in the hood, and since Stump's death, there wasn't any threat of a worker getting robbed or killed while they were out making money.

People in the hood were treating Rock and Junior differently. Both guys had become ghetto celebrities. After what happened to Lakim and Drez, it seemed as if everyone knew they were responsible, but no one was willing to snitch because they feared death would be the retaliation and rightfully so. Rock figured out how thorough Junior was from Stump's murder. Junior was the one that devised the ambush on Stump. When Rock told Junior that Lakim wanted him to do the hit on Stump, Junior told Rock to go ahead with it, but he wanted to be there to make sure everything went right. Lakim never knew Junior was the actual mastermind of the hit. Junior scrapped Lakim's idea once Rock told him, because if Rock did it Lakim's way, he would never have made it out of the building without getting caught. So, Junior planned the murder, right down to the last detail.

***

The phone was ringing, but no one would pick up. This worried Shondra more and more. Her friend wasn't returning any of her calls. She had been calling Gloria's house ever since she heard that KB had come home from the hospital. She wanted to see if she could repair their friendship, but she never could get in contact with Gloria.

Shondra's frustration was amplified by the absence of her man, whom she hadn't seen in months. Junior hadn't spent any time with her since the incident with Lakim and Drez, and when she beeped him, he rarely answered her pages. She was spiraling into a depression and was beginning to question their relationship. This was a time when she needed him the most, and he was unavailable. The fact that she lost her friendship because of her decision to betray Gloria for his benefit weighed heavy on her heart. It seemed like Junior didn't care about what she was going through now that it was all over. She was sure he had things on his mind, too, but she was his girl, his Bonnie, and he wasn't showing her any love or understanding.

The only thing she could think about was him cheating on her with that girl from the club the night KB was shot. Thinking that he was still with that same girl was inevitable. Why else wouldn't he return her calls or come see her? What other explanation could there be? The more she thought about it, the more upset she became, and when a woman started to think about infidelity in her relationship, she was likely to do anything.

Shondra went to the phone and dialed Junior's pager number, putting in 9-1-1. If he didn't call her back, she was going to go find him.

***

KB was still in pain, but he was healing quickly. He was already walking without the cane they gave him in physical therapy. Gloria had stood by him the entire time. From the time he arrived at the hospital to the day he left, Gloria's face was always the first thing he saw when he opened his eyes. She would wash him, read to him, and feed him. His mother wasn't even there as much as Gloria. She was there so much that the nurse brought a recliner into his room so she could be comfortable when she slept there overnight. KB was grateful she was by his side. There was no doubt in his mind that she loved him. She kept her ear to the street and kept him abreast of what was happening in the hood. She informed him of how many people died the night he was shot.

She told him that Stump got murdered in his building and that the police had no witnesses, and most recently, she told him about the incident that happened with Lakim and Drez in her projects. The image of the girl pointing the gun at him was ever fresh in his mind, and he was lucky to be alive.

With Stump, there was a certain honor he had when it came to his crew. There was seventy-five thousand dollars cash with a gold chain in a bag on his bed when KB came home from the hospital. It was from Stump. That's why it bothered him to hear of his brutal murder, but for some reason, he felt free, as if he was released from some invisible bondage. KB felt his life was spared for a reason, and he mentally made a pact with himself to live a safer existence. Sometimes people didn't get second chances, but for whatever reason, he was granted one.

KB looked over to Gloria who lay across the bed in a deep sleep. He was supposed to be going to therapy in a little while, but he didn't want to wake her. She looked so peaceful. She had literally been taking care of him with no complaints, and he wanted her to rest.

He walked to the mirror and pulled up his T-shirt, looking at the bandages that went around his mid-section and over his chest and shoulder. He stared at himself in the mirror and internalized the drastic change his body had been through. His health had changed in the course of one night. He lost a lot of weight while in the hospital, and he wasn't able to get around as easily as he used to. KB was afraid. He didn't know if he would ever recover one-hundred percent, but he was grateful to be alive. A single tear formed in his eye, then rolled down his cheek. Since being shot, he found himself more emotional and somewhat religious. Gloria's weekly Bible readings may have contributed to this new behavior. He wiped his cheek and grabbed the cane from off the bed.

"Hey honey, whatcha' doin'?" Gloria asked, waking from her sleep.

"Nothin', ma. Get your rest, I'ma go to therapy," KB told her.

"Okay, wait. Let me get dressed." She rose from the bed and headed for the bathroom.

"Look, ma, I appreciate all you've been doin' for me. Just let me go to therapy myself. I'll take a cab there and back. You stay here and rest. Okay?" KB wanted to do something on his own without help. He was beginning to feel like a handicap.

"It's okay, baby. I don't mind," she yelled from the bathroom with toothpaste in her mouth.

"Nah, ma, let me do this on my own. It's been a while since I did shit for myself, you know. I wanna know that I can, baby. Feel me?" he asked her, as she gently put her arms around his waist.

"I'm sorry, baby. I've been so caught up in trying to get you back to how you were that I ain't realize the improvements you've already made. You right. You should go to therapy by yourself. Shit, it'll give me a chance to clean up this damn room." Gloria kissed him gently on his back, got his sneakers from the closet, and placed them by his feet.

KB loved the fact that his girl understood his needs. She really understood how he felt without him really getting into it with her. He put on his sneakers, wincing when he bent over to tie them.

"Aaaah! That's why I gotta keep goin' to therapy. I gotta get used to bending ova without feeling so much pain," KB moaned.

"Well, baby, you've had plenty of bedrest. You've been eating right, and you've even exercised while you were here, so you are definitely improving faster than they expected," Gloria told him.

"You right. Call me a cab now so by the time I get downstairs, it'll already be there," KB instructed.

"All right. I'll just clean up your room for you while you're gone and run down to my house and get some more clothes. You don't mind that I've been stayin' here with you this long, do you, baby?"

"Come on now, is that a trick question?" KB asked, staring lovingly into his woman's eyes.

"Just had to make sure, baby," Gloria beamed.

***

Gloria was surprised to see Shondra standing in front of the building when her cab pulled up. She hadn't spoken to Shondra since the day she dismissed her when she came to KB's room and

acted like she was so concerned about him. Gloria vowed she would never forgive her for her blatant betrayal of their once solid friendship.

Shondra noticed Gloria as she emerged from the cab. She watched as her friend stepped out of the cab wearing a tight-fitting sweat suit that showed off the perfect form of her body. As Gloria approached the building, Shondra could see she wasn't looking at her. Shondra figured Gloria might still be mad, but she felt Gloria could at least acknowlege her existence. As Gloria got closer, Shondra stepped in front of her, partially blocking the entrance so Gloria was forced to face her. Gloria walked past her, shoving her aside. Shondra lost her footing and stumbled over to the wall. She didn't get upset, but she felt she deserved a spoken word if Gloria was going to do all that.

"Damn, Glo, if you gonna push me, you can at least speak to me!" Shondra remarked.

Gloria walked to the elevator and pushed the triangular button to summon its arrival. She refused to recognize Shondra's presence. Shondra followed her into the building and stood behind her.

"Come on, Glo, I know you're still mad, but please give me a chance. I'm so sorry! I really am!" Shondra pleaded.

When the elevator door opened, Shondra grabbed her arm, preventing her from getting on. Gloria turned around and slapped Shondra hard in her face.

"Don't touch me, bitch!" Gloria spat. "Don't ever put your raggedy-ass hands on me again!"

Shondra's face shifted violently from the force of the slap. In that instance, she forgot the purpose of her standing there with Gloria and became defensive, an instinct she had inherited from the many fights and scuffles she had in the past. She swung her fist, connecting to Gloria's face, and continued her assault until Gloria found the power to push her off momentarily. Shondra backed up but was back on Gloria like a cheetah on a gazelle. She punched her in the face and pulled her hair, trying to get her off balance. She swung her into the mailboxes, then stomped Gloria as

she tried to cover up. Shondra was screaming as someone came into the lobby and pulled her off of Gloria.

"Bitch, you crazy! You musta bumped your fuckin' head thinkin' you could slap me and not catch a beatdown! You really musta forgot who the fuck I be, bitch!" Shondra said menacingly.

Some guys that came in the building to see what was happening were helping Gloria to her feet as she tried to regain her composure. She looked over to Shondra, who was still going off in a tirade about how bad a bitch she was when it came to fighting. Gloria was furious. She didn't have any wins with Shondra on a physical level, so she decided to beat her with words.

"You stinkin', bitch. You 'posed to have been my best friend. How the fuck could you do me the way you did me? You is a lyin' bitch," Gloria started.

Shondra suddenly stopped with her ranting and raving and calmed down, remembering her purpose for stopping Gloria in the first place. She listened to Gloria go on about their friendship.

"You acted like your relationship with Junior was so fuckin' good, and the whole time you was frontin', bitch. That's why you was willing to fuck up what I had with my man, because your shit was already fucked up. You was getting info out of me about my man and running back and telling that muhfucka, thinking that would make shit better between y'all. You stupid bitch! That muhfucka still was fuckin' around on you, and when you seen me happy with my man, it made you mad. Why, bitch? Why didn't you want to see your *best friend* happy? You played it off like he was such a good dude to you, and the whole time he was fuckin' around on you. I never knew you was jealous of what me and my man had. I didn't know that you hated to see me happy. Now I know the truth about your miserable ass. You can't live a lie, you dumb bitch, 'cause it's bound to come out."

Shondra was standing there with her mouth wide open. She was shocked Gloria was putting all her business in the street like that. There were a lot of people from around the way that didn't know anything about her personal life, much less her relationship with Junior. She was embarrassed and wanted to just go in the house and forget everything, but she couldn't let Gloria get the last word.

"You don't know what the fuck you talkin' about, bitch. I always looked out for you, you stupid ho! You was always jealous of me, you black bitch. You always wanted my life. You always wanted to be me, but you couldn't. Well, fuck you and that muhfucka you fuckin'. I wish he did die!" The last part of that statement was meant to pierce Gloria's heart.

Gloria rushed Shondra at full speed, but Shondra sidestepped and uppercut her, then kicked her in the ass as she fell to the ground.

"You can't win, bitch, so you betta stop while you ahead," Shondra hissed.

"Shondra, you wish my man died? Well, I hope they get your bitch-ass man for all the shit he did. Everybody knows he had something to do with that shit that happened in the back of Lakim's building. When my man gets better, I'ma tell him to slap the shit out of you for tryin' to set him up, you dirty, stinkin' bitch!" Gloria's voice rumbled.

"You threatenin' me, bitch! You wait 'til my man get ova here. I'm gonna get him to kill that bitch-ass man of yours, and after that, I'ma stomp your black ass out!" Shondra threatened.

"Shondra, the telephone!"

Shondra's brother had opened the door and yelled out into the hallway to his sister, unaware of the commotion going on.

"Oh yeah, bitch, that's my man right there. I'ma tell him what's goin' on, so you betta be gone by the time he gets here!"

"Whateva, bitch. That muhfucka probably won't even come, with his faggot ass!" Gloria screamed loud enough for Shondra to hear before she closed her apartment door.

Shondra was on fire when she grabbed the phone that was dangling in the hallway.

"Hello?" she screamed into the receiver.

"Yo, what the fuck is wrong?" Junior asked, taken off guard by her aggressive tone.

"Why the fuck it took you so long to call me back? I been beeping you all week and you ain't return none of my calls. Why!"

Shondra was upset. She was furious because what Gloria had said to her was all true. She was sure Junior was seeing that girl, and she didn't know what to do.

"I told you why, ma. I'm busy takin' care of shit out here. I gotta make sure shit is going right out here or I'll fuck around and lose e'erythin'," Junior half explained. "What's wrong? You put 9-1-1."

"I just got into it with Gloria. She threatened me. She said that she gonna tell KB that I was the one that tried to set him up and get him to kill me. She said she gonna tell him to get you, too!" Shondra lied.

"Word? Where they at now?" Junior asked, fury in his voice.

"She just went upstairs. He wasn't with her, though. She mighta been comin' from his house 'cause she was gettin' outta a cab when I saw her," Shondra told him.

"Well, I'm on my way ova there. I'ma pistol whip that bitch and make that muhfucka come see me. He know what it is wit' me. He got blasted and he still poppin' shit. That's my word. I'ma bury his ass, too! He gonna wish the devil took him when he had him the first time," Junior growled into the receiver. "Look, just stay inside 'til I get there. Make sure you leave your door open. I should be there in like fifteen minutes. Don't forget to leave the door open, Shondra."

"Okay, but when you get here, we need to talk 'cause I'm tired of your bullshit!" she added.

"Whateva. I'm on my way! Just be sure you leave the door open!" Junior reiterated.

Muffin was standing at the door while Junior was talking on the phone. She had a feeling he was going to sneak off and call Shondra sooner or later, but she didn't think he would be so disrespectful and call from her bedroom. She heard the whole conversation and was pissed off when he came into the living room where she was sitting. She prepared herself for the lie he was about to tell her about why he had to leave so abruptly.

"Ay Muff, I gotta go check on somethin' 'round the way. My boy got some problems," Junior said, putting on his black leather jacket.

"Your boy, huh?" Muffin asked, being cynical.

"Come on now, ma, don't give me that. Soon as I take care of this business, I'll be back here with you and we can finish what we was doin'," Junior promised.

"I ain't worried, baby. Take your time and be careful out there," Muffin told him.

Junior kissed her gently and walked out the door. She walked to the window and waited until he got in his car, then went into her bedroom and pressed redial on the telephone.

"Hello?" Muffin said when Shondra picked up the phone.

"Hello, who is this?" Shondra asked.

"It's me, you ugly bitch!" Muffin responded.

"Who the fuck is this?" Shondra asked, her heartbeat and pressure increasing.

"You know who this is, bitch! Why the fuck do you beep him so much? Don't you get the message when he don't call back. HE DON'T WANT YOU NO MORE, BITCH. GET OVER IT ALREADY!" Muffin screamed into the phone.

"You fuckin' ho! Why don't you tell me where you at so I can finish fuckin' you up? You was lucky last time, bitch!"

"No, bitch, you the lucky one. Look, when my man get ova there, please tell him when he's finished helping your measly, broke-down ass, to hurry home and don't forget to bring me a shrimp roll back," Muffin teased.

"Ooooh bitch! Why don't you come here and tell him yourself, or are you scared?" Shondra challenged.

"The only thing I'm scared of, bitch, is looking at yo' ugly ass. Give it up, Brusilla. He mine now, and you can't do shit 'bout it. Junior like pretty things, sweetie, and ain't nothin' pretty 'bout you Magilla gorilla." Muffin laughed.

"I'll find out where you live when he comes here, bitch. And when I do, watch your back and front," Shondra said. "If you think you're so cute, I'll change all that when I slam your face on the concrete!" Shondra slammed down the phone.

Muffin laughed, but she was furious with Junior when she sat down on the couch and thought about how deceitful he was to her.

Shondra was going to stand outside and wait for Junior. Her anger wouldn't allow her to stay in the house and wait. When she went into her room to snatch her jacket off the hanger, a card fell on the floor. It was one of the cards the detective had given her when they came to her house asking about Junior. She bent down slowly, picked it up, went in the hallway, and paused by the telephone. Hell hath no fury like a woman scorned.

***

Junior didn't have a gun on him at Muffin's house. Therefore, he had to call Rock so he could get strapped before he went over to Shondra's.

"Yo, you got a biscuit in the crib, right?" Junior asked Rock over the phone.

"Hmmhmm. What's up, man? You got some beef?" Rock asked.

"Nah, not really. I gotta take care of something. I'll tell you when I get there," Junior said.

Junior pulled up in front of Rock's crib and went upstairs to get the gun. He knocked on the door, and Rock opened it and let him in.

"So tell me why you need toast. You need me to go with you?" Rock asked.

"It's that bitch Gloria. She fuckin' with my girl, but I can handle it," Junior told him. "By the way, how shit goin' out here?"

"It's goin'. I'ma need to see you in a minute," Rock responded.

"Cool. I'll take care of you after I take care of this bullshit with this stupid bitch. Where the iron at?" Junior asked, as he followed Rock to a back room of the apartment.

"Right here." Rock passed him a nine-millimeter.

"Let me pick what I want, muhfucka," Junior said, trying to see if there were any other guns Rock had available.

"This the only one I got up here," Rock said with a suspicious look on his face.

"A'ight, fuck it. I'ma dirty this shit up, so don't expect it back," Junior said.

"It's yours," Rock replied, shrugging his shoulders.

"I'm out. I'll get wit' you lata." Junior slapped him five.

Rock had given Junior the gun he had used to kill Stump.

Junior decided to enter through the back of Shondra's building in case KB or Gloria was in the lobby. He pulled out the gun and opened the door to the hallway slowly, peeking in to see if anyone was in the vestibule. Seeing no one, he holstered his heat, proceeded up the three stairs to Shondra's door, and turned the knob. When the knob didn't turn, Junior immediately became upset because he specifically told Shondra to leave the door open for him. He knocked with his special knock and kept turning around to make sure KB wasn't lurking in the stairwell while he waited for Shondra to open the door for him.

Shit, she knew to keep the door open for me. She knew I was coming, he thought, as he stood there waiting for her to open the door.

"Freeze! Police! Don't move, motherfucker, and don't turn around!"

Fuck! Junior thought. *How the fuck...who the fuck...Damn! Somebody set me up.*